With shaky fingers she pressed the button...

The lights flickered on and off. A pulsating, purplish mist erupted in her hands and lit her entire kitchen. Startled, Julia jolted to her feet, dropping the jewelry box. It landed on the tabletop with a thud. She tore her gaze from the box...and froze.

A man—a very large man—stood in front of her. He wore nothing more than a pair of black skintight pants. A sword dangled at his waist.

The man was gorgeous. His seductiveness hit her like an uncontrollable whirlwind. His skin was bronzed, sexy and ridged with muscle. Everything about him oozed carnality.

"You summoned?"

Summon this gor̶̶̶̶̶̶̶̶̶̶̶̶̶̶̶̶̶̶̶̶sies, perhaps. "Me, su̶̶̶̶̶̶̶̶̶̶̶̶̶̶̶̶̶̶̶̶ thing."

He ignored her denial. "What do you wish of me? Tell me what you desire. Caresses? Erotic words? Do I now kiss your naked body or let you kiss mine?"

"Sexy, funny, and downright magical! Gena Showalter has a lyrical voice and the deft ability to bring characters to life in a manner that's hilarious and absorbing at the same time."
—Katie MacAlister, *New York Times* bestselling author of *Sex and the Single Vampire*

gena showalter

the pleasure slave

HQN™

ISBN 0-373-77032-4

THE PLEASURE SLAVE

Copyright © 2005 by Gena Showalter

To Shonna Tolbert-Hurt, Michelle Tolbert,
Heather Showalter (and her donkey pal)
and Kemmie Tolbert for the love, joy and laughter you bring
to my life. And of course to Debbie Splawn-Bunch, who
wouldn't let me title this book *Handcuffed to the Headboard*.

A special thanks to Deidre Knight, Tracy Farrell
and Jessica Alvarez. I am blessed to work with you.

the pleasure slave

PROLOGUE

Imperia
The Fifth Season

"I WANT YOU AGAIN, Tristan."

Waves crashed against the cliffs outside, their lulling rhythm floating upon the sea-kissed beams of moonlight filtering through the arched windows. The sweet scent of *gartina* and *elsment* filled the chamber, a palpable omen of magic few could comprehend or even acknowledge.

Zirra leaned naked against the window frame, the exact place her lover had taken her moments ago. When he failed to respond to her words, she seductively arched her back and skimmed a hand down the flat plane of her stomach.

"I want you again, Tristan," she repeated, a husky edge to the words. Her body still hummed from his touch, but she needed more of him. She *always* needed more of him.

The darkness of his hair hung in wild disarray over his shoulders as he fastened his black, warrior drocs around his waist. He eyed her with amusement. "You know I must go, *nixa.*"

"Why?" Annoyed, Zirra abandoned her pose of re-laxed beckoning and stalked to the bed. She didn't bother covering herself with the silky white sheet, but left the plump mounds of her breasts bared for his view. "Why do you deny me the pleasure of your touch?"

He closed the distance between them and eased atop the bed, mere inches away from her reach. "You know I must journey to the palace for instruction from Great-Lord Challann. A rebellion brews in Gillirad."

"But I—"

"I cannot disobey a direct command from my sover-eign. This you know, as well."

Her brow knit in annoyance. Tristan acted as if her nakedness no longer tempted him.

Mayhap it didn't.

Tendrils of fury danced along her spine. Earlier she had kissed and licked a path down his entire body, had taken him deep into her mouth as she'd never done for another man. When she finished, he had slid himself in-side her, pumping and gliding erotically, giving her a rapture so complete she had begged for mercy. Yet he had yawned. Yawned!

Her fists clenched so tightly her knuckles whitened, and her long oval nails dug into her palms, cutting deeply into the skin. She had given Tristan everything she had to give, and yet she, a priestess of the Druinn, had failed to truly satisfy him. And because of her fail-ure, she would soon be discarded like a worthless piece of garbage.

That image burned in her mind, and the urge to hurt

Tristan, to destroy him in some way, coursed through her. For eight cycles he had come to her, giving her incomparable pleasure, and for each of those eight eves he had left her here afterward, alone in the vast emptiness of her bed, desperate for more of him. Dying for more of him.

He must suffer as I suffer, she thought. Yet…

Her need for his affection proved a vehement ache she could not ignore, and she found herself reaching out, gripping his muscled forearm. Even now, his features drawn tight with annoyance, he exuded the sensual eroticism of a man who existed only to pleasure his woman. She wanted, *needed,* to be the one who obtained his eternal devotion. Mayhap then the constant ache inside her heart would be filled.

"We belong together," she said, her words emerging on an ethereal wisp of breath. "Life-join with me and I will give you more carnal pleasure than any other woman is capable of giving."

He did not even pause. "Nay."

"Treasures. I will give you treasures beyond your deepest imagination." With a desperate flick of her wrist, she tossed her long black hair over one shoulder. "Even, if you so desire, a planet of your own to rule."

"Zirra," Tristan chided softly. Watching her, he lounged across the bed and propped his weight on his elbow. "Best you recall my words before I ever came to be your lover. I told you I could never be more than a passing fancy for you."

"Aye, I remember," she admitted through clenched

teeth. But she hadn't let it stop her from having him. One look at Tristan's male perfection, at the way his pale violet eyes promised untold passion, at the way his hard, muscled body moved with sinewy grace, and she'd been lost. Lost as if her mind and heart were separate entities.

"Nothing has changed," he said. With a touch as gentle as his tone, he ran a fingertip down her cheek. "Nor will it ever. You are Druinn, and I am mortal, and permanent ties are forbidden. I am sorry."

Once again, fury blazed through her, hot and hungry. No one treated her this way. No one. "I will give you but one more chance to bind yourself to me."

He pushed to his feet, uttering a husky chuckle that usually made her shiver with delight. Now the sound merely fueled her anger.

"Or you will what, *nixa?* Boil my eyeballs in water? Render my manhood flaccid for all time?"

"Oh, no, my fine warrior. I will do much, much worse."

Not the least affected by her ominous warning, he lifted his gleaming silver blade from its inclined position against the wall and hooked it to a metal loop on his belt. He bent down and placed a quick kiss upon her cheek. "Mayhap later we will work off this energy you seem to harbor, hmm?"

Without waiting for a reply, he turned on his heel and strode to the door.

"You desire women above all things, Tristan," she said, "and now I will make you a slave to them." Scowling, she snatched up the jeweled trinket box he had given her mere hours ago and hurtled it at him. It sailed past his ear and crashed to the floor, unharmed. She vaulted up. "I will make you a slave to *me*."

Tristan spun and faced her. His expression no longer boasted of easy confidence but of incredulity, and just a little fear. "What are you doing, Zirra?"

A rush of excitement pooled between her legs, for *she* had made this mighty warrior afraid. "No one refuses me," she told him, her body remaining taut as she stood in all her naked glory, fury and indignation her only cloth. "And you, my handsome mortal, shall pay for doing so."

"Mortals have vowed never to destroy your people's Kyi-en-Tra Crystal, and in return the Druinn have sworn never to use their powers against us. You yourself agreed to this. If you break your oath you will break the Alliance between our people and war will erupt. You *will* honor your word. No sorcery. I forbid it."

"You, a mortal? Forbid me? I think not." She laughed, yet the sound lacked humor. "How will your Great-Lord ever discover what I have done to you if you cannot tell him?"

"Zirra—"

"Beg me to become your life-mate, and I will swear never to harm you."

Lavender fire instantly blazed in his eyes. "I will never beg you, or anyone, for anything."

"Then you have brought this on yourself, Tristan ar Malik." Her dark brows arched in mocking salute, she raised her hands in the air, palms up.

Tristan growled low in his throat and advanced, his

intent to immobilize her evident with every step. A simple wave of her hand froze his feet in place.

Surprise flashed across his features a split second before he glared at her with such hostility she shivered. She refused to allow a mortal to frighten her. She closed her eyes, splayed her fingers wide and began to chant. "From now until love finds you true, a woman's slave I shall make of you."

Wind howled in swirling procession, thrashing and clawing throughout the spacious chamber, whipping the white gossamer cloth over the windows and rattling the very foundation of the floor. Energy erupted and glowed all around, striking like bolts and war spears. A rumbling boom echoed in her ears. She raised her arms higher.

"Into a trinket box you shall rest, answering each summons as it suits best. This I bind, this I speak, your will matters none. So said, let it be known. So said, let it be done."

One moment Tristan stood before her a strong, virile man, the next he was gone. Only the small jewel-encrusted box she'd thrown rested on the floor. Grinning slowly, she hopped from the bed, bent down and clasped the box in her hands. A wave of giddiness swept through her. Tristan now belonged to her—only to her. And over the next thousand years or so, she would enjoy letting him make up for his behavior today. He would learn well his mistake in refusing a priestess of the Druinn.

CHAPTER ONE

Sante Fe, New Mexico

Ways Of The Pleasure Slave

*The Slightest Whim Of Your Master
Is Your Highest Law*

THE BLARE OF A HORN SOUNDED. Again.

Julia Anderson gripped the wheel of her sedan and glanced down at her speedometer. Six miles per hour over the speed limit. The driver behind her found this completely unacceptable and honked yet again, a demand that she get out of the way or hit the gas.

The morning sun had yet to make an appearance, but the waning moon and towering streetlights revealed two open, easily accessible lanes. There was no reason to ride her tail like this.

Still the honking persisted for another mile.

By that time, Julia's nerves were frazzled and her foot was shaking on the gas pedal. She rolled her shoulders and drew in a deep breath, but neither action managed to relax her. She cranked up the volume on *La Bohème*.

That didn't help, either.

I'm a calm, rational woman, she reminded herself. *I will not become unnerved by a little honking.*

Honk. Honk. Hoooonk.

Her teeth gnashed together. She didn't have a temper; she really didn't. Not usually anyway. But right now she wanted to slam on her brakes and give that driver a crash-test-dummy demonstration. Instead, she allowed her car to gradually slow.

"What do you think of that, Speedy?" she asked smugly.

Apparently, he didn't like it. His little Mustang finally whipped into another lane, accelerating quickly. When their cars aligned, he rolled down his window and began shouting and waving his fist. The moment she recognized him, Julia forgot she believed in thinking before acting. She forgot that she preferred to act rationally in all situations.

She gave him the bird.

That's right. She held up one hand and extended her middle finger. In a hiss of fury, the red sports car roared away.

Shock was still coursing through her when she reached her destination. She, a woman who prided herself on her calm, rational behavior, had just flipped off her biggest competitor.

And it had felt good. So deliciously good.

Chuckling, she parked her car. Her amusement faded, however, when she saw that there was one other car in the lot—a red Mustang.

A groan worked its way past her throat as she gathered her purse and stepped into the frigid Sante Fe morning. A strong wind immediately blustered by, making her shiver. She tugged the lapels of her coat tighter and hurried toward the only building in sight.

The Mustang's owner was waiting near the metal doors. When he spotted her, he glared at her through small, dark eyes. Hostility radiated from him.

She came to an abrupt stop and watched him warily. At five foot six or seven, he wasn't much taller than she. His thin cap of hair gleamed with a thick film of mousse, and a round belly protruded over the elastic waist of his wrinkled pants.

The same wild impulse that had hit her in the car hit her now. *He's going down,* she decided, squaring her shoulders. *And I'll be the one to give him the final push.* He must have sensed her determination to outmaneuver him, because he placed one foot in front of the other and crouched down ever so slightly. The classic fighting stance.

This meant war.

She stiffened her resolve, refusing to run back to the safety of her car. She stared at him through slitted eyes, not willing to look away or even blink. To do so showed weakness, and the desire to win this battle had suddenly grown to unimaginable proportions. While he was closer to the door, she was a good twenty years younger and a hundred pounds lighter.

He didn't stand a chance.

Suddenly a click reverberated through the cover of silence.

The Kreager Flea Market had just opened to dealers.

Jumping into action, Julia pushed and elbowed her way past the man. She glided through the double doors a split second before he did. Yes! Victory. Smiling with pride, she grabbed a basket and began her treasure hunt.

Antiques. Ah, that one word had the power to send ribbons of delight down her spine. Over the years she'd been called many things. Garage-sale junky. Thrift-store devotee. Auction-house addict. She had accumulated so much stuff she'd had two options: buy an antique store to sell her wares or become buried alive in her collection.

She'd chosen to set up her own shop.

Julia's Treasures opened the day of her twenty-third birthday and had flourished in the two years since. It was her pride and joy, a place where she found success and happiness. *Unlike the rest of your life,* a hidden corner of her mind supplied.

"Hey," she said, then pressed her lips together. *I'm happy with the rest of my life.* So what that she had plain brown hair, nondescript green eyes, and a short, rounded body that failed to gain admiration. So what that she had no fashion sense and didn't know how to attract a man. "I'm happy," she repeated firmly.

As she wandered through the market, her old, ratty sneakers squeaked, drawing the attention of several sellers intent on luring her over. Knowing exactly what she wanted to buy—and what she didn't—she ignored them. She bypassed a table of porcelain dolls and didn't look twice at the stand laden with Depression Era glass.

In the back, next to a slightly worn cherry vanity, she

spotted an old corncob pipe. She studied the aged wood from every angle, then lifted it to her nose and sniffed. The faint scent of tobacco drifted to her nostrils. She grinned, the perfect customer in mind.

Elated, she carefully placed the pipe in her basket. Next she examined a colorful blown-glass carousel, but decided to forgo purchasing such an expensive item when she didn't have a buyer already lined up. The rest of the items on the table received a cursory perusal before one object in particular drew and held her gaze. She set aside a collage of plastic flowers and stared down at what looked to be an old square jewelry box.

The sides were chipped, and the outer layer, which at one time had probably been a glossy ivory, was now a dull yellow-brown. There were several holes where colored glass, or maybe even precious gems, once resided. Overall an extremely ugly piece, yet something about it called to her. Biting her lower lip, she ran her fingertips over the surface. Unexpectedly, the cool exterior sent a shaft of warm, inviting heat up her arm. Tingles raced down her back, making her shiver. Intrigued, she tried to raise the lid, but the stubborn thing refused to budge.

That didn't dissuade her. She wanted this box. Badly.

"See something you like, lass?" asked a voice with a slight Scottish accent.

Julia glanced up. A man who appeared to be in his early sixties with a beaked nose and eyes that drooped low on his cheekbones regarded her expectantly. Those eyes, she thought…they were as fathomless and blue as an ocean, and she would swear they saw into her soul. She shook off her unease.

Not wanting him to know just how much she desired the item, she schooled her features to show mild curiosity, nothing more. "How much for the jewelry box?" she asked.

He smiled, causing the puckered skin around his lips to deepen. "Today only, lass, I'll let you have it for fifty dollars."

"Fifty dollars? When the stones are missing and the lid is broken?" She laughed. "I'll give you five."

He made a choking sound in the back of his throat, and when he spoke again, his burr was more pronounced. "No can do. I canna let a prize like that go for such a paltry sum. Not when there's a tale that comes with it." He wiggled his bushy, silver brows. "Verra intriguing."

"Well…" Confident he simply wished to drive up the price, Julia pursed her lips and donned a nonchalant air. "I'm not really into fairy tales."

"Oh, you'll like this one. There's none like it. That I promise you."

After a sufficient pause, she said, "Sure, why not?"

His eyes lit with amusement, as if he knew her game. "Story is, that when a woman owns this here jewelry box, she'll find the greatest pleasure ever known."

Julia waited for him to continue. When he didn't, she said, "That's it? That's the big story? Own the box and find great pleasure?" For fifty dollars, she'd expected a story about naked dancers, bowls of cocaine and wild orgies. Disappointment coiled through her. "Just what *is* the greatest pleasure ever known?"

"I don't rightly know." He scratched his beard, and a rain-scented breeze, like the calm after a storm, accompanied the movement. "I guess pleasure's different for everyone. Who's to say?"

"The last female owner."

"Well, now, she lost her soul long ago, so I canna be asking her, can I?"

"Lost her—oh. I'm so sorry for your loss," she said softly. "I didn't mean to bring up painful memories."

"No, no. No need to be sorry. She was an ancestor of mine, you could say. I like to call her Granny Greedy." He chuckled at his own joke. "Family legend says she created the box and kept it with her at all times, never letting it out of her sight. When she died, the damn thing had to be pried out of her fingers." He barely paused before adding, "What's your name, lass?"

"Julia Anderson."

"Well, Jules me girl, I'll be honest with you. I think you need this here box more than you realize. Great pleasure will put some color in your cheeks. Maybe put a sparkle in your eyes. So are you interested in buying or not?"

Julia tried not to be insulted; she really did. She might not have any hobbies outside of work, and she might spend every evening in bed, reading sexy romance novels and watching made-for-TV movies, but she *did* have pleasure in her life. At the moment, though, she just couldn't recall where.

"Thirty," a nasally voice said from behind her. Julia spun around. The Mustang's owner gave her a smug I've-got-you-beat-this-time grin. "I'll pay thirty."

"Well, lass?" the salesman prompted, giving her a chance to outbid.

After haggling for half an hour over the price, Julia finally paid seventy-three dollars—plus fifteen for the pipe. She'd been robbed. She knew it, just as she knew her opponent hadn't really wanted the box. He'd wanted retribution, and she hadn't been able to walk away without owning the "greatest pleasure."

The moment she arrived home, an all-too-familiar anticipation filled her. She carefully placed her new purchases on the kitchen table, then gathered a rag and cleaning supplies. The bark of a dog pierced the air and the midday sun dappled through sapphire curtains covering the large bay window on the far wall. Settling into a high-backed gold velvet chair, she focused all of her attention on the jewelry box, cleaning every inch with painstaking gentleness. There was something almost...*magical* about it. And she would swear to God it purred every time she stroked the corners.

Just as she began adding polish to the outer surface, she zeroed in on a tiny button hidden beneath the rim. Her fingers stilled and her heart drummed erratically in her chest. Excitement pounded through her veins. Would this open the lid? And if so, what would she find inside? Jewelry? Love letters? Nothing?

With shaky fingers, she set aside her rag and pressed the button.

At the moment of contact, lights flickered on and off throughout the house, dancing shadows and light on the rose-tinted wallpaper. A pulsating, purplish mist erupted in her hands and lit her entire kitchen.

Startled, Julia jumped to her feet, dropping the jewelry box as if it were nuclear waste. Instead of shattering, it landed atop the honey-oak tabletop with a thud. She tore her gaze from the box…and froze in terror.

A man—a large man—a *very* large man—stood just in front of her. He wore nothing more than a pair of black, skintight pants and—Omigod! A long, menacing sword dangled at his waist. A scream rose in her throat at the exact moment a hard lump formed, preventing any sound from emerging.

Terrified, she scanned the kitchen, looking for a way out. The back door was bolted shut. The windows were closed. Sweat beaded across her forehead.

It didn't matter that the man was, well…gorgeous, that his seductiveness hit her like an uncontrollable whirlwind. He didn't belong here, didn't belong in her home. Alone. With her. With her panic intensifying, she assumed a karate position and prayed with every fiber of her being she appeared menacing and lethal.

Why had she never taken self-defense lessons?

Stupid, stupid, stupid.

"I know karate," she forced out. "My body is a dangerous weapon."

He merely arched a brow.

He knows I'm lying. At least she could memorize his description—just in case she survived. Concentrate.

Concentrate. His towering height pushed toward the ceiling. Inky shoulder-length hair framed a strong forehead, a straight nose and high, bladelike cheekbones.

Yet it was his eyes that truly drew her attention. They were pale violet, almost lavender—wait. They were blue, a light aqua. No, no. They were emerald green. But that wasn't right, either. She blinked, shook her head and realized his eyes weren't one color. They were *all* colors, shimmering like a sea of constantly changing purples, blues and greens. Glowing with a life of their own, catching her attention until she almost forgot where she stood—and why she was standing there.

Look at the rest of him, Anderson.

His skin was bronzed, sexy and ridged with muscle. Lord, what strength! His stomach muscles formed a vee that pointed her eyes lower, lower still, directly between his legs. She gulped. He was like a savage romance novel warrior come to life in her home. Everything about him oozed carnality yet screamed with danger.

He stared at her a long while before taking a step toward her.

She recoiled.

The chair stopped her retreat. A slow grin lifted the corners of his full, mouthwatering lips, revealing perfect white teeth. For some reason, the smile seemed less than genuine. Almost predatory.

Her heart galloped then skipped a solitary beat.

"You summoned?" he asked.

Summoned this gorgeous warrior? In her wildest fantasies, perhaps, but not in reality. She hadn't even known such beauty existed. Besides, the man had a sword that looked like it could chop her in half in less time than was required to blink. He wanted to kill her, or worse, so no! Julia hadn't summoned him.

"Me? Summon you?" Eyes impossibly wide, she shook her head. "I promise I did no such thing."

He ignored her denial as if he hadn't heard her or didn't care. "What do you wish of me?"

She had to escape. With the back door locked, she had only one option—the front entrance. Perhaps if she inched around the chair... She managed one tiny step to the right. Two.

"Do I now kiss your naked body or let you kiss mine?" His slightly accented tone dripped with boredom and still managed to be the most compelling, erotic voice she had ever heard. Honey-rich, warm, like refuge on a stormy night.

Even still, the word *naked* twisted terror through her stomach.

She gained another step. Did he plan to rape her? She had to know, had to prepare. "What do you want from me?" Each word ripped from her throat. "Why are you here?"

"To please you, of course."

"I don't want you to please me. I don't even want you within a hundred yards of me." Another step.

He studied her and frowned. "Do I frighten you?"

Never admit your fear. Over and over her sister's words drummed through her mind. *Never admit your fear.* Julia gulped, inched to the right just a bit more.

"Yes. I mean, no! I'm not afraid of you. I'm not afraid of anything."

"That is good." He nodded. "For I would never hurt you."

"I don't know you. I've never seen you before. And you're in my house." She gave a half hysterical, half desperate laugh. "I didn't invite you, yet there you stand. No, I'm not afraid. Nothing to be afraid of. Nothing at all."

A mocking smile played at the corners of his lips. "Then why, my fierce little dragon, are you widening the distance between us, even as we speak?"

She froze, unable to reply.

"My word has been given," he said. "I will not hurt you." Then he winked, causing her stomach to flutter. "Unless, of course, you ask me to."

"No, no." She raised her arms higher, placing her weapons of mass destruction, aka her fists, directly in his line of vision. He didn't seem impressed. "I definitely do not want you to hurt me," she said. "I definitely don't want you here, either. I just want you to leave. Please."

Looking confused, he folded both arms over his muscled chest. "I am bound to you. I stay where you are."

Bound. "Let's not be hasty," she rushed on, trying for an easy, carefree laugh. She sounded more like an asthmatic running through a pollen field. "No one needs to be tied up, okay."

"I have already told you no harm will befall you at my hands."

She hadn't believed him the first time he said it, and

she didn't believe him now. The man had a freaking sword the size of a small country.

"Come now, little dragon. Tell me what you desire of me. Caresses? Erotic words?"

Julia scoured her mind for something that might keep him from "caressing" her body and talking dirty while he did it. "Look, I just started my period and I have cramps and I haven't shaved my legs in three weeks. I haven't had a bath, for that matter. Trust me, you do *not* want to caress me."

"Then I will entertain you in other ways." He uttered a resigned sigh. "I am not simply here for your sexual pleasure. I am here to entertain you, converse with you and protect you."

"Uh, well…"

He persisted. "Shall I dance naked upon the table-top? Feed you by hand? Pose so that you may paint my likeness?"

While all of those scenarios sounded quite nice for any other circumstance, they didn't appeal to her now. "My husband is in the living room. He's big. And mean. And he hates when other men come near me. He killed the last one who tried. It was a violent death. Very bloody."

Indifferent, the intruder shrugged. "I am here for your pleasure. Not his. Besides, your husband's strength is no match for mine." His tone held no hint of pride. Only truth. "Unless that is your hope," he added, his pale violet eyes accusing, yet acceptant. "Do you wish me to kill your mate?"

She almost fainted right then and there. "I prefer no one be murdered in my home," she managed to squeak out.

"It will be as you desire."

"Uh, thank you?"

He shifted impatiently from one foot to the other. "Decide what you wish me to do. I do not like this waiting. I will do whatever you like. To you," he added, "and no other. Not even your mate."

The man probably planned to torture her—*her,* mind you, not her nonexistent husband—and he definitely planned to kill her. Yet there he stood, speaking to her as if she were his master and he were her slave.

"I will do whatever you like," he repeated.

Surely that statement was too good to be true. She arched a brow and studied him. "Anything? Anything at all?"

"Aye." His jaw clenched, as if his next words were somehow painful. "Your every desire is mine to fulfill. Whatever will please you, that will I do."

Well, she knew exactly what she wanted. "You want to please me? Then get out of my house. That's all I want."

His eyes widened with surprise, then quickly tapered to half-mast with suspicion. "You have not yet tasted the bliss of my touch, and yet you command my absence?"

No, stay and kill me, she almost shouted. Dying might be worth the price of this luscious man's touch.

"Look, the sooner you go," she said, surprising herself at the evenness of her tone, "the more pleased I'll be."

"Leave? Without touching you?"

She held up her right palm. "I swear I don't want you to touch me."

Everything about the intruder relaxed. He grinned again, this time wider, more genuine. "You shall have your wish, little dragon." With that, he disappeared, leaving a scented cloud of masculinity in his wake.

Julia's eyes darted around the kitchen, going from one corner to the other. Okay, what had just happened here? How had Mr. Let Me Touch Your Naked Body simply appeared, then vanished? One second she'd been alone, the next she hadn't, and now, in less than a heartbeat, she was alone again.

Totally confused, she sank into the chair behind her. There were only two explanations for what had just happened. Either a large man with very quick reflexes and a deadly sword had, indeed, invaded her home. Or she needed intense psychotherapy.

After a moment's thought, Julia settled upon the second. Hearing the legend associated with the jewelry box must have somehow caused her mind to try to prove it. Hence, all that "pleasure" and "caressing" nonsense. It also explained the purple mist, because what fantasy was complete without erotic lighting?

Relief surged through her, but quickly evaporated.

A perverted killer hadn't invaded her kitchen. Oh, no. She was simply insane. Wonderful. Just freaking wonderful.

CHAPTER TWO

*Regardless Of Personal Feelings, Your Master Must
Be Treated Respectfully*

MONDAY MORNING Julia opened her shop thirty minutes
late—a first for her since she usually arrived an hour
early. The problem? She'd overslept. All the blame fell
on Mr. Half-Naked Body's massive sun-kissed, delectable, mouthwatering completely lickable shoulders, of
course.

All night she had endured vivid, realistic dreams
where he did, in fact, please her body, touching her, caressing her. Pleasuring her. Several times! When her
alarm clock erupted in its shrill ring, she'd simply been
too tired to rise.

At least she'd been smiling.

She wasn't smiling anymore.

With her thoughts so fixated on Mr. Body, she'd
scratched a late Victorian walnut chair, decreasing its
value by at least a hundred dollars. Next, she had
dropped a 1950s vase, shattering the precious crystal
into a thousand tiny pieces—another three hundred dol-

lars in the garbage. But best of all, she had stepped in a pile of dog poop on her lunch break. Now, even though she'd scrubbed her shoe clean, the scent of puppy à la manure followed her everywhere.

Julia uttered a sigh. She needed a distraction to keep her mind off this increasingly atrocious day.

As if hearing her silent plea, an eerie whistle drifted from the back of the shop and greeted her ears.

"No, no, no," she muttered. With a grimace, she massaged her temples to ward off the sudden ache. The store's bathroom pipes were acting up again. She almost stomped her foot. This wasn't the kind of distraction she wanted. Left with no other choice, she gripped the phone and punched in her landlord's number. After the third ring, a gruff, craggy voice answered.

"Hello."

"Hi, Mr. Schetfield. It's Julia Anderson. I'm calling to see if you've hired anyone to fix the plumbing here at the shop."

"The plumbing's broke?" A stream of air crackled over the line, and she pictured him smoking one of his cigars. "When did that happen?"

Deep breath in, deep breath out. *Stay calm. Try to forget that you've phoned him three times in as many weeks about this problem. Could be worse, Julia. You could be imagining Mr. Body's luscious navel and the dark hair that plunged...*

Argh.

"The toilet doesn't flush," she reminded her landlord. "The sink turns on and off of its own free will, and the pipes are making that noise again. Something needs to be done, Mr. Schetfield. Soon." She pinched the bridge of her nose, imagining another week of closing the shop to run next door every time she needed to pee.

In such a prime location, gaining business from surrounding restaurants and boutiques, she paid an exorbitant amount for rent. An exorbitant amount she didn't mind paying because she loved the old Mexican-style building. Plus, she hoped to expand one day soon, and there was enough space here to do that. But Mr. Schetfield's miserly ways were pushing her to the edge of her tolerance.

"I'll take care of the problem," he said. "Don't you worry."

Since that was exactly what he'd told her the last time she called, Julia didn't allow herself to hope he spoke the truth. "Why don't you tell me how much you're willing to spend. I'll call a plumber and make sure he doesn't exceed your limit."

"No. That just won't work." The old man's rough voice crept a notch higher. "I want my son, Morgan, to do the job. Good boy, my Morgan."

"All right." She sighed. "Please call me in the morning and—" The bell over the door chimed, signaling the arrival of a customer. Julia hurried to end the conversation. "Just let me know what time Morgan will arrive, okay?"

"Can do."

The connection severed. She replaced the phone in its cradle and strode to the front of the store. A tall pleasant-looking man dressed in a suit and tie stood in the entryway, a bewildered, what-do-I-do-next expression on his face.

"Is there anything I can help you with?" Julia asked, drawing his attention.

"Yes. Yes, there is." His lips lifted in a relieved smile. "This is going to sound strange, but I'm searching for a glass donkey. My mother collects them, and her birthday is tomorrow."

"Any color preference? Or era?"

Surprise flashed in his big brown eyes. He shook his head. "No. I'll take whatever you have in stock. I've been to six different antique dealers. You're my last hope."

"I have two here," she said, her pride evident. "Does your mother prefer blown glass or etched?"

"I'm not sure." He ran his tongue over his teeth. "Why don't I buy both?"

"Excellent choice." In the center of the store, Julia climbed a gray step stool and rooted around a shelf for the desired items. A few seconds later, the tinkling of the doorbell sounded again. She glanced over her shoulder and smiled warmly when she saw who had arrived. "Good morning, Mrs. Danberry."

"Morning, dear." Mrs. Danberry, a regular customer of Julia's Treasures, gave her quintessential "old woman" curls a pat. Immediately the springy silver bob bounced back into place. "I came to see if you have anything new."

"Yesterday I acquired a corncob pipe that I know you'll love. I'll have it ready for viewing in a few days."

"Oh, wonderful. I'm still going to have a look

around, though. I might've missed something the last time I came in."

"Of course." Still grinning, Julia returned her attention to the shelf. When she found what she needed, she lifted the donkeys from their perches and eased to the floor. "Here you go," she told the man, bequeathing him both items. "Are these what you had in mind?"

He palmed each one in a different hand. After studying them, he blew out a satisfied breath. "Yes, they are. They're perfect, actually."

"The first is a seventeenth-century model made from—"

"No need to explain," he interjected. "I'm already sold on them. You just saved me a lecture about a son's responsibility to his family."

A chuckle tickled her throat. "Glad I could be of assistance."

He tilted his chin and gave her a lingering once-over. He cleared his throat. "You know, you have very pretty eyes."

His words, though innocent, caused her tongue to thicken, a familiar sensation whenever she spoke with the male species about, well, anything remotely flirtatious. She quickly lost her good humor. "Uh, I—uh—thanks. You, too." After that, speech became impossible. She tried anyway, managing another "uh" and two grunts.

"Are you all right?" he asked, concerned.

Her cheeks warmed. She nodded, though what she really wanted to do was slink away and hide. The admiration slowly faded from his expression. He gave her a strange perusal, paid for his donkeys and left without another word.

"You really should work on your technique, dear," Mrs. Danberry said, strolling to the cash register. "He might have asked you on a date."

Julia squeezed her eyes shut and let her head sink into her upraised hands. Was it too much to ask for God to strike her down with a bolt of lightning?

THAT NIGHT, Julia lay underneath a downy comforter, tossing and turning. When she actually slept, she once again dreamed of Mr. Half-Naked touching her. Kissing her. Their naked, sweaty bodies tangled together in passion. She'd lost count of how many "Oh, Gods" she'd uttered.

Why did her dream lover refuse to leave her mind? And why was she still lying in bed, allowing him to slide those phantom hands over her nipples, down her stomach and slip inside her panties? Circling, grazing, sinking deeply into her. After two more "Oh Gods," Julia scowled and lumbered wearily to her feet, sweeping aside the gauzy, cream-colored canopy that enclosed her bed. She needed something to do, something that was totally and completely *un*pleasurable.

Her taxes! Yes, that was it. She marched into her office, grabbed her books and carried them to the kitchen, where there was more room to work. She plopped into the nearest chair, an eighteenth-century brocade bench she'd acquired at an estate sale several years ago.

Five minutes later, she shoved the books aside with a growl. She was tired, cranky—okay, she was still aroused—and the numbers were blurring together. She needed something else to do.

Since her newest acquisitions were still strewn across the table, she picked up the jewelry box. She'd never discovered what lay inside, had she? She tried to depress the lid's latch, but her finger shook and refused to make contact. Brow puckered, she tried again. Once more, the shaking stopped her. What was the problem? It wasn't like Mr. Half-Naked and his sword would reappear.

You're thinking about him again, her mind tsked.

"For God's sake," she muttered, jabbing the button. "This is ridiculous."

Lights flickered throughout her house. Purple mist drifted upward. An intoxicating scent of masculinity surrounded her. This time, Julia didn't jump up, didn't drop the box atop her hard-carved tabletop. She simply bit her bottom lip, staring wide-eyed as Mr. Half-Naked did, indeed, appear. He was still half-dressed—and he still carried a sword.

"Omigod." And not a good, this-feels-so-wonderful omigod, the kind that had filled her dreams. But a bad, what-the-hell-is-happening omigod. Julia gulped. "I'm having a nightmare. That's all it is."

She rubbed a palm down her face, blinked her eyes and shook her head, thinking such a gorgeous creature would vanish by the time she refocused.

His extraordinary image never even wavered.

He isn't real, she mentally chanted, slowly rising to

her feet. *He isn't real, he isn't real, he isn't real.* Step by agonizing step, she approached the wildly savage apparition. He wore a let's-get-this-over-with expression...and not much else. Those pants. That sword. Slowly, shakily, she reached out and poked his chest once, twice. The heat of his skin singed her both times, and she finally jerked back, jaw slack.

This wasn't her imagination. This wasn't a dream.

What kind of man could appear and vanish in less than a single breath? Man...was he even human? Could he be a genie? Yesterday he had vowed to fulfill her every wish and desire.

No, she thought. That wasn't possible. Genies were a myth.

But what if genies did, in fact, exist? The thought continued to tease her mind, battering against her beliefs. Didn't her sister, a highly respected archaeologist, often say there was a bit of truth to every tale?

There was only one way to find out.

"Leave," she whispered to him. "Leave right now."

His scowling countenance disappeared in a cloud of smoke.

Three minutes passed, then four. The only sound was the ticking of the clock, and each tap pounded in her ears like a war drum. When she felt enough time had elapsed, she sucked in a deep breath, reached out and jabbed the button again. Just like before, the lights flickered. Purple mist erupted. Mr. Half-Naked's clean, unique fragrance invaded her nostrils.

Then, suddenly, he was frowning down at her, his

swirling violet eyes alight with irritation. "What is it you wish now, little dragon? This coming-and-going nonsense must cease."

A genie, she thought, awed. She couldn't deny his existence and wasn't even sure why she'd wanted to. He was an exquisite specimen of manhood. So exquisite, in fact, she wouldn't be surprised if he had "grade A one-hundred-percent pure beef" stamped on his butt.

Gathering her courage, she spoke. "Welcome to my home, genie."

His brows knit together in confusion, and for the moment, he didn't appear quite so menacing. "I am a man. A warrior."

She paused. "But you have magic powers."

"Only in the art of seduction."

"So you don't grant wishes?"

"Nay. I do not."

"Oh." Her shoulders sagged in disappointment. "What exactly do you do?"

"This I have told you once before. I entertain, converse and protect. But most importantly, I supply the female body—your body—with untold bliss."

He could have been filing his fingernails for all the excitement in his voice. Still, the man flat out admitted he wanted to…wanted to… Her tongue began to feel heavy, preventing speech. This man, this nongenie, wasn't hitting on her, she reminded herself. He wasn't asking her out on a date. More than likely, such a dangerously handsome male found her unattractive. Repulsive, even. That thought eased her discomfort, making her tongue feel normal again, but a hollow ache sparked to life in her chest.

She studied him. He looked capable of anything, anything at all, and she found herself wondering what his limitations were. "So you're saying that if I want you to clean my toilets, you will?"

"Toilets?"

"Lavatory. Chamber pot. Powder room."

"Aye, I have cleaned many of those."

She wanted to laugh at his disgruntled expression, but the sword strapped to his waist kept her quiet. Surely he didn't have to obey her *every* whim. "What if I want you to crawl on your hands and knees to polish my floor? Or what if I want you to dust every single one of my antiques with your tongue? Or…eat a mud pie because I spent an hour baking it?"

"Would those things bring you enjoyment," he said, a feral glint entering his mystical eyes, "they would be mine to do."

His words surprised her and should have made her happy, but suddenly Julia was overwhelmed with pity for him, to always be reliant on someone else's pleasure. Other men probably dreamed of being caught in just such a circumstance. A sexual object. Not this man. He was tense and edgy, and self-loathing radiated from the hard stance of his body.

Silence permeated the room for a long while.

Julia didn't know what to say, didn't know what to tell him that could make the situation more bearable for him. She felt a bombardment of guilt for even suggesting he do those awful things for her. Well, no more. Really, what did she need a slave for? Nothing, that's what. She enjoyed cleaning her home, cooking her own meals—not mud pies—and she didn't like others handling her antiques, unless they planned to buy them.

She would *not* treat this man as a slave. He was a human being and deserved more. She'd treat him like the big brother she'd always wanted.

Just admit it, Julia. You simply don't have the courage to take him up on what he's really offering.

She gulped. "What's your name?"

"Most call me Pleasure Slave, or simply Slave."

Pleasure Slave? "I'm not calling you that." The name was too erotic, too sexual. "Do you have a name that doesn't have anything to do with the bedroom? Like John or Phil."

A pause, then, "Tristan."

"Tristan," she repeated, liking the sound. It suited him, being both sensual and unique. "That's what I'll call you."

"If that is your desire." He gave her a slow, leisurely smile that held a hint of genuine appreciation.

Her heart rate kicked into overtime, the impact of that take-no-prisoners grin leaving her reeling. Good Lord, the man belonged on the cover of *GQ*. Julia glanced at his sword. Okay, scratch *GQ*. He belonged on the front page of *Hunky Barbarians*.

"I will hear your name, little dragon."

Annoyance replaced her admiration and launched her quickly to her feet. "You can stop referring to me as a tiny fire-breathing lizard. I'm not *that* unattractive. And for your information, I'm not little. I'm normal. You just happen to be excessively tall."

His lips twitched, and his eyes went from lavender to the purest blue. "So I say again—I will hear your name."

"Call me Julia," she replied grudgingly. "Or Jules, if you must."

"I shall keep that in mind." He clasped his hands behind his back. "I am now ready to hear what you desire of me."

"I want nothing from you," she hastened to assure him. "Absolutely nothing."

Features tightening, he said, "Why did you summon me on three separate occasions if you wished not to make use of me?"

She shrugged. "The first time I thought you were an intruder."

"Ah." Like the flip of a switch, he lost his dark glower and his lips once again twitched with amusement. "And you thought to defend yourself from an Imperian warrior with this karate of yours?"

Bristling at his superior tone, she locked her fists on her hips and glared. "My hands are deadly weapons, you know. You would die if I karate-chopped your neck."

"I believe you," he said. "I am quite sure I would die of laughter."

Even as her heart accelerated at the sheer masculine beauty he represented, Julia fought a surge of anger. The man had a lot of nerve! First he scared the crap out of her. Then he called her a tiny dragon—did she really look like a lizard? Now he had the gall to insult her self-defense skills.

I would die of laughter, she silently mimicked.

A hidden part of her wanted to slap Tristan upside the head with a jackhammer. Since physical violence was against the law—and she didn't relish being locked inside a cell with a woman named Big Bertha—Julia opened her mouth to offer him a stinging retort. His next question stopped her, however.

"Where is your husband?" He uttered a low, rumbling chuckle that purred and soothed and probably sent women to their knees. "You did not kill him with karate, did you?"

Uh-oh. Caught. Julia's animosity toward Tristan drained as *her* sin surfaced. A piece of lint on the hem of her white tank top suddenly became fascinating.

"Did you kill him?" All traces of humor vanished from Tristan's voice. "By Elliea, you did! Where did you place the body?"

"Look," she said, twisting the sheer fabric in knots. "I'm not actually married."

Tristan blinked. "Then where is your man?"

"Technically, I don't have a man."

"Not a father? Brother? Protector?"

Jaw clenched, cheeks red, she shook her head.

"So you spoke an untruth." It was a statement, not a question, laced with puzzlement rather than ire.

"I thought you were an intruder, remember? What else was I supposed to say? We're all alone so don't worry about the neighbors hearing my screams while you kill me?"

"I am glad you do not have a man."

Julia gulped, not liking the sudden, possessive perusal he gave her. "Mind if I ask why?"

"Jealous husbands are a nuisance."

Not exactly the answer she expected. In fact, she was offended for married men and women everywhere. Because of Tristan's profession, he probably didn't know much about relationships. To arm him with knowledge, she launched into a speech about vows, monogamy and the joys of commitment. Her sister often said Julia should have been a lawyer. Tristan's eyes soon glazed and a yawn hovered at the edges of his mouth. "Don't you believe in the sanctity of marriage?" she ended.

"Aye. Yet I must do as my *guan ren* commands." His steely tone scraped the very air around them.

She had to assume *guan ren* meant master. "I'm sorry," she said, hoping to soothe him. "Being a slave must be difficult at times."

"Such a life is not difficult," he grumbled. "Such a life is torture. Every minute of every day."

Lord, there had to be some way to help him. The prospect of owning another human being was beginning to make her queasy. "Is there any way I can free you?"

He didn't answer for a long time, his features changing expression like the click of a camera. Hope. Disappointment. Anger. Finally all emotion cleared and he said simply, "Nay, you cannot. What is required is impossible. I must find my one true love."

"Why is that so impossible?" Surely this man had

loved, and been loved, by thousands. For people like him, gorgeous and self-assured, love acted as a magnetic force. He would have no problem finding his soul mate. If he were plain like her, however, she would understand his difficulty.

That muscle was ticking in his jaw again, and she could tell he didn't want to answer. Then, as if propelled by a force greater than himself, he spoke. "Love is an emotion I am unable to experience."

She blinked up at him. "You're joking, right?"

"Nay, I am not."

He was serious—deadly serious—and since he had a sword, she wasn't going to try to change his mind. Julia rubbed her temples. *What am I going to do with this tall, dark and sinfully delicious pleasure slave?*

She could panic.

No. That wouldn't do. Having grown up with extremely volatile parents, she preferred to calmly wade through her problems.

She could return the box to the flea market.

No again. The dealer's market only ran once a month, and the vendors always changed. The previous owner might not be there and, more than likely, he wouldn't refund her money. Besides, she felt sorry for Tristan. No telling what another woman might force him to do. Kiss her, lick her, touch her…

Julia's back straightened and she squared her jaw. No question about it, she was keeping him.

"Look," she said. "I'll be honest. I'm not interested in having a slave, but I'd love a big-brother type." Ignoring his dubious expression, she continued. "Anyway, we need to talk, to iron out some details."

"Such as?" he asked, though his expression made it quite clear he was really thinking, *Hush your mouth, wench.*

"We need to discuss exactly what we expect from each other. Where you'll stay, what you'll do. That sort of thing." She motioned with a wave of her hand, indicating the chair directly across from her. "Please, have a seat."

Though the scowl he offered her said he'd rather skin her alive with his sword, he folded his long, gorgeous legs under the table. The chair creaked in protest.

Giving him a grateful smile, she sat down, as well. "Where to begin?" she muttered. She'd never been in this situation before, with a half-naked man across from her. Should she begin with the sleeping arrangements, or casually work her way around the subject?

A moment later, he grabbed the reins of the conversation himself. "Where am I?" he asked.

"America. Sante Fe, New Mexico, to be exact."

"Santa Fa? Am-erica." One dark brow arched, and confusion flittered in the crystalline pools of his eyes. "I do not know of these places."

Not know of the mighty U. S. of A.? "How long were you trapped inside that box?"

"I last emerged eighty-nine seasons ago."

"And before that?"

"I was blessed with twelve seasons alone, then emerged in Arcadia. Before that? I hardly recall."

Seasons must be years, Julia thought. She studied the smooth skin of his face. "Just how old are you, Tristan?"

"Almost one thousand and five hundred seasons, I think." He shrugged. "I stopped counting several centuries ago."

Her jaw nearly dropped to the floor. She hadn't expected that. He was a living, breathing antique, yet he looked so handsome, so virile. "Do you eat lots of bran or something?"

His chin tilted to the side. "I do not understand."

"It's just that you appear so young. Too young to be so old."

Bitterness hardened his features, like clay drying into pottery. "Once the binding spell was cast, I ceased aging. A *courtesy* of the black-haired sorceress, Zirra."

Sorceress? Binding spell? "She cursed you? But… why?"

"Why does any woman curse a man?"

Because she'd been spurned hung in the air unsaid.

"This Arcadia you mentioned," Julia said. "Is that where you're from?"

"Nay. I hail from Imperia."

Arcadia. Imperia. Both were names she didn't recognize. Julia's stomach tightened as her thoughts spiraled off in a direction she didn't like. "Are either of those places, um, on Earth?"

His lips thinned into a tight line. "Nay."

Okay. The thought of life on another planet or dimension or *whatever* stretched her imagination to the limit. *Remember, Julia, your own personal pleasure slave is sitting mere inches from your reach. So...interplanetary travel? Not too hard to believe, actually.*

"If we're from—" she had to swallow her disquietude before she could continue "—from different planets, how do you know my language?"

"Another spell, this one cast by an exiled member of Gillradian society. Whatever land I visit, that language do I speak."

"Magic language. Of course. I'm surprised I didn't guess."

His warm, rich chuckle rained over her like a silky caress. "I think you speak another untruth, little dragon." Still grinning, his gaze circled the kitchen. "What manner of home is this?"

"What do you mean?"

"It is...so small."

"Small?" A laugh bubbled past her throat. "You've got to be kidding. This place is three thousand square feet."

"Of your feet, mayhap."

Considering she'd grown up in a two-room adobe hut, this place suited her to perfection. "I'll have you know my house is not small. In fact, it's the biggest house in the neighborhood."

"I am sure this is fine for one so tiny as you."

"I am not tiny, Conan."

He shook his head. "I am Tristan, not Conan."

"Never mind." She waved a hand through the air. "You know, for a pleasure slave, you lack certain pleasuring skills."

"Do I?" With a lascivious grace at odds with the

sheer size of him, he eased to his feet. "Well, then, I will have to remedy that impression immediately."

Julia almost jumped out of her skin. "I don't know what you're planning, but I know I won't like it."

"You will like it," he vowed. "I have been pleasuring women for centuries now, and know exactly where to touch you to make you scream."

Oh, my holy Lord most high. "I'm sure you do, but I swear to God I don't need a demonstration."

"Oh, I think you do." And with that, he approached, striding around the table and straight toward her.

CHAPTER THREE

*Always Gain Permission Before
Touching Your Master*

WITH A SPEED Superman would have envied, Julia's guilt fled, replaced by confusion, panic and just a dash of eagerness. "What are you doing?" she demanded as Tristan continued his wicked-minded approach.

He stopped, only a whisper away, and positioned his hands on both sides of her chair. His hard body ignited a fiery heat deep inside her, a heat that, once kindled, might never be doused.

"I am giving you a demonstration," he said huskily, "of the pleasure I can give."

Omigod, omigod, omigod. Her heart pounded sporadically in her chest, a pitter-patter of conflicting emotions. Did he plan to kiss her? Or…more?

Before her tongue could turn to mush, she blurted out, "There will be no pleasuring me in this house!" The prospect of bodily delight both frightened and intrigued her. He was a stranger, after all, but dear God, he was handsome.

He uttered another sexy, rumbling chuckle. "As I am yours to command, I will simply have to see to your *displeasure*."

"Wait! That's not what I meant."

When he leaned down, his lips softening for a kiss, she hastened to add, "I meant to say you *will* pleasure me right now."

"That is all I desire, little dragon. That is all I desire."

Irritated with him—and herself—she wrapped her arms across her chest. Why did this always happen to her? Why did her brain refuse to work properly in the presence of a romance-minded man?

"You will please me," she said carefully, "by staying on your side of the kitchen."

One of his dark brows arched. "You are sure?"

"No. Yes. Yes, I am sure. You stay on your side, and I'll stay on mine."

"Such is your command, and such will I do."

Tristan moved two small paces back. His very presence flustered little Julia, and he would be lying if he claimed he did not like her reaction to him. The slight trembling of her body, the parting of her lips. The deep color in her cheeks. Oh, he liked. He liked very much indeed.

The knowledge made him curse inwardly and he struggled to fortify himself against her appeal. Over the years, he had served many women of many different worlds. Except for a rare few, all of his *guan rens*—his female masters—had been selfish and vapid, expecting him to give total and complete obedience while they gave only commands and empty promises. Those demands always began immediately. Some hadn't wanted him sexually, but they certainly took full advantage of their ownership.

Clean this, slave. Massage me, slave. Caress me until I scream with pleasure, slave. He'd heard every demand imaginable.

Nay, he shouldn't like this woman, not any part of her.

Still…little Julia had yet to request anything except his absence. And his friendship.

Mayhap he had lived inside the box too long, and that was why she seemed so alluring. Or mayhap she simply reminded him of his homeland with her flashing dragon eyes—green, lush and intense.

For a moment, he allowed himself to imagine that things would be different with this woman, that she truly wanted nothing more from him than his company. However, cynicism soon overrode his optimism. How many times had he dared hope for a measure of compassion only to find indifference?

Countless.

Give this one time, he thought, and she will demand submission just like the others. At least bedding her would be no hardship.

Right now, the little dragon wore only a pair of panties and a thin white chemise held in place by tiny scraps of material, leaving most of her creamy skin visible for his perusal. She possessed a curvy waist and full, luscious breasts, as mouthwatering and sensual as her exotic feminine fragrance. Her hair hung down her back in a symphony of colors. From glossy dark brown, to gold, to the pale locks that framed her face.

Her cheekbones were high, and she had a small nose. At first glance, and maybe at second, her prettiness wasn't readily apparent. The more he had studied her, however, the more he liked what he saw. She was an intriguing blend of courage and timidity, prudishness and sensuality.

It was the prudishness that drew him most. That stay-away, do-not-please-me demeanor of hers challenged him in a way nothing had in centuries. Every time he hinted at carnal indulgence, she became agitated.

He considered that. He had been forced to pursue women before. Some simply liked to be chased. Was this a game Julia liked to play, then? After all, bed sport began long before the first piece of clothing was actually removed.

Nay. No game, certainly. The woman radiated fear. She was like a newborn dragon unable to fly away from approaching danger. Was she simply surprised by his intent? Or, if he approached once again, would she retreat? Finding out…hmm, the prospect intrigued him.

Grinning, Tristan closed the distance between them for the second time. Before she could order him away, he leaned down and sniffed. "I see you have taken care of the smell." Stroking his chin, he studied her from top to bottom. "It does not seem as if you are in pain, and the hair is gone."

Her face scrunched up adorably in confusion, and she

dropped those fringed lashes in shy perusal. "What are you talking about?"

"Earlier you mentioned needing a bath, having your woman's time and manlike legs." He stared down the length of her. "I must say, they appear perfect to me. Slender. Smooth. The kind that lock a man in place until he gives you full pleasure. I am most thankful you are no longer wearing drocs."

Her gaze collided with his, her eyes alight with aroused wonder. "Drocs?" she asked, breathless.

He smiled, drawing out his next words and finding more excitement in this one act than anything he could last recall. "Drocs are leg coverings, little dragon. Leg coverings."

"Leg…" Slowly realization set in. Red-hot color licked a path from her forehead to collarbone. "I'm in my pajamas," she said. "I'm in my freaking pajamas." Wide-eyed, she rose from her seat and raced out of the kitchen, both delicately shaped hands over her buttocks to shield his view.

Tristan chuckled.

But slowly, with the release of a breath, his humor abandoned him. This *guan ren* might be entertaining, but being owned, being chained to another, was far, far from humorous.

Once Percen, High Priest of the Druinn, had learned of Zirra's curse, the High Priest had cast a spell of his own, hurtling Tristan's box away from Zirra, where he traveled from world to world, by fair means or foul. From one cruelty to another.

Tristan knew why Percen had cast such a spell—to prevent the mortal Great-Lord from discovering that Zirra had broken the Alliance, already a fragile treaty at best, yet one that had at last ceased the war between their people. If word escaped that the Alliance had been broken, war would have once again raged.

While Tristan loathed the High Priest's reasoning, he understood his actions.

Mortal rebels wanted control of the Druinn, and in turn, Druinn rebels wanted control of the mortals. In their attempts to dominate each other, they killed innocent people and destroyed a once-prosperous land. Before his curse, Tristan had looked forward to quashing them both, for he enjoyed the peace and harmony the Alliance promised.

Peace…ah, would he ever know its sweetness again? During the centuries of his enslavement, he had endured such anguish, such humiliation, the memories still made him shudder. He was forced to wonder, always wonder, how many more women he would serve in his infinite lifetime. One thousand? Two? He scowled. After so many *guan rens,* he should have been used to his bondage, should have shrugged at the thought of one more woman. He could not.

He could only pray for his freedom.

But he knew it would never come.

In the beginning, he had searched for a woman to cherish, a woman to entrust with his heart. Then he had realized that if he fell in love with a woman and uttered a true declaration, there would be no magic to hold him to whatever planet he found himself on. He would hurtle back to Imperia. Alone. Forced to live his life without his true love.

"Love," he spat. The word was a curse more foul than the one he currently endured. To love a woman was to live without her.

Nay, love was not worth the hardships it brought.

Tristan surveyed the room, taking in details that had been overshadowed by Julia's presence. The small space and low ceiling did not hamper the artistry of her decor. Fresh flowers overflowed from colorful vases. Elegant chairs pushed against a dark, ornately carved table. A finely woven rug lined the polished wood floor. Delicate, all. His large frame simply did not fit within the constrictors of this home.

What kind of place was this Am-erica? Were all the inhabitants as small and fetching as Julia? Thinking of her sent a wave of anticipation through him, and he wondered just what the little dragon had planned for him this night.

He was about to find out.

She returned, rosy color blooming in her cheeks; she refused to meet his eyes. Disappointment struck him when he spotted her new clothing. Long black drocs. Neck to waist covered by a thick black chemise. Save for her face, not an inch of skin remained visible. Pity.

"We need to put you to bed." She kept a wide distance between them, remaining in the doorway, as if she didn't dare get too close.

He might have eased another woman from her embarrassment. Yet glowing such a creamy shade of pink, Julia appeared freshly roused from a vigorous bout of lovemaking—and ready for more. Tristan refused to do anything that might disturb that image. Thus, he said nothing.

"Well?" she said, a hint of exasperation underlying her tone. "Aren't you going to say anything?"

"I shall sleep with you."

"No!" With her mouth tightly compressed, she closed her eyes, blocking all trace of her emotions. A moment passed in silence. When she regarded him once more, determination etched every line and hollow of her expression. "Sleeping in the same bed isn't necessary. I have a spare bedroom. You can use that."

"I am your pleasure slave. Sleeping with you is my obligation."

"Your obligation?" She looked insulted. "I don't think so."

Tristan crossed his arms over his chest and leaned one hip against the speckled counter beside him. Seducing women was second nature to him, instinctive and usually boring. Any pleasure he once received out of the game had long since deserted him and now seemed a chore. Most times, he'd rather count grains of sand. Except...he was not bored right now. Excitement pounded through him. He'd forgotten how it felt to take a woman simply because he desired her.

"Why sleep alone when you can partake of my warmth?" His voice dipped low and seductive, something that caused most women's eyes to close at half-mast, their knees to go weak and their resistance to melt. "I am here for your needs, little dragon."

Julia screeched, an all-out, honest-to-Elliea, I've-had-enough-of-you screech. She even stomped her foot. "How many times do I have to say it? I don't want any pleasure."

"Ah…so you enjoy sensual pain?" he asked, purposefully misunderstanding. Never had a wench been so fun to tease.

Her mouth dropped open with a strangled gasp.

He gave her a sublimely immoral grin. "Do you prefer I spank you with my hand or a paddle?"

"We are not having this conversation," she said.

"I have need of clarification." He took two steps forward. "For some, the hand provides enough stimulation. For others, only a paddle will do."

Julia slapped a hand over her eyes. "This isn't happening to me. I am not standing in my kitchen with a man who has seen my butt and thinks everything I say is a sexual come-on. I'm dreaming again. That's it. This type of torture is too cruel to be real."

"Oh, no, little dragon. Right now, I am not torturing you. But do you say the words, I will give you the sweetest torture your body has ever known."

"Enough!" Scowling, she jabbed a finger in his chest. "You will stop that right now, Mr. I'm So Sexy."

"Nay, I am Tristan."

"And you are completely missing the point. No more talk about sex. In fact, if you utter one more word about dirty, rotten monkey love, I will personally cut out your tongue. No, don't say it." She held up one hand, palm out, when he opened his mouth to reply. "Don't say anything for at least sixty seconds."

He waited the allotted time then said, "This dirty, rotten monkey love sounds interesting. Mayhap you should explain."

Argh! "Why can't you understand? I'm not interested in you *that* way."

That gave him pause. "You have no liking for me?"

At his words, she turned her head away, staring anywhere but at him. "You just aren't the kind of guy I'm drawn to, that's all."

Hmm…Tristan frowned. Had things changed so much in the past eighty-nine seasons? He gave himself a once-over, yet found himself lacking in absolutely no way. His body appeared as strong as ever, and he still possessed all of his hair and teeth.

Did the women of her world prefer fat, balding, toothless males?

He wanted Julia, and he liked not the fact that she found him unappealing. But oh, the challenge of changing her mind enticed him on every level.

His friend Roake would have laughed right now had he been here. The scarred, battle-hardened warrior had often commented that Tristan needed a refusal or two. Built character, he said.

"Do you find me ugly?"

"Ugly?" Julia stared up at him. How could he possibly think she found him ugly? He was like a nineteenth-century porcelain hand-painted dessert plate topped with chocolate éclairs. "You aren't ugly."

His baffled and slightly wounded expression didn't waver.

She knew exactly how it felt to be found unappealing and lacking, and the thought that *she* had caused someone to feel that way pained her greatly. "I mean it, Tristan. You aren't ugly, and I'm so sorry I gave you that impression. To be honest, you're one of the most beautiful men I've ever seen."

"I see."

She lifted her lashes and looked up at him imploringly. "I truly am sorry that I upset you and made you feel unattractive. I didn't mean to. Honest."

Tristan tried not to let her ardent apology affect him, but it seeped into his bones like the sweet nectar of *gartina* petals. As he had never witnessed its like, such genuine concern for his feelings mystified him. "If I am so desirable, explain why you do not like me in *that* way."

"You're just so…well, you carry a sword." Finger shaky, she pointed to his talon.

Ah, she feared his mighty blade.

The double entendre made him smile inwardly. Women of every world had adored his weapon, clinging to the danger and excitement it added to their seduction. For Julia's benefit, he uttered a long-suffering sigh, gripped the talon by its handle and unhooked it from his belt.

"One blade is hardly a thing to fear," he told her. "When I lived in Imperia, I strapped weapons all over my body."

"Good Lord. Why?"

"To execute my enemies, of course."

She blinked. "Please tell me you're kidding."

"Worry not." He smiled reassuringly. "You are not my enemy."

"I'm thankful for that, at least."

"You will soon be thankful for many things," he muttered. The silvery metal glistened as he laid his weapon across the table—close enough that he had only to reach out if he needed it. He arched a brow. "Does this satisfy you?"

Her relief pounded through the room like a palpable force. "Yes, thank you."

"You are most welcome." With her one objection to him obliterated, she would want him in *that* way. He was sure of it. She confirmed his thoughts by moistening her take-me-now lips with the tip of her tongue.

Unable to stop the action, he drew in a breath. He became trapped in her sorceress-like spell, craving another glimpse of that pink tongue, unable to blink, much less look away. His groin tightened painfully with need, and he fought a wave of confusion. More than six hundred years had passed since he'd experienced an impromptu erection—and now he did because of one glorious little tongue. 'Twas shocking, that.

"Now that we've got everything settled," she said, reaching down and gripping his jewelry box in her hands, "we can go to bed. If you'll follow me…" She turned and strolled away, swaying her hips in rhythm to a mating call.

A call he had every intention of answering.

CHAPTER FOUR

Your Master Is Never Wrong

WITH ONLY A BACKWARD GLANCE to his talon, Tristan trailed behind Julia. He continued to watch her buttocks as she moved. Very nice. Very nice, indeed. By Elliea, he wanted those hips under him…over him…beside him.

He was actually excited about bedding a woman. He was still shocked by that fact.

By her next words, she was obviously as excited as he was.

"I am so ready for bed," she muttered.

"So am I, little dragon," he said. "So am I."

They passed through a room crammed with treasures. There were paintings, dolls and books. Jewelry, pots, pans and glassware. Had he not been so eager to lose himself in Julia's body, he would have wanted to explore this haven. But that, he decided, would have to wait until he and Julia found release. Twice.

Abruptly she stopped in the center of the room and turned to face him. "Close your eyes, please."

He did so immediately, without question, and hated

himself for it, but over the years he had learned his lessons well. Obey the spell and, in turn, his *guan ren*, or suffer. He heard the rustle of paper, the scrape of…something. What was the woman doing?

"You may open your eyes now," she said.

She was standing before him as if she hadn't moved, yet she was no longer holding the box, and she was blinking up at him as if she expected him to balk. He didn't. How could he? Hiding the box was the action of an intelligent woman. He'd lost count of how many greedy, pleasure-minded women had stolen him—mayhap because he no longer cared who he belonged to.

"This way," she said, continuing her journey. She led him into a dark, narrow corridor. There were no trinkets here, only candles lined against the walls. A soft, sweet fragrance, like sugar and spice, overlaid the air. From there, Julia showed him into a tiny bedchamber.

"This is where you'll sleep," she told him.

He glanced around, taking in the furnishing. A redwood dragon cabinet, a mirrored dressing table, ethereal wine-colored drapes and turquoise decorative pillows. "What type of animal is that?" he asked, indicating to the far wall where an alabaster beast sprouted green leaves.

"That's an elephant plant stand."

"And what is that?" Frowning, dreading her answer, he pointed to a small boxlike structure.

"That is the bed," she told him.

Just as he'd suspected. "A child would not fit in such a contraption, much less two people."

"You—you're sleeping alone," she said. "The bed *is* big enough for one."

She began chewing on her mouth, an action he was beginning to loathe almost as much as he liked it. Her lips were spectacular—lush and soft and pink. They were the kind of lips that made a man willing to battle a thousand armies for a single kiss, and Tristan swore to Elliea the next time she nibbled on those delicate morsels, he was going to soothe them the only way he knew how—with his tongue.

"Nay. I am not sleeping alone. I am sleeping with you."

Her eyes darted around the room like those of a trapped animal searching for escape. "I thought you understood the sleeping arrangements."

"I understand that I do not want to pleasure you in such a small setting. We must find larger accommodations since I plan to bring you to climax over and over again."

"Climax?" She made a strangling sound in the back of her throat, and even folded her hands around her neck. "Over and over again?" More strangling sounds.

Had he frightened her to the point of choking? Concern rushing through him, he pounded her between her shoulder blades.

"I'm...fine...thank...you.... Stop!" she managed between blows.

He did as instructed, though his palm lingered on her back. "You are unharmed?"

She arched her back, then twisted about at the hips, maneuvering each section of her spine. "Except for a few broken bones," she said dryly, "I'm okay."

Broken bones? Tristan ran his hands up and down her body. And what a body it was, all soft curves and feminine roundness. Her shoulders were small and fragile, her hips soft and voluptuous. Her breasts were full and heavy, and the plump mounds overflowed in his hands.

Were her nipples pink or brown or a color in between?

He caressed one peaked tip with his fingertip. She sucked in a breath but never once uttered a protest. Encouraged, he traced his finger over the other tip. "Your bones do not feel broken," he whispered, letting the warmth of his breath fan her ear.

"I was joking," she said, the words barely escaping.

"So you are well?"

She nodded, nibbling on her bottom lip. "Promise."

There she was, chewing on her mouth again. Always a man of his word, Tristan leaned down until his lips were only a rustle away from hers. "This I am glad to hear…because now I am going to taste you."

She didn't pull from his grasp, nor did she attempt to push him away. She merely blinked up at him as if he'd spoken a foreign language. Then her eyes widened. "I'm not sure—"

"No lecture." His fingers tangled in her hair, dragging her deeper into his embrace. "Not now."

She gulped and tore her gaze away.

"Look at me, Julia."

Slowly, so slowly, her long, sooty lashes swept upward until she met his stare. He knew what she saw in his eyes. Hunger. Raw, primal hunger. He wanted her, wanted to forget his surroundings, wanted to forget who and what he was, wanted to lose himself if only for a moment and find strength in the familiarity of a woman's arms.

"My tongue burns for the taste of you. My hands itch for the feel of you. And my shaft screams for the core of you. Let me have you."

Lust flared in *her* eyes, causing the deep, dazzling green irises to darken and the lids to lower halfway. She was desire incarnate just then, and an invisible force seemed to draw her closer, closer still until his hardness nestled her softness. Her exotic scent, like moonlight and stars, wafted to his nostrils.

He moved his hands lower and palmed the soft skin at the back of her neck, guiding her face inches from his. Her small, soft body fit perfectly against him, and he knew instinctively that he would fit even better inside her. Once, twice, his lips brushed hers, lingering, hoping to absorb her sweetness.

His breath caressed her nose, her cheek, as he waited for an invitation to partake of what waited within. When she didn't open, his tongue flicked out and traced the seam of her lips. She moaned, a low, shimmering sound that weakened his knees as it washed over him in slow, erotic waves.

"Open for me," he said.

Surprisingly she did so without hesitation.

His tongue slipped easily inside, and he began a slow dance of touch and retreat. She moved with his mouth gently at first, as if exploring and learning, but soon her dam of restraint collapsed and she increased the pace.

She thrust hard and fast. Her lips meshed against his, and her arms locked around his back, her nails clawing at his flesh. She moaned, trying to sink all the way past his skin. Her taste deepened with passion, a heady combination of savage desire and untapped wildness.

"Delicious," he whispered, forcing himself to disengage from her for a moment to gain perspective. "I want more."

"More. Lots more." She jerked him back to her, holding him tight and keeping him close to her as she rocked her hips forward, sank back and rocked again—no longer acting the innocent.

She was feral with the force of her need. His brow furrowed with confusion. He'd never before encountered a woman who erupted so quickly. "Julia?"

"Don't stop," she said. At each point of contact, each time the apex of her thighs brushed his erection, her hands clutched him tighter, a little more desperately. No matter Julia's former protests to the contrary, these were the actions of a woman in need of immediate fulfillment.

She liked him in *that* way.

Satisfaction swept through him as he imagined fulfilling her in every fashion he knew.

"I can't get enough," she panted, her breathing labored, her eyes still closed. She continued to gyrate against him. "You promised more. I want more."

Her words went straight to his shaft, making him harden and swell to the point of pain. He knew she was wet, so wet he would have no trouble sliding his width inside of her.

"I'll give you everything," he said. His own breaths were coming a little too quickly. "This I swear to you."

This time when he claimed her mouth, he did not have to request that she open for him. Eagerly her tongue swept out to meet him, rolling and sparring with his. Even their teeth clashed with the force of their need. She nipped at his bottom lip as if she wanted to devour him. Her legs entwined with his, and she rubbed more forcefully against his erection. She gripped his buttocks, then reached around and cupped his heavy sac through his drocs.

He sucked in a breath. She was like liquid fire and a wild storm combined. At that moment he wanted to push so deep within her she could only gasp his name. He wanted to feel her inner walls clench as she searched for release, wanted to feel that powerful surge of pleasure while he held her naked and spent himself inside her.

He wanted all of that from one simple kiss and a few caresses. Inconceivable.

A kiss shouldn't be this good, this *magical,* he thought. A kiss shouldn't consume him, shouldn't make him yearn for impossible things. But it did. Suddenly he yearned. With each press of their tongues, with each brush of their bodies, he yearned for their souls to connect, for their hearts to beat in sync.

He yearned for forever. No, surely not.

He had never felt this…pull before. This *need* for another to be a part of him. Surely this had nothing to do with Julia herself, he rationalized, but everything to do with a man's desire to conquer.

Aye. That was it. Little Julia was proving to be more

enticing, more *exciting,* than he'd first imagined, and his warrior's instinct demanded he conquer her. That was all. She might taste like ambrosia and feel softer than *gartina* petals, but she meant nothing more to him than the rest of his women.

She was not special.

Determined now to prove to himself that he could take her and remain emotionless, he trailed kisses down her jaw, her neck, her collarbone, all the while keeping his mind detached. *She is nothing,* he told himself, *merely a* guan ren.

"I'm going to remove your clothing now, *nixa.*"

"Yes, I—" Julia paused. Something wasn't right, she realized. Something was different now. He sounded cold and callous, completely uncaring.

She shoved her way out of the sensual fire raging inside her mind and slowly regained her common sense. Details danced within her grasp, then solidified. Tristan wasn't breathing hard, wasn't even winded, while she labored for every breath. He appeared perfectly skilled, dispassionate and restrained while she arched and writhed for more.

His expression was impassive, his eyes devoid of emotion, his lips firm, hard. He did not look like a passionate lover. He looked…removed. Like a slave doing his master's bidding. He didn't really want her, she realized. He merely played a part. Nausea and embarrassment churned in her stomach.

With calm, sure movements, he began to work her shirt over her head.

"No." Julia jerked backward, away from Tristan and the magnetic force of his body.

I'm an idiot. Why hadn't she pushed him away the first moment he touched her? But she already knew the answer. When his hands had moved over her body checking for injuries, she'd found herself confronting every fantasy her mind had ever conjured. Pure sensation, raw maleness. Total desire.

How she'd craved—how she *still* craved—more of his caresses, more of his taste. Lord, he had stroked his tongue across her lips while his hands kneaded her. Tingles and need had shot straight through her like the lightning bolt she'd wanted God to strike her with. Desire had pooled deep in her belly, between her legs, and her nipples had pearled tightly. She'd simply reacted.

For the first time, she'd known true, consuming desire. Every cell in her body had gone on alert, ready for sensations she didn't quite understand but wanted to. Desperately. His flavor…well, chocolate didn't compare. He'd moved his tongue, body and hands so expertly, bringing optimum pleasure. As she remembered, a dreamy sound of promise and passion slipped past her lips. She craved another kiss, another taste. Would do almost anything to experience one more. Just one more kiss….

Julia blinked, realizing she was once again losing herself in Tristan, and this time he hadn't even touched her! How could one man affect her so strongly? And how in God's name could Tristan remain so unaffected?

Was she *that* undesirable?

I am, she thought, battling a sudden torrent of self-pity and sadness. *I truly am.* If she'd had more experience, she might have bolstered her confidence with memories of all the men she'd left in satisfied comas of sexual bliss. But she didn't. And she couldn't. Tristan probably had more experience than most porn stars, while she kissed like a ninety-year-old grandmother suffering from heart disease.

At that thought, what little confidence Julia had left shattered. Self-consciousness snaked stronger coils around her spine, quickly tightening its grip. This was exactly why she couldn't ever kiss Tristan again, no matter how much pleasure his slightest touch gave her. With him, she would always worry that she wasn't doing things right, wasn't satisfying him. Wasn't woman enough.

Except, oddly enough, when his lips first met hers, she hadn't thought about anything except the hot press of his body and all the wicked things they could do to each other.

No. She shook her head. A fluke. Had to be. Were this detached lover to kiss her again, she'd worry, worry, worry that her breath smelled bad, or that he didn't like her body, or that she'd bore him to death.

What if she'd done that this time?

Oh, God, he wasn't even kissing her right now and she was beginning to worry. He found her lacking in the sexual arena. She just knew it. That's why he'd become so unresponsive, and he was probably laughing at her pitiful attempt. Julia studied his face, searching for amusement. She saw confusion…and desire?

No, he didn't desire her. She only saw what she wanted to see, instead of what was really there.

"Let us go to bed," he said, his honey-rich voice breaking the stretch of silence. He clasped her arm.

She wrenched away, using anger as a shield. Anything to prevent herself from flying back into his embrace. "You'll be sleeping—or whatever else you want to do—alone."

His teeth flashed in a scowl. "Alone? I think not. You do not kiss a man with such passion unless you want him in your bed."

"Really? Passion?" Delight shimmered through her. "You're not just saying that?"

He worked his jaw left and right, and didn't stop until the bone popped from exertion. "You would be happy with such an occurrence?"

Not a denial, but not an agreement, either. "Forget it," she grumbled. "Just go to sleep. I'll see you in the morning."

"Must we go over our sleeping arrangements yet again?"

"We'll go over it until you get it right." Her chin tilted stubbornly to the side. "This—" she motioned in a circle with her hand "—is your room. That—" she pointed down the hall "—is mine."

"I removed my weapon. Now you will spend the night with me."

Jeez, for a man who catered to the desires of women, he sure needed constant instruction. Her exasperation must have given her strength, because she managed to say quite forcefully, "We're not sleeping together."

"Julia," he muttered softly, all traces of ire melting from him as swiftly as ice cubes in a desert. His lashes swept low over his eyes and his lips parted. "There is never a good reason to deny ourselves pleasure."

"I told you, I'm not interested in you sexually." She sounded strong and self-assured, like a woman who knew what she wanted and what she didn't. So why didn't she *feel* that way?

"I have already proven your words for the untruth they are. You became liquid fire when I touched you. Your legs wrapped around mine, locking me against you, your lips to mine, your body to mine. Were I to touch between your thighs now, you would be wet for me. So do not tell me you want nothing to do with me sexually."

Because her tongue was now glued to the roof of her mouth, Julia opted for the coward's way out. She didn't offer a reply; she simply turned and ran to her room, shutting the door firmly behind her.

Closing her eyes, she sank onto the bed. What had she gotten herself into?

Trouble, her mind immediately answered. *You've gotten yourself into a whole lot of trouble.*

CHAPTER FIVE

*You Have Only Two Words To Offer Any
Conversation: Yes And Master*

TRISTAN PACED the small hallway for a long while. And with every step, he cursed women everywhere for their fickleness. He cursed himself, as well. He hadn't remained detached. He wanted Julia, had tried to force her to see his way. A small sin, really, when compared to hers. *She* had made his body burn for completion, and then turned him away.

This would not have happened on Imperia, where women flocked to his side.

Imperia. Just thinking the name caused a wave of loneliness and loss to crash through him, cutting so deeply it nearly cleaved him in two. Never again would he see his home, the billowing white grass, the multi-hued sky. The soaring dragons. Never would he watch the four suns rise separately and the moons rise together. Never would he know if his friend Roake had taken a wife, if he had children.

Never would he know the life—and death—his dearest friends and family experienced. Or rather, *had* experienced. They were dead to him now, for they'd lived over a thousand years ago in his other life. The people and places that had been so important to him were now like mist in his mind—sometimes thick and tangible, and at others so sheer he would not know they were there if not for a lingering, ever-present fragrance.

Still he ached at their loss. Ached because he would never again know true friendship or have a home of his own, but would know only the whims and ever-changing desires of his *guan rens*.

Bitterness roared to life, an emotion he rarely allowed but could do nothing to stop now, wrapping him in despair so absolute he almost moaned in physical pain. With a virulent expression, he gazed at the empty area surrounding him—an emptiness he found mirrored within himself but usually managed to hide. He'd lost his future. His loved ones.

Mayhap even his soul.

What did he have now except an eternity of slavery? Hopelessness joined ranks with his bitterness, waging a desperate war against his resolve, each emotion clawing inside him, leaving him raw and wounded. Only his pride kept him from capitulation, kept him defiant and prevented him from crying out to the heavens and begging Zirra to free him. Not that she would hear him, but the desire sometimes remained. Aye, only pride stopped him, a thing that had earned him so much despair…yet the only thing that had kept him sane.

As he continued to pace, his steps became agitated,

clipped. His very bones burned with the torment of emotions he felt. He had to distract himself, had to lose himself in a woman's—in Julia's—body. Sex wiped the acrid knowledge of his past, and his future, from his mind, if only for a moment, for he controlled the pleasure, therefore he controlled the woman.

But Julia didn't want him.

His hands curled at his sides. Well, he would just have to use every sensual weapon at his disposal to seduce her. All the while keeping his emotions untouchable.

Scowling, he stalked to her door and paused. Without her permission, he could not enter her room. That thought irritated him even further. By Elliea, he loathed being told what to do. He always had. He had been a soldier, leader of the Elite, and all of these years of enslavement had not destroyed his warrior instincts.

A warrior gave orders, he did not take them.

Body tight with frustration, he tested the handle and found the silver metal turned easily. "May I enter, Julia?" The words left his mouth quickly, for he despised the taste of them.

"Why?" came the muffled reply. "I've already told you. You and I are not…we aren't…"

"I did not come to beg for your favors, if that is what you desire." He'd spent too many years of his childhood on his knees, begging for clothes, food and affection, his efforts rewarded with pain and humiliation. To willingly hand that power to another… Nay, he would not. He had proven that to Zirra, and he would prove it now to Julia.

"I don't want anything from you," she called. "I just want to sleep. Alone."

She didn't want him to grovel, then. His muscles released their viselike grip on his bones. "I must ascertain your chamber is properly bolted against intruders." *Before I strip you naked and seduce you.*

A heavy pause thickened the air. Finally she uttered a long-suffering sigh. "All right. You may enter."

He pushed his way inside. Light dripped like crystal tears from an overhead source, brightly illuminating the small room. Imperian light stemmed from *lamori* gems, stones that were alive, yet in his otherworld travels he had seen such light sources as this before, some much more elaborate, so he paid this one no heed. Julia sat atop a sinfully decadent four-poster bed of pink silk sheets and mint-green shams. Her knees were pulled to her chest, and her long honey-colored hair cascaded like rays of sunshine around her face, shoulders and slender arms.

For an instant, her eyes met his, but she quickly glanced away.

After a determined inhale, exhale of breath, she once again faced him. "I haven't meant to be so ill-tempered," she said. "I'm just...I don't know. Two days ago I flipped a man off, then shoved him at the flea market just to beat him past the doors. Then I yelled at a perverted killer with a sword—that's you, though I don't think of you as a killer anymore."

He arched a brow. "But you still think of me as perverted?"

"No, of course not." She gave a dejected sigh.

"What's wrong with me? I'm usually very reserved. I never speak out of turn. But I've managed to insult you over and over again, and I'm sorry. So very sorry. I don't want to hurt you."

He had expected anger and resistance from her, yet she displayed repentance. She was the only woman ever to offer him such a thing. For a moment, he closed his eyes, unsure of how to respond.

What was he going to do with this woman? Seduction somehow seemed wrong. She deserved so much more than he could give her.

"You have nothing to apologize for, little dragon. I have enjoyed my time with you."

"I know you're just saying that," she said shyly, hopefully contemplating him, "but I thank you, anyway."

He opened his mouth to comment, but her next words stopped him. "I'm sorry for the kiss, too. I didn't mean to let it get out of hand, or to lead you on."

She looked so earnest, so concerned for his feelings. First her apology, now this. A *guan ren*'s concern…so new to him, and yet it was the second time Julia had sought to soothe his ego.

"Do you forgive me?" she asked.

He could not refuse her. "You are forgiven, Julia. As a novice, you knew not what you were doing."

Her features crumpled, and her chin began to tremble. "You noticed, huh? That I'm a novice, I mean?"

"Aye. Our kiss ended too quickly. A woman of more experience would have known this and continued kissing me."

"Oh...oh." Understanding dawned.

Her chuckle rang in his ears as he checked both windows, making sure the locks worked properly and were bolted securely. He searched under the bed, finding nothing but old, dusty boxes. He circled a dark mahogany chest and rummaged through her closet. The amount of clothing contained in the tiny space almost swallowed him whole. Could one tiny female possibly wear all of these garments?

"Um, excuse me," Julia said, all traces of humor now gone. "That's my stuff you're going through. My personal belongings."

"Your personal belongings need organization. Ten men could hide in here and you would never know it."

"No one is hiding in my closet."

"Such is the thought of one who will soon be caught unaware."

She stiffened. "For your information, I look in there every morning."

"Then tell me, little dragon, what this is." He emerged holding a yellow, green and orange floral-print gown. A large mass of painted foliage covered one side. "This is the most hideous garment I have ever beheld. Do your people truly wear such things?"

Offended, she lifted her nose high into the air and he had the distinct impression she wanted to give him another lecture. She didn't. She settled for "That's an authentic baby-doll dress from the sixties."

"It is authentic dung." He knew his eyes were gleaming with mirth as he tossed her the gown. "Put it on."

"I most certainly will not," she said, catching the material with a *humph*. "Why don't you try it on?"

"Men wear armor and weapons, Julia. They do not wear women's clothing."

"Some men do."

Surely she jested, yet her expression held no trace of humor. "What man struts around in his woman's gowns?" he demanded.

"Some men like to wear dresses, okay? Let's just leave it at that. Now, will you please leave my room? It's time to go nighty-night. And do not come back in here for any reason," she added for good measure.

"Not for *any* reason?"

"That's right."

He crossed his arms over his chest. "What if a witch tries to boil you alive?"

"I'll beat her over the head with her broom."

"What if demons of the night attack?"

"I'll scream my head off."

He clicked his tongue. "Nay, if I were with you, little dragon, you would scream—again and again. Since you will be alone, you will do nothing but imagine."

Tristan left her with those words, firmly shutting the door behind him.

CURSE THAT MAN, Julia thought.

You will do nothing but imagine, he'd said, and by God, he was exactly right.

All through the night she tossed and turned, imagining his naked body pressed to hers, his tongue and hands doing wicked things to her. In these fantasies, she was a wild woman. Totally insatiable. She clawed at his back, screamed out his name and sucked the entire length of him into her mouth.

In her dream, she whispered, *"More. Give me more."*

"For you and no other," he replied silkily.

"Harder. Harder," she begged.

He softly laughed. "Oh, but I do love to please you."

"No talk. Only pleasure."

Several times she almost called out to him and begged him to turn her dreams into reality. In the end, she suffered in silence. Stupidity on her part? Probably.

Her body might crave the man, but her pride demanded she only give herself to someone who truly lusted for her. As a pleasure slave, Tristan was forced to please his mistress even if he found her unappealing, and Julia didn't want to be just another let-me-get-this-over-with obligation. How pathetic if she were.

Yes, how pathetic. In a secret part of her heart, she'd always longed for a fairy-tale existence—a man who thought her the most beautiful woman in the world, who loved her madly and deeply. Who worshiped at the altar of her loveliness. Okay, the last was a bit much, but that dream of happily-ever-after had never faded and *would* never fade.

There had to be someone out there for her. *Please let there be someone out there for me,* she prayed. If she found him, maybe then she could regain her sense of contentment.

Closing her eyes, she blocked the image of Tristan

from her mind and pictured the type of man who would find her desirable, yet wouldn't intimidate her. His features were plain, but he had an easy, gentle smile. Heightwise, he stood below average, not much taller than she. He was kind and tender and just a little shy. Most importantly, he never once made her feel stupid or unattractive or unworthy.

Was that asking for too much?

"No, it's not," she muttered. In fact, the more she considered this paragon of manly virtue, the more he took the shape of her new next-door neighbor, Peter. Peter had brown hair, kind hazel eyes, and always wore a good-natured grin. Oh, she wasn't attracted to him physically, but she did feel comfortable in his presence. The only problem was, the few times they'd spoken, Peter hadn't acted as if he was interested in her.

You didn't act as if you were interested in him, either, she reminded herself.

A sigh slipped past her lips. How would Peter react if she called right now and asked him out on a date? Fall to his knees and thank her? Or demand she never call him again? In a spurt of determination, she decided she didn't care how he reacted. She would simply pick up the phone and invite him to dinner. Now. Today. This very second.

Well, maybe in the morning.

Confidence swiftly draining, she burrowed deeper into the covers and recalled the first and only date she'd ever experienced. She'd been sixteen, very shy if a bit mischievous. Brian Davidson, the most popular boy in school, had invited her to dinner. Since she'd had a crush on him for years, she foolishly agreed.

The night of their date, they shared a pizza at the local hangout and talked about their lives. He treated her with such care, was so complimentary, she floated on a rainbow of dreams, imagining the flowers, candy and romance in her future. She'd placed no significance on his glances to the door, or on his laugh, which had rasped a little too high, a little too forced.

Later in the evening, Brian drove her to his home. His parents were out of town, so they were alone. Or so she'd assumed.

They talked some more, and Julia shyly admitted how much she liked him, how she wanted her first time to be with him. He smiled, his eyes cold, and leaned down to kiss her. A heartbeat before his lips met hers and all her dreams came true, she heard a deep voice say, "Gross, Bri. You're not actually going to kiss Julie Ghoulie, are you? We dared you to be seen with her in public, not to make out with her."

Hunter Stevens, Brian's best friend, stood in the hallway, three other boys behind him. All of them doubled over with laughter.

"Brian, you're so wonderful," one of the boys mimicked. "Man, if I heard her say that one more time, I was going to puke."

Brian jerked back, his gaze flitting guiltily from hers. "I had to shut her up, didn't I? What took you guys so damn long? Another second and I would've had to do something desperate."

While the boys continued to laugh and taunt her, Julia had gathered her pride and run out of the house, head high. Each step home, the dam holding her emotions together cracked a bit more. Finally, humiliation and despair consumed her. She had sunk to the ground and sobbed until her tear ducts threatened to burst from the strain.

That one night had destroyed every ounce of self-confidence she'd possessed—and there hadn't been much to begin with. She'd been shy before, but she'd soon become the tongue-tied idiot she was now.

How could a man fall in love with a plain, jittery, awkward woman?

He couldn't.

But...

Perhaps now, things could change. Her shoulders straightened, and she blinked up at the ceiling, hope unfurling in her stomach. Yes. *Yes!* Things *could* change; Tristan could help her. He possessed a vast amount of experience dealing with the opposite sex, and she could make use of that knowledge. Not the way he wanted, of course, spending hour upon hour burning up the sheets, but in a better way. Better? Make that a more productive way. He could teach her how to attract a man... How to attract Peter.

And if she didn't desire her neighbor the way she desired Tristan, well, that was her cross to bear. She needed Peter. He was so much like herself, so reserved and lonely, plain and inexperienced. So safe.

The question was, would Tristan be willing to help

her? She absolutely refused to force him under the Pleasure Slave code of behavior. Unsure, Julia stared out the window, a pillow clutched to her chest. Stars twinkled in the black velvet sky. Tristan had made his intentions toward her very clear. She was his master, therefore he thought she belonged in bed—with him. And no other. So how was she going to convince him to help her entice *another* man?

CHAPTER SIX

*A Slave Must Never Hesitate
When Given An Order*

SUNLIGHT POKED unwanted fingers through Julia's bathroom window, brightening the spacious haven and highlighting her fatigue. She stared at her pale, tired reflection in the vanity mirror. Red eyes. Frowning lips. A leisurely shower had done nothing to improve her I've-been-up-all-night-imagining-Tristan-naked appearance.

"Coffee," she told herself. Her voice cracked and her mouth watered in homage to the beverage. "I need coffee." Then, God help her, she'd talk to Tristan about Peter.

Just thinking about the upcoming conversation caused her stomach to churn with anxiety. She tried to ignore the discomfort and told herself there was no reason to agonize. She had a plan, after all. She was going to treat Tristan as sweet as a brownie-fudge sundae with extra whipped cream. She'd use lots of smiles and a gentle tone of voice.

How could he refuse her?

How could he not?

Focus, Julia. You can do this. You can. Determination pushing her onward, she wound her still-damp hair in a ponytail, shimmied into a pair of beige dress slacks and a white, button-down shirt, and strode to the door.

Sweet as a sundae, sweet as a sundae, sweet as a sundae....

Two steps into the hall, her foot hit a large, immobile object. She plummeted face first and landed with a thud on the hardwood floor. Air shot from her lungs like a Fourth of July rocket. Dazed, she shook her head, blinked her eyes several times. Finally she recaptured her breath and her vision cleared. When she focused, she realized Tristan's sword lay just in front of her, glistening menacingly.

"Julia," he said, concern tinging his voice. "Speak to me. Tell me you are unharmed."

"What the hell are you doing on the floor?" She glared up at him. "I told you to sleep in the guest bedroom."

"Nay, you said the guest chamber is mine, not that I *had* to sleep there."

"Why do you still have your sword? You were supposed to put it up."

"And just where am I to place such a large weapon in such a small home?"

"In your box."

"Is that an order?"

"A request."

"'Tis the same, really." His lips dipped into a fierce frown and as she watched, the air around the sword wavered, thickened like dappled water, and then the silver metal vanished in a puff of smoke. "Done," he said.

She should have been shocked by the disappearing act, but she was too relieved. She vaulted to her feet, keeping her gaze locked with his. This was not the way she imagined them starting the day. *Sweet as a sundae, remember?* Except, now the whipped cream was splayed across the floor. She forced herself to smile, as if practically slicing herself in half was an everyday occurrence.

"We have to talk." Gentle voice. "There's something I need to ask you."

"My attention is yours." He stood with his legs braced apart, arms folded. A prebattle stance, she was sure. "You may begin."

Running a hand down the length of her ponytail, she mentally catalogued her planned speech. She drew in a deep breath and then slowly released each molecule of air. "In America, when a man and woman are attracted to each other, they begin to date. Dating might include a romantic dinner, followed by a walk on the beach, or a—"

"Halt there, little dragon," he said, silencing her words. "We must eat ere you lecture me, for I am in desperate need of sustenance."

She frowned. "I'll have you know I do not lecture. I simply state facts."

"These facts can be stated after we dine."

True, but her nervous system might collapse by then. Still she muttered, "Of course," like a good little brownie sundae.

In the kitchen, beams of sunlight filtered through the

large bay window, enveloping the room in a cheerful ring. She grabbed a blueberry muffin from the counter and turned, holding out the offering like a priceless treasure. "Here you go…" Her words tapered to quiet. A shaft of light illuminated Tristan's hair, creating a glossy halo around his face. He was Hercules come to life just then, only he had a bigger…well, a bigger *everything*.

How sickening, she thought, that one man could be so gorgeous.

"I thank you," he said, accepting the muffin.

Sighing, she pivoted to the counter and began her morning ritual. Fill coffeepot with water. Drain water into percolator. Scoop grounds.

"Sit," Tristan ordered. He set his muffin aside and pried the coffee tin from her hands—an action no one else had ever done and lived to tell the tale. His fingertips brushed her palm, causing shafts of electricity to rush up her arm. "I shall do this duty."

She gulped and pulled away. "Do you know how to make coffee?"

His features lit with wry amusement. "The knowledge I gained on other planets far surpasses that of Am-erica."

"Your knowledge stems from almost a century ago," she pointed out.

"That is sufficient."

"So you know what to do?"

"I have traveled the ages, little dragon. I can manage to concoct one morning beverage."

Okay, then. Without another word, Julia plopped down on the stool behind the counter. Her new position gave her a better view, anyway. Crossing and uncrossing her legs, she watched the corded muscles of Tristan's stomach tighten with every move he made. She watched the way his nipples puckered in the cool, early morning air. Then she watched him saunter across the tile barefoot and stop at the faucet, revealing his naked back.

She gasped. To cover the sound, she uttered a quick cough. Thankfully he didn't seem to notice, and she was able to study his back in more detail. Thick, jagged scars laced every inch of flesh. Some intersected, some stood alone, but all of them were badges of pain. She'd noticed the slight marks on his chest, but these… What had he suffered?

As she studied his back more intently, she noticed a small tattoo rested on the upper left side of his shoulder blade. A black symbol, almost Oriental in appearance, utterly provocative and endearingly sexy. Another tattoo, very similar in appearance, decorated the curve of his lower back and dipped past his pants.

"What do those symbols mean?"

He glanced at her over his shoulder. "Conquer and destroy."

How appropriate.

"Do you usually rise this early?" he asked.

She tore her attention from his back and glanced at the wall clock. Six-thirty. "Today is a work day. I have to get up early."

"Yet you hardly slept last night."

Her eyes narrowed. "How do you know I didn't fall asleep? Did you enter my room?"

"Nay. I heard you through the door. If you were not sighing, you were punching your pillow." He cast another glance over his shoulder, his pale, otherworldly eyes filled with knowing pleasure. "Did I not tell you, little dragon? Without me, you will be unable to sleep."

"If you heard me, that means you didn't get any rest, either." Ha! She mentally patted herself on the back for that observation.

"I am used to going without slumber. In Imperia, I stayed up most nights to debauch and devour."

I might have to try that sometime. After the words flittered into her mind, she shook her head in surprise. Such a thought wasn't like her. Perhaps a wild side lurked inside her, waiting to break free. Why else would she tingle every time she imagined acting naughty with Tristan? Of course, if she ever tried debauching and devouring, it would have to be with Peter, not Tristan.

As the coffee percolated, filling the house with the fresh scent of caffeine, Tristan sat beside her and consumed his muffin with the gusto of a man just off a year-long fast. When he finished, he asked for another. And another. And another. He chased each one with a glass of milk.

"Would you happen to have another?" he asked hopefully, after he had swallowed the final crumb of the fourth.

"Sorry. That's all I have," she said. "How can you hold so much food, anyway?"

"By eating it."

She rolled her eyes. "How did you eat inside the box?"

"Magic sustained me." With a contented sigh, he settled more comfortably in his chair. "You may now lecture me."

I'm not ready. "Yes, of course." She cleared her throat. "I need you—" Wait, that didn't sound right. "My next-door—" That wasn't right, either.

"Surely your powers of speech have not deserted you."

Heat scalded her cheeks.

And as her color deepened, so did his amusement. Humor flickered in the depths of his eyes, making them appear as clear and light as an ocean at sunrise. "Whatever has put that blush on your cheeks has roused my curiosity."

"It's just that dating is—"

"Oh, no. This is beginning to sound serious. If you wish to ask me on this date of yours, then you may do so. I might even say aye."

He was teasing her. Julia knew it, but let it scrape against her already-raw nerves unchallenged. She yearned to blister his ears with scorching words. Instead, she used her sweetest tone of voice when she said, "Before I begin, let's have our coffee. Okay?"

"A fine idea," he said, parroting her overly polite tone.

Besides being too *sexy,* too *perfect* and a *sexual master,* he was a freaking comedian. Fabulous.

"I shall fetch your beverage this instant." He stood, turned toward the coffeemaker, stopped, then faced her once again. His expression suddenly serious, he said, "Have I told you yet that you look very beautiful this dawning? Your lips are pink and dewy, your eyes are drowsy and you smell like *gartina* petals."

"What do *gartina* petals smell like?" she asked. Please don't let him say *moldy cheese*.

"Like a gentle rain just after a tempest."

Oh, my. Even though he probably said that to every woman who owned his box, Julia felt herself melt under his spell. That was the nicest thing anyone had ever said to her, and she savored the words, no matter if he meant them or not.

"Thank you," she said, her voice cracking slightly.

"You are welcome."

Giving her another glimpse of his back, he poured her a steaming mug of coffee. Her mouth watered, but not for the liquid. For Tristan. He was pure male per-·fection. His muscles were so…yummy. His bronze skin resembled satin, rippled in some places, smooth in others. For a man his size, he moved with such grace and agility, managing to look both angelic and devilish all at once.

And right now, he belonged to her.

She licked her lips. For a second, only a second, she allowed herself to mentally strip away his clothing. Off came the belt. Down went the pants. Oh, yeah! Such a tantalizing taper of dark hair…so many rippling muscles…a thick, hard erection aching for her touch. Only a moment passed before she realized the big, hard erection in her imagination was actually big and hard in reality and straining against his black leather pants.

"Like what you see?" he asked on a wave of laughter.

Her gaze jerked from his crotch. She stared past him, past the window. "Uh, I was just—"

"Admiring the view?"

"Absolutely not. There are rules on this planet, you know. Rules about being seen in public with an—an engorged appendage. I was simply deciding whether or not to give you a citizen's citation."

He offered her a shameless, sexy grin. "Tell me, little dragon. How do you like it?"

She gasped. "I can't believe you just asked me that."

"It is a perfectly innocent question. I simply wish to know how you want me to give it to you. Hot? Most definitely. Sweet?" He winked. "Maybe. If you ask nicely."

She had trouble dragging in a breath and tugged at the collar of her shirt. "Discussing sex at the kitchen table might be okay where you're from, but not here."

"Julia, Julia, Julia. What a naughty mind you have. I spoke only of your beverage. Since you have no liking for the subject, I will certainly discuss sex with you."

"No, thank you." *Coffee.* He'd wanted to know how she took her coffee, and she had assumed he wished to know how she took her men. Well, that certainly clenched it. Her mind officially resided in the gutter. "I'll take cream and sugar, please."

Seconds dragged by as he placed a steaming mug in front of her. Grateful for the distraction, she latched on to it with a vengeance. She blew on the top, then allowed herself a tentative sip—and almost gagged. Her eyes watered, and she bit back a cough. This was by far the worst coffee she'd ever tasted. Had he even used a filter? Yuck!

Tristan eased into the seat beside her and swiveled

her chair until she faced him. "Now you have your drink," he said.

"Yeah," she assured him, hoping her distaste remained hidden. She didn't want to hurt his feelings by insulting his beverage-making skills. "I do."

He chuckled, and the deep rumble poured over her as smoothly as melted butterscotch. "You may begin your lecture."

Julia slowly pushed out a breath. The moment of reckoning had arrived. Either she asked Tristan to teach her how to entice Peter, or she forgot the plan altogether. Was she a woman or chicken?

One glance at the chiseled perfection of Tristan's features and she knew her answer.

Chicken. Definitely chicken.

More than likely, her pleasure slave had never faced a moment of rejection in his life. He didn't know how it felt to have others make fun of him, call him mean names and torment his every waking hour. She did. She knew. Her emotions bore the scars.

"When I said we should have our coffee first," she told him, "I meant the whole cup." Though the thought of drinking the entire contents of her mug made her shudder. Owning her own shop meant she couldn't afford an overnight stay in the hospital due to food poisoning.

"I do not wish to wait," Tristan said. "I am anxious to learn more about this dating."

"Okay, okay." Concealing another shudder, she scooted her coffee away. "I have something to ask you."

"You have told me that much already."

"I have?"

"Aye, you have."

"Well, here goes." Julia mentally rehearsed her speech one last time. *I can do this,* she thought just before a jolt of pure panic shot through her body, shaking her resolve. Her heart rate increased; her breath came in short, erratic pants. Was the light coming in from the window suddenly brighter? "Do you like cinnamon rolls?" she blurted out. "No. What about croissants? I make them from scratch."

"I am no longer hungry."

"What about—"

"Julia." Her name left his lips on a sigh of exasperation.

"Okay." By focusing all of her energy on her next words, she managed to temper her body's trembling. She kept her eyes to the floor and sat perfectly still. Tristan held his cup to his lips, and she felt him expectantly watching her. Waiting.

A woman's need for romance, she thought, facing him, left no room for pride. "Will you teach me how to seduce my next-door neighbor?"

CHAPTER SEVEN

You Live Only To Pleasure Your Master

TRISTAN NEARLY CHOKED from fluid inhalation as a gamut of questions swept through his mind. Astonished and praying he had misheard, he demanded, "Repeat your last words."

A visible force of determination suddenly surrounded Julia. "I want you to teach me how to entice Peter, my next-door neighbor."

By Elliea, Tristan had never expected this. When she had mentioned men and women and dating, he'd foolishly assumed she desired to ask him on a date.

Him.

"Do you wish to assuage your body's needs, Julia? *I* am here. Peter—" he spit the name "—is not needed."

She sputtered, opening her mouth, closing it with a snap. "This isn't about bodies and needs. This is about love. So yes, Peter is needed."

"Love?" Tristan scoffed, not liking the idea of another man holding Julia's affections, and liking even less that he cared. "You are being ridiculous."

"Why?" She bristled, and if she'd had a sword, he felt certain she would have sliced off his favorite appendage. "Because I'm unattractive?" she demanded to know. "Because I don't always say the right thing?"

He bared his teeth in a scowl. How dare the woman say something so ludicrous about herself. "You are perfect just the way you are and anyone who says otherwise needs to swing from a pike. I am simply unsure this neighbor of yours can appreciate you."

Her shoulders relaxed, and the lines around her lips softened. "You've never even met him, so how do you know what he's like?"

"I need not meet him to know he is a coward. Why has he not beaten down your door and demanded that I leave?"

She rolled her eyes. "He doesn't know you're here."

"Such a thing would not stop me from claiming what is mine."

"That's the most illogical thing I have ever heard. Besides, this is America. We do not beat down doors."

"Over the centuries I have learned that origins matter naught. If a man has not the bravery to fight for his woman, then he is no man at all."

"He'll fight for me one day," she said, her words assured but her tone doubtful. Hesitant. "So will you help me or not?"

Tristan watched Julia's chest rise and fall with her breaths. Throughout the night, a dark carnal craving had grown within him, and he now wanted her with a hunger that surpassed reasoning. He wanted to enjoy her complexities and contradictions for what short time they had together. And even knowing she longed for another man failed to abate his hunger. Nay, he yearned for her all the more. He desired this amusing, compassionate woman, and by Elliea, he would have her. So would he help her win another man? Nay!

"Why can you not lure this Peter on your own?" he demanded, one brow arched. "Have you tried and failed?"

"No, I haven't tried."

"Why not?"

A long while stretched. She ran her tongue over her teeth and fidgeted in her chair, her cheeks glowing with rosy embarrassment. "I don't know how," she finally whispered.

"How do you not know how to please a man, little dragon? You are of age."

"I'm shy."

"You? Shy?" Certain she jested, he laughed. "You are many things, little dragon, but you most definitely are not shy."

Tendrils of her hair, the palest locks of all, escaped the band and danced around her temples as she shook her head in denial. "If I were outgoing and bold, wouldn't I know how to talk and act around men? Wouldn't I go on lots of dates instead of spending every night at home alone?" Scowling now, she stamped her foot. "I'm shy, I tell you."

This woman who made his body harden and ache, and who made his blood quicken, thought she needed help winning a male's affections? Unbelievable. "You have done just fine with me," he grumbled.

"But you're different."

"I am no different from any other man."

"Yes, you are. I don't know how to explain it, but you are different."

Tristan wanted an answer, not an evasion, but the stubborn set of her jaw told him he wouldn't acquire what he sought any time soon. So he abandoned that particular line of attack for another. "Has Puny Peter ever tried to win *you?*"

Her chin rose a notch. "No, he hasn't."

"You mentioned love. Do you love him?"

She caught her bottom lip with her teeth, watching as her fingers pinched the edge of the counter. "That's none of your business."

"If you desire my aid, it had better become my business."

"Fine. I'll answer you. Do I love Peter? No, not yet. But he's perfect for me. We're alike in so many ways, and I can grow to love him. I just know it." Before he had time to dissect her words, she sent him an imploring look through her lashes. "I need your help, Tristan. Help me."

His teeth gnashed in irritation. Finally she proved that she was just like the others, putting her will before his own. And he was helpless to do anything to change the circumstances, helpless to do anything but obey. "I will do as you demand, of course," he replied, his tone stilted.

"No." Slowly, with an almost imperceptible motion, she shook her head. "I'm giving you a choice. I won't force you to do this. If you help me, it will be because you want to, not because you're my slave."

Shocked, disbelieving, Tristan could only stare over at her. "You are giving me the right to say nay?"

"Yes."

How…unnerving. He tangled a hand through his hair and cursed under his breath. Such benevolence proved stronger than any command, leaving only one choice. "I'll do it," he drawled, wanting to snatch the words back as soon as they left his mouth.

"Oh, Tristan." Grinning, she clasped her hands, jumped to her feet and spun around. Then she plopped back into her chair with a happy *whoop*. "Thank you. Thank you so much. You won't regret this. I promise. I'll be the best student ever."

"I'll do it," he repeated, suddenly inspired. "But on my own terms."

Her grin slowly faded, and she lost her excited glow. "What do you mean?"

"Like any teacher and student, we must set the parameters of our relationship."

Her neck elongated ever so slightly as she straightened in her chair. "Just what are these *parameters?*"

"You may not see or otherwise engage in any type of activity with another man until I say you are ready." Which meant she would never see Peter the Weakling again!

"I don't think—"

"I am the expert," he interjected. "Therefore we will

do this at my pace. During a lesson, you will do what I say, when I say and how I say. No arguments."

"Now hold on just a damn minute."

He never even paused. "You will allow me to sleep in your chamber."

She gasped. "That's not going to happen. I'm asking for flirting lessons, not Dresden crystal." Seconds ticked by but he didn't respond. He merely watched her, expectant, determined. Finally she conceded, albeit reluctantly.

"Fine," she snapped, "you win. Is that it?"

"No. You will remember the first parameter at all times."

She folded her arms across her middle, causing her shirt to strain, emphasizing the fullness of each breast. "Is *that* it?"

"For now."

"What about this? I'll agree to your parameters, if you agree to mine."

Tristan almost smiled. He forced his lips to remain in a straight line, however, hoping he appeared stern. "I am listening."

"*You* may not date, see, or otherwise engage in any type of relationship with another woman while you're teaching me," she said, mimicking his domineering tone.

"Agreed." He refrained from mentioning that because she owned his box, he wasn't allowed to attend to other women. That would have spoiled the fun.

"You will treat me with respect at all times, especially in the presence of others."

He didn't have to fake a frown this time. Her words irked his masculine pride. "That is something you need not ask for."

"Nonetheless, I'd like to hear your agreement."

He gave a stiff nod. "You have it."

"You can tell no one of our arrangement."

"Agreed." Who would he tell?

"You will…you will…never wear your sword in my house." She smiled triumphantly, and he knew she expected him to balk or, at the very least, to bargain.

He wanted to. Being without his weapon made him vulnerable to attack, and he knew nothing of this world, nothing of its people. The knowledge frustrated him, yet he said, "I agree to all of your conditions, Julia."

She paused. Surprised flickered in her beautiful fey-green eyes before she once again rewarded him with a smile. "Thank you, Tristan."

"Do not thank me yet." He stood, then paced back and forth in front of the kitchen counter. "Lesson one will be how to dress properly. If the garments I found in your closet are any indication of what you normally don to impress a man, you need guidance. And this," he indicated her slacks and blouse with a sweep of his hand, "is attire only a man should wear."

"We can go to the mall. It will have the largest assortment of clothes to choose from."

"What is this mall?"

"A big building filled with clothes, food and other necessities for the public to purchase."

"Ah, a market," he said, his tone both wistful and re-signed at the same time.

"We'll go this evening after I close the shop," she said, then paused. She had to open her store in an hour. Just what was she going to do with Tristan while she worked? She could leave him here where he'd grow bored and execute something. She could send him back inside his box, but he'd hate her for the rest of her life.

She wanted so many things from him, but hate wasn't one of them.

She was going to have to take him with her, she re-alized with a shiver of anticipation and a shudder of dread. First, however, he needed new clothes.

Having a pleasure slave grew more complicated by the second.

Looking him over, Julia chewed on her bottom lip. "Before you can leave the house, we'll have to find you more appropriate clothing." Preferably something less sexy, something that covered every inch of his bronzed, come-and-lick-me skin.

"What is wrong with my drocs?" he demanded.

She gave him another once-over. In those leather tights, with no shirt, he resembled an exotic dancer playing the part of a rogue pirate, and perversely, she wanted him to stay that way. Except, equally perverse, she didn't want any other woman seeing him like that.

"They're too tight," she informed him. "I can see the outline of your…your… I can just see things I'm not supposed to see, okay?"

His arms crossed over his chest, and he uttered a patronizing snort. "If a warrior's clothes are loose, they are easily grabbed by his enemy."

"We're not at war."

"Silly dragon. Enemies are all around us, some seen, some hidden."

"Fine," she said on a sigh. "Keep your pants. You still need a shirt, though."

"Mayhap it would be easier if we simply stripped naked and stayed here."

"No!" she shouted, though her body screamed, *Yes. Oh, yes.*

"Will you find me appropriate attire, little dragon?" His voice was pure, unadulterated sin, and seemed to suggest he could wear *her.*

Images of her naked body covering him, of her arms draped around his shoulders and her legs wound around his waist, flashed inside her mind. A delicious shiver danced along her spine, and she sucked her lip into her mouth.

"Do not do that," he suddenly growled, all traces of seduction gone.

Confused by his abrupt mood shift, Julia blinked up at him. "Don't do what?" *Don't imagine myself draped over your hot, sweaty body?* Too late.

"Do not bite your lip. It is bad for you."

"It is not."

"If you continue, I might add another parameter. No biting of the lips—I mean, no biting of your own lip. You may bite me as much as you like," he said. "Now, about the clothing. I require that you fetch me a shirt."

"There's a store a couple miles from here that's open twenty-four hours. They'll have everything you need." Again she glanced down his big, hard body. "I just hope they have big enough sizes."

"We will leave immediately." Without waiting for her reply, he pivoted on his heel and stalked to the door.

"Wait!" Julia leapt up and bolted after him. She grabbed his arm, a puny action, really, when dealing with a man his size, but it had the desired affect. He stopped.

"*You* can't go," she told him. Thankfully, she'd only be gone an hour, probably less, and that didn't leave much time for him to get into trouble.

He faced her, both brows winged upward. She'd known him such a short time and already she could judge his moods. Arched eyebrows meant one of two things: He was confused, or he was angry. Either way, she suffered.

"Why not?" he demanded.

Angry. Definitely angry. Hoping to soothe him, she gentled her tone. "Here in America, we can't go into a business establishment without being completely covered. We have a policy of no shirt, no shoes, no service."

"This policy mentions nothing of leg coverings. Does this mean that once you find me a shirt and shoes, I must remove my drocs?"

Hormone overdrive, she thought. "You must wear all three items at the same time."

"I do not like the rules of your world."

"You may not like them, but you still have to obey

them. So you'll stay here, and I'll go. No exceptions. When I return, you'll change and then we'll go to my store."

"This I will not allow, for a woman must never travel alone."

"I know how to take down a bad guy."

"Your karate would not hurt a defenseless babe."

"I'm going to pretend you didn't say that. Now, if I'm going to open the shop on time, I have to hurry. You'd only get in the way. And for your information, I am a black belt, the most lethal of all." A small lie, really. She did own a black belt—it was leather with silver tassels at the end. "You will stay here." Cringing inside and hating her next words, she straightened her shoulders and stared up at him. "I—command it."

His jaw hardened instantly, and the heat in his eyes became glazed with frost, turning the violet to icy steel. He no longer resembled the warrior she'd come to desire, but the slave he professed himself to be. Disappointment thundered through her, as potent and alive as her sudden sorrow.

"I shall do as you command, of course," he said, his tone devoid of emotion.

How could he look so…cold, almost brutal in his lack of sentiment? *I have to do this,* she reminded herself. He couldn't leave the house dressed as he was.

Knowing there was nothing she could say to ease his pride, she gathered her purse and keys. Tristan was a hard man, one who obviously yearned for the full measure of his authority. Though the curse demanded he obey her orders, he didn't back down until the end. She couldn't help but admire him and wish she possessed some of his inner strength.

He'll have fun while I'm gone, she assured herself. He'll play with his sword, maybe take a walk…and demand to pleasure every woman he encounters. Fighting back a wave of jealousy, she pinched the bridge of her nose. Maybe leaving Tristan here, alone, wasn't such a smart idea.

She could order him back into his box. One heartbeat passed. Two. With a sigh, Julia again discarded the idea. How could she, in good conscience, ask another human being to lock himself within a tiny crypt? Tugging her lip into her mouth—and for the first time realizing how often she actually did it—she slipped on an old pair of tennis shoes. She glanced up, only to find Tristan watching her, his expression still blank.

"I shouldn't be gone more than half an hour," she said, a catch in her voice. "Don't answer the door and please, *please*, don't use your sword on anyone."

"Whatever you desire…master." He sneered the last. "Didn't I already swear not to use my sword in your home?"

"Tristan—" She closed her mouth with a snap. He didn't want an apology, he wanted to go with her. However, she refused to change her mind. And as the ticking of the wall clock filled her ears, she slipped into her coat. "I'll be back soon," she said. "I promise."

He turned from her, giving her his back.

The urge to stay bombarded her common sense. Regret burned hot as she forced one foot in front of the other. Outside, a crisp gust of wind hit her full force. Going from contentedly warm to impossibly cold played havoc with her internal thermometer, and she shivered. After pulling the lapels of her coat closer together, she palmed her keys and hopped down the porch.

Her gaze automatically sought her shrubs. Thankfully, they were still alive. Her sister was fond of telling her that she possessed the Black Thumb of Death. Anything green and leafy that was left in her care was sure to die. Julia sighed. Tristan wasn't green, but she was having trouble taking proper care of her alien.

TRISTAN FOUGHT against his fury as the silence of the house enveloped him. Julia had commanded her will to his again, just as he'd expected. Just as all the others he had served. Her careless disregard for his wishes made the beast inside him roar and paw for release. But he was a warrior, first and foremost, and a warrior knew when to allow the beast release and when to force him to heel.

Right now, he would heel. He would obey and offer no more of himself than was demanded.

He'd wanted Julia to be different, he thought with clenched fists. She wasn't.

He would do well to remember that.

He would do well not to place too much significance on the sweet things she'd done for him, on the fact that thoughts of her with this other man, this Puny Peter, awakened his deepest possessive instincts.

Even now, his blood boiled.

He needed something else to do, something to occupy his mind until Julia's return. He scanned the chamber. Mayhap he would assuage his curiosity and search the home from top to bottom. His eyes lit on the tapered window alcove that allowed the morning sun to flood into the room, and he nodded. Aye, he would learn the layout of the house, and discover more about his newest *guan ren*.

Ebony framed mirrors with gold-plated edges hung at each corner of the wall. Bright pillows of turquoise, emerald and lavender were scattered across a plump lounging dais and a thick carpet draped the polished wood floors. A cobbled hearth sat devoid of any embers, but glistened all the same. A place of depth and hidden sensuality, most assuredly. The woman who had decorated this room was not cruel or malicious. She was bold and passionate and a maze of untapped delights.

Unbidden, he felt himself once again soften toward her, helpless against the sensation. How did she do this to him? How did she tie him in so many knots?

He sighed. The overflowing boxes that had failed to gain his notice yestereve now received his full attention. He bent before the closest one and shuffled through the contents. There were toys, clocks and silverware. In another were books—all had pictures of half-naked men and women and garnered much interest from him, for these were exactly the positions he craved with Julia. Him looming above her half-clad bosom while her lips parted with passion.

In still another box were dishes, porcelain flowers

and vases, all carefully packaged. A treasure connoisseur, she was, and no wonder she had purchased his box. She had recognized the value—of him? His respect for her grew.

What else would he learn about Julia? Inspection finished here, he journeyed throughout the house, bypassing the kitchen, for he'd already seen it. Too, he'd surveyed the downstairs bedchambers. So he found himself padding up the creaking stairs and following a path that led to two bedchambers with closed doors. He opened the first...and cocked his head to the side, unsure he was seeing what he thought he was seeing.

The chamber was filled with old toys and a cradle. A tomblike silence greeted his ears. The walls were white, the floors unpolished. And the next chamber appeared exactly the same. Toys, a cradle, a crib. Cracked paint and splintered wood. Below, she had carefully arranged her trinkets and furnishings to reflect a certain ambiance. Yet here she had left the room in disarray, choking the life from the light.

A loud, shrill noise ruptured the silence, like a messenger of death come to claim him.

Alert, ready for battle, Tristan raced down the stairs.

CHAPTER EIGHT

Your Body And Mind Belong To Your Master

AT THE SUPER CENTER, Julia grabbed Tristan a bit of everything. Jeans, sweatpants, T-shirts, shoes and underwear (in every style and all extra-extra-large, of course). She only prayed they fit. A man that big and that sexual needed extra room to breathe.

On her way to check out, she passed the hunting and fishing section where she spotted a display case of weapons. One knife in particular drew and held her gaze. She paused, studying the intricately carved hilt, a pattern of slashes and symbols. The metallic blade gleamed sharp and deadly.

She knew instinctively that Tristan would cherish the weapon. Was it smart to purchase a lethal blade for him, though? One so easily hidden? Drumming her fingers against the glass, she imagined his reaction if she presented him with this gift. He'd smile, then tug her into his arms. He'd plant a lingering kiss on her lips and whisper exactly how he wanted to thank her.

"I want that one," she told the clerk in the next heart-beat of time.

"Excellent choice, ma'am," he said. With a face smothered by freckles and bright, silver braces covering his teeth, he looked about twelve years old. The giant tattoo on his forearm—a squirrel eating a pair of nuts—upped his appearance to seventy. "The handle is a wicked work of art."

"Wicked, you say?"

"Oh, yeah. Totally bitchin'."

She'd have to remember to tell Tristan that.

Julia paid for the rest of her purchases, spending over three hundred dollars. "You better appreciate this, Tristan," she muttered, wheeling the basket to her car.

Within ten minutes, she eased her sedan into her drive-way. One of the bags tore as she lifted its weight from the trunk. "Argh." Frowning, she gathered everything to-gether as best she could and stumbled inside the house.

Tristan was perched on the living-room couch, his sword on the woolen rug in front of him. He leaned over the coffee table, his fingers picking at her phone, which was now in more pieces than a jigsaw puzzle! Mouth agape, Julia dropped her purchases on the floor with a hard thump.

"What have you done to my telephone?" she de-manded, hands anchored on hips.

"I have conquered it," he said, looking up at her with pride. Worse, his tone carried the unspoken words, *Bow to your knees and thank me for this great service.*

At least he was no longer distant and emotionless.

"I don't have another phone in the house," she growled.

"Then my work here is done."

What did I do to deserve this? she thought, shaking her head in bewilderment. She didn't kick puppies, or run over children who played in the streets. She lived an honest life and even made a yearly contribution to charity.

"I thought the knowledge you gained from other worlds far surpassed mine," she said dryly.

"That it does." He leaned into the pillowed chaise, his arm draped over the edge, both his hand and the veer of the chair curling like a lover's palm just after an erotic caress. He locked his other arm behind his head and slanted her a glance between half-lowered lids. The pose was carnal. Seductive. "There is much you have to learn."

She heard his true meaning: *There is much I can teach you.*

Her breath caught in her throat at the sheer magnificence of the man. When she drew near him, inexplicable things happened to her mind and body, and she could never quite gain the upper hand. He had only to speak; hell, he had only to glance at her, and she craved the forbidden. Craved him.

Physically, he was faultless, majestic and regal, and his wild fall of hair proved the perfect frame for his chiseled features. How easy it would be to go to him now, to straddle his legs and sink into—onto—him. To demand the pleasure he offered so willingly.

Her face must have betrayed her thoughts because the moment their eyes locked, his nostrils flared. His sensual lips parted.

She gulped.

Change the subject, Julia. Change the subject now. "Um, I bought you some clothes," she managed to croak. "I hope they fit."

"I'm sure they are fine." His tongue swept over his lips, an intoxicating invitation she struggled to ignore.

When he made no other reply, she prompted, "Put them on. We need to leave." Staying here, no matter the deliciousness of the reason, wasn't an option. "We've only got twenty minutes to get downtown. I always open the shop at eight o'clock, and not a minute later." Well, except for yesterday, she silently added, but he didn't need to know that. "Oh, I almost forgot. I bought you a present, too."

"A gift?" His eyebrows drew together, and a flicker of surprise darkened his eyes, chasing away his seductive intent. "For me?"

"Yes, for you." Grinning, she handed him the bag that contained the knife.

He glanced at her, then the bag. Her, then the bag. Finally he hesitantly accepted her offering. "I do not know what to say."

"Don't say anything. Just open it." Eagerness flooded her veins, almost bubbling over. "Well? What are you waiting for?"

Slowly he smoothed the plastic aside and lifted a long, shiny black box. With exquisite care, he withdrew the blade from the velvet center and studied every angle. The sharp-edged metal winked in the light and fit perfectly in his hand.

Silence surrounded them.

She waited, watching as his lips tightened into a fierce frown. Still she hoped for more of a reaction, but her excitement drained little by little. He didn't like the gift. The knowledge caused her shoulders to sag. Maybe she should have gotten him a leopard-print thong instead.

"Thank you, Julia," he said suddenly, his voice laced with reverence. His lashes swept upward, and he pierced her with such gratitude she wanted to promise to buy him an entire arsenal—guns, grenades and all. "Where I am from, weapons such as this cost more than living quarters."

He'd never received a gift before, she realized. How…heartbreaking. This wonderful man had lived over a thousand years, yet no one had thought to buy him a present. She sank to the carpet and rummaged through the surrounding sacks. After a few moments, she withdrew a shirt, a pair of jeans and boxers. Delighted she had other items for him, she handed him the bundle.

"Here, these are for you, too."

"I—thank you," he said again, then placed the clothes beside him on the couch and continued his scrutiny of the knife.

"You're welcome. We need to leave in five minutes," she hinted. "I don't want to be late."

"Tardiness can be a benefit, little dragon, especially if the time is spent in bed—or on the kitchen tabletop. Or on the floor. Mayhap one day you will allow me to prove *all* of this to you."

Each word he uttered made her body ache in a different place. Her left nipple. Her right nipple. Between her legs. Behind her knees. Practically in a trance, she watched as Tristan set his blade carefully to the side. He eased to his feet. Tie by tie, he unlaced his pants, then inched them down his hips, revealing more and more skin.

"Tristan!" she gasped, realizing he didn't plan to stop any time soon. "What are you doing?"

"I am undressing."

"I can see that." And a lot more.

With her sitting, and him standing, their positions gave her a dazzling view of his assets. He was all taut male, hard muscles and, yes, he was large all over as she'd suspected. But she would never have imagined… Julia gulped, felt her body pulse with need, and gulped again.

"Is something wrong?" he asked innocently.

"No, nothing's wrong." Nothing except the fact that she needed to catch her breath—and she would, just as soon as she looked away. But she couldn't seem to remove her gaze from his body. The phrase "mighty sword" suddenly made sense.

"You are staring, Julia," Tristan said, an underlying "tsk" to the words.

Yes, she was staring, and she wanted to continue doing so. Since he had been rude enough to point it out, she couldn't continue without being, well, rude.

"Uh, I'm going to get my briefcase." Did she even own a briefcase? Slowly she rose and inched from the room. She only tripped once, though her attention stayed glued to him until the very last possible second.

TRISTAN WATCHED Julia's retreat. Alone now, he allowed a slow, devilish smile to lift his lips. Very interesting. Very interesting, indeed. Julia found his nakedness appealing. So appealing, in fact, she had been unable to glance away from him. That pleased him on every level, considering she had told him only last eve that she did not like him in *that* way. The little dragon more than liked him; she was transfixed by him.

Ah, what a sweet revelation.

Slowly his smile faded. Was that why she had bought him a gift? Because she wanted him? Nay, not so, he thought. In all of his existence, no other woman had ever given him a present—and all of his women had desired him most forcefully.

So what had prompted Julia to do such a thing? The answer continued to elude him. He finally sighed and pushed the question to the back of his mind. He, a master of female passions, did not understand the workings of Julia's mind.

He tugged on his new clothing piece by piece. If he'd had the currency, he would have bought her the finest jewels, the purest stones to match her eyes. Had any man ever bought her such a gift? His fingers clenched, and he realized he wanted to be the first. The only.

He shook such a dangerous thought aside, wondering instead what he was going to do with this woman who defied him like a warrior, kissed him like he possessed the last breath of air for survival and treated him as if he were a man, not a slave.

CHAPTER NINE

Imperia
The Sixth Season

"WHAT DO YOU HERE, Zirra?"

Rivulets of light trickled like liquid gold from the four suns, past the arched, beveled windows, encircling the tribunal chamber and giving it the appearance of a holy sanctuary. Two towering thrones perched on the verdant dais before her, both inlaid with precious stones from other worlds—ebony, ivory, assyri and merdeaux. Winged figures carved from the purest alabaster decorated the legs and seemed ready to burst into the heavens.

The gleaming cream-and-rose marble flooring cooled her bare feet and reminded her of the cold emptiness within herself…and the reason she was here. Her ears filled with the crashing waves just beyond the palace's gates outside, a potent reminder, as well.

The High Priest sat beside his queen, regarding Zirra intently, his eyes a deep, fathomless blue. Mystical power charged the air around him, surrounded her, moved through her, a power so much greater than her own.

Her fists clenched. Four cycles ago Percen had stolen Tristan's box from her and cursed the pleasure slave to another world with a spell of his own. How infuriated she'd been. How infuriated she *still* was. She'd wanted to retrieve her slave immediately, but Percen had stopped her. He had snatched away her powers, wrapping her in a cloak of mortality so complete she could not summon any of her mystical abilities. Not a single one.

'Twas her punishment, he'd said, for nearly ruining his precious Alliance with the mortals.

Bastard.

"I will ask but one more time," Percen said, a steely edge underlying his tone. "What do you here, Zirra?"

Chin high, she stood in the center of the room, a gossamer froth of cerulean draping her body, her hands at her sides. She kept her expression impassive, though she could barely stand to look upon the High Priest. With the wild fall of his inky hair, the strength of his magic, and the blue pools that were his eyes, he should have been a beautiful man. Instead he was hideous. His body was twisted, and his left eye drooped low on his cheekbone. His nose was sharp and beaked.

A pity he was not tolerable. She might have tried seducing him to her will, even though she'd vowed long ago never to take another Druinn as her lover.

"I have come to demand the return of my powers," she said defiantly.

A chorus of "ooh" circulated across the swell of talon-carrying guards positioned strategically around each corner before an arduous silence sharpened its claws. The sound and the lack of sound grind together in disharmony like shards of broken glass.

"You? Demand me?" he said, uttering the very words she'd once uttered to Tristan. "I doubt I will ever return your powers. You would attempt to retrieve Tristan, and that I cannot allow."

"He belongs to me."

Percen's brows furrowed together high on his forehead. "If I were capable of breaking another's curse, I would have done so. As that is something no Druinn can do, I simply sent him away—where he will remain. Be glad I did not kill you."

Be glad I did not kill you, she silently mocked. "I demand you return him to me at once."

"More demands?" His tone sharpened with deadly precision. "There is a war brewing, Zirra. Many of my favored sorcerers have already joined the rebels in hopes of destroying our tentative bond with the mortals— something you nearly did all on your own. I punished you for your actions, and yet you continue to think only of yourself and demand I reward you. My answer," he added casually, almost pleasantly, "is nay. And any who seek to aid you will suffer my wrath."

Dread fluttered sharp wings inside her stomach, cutting, slashing at her sense of hope. Her gaze flickered to the queen, poised lovingly beside the High Priest. Heather was the only one who held any sway with Percen.

Zirra prayed the queen would aid her cause.

"I agree with my life-mate," Heather said, the sweetness of her voice as lyrical as a song. Almost absently, she reached out and squeezed Percen's hand. "You would do well to leave this matter alone. To leave Tristan alone."

Curse them, Zirra fumed. So self-righteous they were, thinking they knew what was best. Well, *she* knew what was best for herself. Tristan. Only in his arms did she feel beautiful and strong. Only when he obeyed her did she feel alive and wholly fulfilled.

Through slitted eyes, she returned her attention to the High Priest, and their gazes collided, an icy clash of blue against blue, a stormy sea against a tranquil breeze. "You once cursed your own brother to a life of stone. My actions are no worse than yours."

"I made reparations for my sins. My brother now lives quite happily with his life-mate and their children."

"Then allow me to make reparations with Tristan. I will become his life-mate and give him as many children as he desires."

"Nay," Percen said.

She nearly screeched as her rage leapt to another plateau. How easy it would be to reclaim Tristan if she possessed her powers and knew where he now resided. All she would have to do was open a vortex. Since she could not, her only hope lay with the High Priest. She *must* convince him to help her.

"I have suffered my punishment for many cycles. Surely that is enough."

"Nay, 'tis not." He paused, his expression pensive. "Mayhap I should give you to the mortal Great-Lord and allow *him* to punish you."

"You would not dare. For you do not want him to know what became of his finest warrior."

"I would dare, Zirra. Doubt me not."

As her hope faded, longing stirred inside her. Tristan's beautiful face flashed before her mind. She needed him again. Must have him again. For Tristan was like an aphrodisiac and, once ingested, nothing else mattered but another taste. She hated him for this *need* he made her feel, but she was helpless against her craving.

She had tried to humble him, to prove her mastery over his every action, yet each and every day that she'd owned his box, he had defied her. Aye, he'd ravished her body whenever she commanded, but he'd never given anything more of himself. He had spoken of her death while his hands glided over her body. He had glared at her with hatred while his tongue licked her skin.

And yet, memories of his magnificence had the power to make her shiver with delight.

"Tristan is but a mortal," she ground out. "He is nothing to you."

Heather, a mortal herself, narrowed her eyes. "He is a mortal, yes, but that does not make him a lesser being."

"He fought for his Great-Lord," Percen said, "and he has fought for me, as well. He killed his enemies without hesitation or regret. He is loyal and trustworthy, a king at heart and a true legend among any race. What are you but a pitiful excuse for flesh, blood and magic? Well, magic no longer," he added smugly.

Though shaking with the force of her hurt and fury, she ignored his taunts. Percen wanted to humiliate her, she could only guess, because she had once spurned him, had once spit in his ugly face and refused his touch. She would not allow him to injure her spirit.

"Tristan is all that you claim," she said. "I admit that. But he is also mine. He belongs to me."

Heather uttered a tinkling laugh. "He was never, and will never be yours."

Zirra's teeth bared in a scowl.

"Do not fear," Percen told her. "One day he will return to our land. Yet he will return when Elliea has decreed it, and not a moment sooner."

Joy and despair, impatience and delight all pounded through her. "If you bring him back now, I can make him love me. I know I can. He will even thank you for returning him."

A laugh boomed from Percen, a cruel reverberation that struck and destroyed her pride. "Why do you persist in this? He will never love you. You are not worthy of him."

I am *worthy,* she longed to shout, though her features never wavered from their tight, emotionless facade, never revealed a hint of her inner turmoil.

"Get you gone from my sight, woman." Regally he waved one hand through the air. "Your greed sickens me."

Fists clenched, teeth still bared in a scowl, she paused but a moment. "I *will* find a way to retrieve him, doubt me not. Tristan is mine. My lover. My property. And he will belong to me once again."

Percen's nostrils flared at such blatant insolence. "You dare contest my will?"

"I dare," she said evenly, glaring up at him. "Oh, aye. I dare."

WHEN THE TRIBUNAL chamber cleared, Percen glanced at his life-mate, the queen of his heart and soul, the woman who had saved him from destruction. "Mayhap I should have Zirra killed," he said on a sigh. "Her treachery will only grow."

"Our son would never forgive you if you hurt her." Concern flashed over Heather's aging features, her brown eyes wide. "Did we do the right thing, sending Tristan away?"

"Aye, we did." A long sigh slipped from his lips. "Worry not, my love. I will think of something to do with Zirra, something that will not upset our son."

ZIRRA PACED the confines of her chamber. Her hands fisted in the silkiness of her robe, and her hair whipped against her back each time she turned. Dark emotions pounded through her, as hot and stifling as the fire burning within the hearth. Heavy clouds, thunderous and gray, covered the four suns, only adding to her riotous mood. With a screech, she kicked a chair from her path and knocked her three-tiered vanity to the floor. Her prized crystal vase shattered, leaving a broken trail of jagged, opalescent shards.

How dare Percen de Locke treat her so shabbily. Oh, how she longed to punish him. To destroy his magic with her own, as he had done to her. Yet, as High Priest of the Druinn, his magic far surpassed hers, and she could do nothing to hurt him or counter his spell. Nothing!

She'd lost her powers. She'd lost the people's respect, becoming nothing more than an amusing tale to chuckle about over meals. And she'd lost Tristan, just as he'd intended.

I must have Tristan back. He's mine. She lifted a jeweled goblet and hurtled it at the wall, where it thumped and fell unharmed. She'd owned her slave only a few seasons. Such a small amount of time, really, yet her need for him had grown to incomprehensible dimensions.

"Where is he?" she cried. What woman owned him now? Touched him? Tasted him? Welcomed his body?

What woman felt the power he incited?

Those thoughts caused tenebrous jealousy to completely awaken from slumber and invite a deep-seated wrath. She felt sick in the pit of her stomach and with another screech of fury, flung herself atop her bed—the very bed on which she'd last enjoyed Tristan. The silky white cloth enveloped her like a lover's caress, mocking her. She pounded her fists into the fur-lined mattress.

"He belongs to me. Me!"

A servant entered the chamber, her gaze wide and uncertain, as if she wasn't sure what fate awaited her. "You called, Sorceress?"

"Nay I didn't, you stupid—" Zirra stopped abruptly. All of a sudden, her breathing slowed, her rage eased. The solution was so simply, really, and she wondered why she had not considered it before. There *was* a Druinn male who would risk Percen's wrath to help her. Oh, aye. The man hungered for her, after all, and with the proper incentive he would do anything that she asked.

She almost laughed.

"Where is the prince?" she asked.

The servant's fingers twisted the plain brown fabric of her gown. "Practicing his magic in the white sands."

"Go to him. Tell him I request his presence in my bedchamber."

The young girl gave a relieved nod and hurried to obey.

"I will have you yet, Tristan." This time, Zirra did allow herself to laugh. She was giddy for the first time since Percen cast his traitorous spells.

Romulis strode into her chamber a short while later, his lips stretched in a tight scowl. His bare chest gleamed with sweat and tiny white crystals. His muscles were laced with sinew and scars.

He looked every inch the savage, dangerous warrior that he was, yet all the more potent because his magic hummed all around him, as sharp and deadly as any talon. His booted feet crunched the broken vase on the floor, when he suddenly halted at the edge of her bed, a dark tower against the whiteness of her walls and furnishings, and stared down at her. His features were bold and striking. Silky black hair hung to his shoulders, framing his golden eyes and bladelike cheekbones.

On numerous occasions, he'd attempted to lure her to his bed. She always spurned him, quite forcefully, and sent him away untouched and frustrated, for she never dabbled with the Druinn males. They were too volatile and uncontrollable, and could curse or bless with the wave of a hand. While she relished that power within herself, she did not welcome it in another. The way Percen had so easily stripped her of her mystical abilities only proved her reluctance to take a Druinn lover was well placed.

Though he knew how she felt, Romulis desired her still. Would always desire her. The knowledge burned in his eyes. Oh, he might despise himself for his weakness, but he was helpless against it. Why else would he be here?

"What is it you wish this time, Zirra?"

Her shapely brows furrowed in a pouty scowl. "Your father has stolen my mystic abilities and sent my slave to another world."

"I know." He paused a moment to rest his hand against the alabaster column rising beside him. "All of the palace knows, in fact, and none of us care."

She forced her expression to remain unaffected. "Will you bring Tristan back to me?" Watching him, she lounged seductively against the furs and traced her fingertips over the curve of her hip. "I would be most grateful."

"Is that the only reason you called me? If so, I will take my leave of you now." He spun toward the entrance.

"Wait!" she called. "Please."

He slowly turned to face her. His lips slanted in an insolent grin. "You have something more to add?"

"Show him to me. Just a glimpse. That's all I ask. Please, Romulis. I will be in your debt, doubt me not."

A flicker of something unnamable lit his eyes like creamy, gossamer cloth against a deadly dagger, then quickly disappeared. "Very well," he said, punctuating each word. "I will give you a single glimpse."

He lifted a large shard of her crystal vase from the tiled floor and used it to scoop a flaming ember from the hearth. Smoke ribboned all the way up to the vaulted ceiling. He muttered a spell and magic's sweet essence scented the air. He moved the fingers of his free hand in a wide arch. Directly above the dark cloud, the air began to swirl and liquefy.

In the center of the dappled liquid, Tristan's image materialized.

Zirra smothered a hungry gasp and forced her body to remain where it was as the mortal she'd dreamed of these many eves filled her vision. He was sitting atop a plain black chair. His arms were locked behind his head as he stared up at a ceiling. He was so deep in thought the fine lines around his eyes were tight, his lips drawn. Her mouth watered for a taste of him.

What thoughts tumbled through his mind? Did he think of her?

She reached out to touch him but grasped only air. Her disappointment was nearly a living thing, and she screeched, "You must get him back for me, Romulis. You must."

His hands lowered to his sides, and Tristan's image floated away. Romulis laughed with forced humor. "You know I will not risk punishment for you. None of us will."

"Percen is your father. He will never punish you."

"My answer is still nay."

"Surely you can do something for me," she cried.

"Aye, I can. But I will not," he said firmly. "Tristan has had many *guan rens* since you and does not need your interference in his new life. The woman he is with now might just set him free."

Glaring at him, she jolted up. One of this Druinn's gifts was the ability to see into the future and know. Just *know*. She didn't doubt he spoke true. "Where is he now? Where? Who dares to claim my property?"

Stubbornly he remained silent. Yet his gaze traveled over her hungrily, desperately.

"Please help me, Romulis. I am not above begging."

"Zirra—" he began.

"Romulis," she returned, gentling her tone. Watching him through the shield of her lashes, she turned to her other side, lounging seductively, her hair draped over one shoulder. She knew she presented a picture of carnality, an image that inspired the lust of legions. "I will give you anything you desire if only you will bring him back to me."

"Nay," he said, though he hesitated this time.

"Anything you desire of me is yours, Romulis. Anything. All you must do is help me."

Minutes dragged by, an eternity. What thoughts swirled through his mind, she did not know.

"You will do anything I ask?" he finally said.

"Aye," she answered without consideration to the consequences. Hope edged within her, and she knew she would pay any fee this Druinn asked.

"My price will be named at a later date. Is that acceptable?"

Again she answered swiftly. "Aye."

Romulis closed his eyes. A war waged within his

mind, she knew. Duty versus desire. His father versus her. Which would emerge victorious? She waited, suspended on the edge of her bed. Her entire existence hinged on his answer.

"Very well," he said softly, facing her once more. Determination shone in his eyes, yet there was a hint of regret. "I will help you."

Triumph drifted through her, as absolute and powerful as the fourth-season winds. "How?" she demanded. "Will you take me to him?"

"Nay, I will not," he answered firmly.

"Why?"

"My answer is of no concern to you."

"Then how will I obtain him?" she asked through gritted teeth.

"I will teach you a spell that will return Tristan to you."

"Had I my powers, I could do that on my own."

"But you do not have your powers. 'Tis why you need my help. If my plan is not acceptable, then consider our bargain null and void."

"It is acceptable," she said quickly. "It is acceptable."

"Mayhap I will even show you how to win back all of your powers."

Anticipation slithered along her spine, wrapping around her like a hungry serpent in search of sustenance. She could barely contain her eagerness. Her body was desperate to reclaim her magic, and her hands were itching for the feel of Tristan, to once more hold him in her arms, to glory in his body pressed against hers.

"Whatever you must teach me, Romulis," she assured him, "I will learn."

He shoved both of his hands through his hair, sweeping the dark locks from his temples. Sweat kept the strands in place. He sighed. "I must bathe ere we begin."

"Hurry," she commanded with a clap of her hands.

His gaze narrowed. "Best you recall who is helping whom."

"Please hurry," she amended.

"I think we will both come to regret this." With a weary shake of his head, he strode from the chamber.

This man was going to be difficult to control, she mused as she lay back on the bed. Were she strong enough, she might have cursed Romulis inside a trinket box of his own. Then she would have two slaves to use at her leisure.

The thought made her smile.

CHAPTER TEN

You Must Accept All Punishment
As Your Due

JULIA'S TREASURES CLOSED at five o'clock, and by that time, Julia felt as if she'd just fought in a world war—and lost. Every time the bell above the door had chimed, Tristan had instantly swooped to her side, hovering over her shoulder and glaring like the wrath of God. He claimed he'd only wished to protect her. Protect her, of all things. She wasn't sure if he meant to protect her from her customers or the door chime. The man did not like loud noises!

Twice she'd watched him stroke his knife and eye the blasted door with a do-you-want-a-piece-of-this glare. Though he hadn't been looking their way, several patrons assumed he meant to commit a mass murder and had hastened away. The memory had her rubbing her temples in a vain effort to ward off the growing ache. She was only surprised the local PD hadn't been called.

Never again would she put herself through this. If America's economy collapsed and the only way to raise money for herself was to nail Tristan inside her display case, she still wouldn't bring him to work with her. Sure, women twittered over him and bought anything he recommended. Sure, she'd sold more merchandise today than she usually sold in two weeks combined. It didn't matter. The man smelled like a buffet of sensual delights and all that hovering nonsense had given her a pheromone overdose.

Now her feet hurt, her stomach was twisted in tiny knots, her headache was already worse, and she was so irritable it bordered on PMS. All she wanted to do was toss back a few pain relievers, soak in a hot, steamy bath, then go to bed.

"Let's go home," she told Tristan on a sigh.

"Aye." He nodded. "This shopkeeping requires more energy than soldiering."

She locked all the doors, and they strode to her car. Tristan handled the ride home much better than he had handled the ride to the shop. This morning his skin had turned an unflattering shade of green and sweat had beaded on his brow. Now he gripped his hands on his knees, but his color remained high. For his benefit, she stayed five miles under the speed limit.

"What type of vehicle did you use in Imperia?" she asked.

"I rode atop horned stags or the back of a dragon."

"A dragon?" Astonished, she flicked him a quick glance. "As in fire-breathing, green scales and wings?"

"The very same."

"Is this the dragon you're so fond of comparing me

to?" she asked with a narrowed gaze, ready to claw out his eyes if he agreed.

"Again, the same," he said. "Dragons are revered for their courage, their defensive skills and their tenacity."

Oh, she thought, melting into her seat and smiling slowly. *He thinks I'm a dragon.* How sweet and absolutely endearing. "I know fifteen hundred years have passed, but do you still miss your home? The magic... and the dragons?" she added tentatively.

"More than I can ever say."

As he sat there, memories filling his eyes and sadness radiating from him, something inside her cracked. Poor man. What all had he lost? She couldn't, or perhaps didn't want to, fathom the answer. At the house, she pampered him a little, letting him relax while she fixed turkey sandwiches. Tristan ate five. So far he'd cost her three hundred and forty-eight dollars, plus the loss of her sanity. A good bargain? Earlier she would have said absolutely not. Now...well, the jury was still deliberating.

"Best we go to the mall now," he said, after putting his plate in the sink. "I do not like these clothes you have provided me with. These—" he motioned to the sweatpants with a wave of his hand "—leave me suspended."

The thought of battling crowds, of having Tristan "protect" her from salesclerks, swept away every ounce of relaxation she'd gained. "Slight change of plans," she said, hoping he wouldn't mind. "We'll go to the—" She paused, the last part of Tristan's speech registering in her mind. "Uh, Tristan, you are wearing the underwear I gave you, right?"

His chin veered to the side, and his eyes changed from green to blue to purple with confusion. "What is this underwear?"

How to explain, how to explain? "It's a protective cloth for your—" She pointed.

"Ah." He shook his head. "A strange garment, that, and one I did not make use of the way you described. I tore strips of the underwear and used them to secure my new blade to my thigh."

Which meant he had spent the entire day with only a pair of sweatpants between his assets and the rest of the world.

Oh, my.

"So you didn't like either the boxers or the briefs?" she asked. When he gave her another confused frown, she explained the difference.

"I do not recall seeing these briefs. Only boxers."

Wonderful. She'd either left them in the cart or her sedan's trunk. "I'll see if I can find you a pair. That way, you won't feel so…suspended." Was she really sitting here, peacefully discussing a man's underwear?

Grinning at her progress, she grabbed her coat and practically skipped outside. She stepped off the porch, looked past her shrubs and froze. There, trimming the hedges surrounding his house, stood Peter, her next-door neighbor. Her love interest.

Julia's happy-go-lucky mood vanished, and her tongue thickened like a block of concrete. She didn't want to face him until her lessons were finished—or had begun, for that matter. Panicked, she scrambled for a hiding place and ended up kneeling behind one of her bushes, not twenty feet away from him.

Several prolonged minutes ticked by, and she watched him all the while. *I'm a coward,* she thought, envisioning the spectacle she must make. However, jumping up and announcing her presence wasn't feasible at this point. Peter might think she was foolish, and she really, really wanted him to believe she was wonderful.

Only one solution popped into her mind: wait him out.

She continued to watch him. In his late twenties, early thirties, Peter resembled the average American male. He had a full head of sandy-colored hair, good skin, and a decent, if a bit skinny, body. He always wore a smile, as if forever pleased with the world around him.

He was reserved, didn't always know what to say, and wasn't so beautiful women would flock to him, trying to steal his affections. He was perfect for her.

And yet…

She didn't feel drawn to him, didn't crave his lips against hers. Didn't dream of him when she closed her eyes. Didn't imagine his body stroking hers. Instead, Tristan occupied her thoughts. She liked the way he moved, sensuous yet sometimes predatory. She liked the way his eyes crinkled at the sides when he teased her. While his muscles bulged with strength, he'd never hurt her. He was always careful of her smaller size.

Shame washed over her as she realized that she was comparing the two men, just as she'd been compared to her sister throughout her entire childhood. "Faith plays the piano so beautifully. Why can't you, Julia?" "Faith won first place at the track meet. Better luck next time, Julia." "All of the boys adore Faith. If you'd just try a little harder, Julia."

So Tristan resembled a legendary warrior king, and Peter resembled a toilet-scrubbing servant. Big deal. Beauty always faded. She *knew* that. Why then did her palms sweat and her heart pound whenever Tristan entered a room? Why did she feel unaffected by Peter, a man who seemed made specifically for her?

Julia didn't have the answers to those questions, and she told herself it didn't matter. Once she spent time with her neighbor, romantic feelings would come. She'd long to strip him naked and have him do the same to her. She'd long to taste his kisses and feel Tristan's—uh, Peter's body pressing against hers. Thankfully, a cool breeze drifted by and calmed the sudden fire in her blood.

Surely Peter possessed *some* quality that overshadowed Tristan. Hoping for a better view, she shoved several branches out of her line of vision. The brittle foliage tickled her check, but at least she now saw him clearly.

He paused, sheers in hand, and turned toward her bushes, his expression curious. "Julia?" he asked, unsure.

Caught in the act of spying! Julia stifled a groan of mortification and crawled out from beneath her hiding place. She jumped to her feet and smoothed away clinging foliage and dirt. "Uh, hi, Peter." She gave him a smile, hoping to cover her embarrassment. "I was just, uh—" Where were her wits when she needed them? "Pruning my bushes."

"Really?" He returned her grin and set his shears aside. "Me, too."

"That's great. Keeps your yard looking fresh."

An uncomfortable silence stretched between them. He rocked back and forth on his feet. His hands dug into his jacket pockets and jiggled change.

"Do you prune often?" she asked, willing to talk about anything at this point. "In the winter, I mean."

"I work in my garden all year round. I find it very relaxing."

Since she knew nothing about greenery, Julia didn't reply, too afraid of what might come out of her mouth. He didn't seem to mind. In fact, he continued to grin from ear to ear as he covered the distance between them. Her stomach churned with nervous anticipation, but she remained in place, determined to converse with him even if God himself reached down from heaven and clamped her lips shut.

"I've been meaning to come by," Peter said. His fragrance, like pine needles and dark wood, followed him on a scented cloud. "We've been neighbors for a few months now, but we've never really talked."

Julia forced her mouth to open and her reply to emerge perfectly, precisely. "I'd love to change that. To talk to you, I mean."

His hazel eyes glowed with approval, and he inched another step closer. "I must admit, I've been curious about you. What do you do for a living?"

"I own an antique store downtown. Julia's Treasures. What about you?"

His shoulders lifted in a shrug. "I do aircraft title searches." He noticed her confusion and added, "When someone wants to buy an airplane, I study the title to make sure there are no outstanding liens. It's the same procedure for buying a used car."

"How interesting."

"Very. I meet fascinating people." He kept shifting from one foot to the other. "Listen, I was thinking—"

"Julia will not be going anywhere with you," a low, sexy voice growled behind her.

Julia whipped around, but not before catching a glimpse of Peter's pale, horrified features. She wanted to assure him everything would be all right, but she couldn't think about her neighbor's sensibilities now. Not when Tristan's arms were crossed over his chest, his feet braced apart, and a dangerous, predatory light gleamed in his eyes. He bore no weapons save his fists, yet he looked ready to kill.

"What are you doing?" she whispered furiously.

"Saving you from yourself." The moment he'd heard voices, Tristan had stepped outside…only to see Julia conversing with the man she hoped to entice. Raw possessiveness had ripped through him, and he'd had to force himself to resist the urge to grab several blades from Julia's kitchen and slice this puny man in two.

It surprised him, this instant, volatile reaction. He'd never felt more than mild affection for any of his other women, if anything at all, and hadn't cared if they entertained other men when they no longer wished his services. But mild affection did not eat at him right now. Fury? Aye. She had told him an untruth, consciously breaking the first parameter of their bargain by talking with another man. Incredulity? Aye, he felt incredulity. Discarded? Absolutely. Julia hungered for the touch of a man—and it wasn't Tristan's.

He growled.

His muscles clenched, his blood boiled and his warrior instincts surfaced in full force. The image of removing Peter's heart—if he possessed one—with his bare fist mollified him somewhat. What was so special about this neighbor of hers? Tristan glared down at him, but saw nothing that might entrance an exotically sensual woman such as Julia to madness.

Julia pivoted away from him and stared at her neighbor, an apology—and something else?—in her eyes. Tristan's rage sparked to life with greater potency; he worked his jaw with a callused hand. Aside from their kiss, she rarely acted as if she wanted him. In fact, she continuously pushed him away, a completely foreign concept. Yet she desired marriage with this man.

What if she truly loved Peter? The possibility angered him more than he cared to admit. Did she not realize love would make her weak? Gave another control over her emotions? Obviously not. Well, as he'd told her only moments ago, he would simply have to save her from herself.

Tristan clasped Julia by the shoulders, melding her body with his own and visibly staking a claim lest Peter doubt the nature of his presence. The puny man's face was pallid by now, and he was backing away. Julia didn't turn or acknowledge Tristan's gesture in any way. At the moment, she was completely oblivious to him as a male, to the raw, masculine intent surging through his veins. He might as well have been a tree stump for all the attention she paid him. Every combative bone in his body demanded he act. Immediately!

By Elliea, he *would* make her want him.

To Peter, he barked, "You will leave us now."

The puny man blanched further, inched another step backward and held up his hands in a peace offering. "I was just on my way home. I swear to God I barely even looked at Julia."

"Please stay," Julia said with a shaky smile. "This will only take a second. My…brother and I just need to chat."

"No, really. I should go."

"Stay!" she commanded with such determination that he froze in place. She whipped around and pinned Tristan with a glare. "I don't appreciate you messing this up for me," she whispered fiercely.

"I require my underwear," he barked, not even trying to quiet his voice.

"Shh," she hissed. "That is not information Peter needs."

"Have you forgotten our bargain already?" His lips thinned, and his nostrils flared. "The first parameter— you will not see or otherwise engage in any type of activity with another man while I am giving you lessons."

Color drained from her face. "Peter and I were just talking."

"Otherwise engaged includes speaking. That you

knew. Mayhap I should bend the parameters and carry my sword." He leaned into her until their noses brushed, until their breaths intermingled. "Shall I retrieve the weapon now?"

Still ashen, Julia shook her head. She blinked several times, watching him, gauging, as if she didn't quite believe what was happening. "You're right, Tristan. You are. But it would have been rude for me to walk away without saying anything to Peter."

"You will be forgiven the moment you inform him that I am not your brother."

"Don't ask me to do that. Please."

"I have already asked, thus you will do it." The beast inside him had emerged, clawing and fighting and demanding immediate appeasing. He cared not at all that Puny Peter had already retreated inside his dwelling.

"I can't tell him who you really are," she said. "He might assume you're my…"

"Lover?" he finished for her. "If you will not tell him who I am, then explain to him that you cannot see him again until your lessons are complete."

"He'll think that's an excuse, that I don't really like him. I can't damage his feelings that way. He's a nice man, and he doesn't deserve to be hurt."

"So you will hurt me, instead?"

She looked away guiltily. "I doubt a woman could ever hurt you," she muttered after a long, defeated sigh. "Go back into the house, Tristan. Please."

He remained in place.

"I said go back into the house. Now!"

Glaring down at her, he waited for her to do or utter more words that would prove she was not as heartless as she sounded. She didn't.

"I live with you," he said quietly, "and as of tonight, I sleep in your bed. I will be your lover, Julia, and I will make sure *he* never once crosses your mind." With that, Tristan spun on his heel and obeyed her command.

CHAPTER ELEVEN

*Your Pleasure Rests In The
Pleasure Of Your Master*

JULIA CURSED under her breath as she stomped to the car. Men were *sooo* unbelievably stubborn.

By ordering Tristan back inside the house without hunting Peter down and telling him the truth, she'd damaged Tristan's pride, treating him as a slave instead of a man. Yet her actions had been unavoidable. Allowing Peter to believe she had a live-in lover was not the best way to win his affections. Besides, she'd wanted to avoid all confrontation, thereby avoiding Peter's execution.

In Tristan's black mood, Peter might have accidentally said something to set him off. Tristan would have unsheathed his dagger, and Peter would have dropped to the ground in a fetal ball, crying for his mommy and sucking his thumb. Then Tristan would have killed him.

Julia snorted in disgust. Men were not a prize; they were an affliction. A disease upon society, and at the moment, she couldn't think of a single reason she had decided to seduce one.

She was better off alone.

Alone.

The word echoed in her mind over and over, chafing against her deepest dreams and desires until she succumbed to the truth. She didn't *really* want to be alone. She wanted romance, damn it, complete with moonlight and candles. Promises of love and forever. Soft, sweet music and wandering hands. Hot, gyrating bodies. She wanted to feel beautiful, admired and gloriously special.

Because Peter was as plain and shy as she was, he would know how it felt to want those things and would do everything in his power to give her what she craved. She *knew* it. Of course, she now had to defuse his fear of infuriating her "brother," which might prove difficult considering Tristan had practically hacked him in two with a mere glare.

Oh, lighten up, Julia. She'd built her business with nothing but her wits, and she could build a relationship with Peter doing the same. So what that her seduction had taken a wrong turn. So what that she couldn't see him or otherwise engage in any type of activity with him until her lessons with Tristan ended. She'd wait, and when the time was right, she'd smooth things over. Perhaps by then Peter would find her so irresistible he'd fall on his knees and beg her to date him.

Feeling lighter, freer, she hummed under her breath as she rooted through the trunk of her sedan. Minutes later, she found the package of black men's briefs, extra-large. Slipping the item under her arm, she sauntered into her house. Tristan lounged on the living-room couch and, even in his relaxed pose, he radiated authority and consuming fury.

Her light mood vanished. She gulped. "I found your briefs," she said, placing the package atop the coffee table.

Without glancing at her, he replied, "Thank you, master."

His steely tone cut like a knife, and shards of guilt uncoiled deep within her. "I didn't want to order you inside, Tristan, but you gave me no choice. You were angry, and I didn't want you to take your emotions out on Peter."

Nothing. No response.

"He's not as strong as you are," she continued, "and if you had hurt him, you would have been arrested."

When Tristan still didn't move or acknowledge her in any way, she struggled against a sharp ache in her chest. Had she caused irreparable damage to his pride? Had she ruined their growing friendship?

"Tristan, please say something."

"Is that a command?"

"No."

Only silence greeted her.

After a brief hesitation, she slipped from the room.

Tristan watched her go, hating his existence more at this moment than ever before. She'd dishonored him, embarrassed him and dismissed him. Circumstances he'd endured a thousands times before, but all the more potent now as they mingled with his need to possess and conquer.

He was letting himself care for her, and he knew bet-

ter. Curse him, he knew better! She might challenge
him, draw him and anger him. She might confuse him
with her illogical speech. And most times, she might
simply captivate him. But none of those things mattered.
He had to remain disciplined, had to keep himself dis-
tanced. One day she would die, or mayhap even lose his
box, and he would continue on—on to another woman.

Every muscle in his body tensed. Relaxed. Tensed
again. The thought of Julia alone, with no one to care
for her, did not settle well within him.

Drawing in a deep breath, and catching a hint of Julia's sweet, lingering fragrance, he leaned forward and
studied the portraits on the small table in front of him.
In one, Julia perched next to a girl who was slightly
older. While Julia's eyes were green, the other girl's
were big and blue. Both looked so young, somber and
defeated, and Julia did not resemble the spitfire he knew
her to be. In another, the same two girls were splayed
atop a bed of bright emerald foliage, their eyes sparkling
and staring up toward the heavens, their lips lifted in
sad, wistful smiles.

'Twas the same smile Julia wore before walking
away from him moments ago.

He could not leave things as they were.

He knifed to his feet and followed the direction she
had taken. What he planned to do with her, or to say to
her, he didn't know.

He found her in the bathing chamber, preparing a
bath. Water burst from a small opening, filling a white,
oblong container. A long, blue robe covered her from

shoulders to toes. Her hair was plaited high at her crown, and a few tendrils cascaded down her temples. She looked so tiny just then, so fragile.

Seeing her like this lanced him with a spear of tenderness. She was life and beauty. She was innocence, utterly and purely. Sometimes, like now, he felt unworthy of the merest glance from her. She deserved only happiness.

The last vestiges of his anger eased, and he shook his head in shock. How did she slay his riotous emotions so quickly? How did she make him feel so conflicted…and yet so content? He knew not the answers.

"I thank you for the underwear, Julia."

With a surprised gasp, she jerked her gaze to the doorway. To him. When their eyes met, her expression softened. "You're welcome," she said. "I didn't mean to hurt you. I—"

"I know. And it is okay," he replied, borrowing one of her favorite words. He propped one shoulder against the door frame. Fragrant steam wafted through the small room, billowing around her like a loving caress.

As she watched him, she wet her lips with her tongue. Just as before, his breath caught. How tempting it was just then to push her against the coldness of the wall and fill her with the heat of his flesh, to drown the mounting silence of the room with the screams of her pleasure. And she would scream. He would make sure of it.

Tristan had to force himself to remain where he was. Control. He would control his reactions to her.

"After you bathe," he said, "I wish to go to this mall

of yours." He missed the excitement and revelry only a market could provide, yet knew visiting such a place would bring memories of his friends, memories that made him long for impossible things. Yet he desired more time with Julia, wanted to make her smile again. Wanted to see her in the clothing he chose for her—but only because he had given her his word, he forced himself to add.

Her grin slipped. "How about we go tomorrow instead? It's been a really long day."

"And if tomorrow is a long day, as well?"

"Why don't I just close the store? We'll shop in the morning. That way I'm guaranteed to be perfectly rested."

Satisfied with that, he nodded. "At tomorrow's dawning, we shall venture to the mall."

When the door closed behind Tristan, Julia sank to the edge of the tub. She never, *never* closed her shop. Not for sickness. Or weather. Or a broken limb. That she even suggested such a thing was shocking.

Tristan had no idea of the magnitude of what she'd just done.

Did she?

CHAPTER TWELVE

*All Of Your Choices Must Be Based Upon
Whether Or Not They Please Your Master*

WHEN THE MALL OPENED the next day, Julia and Tristan were there, waiting at the doors. She tried not to picture the Closed sign on her shop's front window and the customers knocking on the glass, confused and angry.

With a sigh, she strolled beside Tristan. They headed for a chic boutique that carried only the hottest fashions. Even in jeans and a T-shirt—and hopefully briefs—Tristan generated quite a bit of feminine appreciation. Not that she cared. He could entice all the women he wanted with his dangerous swagger and otherworldly eyes.

Julia's nails dug into her palm as she recognized her thoughts for the lie they were. The jerk had better not be doing any enticing, not after he agreed to the first parameter. The death glare she leveled at him contained enough heat to incinerate him. Surprisingly his gaze never once strayed to another woman.

By small degrees, the muscles in Julia's body relaxed. She wasn't jealous, she assured herself. She was simply guarding her investment. Her tutor. If someone lured him away, who would give her dating etiquette lessons? No one, that's who.

I'm pathetic, she thought.

Meanwhile, Tristan dove into their adventure with the eagerness of a teenage boy locked inside a room with naked, horny women. Once they reached Coco's, he hopped from one rack to the other, tossing garments her way.

"You will try this one. And this one. And this one." He held up a short red Band-Aid—such sheer, barely there material couldn't be called a dress—wicked intention gleaming in his eyes. "This one will be fun to remove."

"I'm not wearing that," she told him with a shake of her head.

"Aye, you will."

"That's just so…sexy. Too sexy for me."

"Julia, Julia, Julia. There is no such thing as too sexy for you."

"I need conservative clothing. I wouldn't feel comfortable with three-fourths of my skin showing."

He arched a brow. "Who is the expert here?"

"You are," she grudgingly admitted.

"Exactly." He grabbed another slinky dress, this one a flowing, gauzy white. On and on he went until she stumbled under the weight of the clothing. After a while, her arm muscles shook from exertion.

"I need to work out," she muttered.

"I once served a woman who insisted she have at least one hundred gowns to choose from every day," Tristan said, as he hunted through a new rack of garments.

"Well, hel-lo there, gorgeous," a strong, masculine voice said. "Is there anything I can help you with?"

"Thank you, yes." Relieved, Julia craned her neck until she saw over her bundle. "I need these placed in a dress—"

The salesman never even glanced her way. He stared at Tristan, totally and completely transfixed. She almost laughed. She rolled her eyes in exasperation. The word "gorgeous" should have tipped her off. Men usually referred to her as "Hey, you."

"I'm Gary," the salesman said to Tristan. "I'll be your personal shopper. Or anything else you want me to be."

Gary had beautiful black hair, fashionably styled and cut just above his collar. He wore no jewelry save for the black onyx ring on his right index finger. He stood taller than the average man; the top of his head reached Tristan's shoulders. His clothes were perfectly tailored and overall he presented one very attractive package. It was quite obvious he wanted to slather Tristan's naked body with whipped cream and have himself a double-dip sundae. He gave Tristan a full-body, I-wish-I-had-X-ray-vision once-over.

Tristan didn't seem to notice. "We need no assistance," he said.

"Yes, we do," Julia spoke up. "I'm buying a hip, new wardrobe and I need all the help I can get."

"Excellent, excellent." Too lost in the fantastical maleness of Tristan, Gary spared her the barest of glances, one that asked, *Are you still here?* She couldn't blame him for his inattention. She often found herself in the same predicament whenever Tristan neared. "I'm afraid I didn't catch your name, gorgeous," he told Tristan.

"I did not throw it." Tristan gripped Gary's offered palm, studied it, then dropped it.

"Are you sure there isn't anything I can get for you?"

"Aye. I am most sure."

Julia doubted Tristan realized he was being hit on, and she wasn't going to be the one to tell him. In fact, she needed to rein in Gary's lust before the situation mutated into one of death and disaster. "Would you mind helping me carry these outfits into a dressing room?" she asked him. At last her arms gave out, and she dropped the bundle with a whoosh. "I'd really appreciate it."

Finally he awarded her his full attention. "I'd be glad to help, darling." With an imperial frown, he snapped his fingers and another sales associate flew to his side. "Take these to dressing room four."

The pretty young girl, no more than twenty-two, bent down, hefted up the clothes, then started moving away, albeit slowly.

"Wait!" Gary called abruptly. The girl froze. With his forefinger and thumb, he pinched a white bubble-knit skirt from the top of the pile. "Unless you want to look frumpy," he told Julia, his tone properly disgusted, "this simply will not do. Your body cries out for something elongating. Think stiletto heels. Slimming black pants. Dark gray top. You're about a size—" He wrapped his palms around her waist, taking her measurements. "Eight, right? A snug eight, I'd say."

With a speed and grace at odds with his massive size, Tristan pinned the salesman against the wall, leaving the poor man's feet dangling in the air. He appeared every inch a cold, hard killer, from the predatory gleam in his gaze to the ticking muscle in his jaw.

"There will be no touching my woman. Understand?"

Far from being frightened, Gary closed his eyes in surrender, as if he'd just entered the gates of paradise. "Possessive, are we? I like that in a man."

"Do you understand?" Tristan demanded, enunciating every syllable.

Julia was just about to order Tristan to release the salesman, when Gary spoke.

"Oh, yes, I understand. But what about you?" A slow grin played at Gary's lips, and his eyelids cracked open, revealing a suggestive, eager glint. "Is it permissible to touch you?"

Tristan released him as if he'd just mutated into nuclear waste, and Gary dropped to the hardwood floor with a thud. Thank God she'd taken Tristan's sword away. He might have skinned the salesman alive.

But you gave him a knife, remember?

Her eyes widened. Stupid, stupid, stupid. Sweat popped up on her brow as she glanced around the boutique. People were openly staring, some concerned, others merely entertained. With Tristan's warrior speed, he could slice Gary to ribbons before she uttered a single word to stop him.

"You haven't answered my question, gorgeous." Gary gave Tristan a flirtatious wink. "Is it permissible to touch you?"

"Nay," he growled. "No touching. Not me. Not Julia."

Relief crashed through her like the waves of an ocean. The imminent threat of attack had passed. Everyone would live.

Undaunted, Gary simply continued on. "What about these?" He shuffled through a rack of pants and, with a flourish, swished out a silky black pair. "These will make your woman look fab-oo, darling. Simply fab-oo."

No longer resembling a thundercloud of wrath, Tristan stroked his chin, giving the slacks a thorough inspection. "Nay. I want Julia to wear a gown that is soft and feminine, that flows around her ankles. That means no drocs."

"No pants," she translated.

"If that's what you want, gorgeous, that's what you shall have." With a flick of his wrist, Gary tossed the slacks aside. "This way," he called, sailing off. Julia followed, Tristan close at her heels. "Here you are, dear, and don't be shy. We want to see everything you try on. Absolutely everything."

"I'll show you," she said sternly, and waited, tapping her foot, for him to leave.

He got the hint.

"Of course, of course." Smiling with delight, he

waved one hand through the air. "I'll just keep the big man occupied, all righty?"

Her delight far surpassed his, and she gave him a grin of her own. "I would like that, thank you."

Tristan opened his mouth to protest, but she slammed the door shut and clicked the lock in place. Julia slipped out of her jeans and T-shirt. Clad only in her mismatched bra and panties—next item of business: lingerie—she stole a moment to study herself in the mirror. A single bulb hung straight above her, its bright rays unforgiving. She turned left, then right, then left again. A frown pulled at her lips the entire time. No matter what the angle, the image stayed the same. Unattractive. Diets didn't work for her, damn it, and she would never be model slim. A short size eight was not the same as a tall size eight.

"Mirror, mirror on the wall," she muttered, pivoting for a back view. Her frown deepened. For some reason, her butt seemed extra wide today. How was that possible? Did fat cells reproduce? Before she worked herself into a good panic, she turned her attention elsewhere. Her breasts were nice, a definite handful. Would Tristan like them? she wondered, then scolded herself for even caring.

"Mayhap we should forget the gowns and leave you just as you are. No man could resist you like this."

Heart slamming in her chest, Julia uttered a panicked scream and spun...only to find Tristan watching her. Because of his immense height, his head towered over the dressing-room door, giving him a perfect view inside.

Right now, his eyes burned with the same heat that had flared to life right before he'd kissed her.

"What are you doing?" she screeched, snatching a dress and molding the material to the outside of her body. Her bra and panties covered crucial areas, but that didn't save her from embarrassment. Or arousal.

The grin he gave her reminded Julia of a naughty toddler who had just found a piece of fuzzy candy under the couch cushion. "Think you I would not remain nearby in case you had need of me?"

"I don't need you," she rushed out. "I swear."

The fire in his gaze blazed all the brighter, as if she'd offered him a scorching innuendo and had every intention of seeing it through. "Oh, but you do have need of me, little dragon," he said softly. "You do." The ominous words sounded like a promise and had nothing to do with changing her clothes. "One day soon I will prove that to you."

She decided to change the subject before her tongue turned to rubber and her body to a quivering bundle of need. If only he didn't smell so seductive or look so erotically dangerous. So…yummy. "Wh-where's Gary?"

In the space of a heartbeat, Tristan lost his passionate glow. The hollows of his cheekbones brightened with horror, and he offered in a strangled whisper, "That man desires me, Julia. As a lover!"

"I know," she replied, and prayed he missed the sudden trace of laughter in her voice.

He didn't. His eyes narrowed. "You *know?*"

"Well, yeah."

"And yet you left me alone with him?"

Her lips pressed together, and again she answered, "Well, yeah."

Watching her, he drummed his fingertips atop the door ledge. "Mayhap I should do to you what I did to him."

A gasp slithered out of her throat. The hard slash of his brows had her picturing severed limbs and blood-soaked wood floors. "You didn't kill Gary, did you?"

Only silence greeted her, causing her veins to crystallize with ice.

"Tristan, please tell me you didn't kill him."

"I did not," he grudgingly—finally—admitted. "I bolted him inside a storage chamber."

"Dead or alive?"

His shoulders straightened, and his expression grew shuttered. "I will not kill your people, Julia."

A measure of relief swept through her, but the relief quickly faded, replaced all too soon by consternation as she recalled the state of her undress. She shooed him away with her hands. "Go set him free, Mr. Peeping Tom."

"I am Tristan."

"Look, this is a woman's dressing room." When he didn't immediately walk away, she added, "That means no men allowed."

"During your lessons," he said with an edge of determination in his voice, "I am in charge. Buying new clothes is part of a lesson. That means right now, *you* obey *me*. And I wish to stay."

He had her there, damn him. She couldn't break a parameter, not when she'd broken one this very morning.

So being desperate, she opted for the only option available. Her eyes imploring, she said, "Please, Tristan. I'm begging you. Go find Gary and set him free before we get into trouble." And before she died of mortification.

Tristan stiffened, eyed her with a riotous emotion she couldn't identify, maybe didn't want to identify. Yet she caught a glimpse of shadowed pain, so much pain she wondered how he survived.

"Are you okay?" Concern washed through her, and she closed what distance between them she could. Only the width of the door kept their chests from touching. She clasped the warmth of his hand within her own. "What's wrong? You're suddenly so pale."

Fury and incredulity etched the lines of his face. "You begged me," he stated coldly. "You begged me to leave."

"Of course I did." What did that have to do with anything? Exasperated now, she gave him a stern, no-nonsense glare. "Will you please just go? I want to get dressed."

Without another word, he turned and stalked away.

Hurry, hurry, hurry, echoed in her mind as Julia jerked on her jeans and T-shirt. She tried not to ponder what Tristan had really thought of her poor excuse for a body. Covered at last, she randomly grabbed ten of the dresses he'd chosen, plus swiped several pairs of slacks from a nearby rack and rushed to pay. She was just accepting her change when Tristan approached her side, Gary close behind him.

"It is as you wish," Tristan said stiffly.

"Thanks." She gave the salesman a quick glance—he looked irked but alive—then focused all of her attention on Tristan. "I want to hit a few more stores before we head home." She'd taken the day off, and by God, she was going to get all of her shopping done.

"What about your gowns?"

"I've already paid for them."

"I wished to see you wear them."

Was there a bit of a whine in his tone? "I'll show you later, okay?" *When I can change behind a proper door!*

"Do you not know the meaning of the phrase 'in charge'?" he growled.

"Apparently not," she muttered.

With deliberate leisure, he leaned his hip against the counter. "Mayhap I need to give you a lesson in obedience, as well as enticement."

Julia swiped a stray tendril of hair from her eyes. "Just try it, tough guy, and you'll get a lesson in karate."

"I must admit, I am growing more and more intrigued by this karate of yours. Do you, mayhap, practice the sport naked?"

"Only on rainy days," she replied dryly. "Now let's go." Laden down with sacks, they visited three more shops, buying shoes and accessories and yes, slinky lingerie, which she bought while Tristan was distracted with the "amazing delicacies" of corn dogs and French fries found at the food court.

No matter where they went, he hovered behind her. She needed protecting, he said, therefore he protected her. End of story. If a man glanced her way in a manner remotely unfriendly (or friendly) her charming, playful pleasure slave morphed into a demon from hell. He scowled. Growled. Clenched his fists.

Exasperating. Simply exasperating.

At home, she planted him in front of the TV and took another relaxing bubble bath. Like any man, Tristan became fascinated with the remote control.

Go figure.

CHAPTER THIRTEEN

You Are Always In Submission To Your Master
Whether She Is Present Or Not

TRISTAN EASED back on the velvety soft chaise, fingering his new dagger and staring up at the ceiling. In the center, lights dripped like forgotten tears, their essence draped by burgundy-and-cream-colored glass. A clatter of voices drifted from the talking box in front of him, and he heard the sound of children giggling and racing outside, just beyond the royal-blue stained window.

They were so happy out there. So free. They did not know how it felt to beg for one's desires.

But Julia did. She had begged him.

At the clothing store, she'd asked him to leave her alone, and when he refused, she had begged him.

Begged him.

He hated himself for it, because he knew all too well how it felt to grovel. When the words "I'm begging you" had left Julia's mouth, he'd wanted to rip out his heart and give the offending organ to her.

How many nights had he spent on his knees, hands

clasped, tears streaming down his cheeks as he pleaded with his father for necessities? How many eves had his father taken him into town, tied him to a post, then whipped him until only thin strips of skin were left on his back? All for the sheer pleasure of hearing him cry for mercy?

Innumerable.

The pain of those years even overshadowed the pain of being a pleasure slave. He easily recalled the humiliation. The depravation. If he'd needed to eat, he begged. If he'd needed a blanket to warm his body, he begged. If he'd needed to rest, he begged.

There were days he would have willingly dropped to his knees, all for a simple show of affection from the father who was supposed to love him—affection he never received. As a small measure of revenge, he had learned to repress his body's reactions, never crying out, never showing weakness no matter what cruelty was inflicted. He'd simply channeled his energy into another direction. Seduction. At such a young age, he became a lover of great talents, learning the nuances of the female form, learning every secret place that brought a woman pleasure. In return, he found a short reprieve from the harsh reality that had been his life.

Then at sixteen spans, he met Roake, a boy of sixteen who had endured his own share of pain. The two of them struck out on their own. Together they practiced wielding a sword until their skill surpassed even that of their Great-Lord. They fought for their city, dispatching many rebel troops. And as a reward, Great-Lord Challann gave them land of their own.

Finally Tristan had a home he admired.

Then Zirra had placed him in bondage.

The salvation he had always found in a woman's arms ultimately became his downfall, he thought darkly; his sexual knowledge the bane of his existence, yet his only means of escape. How ironic. How cruel. During the first span of his curse, he had ceased thinking of sex as a pleasure, seeing it as a means to an end instead. Except with Julia. He didn't dread the thought of being with her. Nay, he yearned for her nakedness and touch with every ounce of his manhood, and neither escape nor obligation had anything to do with it.

Why did she continue to resist him?

He was beginning to think that all the knowledge in the galaxies could not win her devotion. And he so badly wanted to win her. She was a woman of surprising depth. Her smile held warmth and sunshine and such captivating beauty he was still awed by its majesty. Her anger held traces of fire and frost, and he often found himself longing to spark her ire simply to soothe her.

Sometimes she seemed a volatile mixture of emotions—need, fear, surety, doubt—as if she didn't truly know her own desires. He'd come to realize that she thought herself shy and plain and unworthy of anyone who was not. How had she ever become so deceived? To Tristan, she radiated kindness, generosity and compassion. Her inner beauty magnified her outer beauty, giving her such luminescence, such tranquility, that no other woman compared. She was precious, worth so much more than she could possibly imagine.

Tristan tangled a hand through his hair, his jaw clenched. He was beginning to realize love was not the monster he'd thought it to be. The moment the thought filled his mind, he blinked and shook his head. He even repeated the phrase out loud. "Love is not a monster."

Every muscle in his body tensed, waiting for him to deny the words, but he could not. Nay, he could not deny them, for he could at last see merits to the emotion. Knowing a woman's smile belonged solely to him... watching passion flare to life in her eyes...tasting her sweetness for the rest of his life.

He knew, though, that loving Julia would be so much worse than any torture he'd hitherto endured. Loving her meant losing her, for there would be no magic to bind them together, and he would hurtle back to his world without her, to never see her smile again, to never breathe in the lushness of her scent.

Nay, love was not a monster, but he still wanted no part of it.

He simply wanted Julia.

Passion lay buried underneath her prudish exterior; he knew it, a raw, primal passion that was so hot it required only one kiss to make her burn. His nerve endings sparked to life with the memory. What would it take for her to catch fire and burn again—for him and no other? What would it take to make her forget Peter?

His fist clenched the dagger so tightly the blade slashed into his skin and a trickle of blood flowed down the length of his arm. Peter must be forced from her mind. The puny man did not deserve Julia's radiance. 'Twas time Julia realized it.

I will give her another lesson, he thought, applauding himself for his own ingenuity. Lesson number two would be anticipation and, as her tutor, it was his duty, nay, his obligation, to make her study. *Find her,* his body shouted.

Following the scent of spices, he strode into the kitchen. The sight of Julia stopped him, held him ensnared. A jolt of tenderness crashed through him as he watched her pad from the stove to the sink and drain a pot of water, her expression one of intense concentration.

His mouth watered for her. "Is our meal ready?"

With a startled gasp, she whipped around. A spot of red sauce dotted her chin. "Everything will be done in about fifteen minutes."

He nodded, wondering what her chin would taste like if he licked the sauce away. The image left him hard and aching, his muscles bunched. Instead of closing the distance between them, locking his arms around her and crushing her lips with his own, he said, "I would like to bathe ere we eat."

"Oh." She placed the pot on the counter. Steam wafted up, a billowing cloud that momentarily shielded her features. "Can you wait until later?"

"Nay." He needed his body scrubbed clean—clean enough to eat off—for what he had planned.

"All right. Fine." She sighed. "You know where the bathroom is." Then she paused. "Do you know how to work a shower?"

"Aye." At least, he hoped he did. A few minutes later, he found that he did, indeed, know how to work the strange knobs. They were similar to those used for a Gillradian bathhouse. He adjusted the setting until water streamed down, pounding against the tub.

Tristan stripped and stepped into the center. The warm liquid caressed his sensitized skin like the hand of a lover. He was still hard, still ready, and as he stood underneath the spray, his arousal became a source of pain. He wanted Julia's hands on him, her fingers curled around his cock while her mouth sucked at his nipples. Then, when he could stand that torment no more, he wanted her mouth and hand to trade places, wanted to feel the hot wetness of her tongue stroke his swollen length over and over, again and again.

His hands fisted. If he did not halt these imaginings, his warrior's training would soon abandon him completely. He might pounce on her, hurt her, and he would no more hurt her than he would hurt himself. But her image refused to leave. Instead, his mind's eye stripped her down and had her stepping into the tub with him. Her smooth, pale skin glittered with moisture, her only color the delicious pink of her nipples and the dark patch of curls between her legs. His mind's eye had her gifting him with a secret little smile as she allowed her fingertips to swirl around his navel…then dip lower. His muscles constricted as a surge of pleasure ripped through him.

He could no more stop his next action than he could refuse to take another breath. With the fragrant steam billowing around him and the rivulets of water stream-ing down his chest, he reached down and clasped his shaft in his hand, picturing her hand there instead. He stroked himself, going from base to tip with a tight fist. He could almost feel her teeth scraping his nipples, could almost feel her lips sliding all over him. Only when he imagined that she moaned with the pleasure of touching him, did he find release.

A paltry substitute, he knew, yet it was effective all the same. He might not feel completely satisfied, but he was calm, once more in control.

Frowning, he emerged from the tub on a haze of mist. Using a thin strip of cloth, he strapped his dag-ger to his thigh. Then he wrapped a bigger cloth around his waist. A desire to see Julia, to hear her voice, filled him and he found himself striding back into the kitchen. Praise be to Elliea, it was time to begin her next lesson.

When he saw her sitting at the table, waiting, dishes and food in place on the tabletop, something in his chest constricted. How he wanted this woman. All of her. Her hands were folded in front of her and she wore an ex-pression of dreamy relaxation.

"I am ready," he said, his tone leaving no doubt as to just what he was ready for.

Her lashes swept up and down as she blinked up at him. Her mouth drooped a bit and a distraught light en-tered her eyes. "Uh, Tristan—"

He cut off her words before they formed. "Every-thing looks and smells delicious, Julia."

She tore her gaze from his towel. "I hope you're hungry."

"I'm always hungry."

"That's good." *Oh, yes, that's very good,* Julia thought, sneaking another peek at Tristan's bronzed perfection. Droplets of water trickled from his hair, ran down his hard, sculpted chest and over the ridges of his abdomen. A plain white cloth shielded his upper thighs, waist and penis.

There. She'd actually used the word in association with him. Penis, penis, penis. The swell of victory gave way to a rise of longing. Her mouth suddenly felt dry and parched.

"Do you like lasagna?" she managed to squeak out.

"I would like anything you prepared." That naughty towel parted slightly as he slid into his chair.

Look away, Julia. No, enjoy. Damn it, look away. Finally she did. "Shouldn't you get dressed before we eat?" As she waited for his answer, her fingers twisted and shredded her napkin to ribbons. Her foot tapped against the table leg as she stifled the urge to wrap them around his waist.

"Nay," he said, not sparing her a glance. "This is appropriate attire for one's home, is it not?"

"I guess so." But how was she supposed to concentrate on dinner while she could very well imagine him sprawled out on the tabletop, a buffet of masculinity for her own personal enjoyment? *I'll never be able to concentrate.* Her appetite had taken a swift turn away from food, and to— she stole another quick glance and felt hot, so hot—to *that.*

He didn't seem to have a problem concentrating, however. Whistling under his breath, he piled his plate high with salad, breadsticks and pasta. His facial features were so relaxed she suspected he might fall asleep.

Throughout the meal, her unbidden gaze caressed his small brown nipples puckered from the cool air, then dipped lower. Lower still. She willed his towel to melt away so that she could run her palms over his abdomen—and anything else she encountered along the way. She even willed his fingers on *her* body, perhaps unfastening her jeans, slipping them from her legs and tunneling beneath her panties. How delightful it would be to have such strength and heat spread all over her.

His knee brushed hers.

The innocent touch propelled spears of fire through her blood. She gasped.

"My apologies," he muttered, never even glancing her way.

"No problem," she managed.

When he did it yet again and again, and then again, Julia dropped her fork with a *clank*. She drew in a shaky breath. *One. Two. Three.* Her body countered with a mantra of its own. *Sex. Sex. Sex.* Every nerve within her suddenly screamed with sensation, and when she discovered that she was caressing a bread stick and Tristan was watching her, her face heated.

"You have no liking for the food?" he asked, all innocence.

"No. I mean, yes. It's fine." Did he know what he was doing to her? No, he couldn't, she thought. He was too busy eating the entire pan of lasagna. *Concentrate, Julia. You are not a nymphomaniac—much as you might wish otherwise.* Her hands trembled as she lifted the utensil and feigned interest in the food.

Twice she managed to steal another peak at him, and twice more he casually bumped her with his leg. He still looked completely relaxed, at ease, while desire kindled within her, embers ready to burst into flame. His damp skin beckoned for caring, gentle hands to wipe away every drop of moisture. His mouth cried out for hot, wet kisses.

She wanted him, was, in fact, just about to leap over the table and rip the towel from his body when the doorbell rang. Saved, she mentally clapped, dropping her fork and jumping to her feet.

"I'll be right back," she said. "We've got a visitor."

Her heart drumming erratically inside her chest, she tugged open the door. The frantic beat slowed, and she dragged in a much needed breath. Peter smiled when he spotted her.

"Hi, Julia," he said, his tone shy and hesitant, yet a panicked light flittered into his hazel eyes. "Your brother's not here, is he?"

"He's in the kitchen. Completely absorbed in his food," she added when Peter backed three hasty steps away.

His shoulders relaxed. He slipped his hands into his pants pockets and jingled change. "I noticed your car in the driveway and wondered if you'd like to—"

Tristan, who suddenly stood right behind her, barked, "We are busy." And shut the door in Peter's stunned, horrified face with more force than necessary.

Grimacing, Julia propped her forehead against the cherry wood with a thump. "That was so unbelievably rude."

"Was it not rude to interrupt our meal? Now, come." Tristan led her back to the table, a silent reminder that they would not discuss her neighbor.

She bit back a sigh and settled into her chair. How would she later explain this to Peter? How would she make him understand it was *him* she wanted? *Liar, liar,* her mind sang, before all thoughts and questions tapered to silence. Tristan touched her knee again, a deeper, more lingering caress, and whether he did it purposefully or accidentally, she still didn't know. And didn't care. Over and over, one part of his body connected with hers, launching erotic shivers down her spine.

When his fingertips brushed the underside of her calf, white-hot need crashed through her body like bolts of lightning. Raspy breaths she recognized as her own pounded in her ears. Beads of sweat popped onto her brow. If only he'd forget about the pasta in front of him and feast on *her.* Lord, when had she become such a sexual being who only considered pleasure? Another tremor raked her, small and deliciously decadent.

"Little dragon," he said languidly.

"Yes," she answered breathlessly. Oh, yes, yes, yes.

"Have you, perchance, found something you desire?"

"Yes." She forced herself to concentrate, to think of something plausible. "You took my bread stick. I want it back."

Light reflected off his eyes, making them twinkle

with an emotion she couldn't quite name. Laughter?
Passion? Mischief? "You have not eaten the one in front
of you."

"Oh." She glanced down, saw her plate piled high
with uneaten food. "I'm not that hungry."

He smiled a slow, sensual smile that held promise
and knowledge, wickedness and allure. "Mayhap I can
interest you in something else, a more appetizing morsel than a mere piece of bread."

"I'm not sure you can, but perhaps you should try,"
she said, dreading—praying—he might say something
naughty.

A lengthy pause left her suspended on the edge of
her chair.

"Mayhap I can interest you in…me."

Was the room suddenly hotter? Brighter? She tugged
at the collar of her shirt and forced herself to remain
seated, lest she throw herself at him. "I made dessert,"
she offered lamely. "Well, I didn't cook it. I just opened
the box and set the bonbons on the counter."

"Bring them to me," he coaxed, his voice like soft,
rich velvet.

Using dessert as a distraction, Julia straightened on
unsteady legs, grabbed the tray of ice cream and set it
on the table with a thud. More balanced now, she re-
claimed her seat. He eyed the chocolate treats with un-
fettered delight, and she suddenly wished she'd smeared
the things over her naked body.

I'm just a guan ren *to him,* she reminded herself. A
means to an end he must pursue because that is his sole

purpose in life. Seduction. To him, she was not special or pretty or even truly desirable. How pathetic she would be if she accepted such indifference and did not demand more for herself—or for him.

Never once taking his violet gaze from her, he lifted a bonbon and licked the center. "Let me feed you dessert," he said so silkily that she swallowed back a dreamy sigh.

Stay tough. Stay focused. "I'm not sure that would be wise, Tristan."

"I care not if such indulgence is wise. I care only about desire." His lids lowered in half-mast perusal, mentally stripping away her clothes and licking every inch of her. "If you cannot accept food from my hand, will you at least accept my kiss?"

Her heart rate quickened with excitement, and the arousal kindling within her burst into hot flames that licked her all over. Prickles of anticipation worked along her skin. Really, what would one more kiss hurt? Just one simple kiss? Nothing, that's what, her mind eagerly answered.

"One kiss?" she asked with breathless longing.

"Just one." He touched her again, this time deliberately, a simple coasting of his knuckles that set off a chain reaction of sensation. How did he do that? How did he make her feel like the most desirable woman he'd ever encountered? Oh, how she wanted him.

Wait! You want Peter.

Peter who?

"There is no room for thought here," Tristan said, as

if he feared she would pull away. "We have defeated your propensity for issuing lectures. Now let us conquer your habit of thinking overly much."

Leaning over, he dipped his index finger into the center of the bonbon, then traced the vanilla cream around the outline of her lips; he stroked a path along the curve of her jaw, then dipped to her neck, touching so softly she felt the coolness of the ice cream rather than the actual touch. Julia shivered as the sweetness melted and spread over her skin. Her breath caught in her throat.

"Come to me," he breathed. His fingertip traveled downward, then around, anchoring at the base of her neck and drawing her forward until she half stood over the table. "I need you so desperately."

It was his words that finally broke her resistance. He needed her. Her! Without breaking contact, she managed to maneuver around the table's edge and close the remaining space between them. He stayed seated, so she peered down at him. His lips looked soft, and she was proud of herself for noticing because at the moment, his erection was pushing against her leg.

"Put your arms around me," he said oh so softly.

Her knees gave out, and she dropped to the cool wood floor, her body positioned between his knees, her face level with his sternum. Both of her hands crept up the taut muscles of his chest, savoring, lingering, then twining around his neck as he'd demanded.

The contact was electric. It felt sinful and erotic and she wanted the moment to last forever. He smelled so good, like soap and chocolate and vanilla. His arms descended to her waist, locking her in place, but such an action wasn't necessary. At the moment, there was no other place she would rather be, and this overly large, overly real man in her arms had long since replaced thoughts of Peter.

Slowly he lowered his mouth to hers, a breath away. "I can feel your body quivering, little dragon. Are you cold?"

She shook her head.

Featherlight, he kissed her cheek, a mere brush of lips to flesh. "Excited?"

"Yes." How could she deny it when her body felt so alive, so eager?

He licked the outline of her lips. "Do you want my mouth on yours?"

Somehow she managed to nod.

"Say it. Say the words."

"Yes, I think I do."

"Ah-ah-ah. No thinking, remember?"

Lost in a world of sensation, where inhibitions and embarrassment didn't belong, she let herself run free. She ached, yearned for him, and finally confessed. "I need your mouth, your lips and your tongue. Kiss me, Tristan. Kiss me."

He chuckled softly, a heady rumble that purred with barely suppressed power. "This is one command I will enjoy obeying." His tongue met hers, blending the chocolate with the vanilla. He thrust into her mouth, all sweetness and warmth, and Julia eagerly welcomed him.

Just as before, the moment he began to work her tongue, passion exploded within her. She moaned. Held him tighter. Tristan must have sensed her desperation because he gripped her from behind and lifted her onto his lap with one swift motion. They were chest to chest. Hardness to softness. Instinctively, she spread her legs, wrapping them under the chair's arms and around his waist. Even through the cotton fibers of his towel, the heat of his erection scorched her. He was thick and hard, and some wanton part of her wanted to take his entire length in her mouth, suck him from base to tip then down again.

I shouldn't be doing this, she thought. *Not with him. I'll stop him in just…one…minute….*

Oddly enough, she felt sexy and desirable and purely feminine, a heady mixture of power, and as these sensations combined, her head swam with confidence. Her fingers sank into his thick hair just as his palm eased under the bottom of her shirt, sliding up to brush the curve of her breast. His big hand cupped its weight and gently squeezed. He rolled the nipple between his fingers.

Then he moved. A simple sway of his hips.

The half crescents of her nails dug into his scalp. Intense, consuming pleasure shot from one corner of her body to the other. That, combined with years of deprivation, pushed her beyond control. She became famished for a touch, *his* touch, and clasped him wildly with her thighs, craving contact. Sweet contact.

As if he, too, were at his limit, Tristan continued to work his open mouth against hers, his tongue aggressive, his taste hot and masculine. He licked, nibbled, sucked, alternating between the three and devouring her one tasty bite at a time.

The kiss was wild and savage and made up for every school dance she'd never attended, every party she'd never been invited to and every night she'd cried because no one desired her. Right here, this moment, she was Aphrodite, pagan goddess of love and beauty, and men worshiped at her feet. Life and vitality beat through her veins.

"Tristan," she rasped. "I need more."

He tore his mouth away, panting, "Then more you shall have." He paused a moment, then, and gazed at her, just gazed at her. Savoring, perhaps? "Had I known how eagerly you would respond," he said, his tone hard, "I would have begun lesson two yestereve."

"Lesson?" she muttered, trying to recapture his lips with her own.

"Hmm, anticipation." The hot wetness of his tongue left a path of liquid fire along her collarbone before he claimed her lips again.

But bit by bit, small measures of sanity returned, clearing her passion-fogged senses. Old self-doubts and insecurities teased the periphery of her mind. Unsure, she loosened her hold on Tristan, forcing herself to concentrate on his words, and not his touch.

Everything came together at once. He'd kissed her as if her mouth held the oxygen he needed for life support because of a lesson. A stupid, stupid lesson. He didn't desire *her*, Julia Anderson. Not really. He'd simply been acting as her tutor. She'd realized that in the beginning, but easily let herself be convinced otherwise. Yet hearing the actual words from his mouth cut painfully.

A jumble of need and mortification, she shot from his lap, conscious now of the sticky chocolate sweetness on her skin. With swift, jerky movements, she shoved her hair from her face and glared down at him. "I changed my mind," she said, trying to sound confident and unaffected, yet not quite managing the feat. All of her residual doubts about why she should resist this man grew in intensity.

Reaching out, he attempted to gather her back into his embrace. She quickly sidestepped his arms.

"Come here," he said. "Your lesson is unfinished."

"I've learned all I need to know about anticipation," she said. *Please, God, do not let my voice sound as shaky and desperate to Tristan as it does to me.*

"There is so much more I can teach you," he uttered, now softening his tone, using each sexy timbre to the fullest.

"I'm not interested."

"That is an untruth, Julia. You *are* interested."

"You're wrong." She tried to stifle the hurt burning in her eyes. She wasn't angry with Tristan. No, she couldn't be angry with him. He'd only been doing what she'd asked him to do: teach her to seduce a man. Yet she'd let herself forget that fact, and she hated herself for her stupidity, hated the ache in her chest. "Very wrong."

"*You* are the one who is wrong, Julia," he said through clenched teeth. He propped his elbows on the armrests and folded his hands together. "You lie to yourself, and I would know why."

"I've merely had enough pleasure for one day, that's all."

He made a tsking sound with his tongue. "Never has a woman needed more, sweet. Twice now you have come apart because of a kiss. And never once did my fingers or my shaft enter your body. You want the pleasure I can give you. Admit it."

Julia whirled, fleeing as fast as her feet could carry her. Where she headed, she didn't know. She only knew that if she didn't leave now, she might cave completely, give Tristan everything he wanted and forget everything she needed. How could he be so passionate one moment, and so frosty the next, as if he were two separate people?

"Julia," he called, racing after her. When he reached her, he gripped her shoulders and spun her to face him. His expression darkened with remorse, and he was once again the tender, fervent warrior she'd kissed. "I did not mean to hurt you."

Forcing a half smile, she looked past him, past the living-room window. "I'm fine. Really."

His strong, callused hands cupped her jaw, forcing her to look at him. "Every warrior knows the words 'I'm fine' from his woman are a death sentence. Tell me what I did wrong, and I will apologize."

"You did nothing wrong." Not purposefully, at least.

He was sorry he had hurt her, but he truly had no idea that he'd just ruined the best experience of her life. "Just tell me when you begin a lesson next time," she said softly. "I thought you really—" Her mouth closed with a snap. She absolutely did not want him to know she'd thought he had kissed her because he wanted to, because he found her attractive.

His brows knit together and his confusion intensified. "What does knowing about a lesson beforehand matter?"

"I have a right to know, that's all."

The fingers on her shoulders tensed, and his gaze slitted dangerously. "This is not about the lessons, is it? This is about Puny Peter. Did you think of him while I kissed you? Did you wish it was Peter touching you? Did you picture him in your mind, and when his image faded, you pulled away from me?"

"So what if I did?" she said, eyeing him with false bravado.

"As your instructor, I forbid you to think about Puny Peter."

"You are not the master of my thoughts. I govern who and what I think about."

"Is that so?" he asked, his tone dripping with deceptive calm.

"Yeah." Standing to her full five-foot-three height, she glared up at him. "That's so."

"Then what think you of this? I liked the way your nipples hardened against my palms. I liked the way you pressed your body deeper into mine. I liked the way you wrapped your legs around me, placing yourself firmly against my cock. *I* liked those things, Julia. *I*. Not Peter."

"I liked them, too," she admitted before she could halt the words. "I liked that you were the one doing them to me."

Everything about him softened. "Then tell me why you ran from the pleasure I gave you."

"I thought you really wanted me, okay?" she whispered. "I thought the lessons had nothing to do with our kiss." Staring down at her fingers, she gave a humorless laugh. "I guess it was stupid of me to hope you could give of yourself and not cater to the whims of a master, huh?"

"What is this?" The words exploded from his mouth. "You think I see your body as an obligation? Curse you, woman. Thoughts of you have fueled my dreams and kept me hard all night long. I crave you, and have not stopped craving you since I first appeared." He jerked her into the hard circle of his arms. "Just as you crave me."

"No, no. Not anymore." *Deny him,* whispered through her mind. If she didn't, she would once again give herself to him completely. He desired her, she conceded that much now. But was that really enough? She would forget her own dreams and neglect Peter. Already her resistance was waning. "No," she said again, more for her benefit than his.

"Peter is not here," Tristan growled. "He is not the one who can give you fulfillment. I am. Your body knows this and will always betray you."

The truth of those words danced through her, and for a moment, only a moment, she thought, why deny the inevitable? But self-preservation won. *Get away while you still can.* "Why don't you believe in love, Tristan?" she found herself asking instead.

He blinked. A muscle ticked in his jaw, and his hands withdrew from her. "The emotion is simply not one I can allow myself to experience."

Silence permeated the room. Their gazes remained locked. Finally she sighed and glanced away. Staying here with him and debating the finer points of love would not change his mind. He appeared too distant right now, too disgusted.

"I've got to balance my accounts," she said, "so I'll be in my office. I don't know what time I'm going to bed, but you can stay up as late as you want." She forced herself to slip from his touch and walk away.

"When you go to your bedchamber," he called, his tone steely, "keep your door unlocked."

A tingle of alarm raced through her and she froze, her back to him. "Why?"

"You agreed that I will sleep with you."

Drawing on every ounce of inner strength she possessed, Julia whipped around and pinned him with her stare. "The operative word here is sleep. And for your information, I didn't say exactly *where* you are to sleep, just that it's in my room. I'll make you a pallet on the floor."

His eyes narrowed. "You have me there, sweet. Next time I'll not leave any room for interpretation."

As TRISTAN LAY on Julia's bedchamber floor, he stared up at the ceiling. He hated that their kiss had ended so abruptly. Yet mayhap that was for the best, he now realized. He'd almost lost control. He'd touched her, tasted her, and had wanted to give her everything he had to give. Julia was quickly destroying that innermost part of him, the part he kept buried.

The part of him that kept him sane.

A cold sweat broke out all over his body.

CHAPTER FOURTEEN

You Must Thank Your Master Immediately
And Frequently For Any Boon Or Punishment

HER RESOLVE TO KEEP Tristan away from Julia's Treasures crumbled.

She didn't want to send him back inside his box, didn't want to leave him at home alone. He would have vehemently protested such an occurrence, anyway, and being the hopelessly infatuated, desperately aroused woman that she was—she'd had to listen to his breathing all night as the raw maleness of his scent wrapped around her—she wanted to make him happy.

So the very next day Julia dragged him to work with her.

How did he thank her? By ignoring her all morning and hacking up another phone.

"Why in the world did you destroy yet another phone?" she demanded the moment her last customer departed.

From his stool behind the cash register, Tristan regarded her with a why-aren't-you-on-your-knees-thanking-me glance. "I would rather walk across a stream of jagged talons than listen to that shrill, bansheelike screech again."

Her nose wrinkled in vexation. "You destroyed my telephone because it rang?"

Unfazed, he lifted his shoulders in a shrug.

"That's the second one you've murdered."

"You are welcome."

"I most definitely am not thanking you." Frowning, she began tidying a shelf of colorful glass vases. "This is a business. Now my customers have no way to contact me."

"A cause for celebration, surely."

"Phones aren't cheap, you know," she grumbled. Okay, so they weren't *that* expensive. "I'm taking this out of your salary."

"Since I refuse to take your money," he said, his tone as sour as her mood, "the situation works to my advantage. And while I am now in the mood to talk, explain to me why you are wearing drocs instead of a new gown."

"These pants are new."

"I did not choose them."

"Sexy clothing is not appropriate in the workplace."

The bell above the door chimed, preventing him from commenting. Tristan and his murderous scowl were forgotten as Julia focused her attention on Mrs. Danberry and the little dark-headed child she held.

"Do you need protecting?" Tristan asked.

Julia leveled him a glance over her shoulder. "No. For God's sake, stay where you are." Forcing her expression to relax, she returned her attention to her customer. "May I help you?"

With Julia distracted, Tristan swept the hacked-up phone into the trash, then settled back on his stool, hands locked behind his head. What was he going to do with this woman? He still did not know.

This dawning, she had bounced out of bed after a peaceful, undisturbed rest. He knew exactly how well she'd slept because he had lain awake on the floor, listening to her breathy sounds of slumber. Several times, while they readied themselves for another day at this shop, she had tried to draw him into conversation about the weather, then about his home, yet he had not responded. Uncertainty still ate at him.

He felt as if he were standing on a precipice, one moment ready to forget his control and discipline and simply enjoy her, the next wanting to prove he was impenetrable to softer emotions. The two needs warred within him, slashing against the other. Whichever direction he jumped, he suspected he would wish he'd taken the other.

How Zirra would rejoice if she knew the extent of his frustration.

He had never been so torn, and a woman had never resisted him quite so determinedly. Where were his legendary skills of seduction that no woman could resist? He had once thought he understood women, and himself, yet he found himself thinking again that he was unprepared to deal with Julia and her hope to win Puny Peter.

A tide of possessiveness crashed through him, whipping with the force of a mighty wave. *I want to enjoy her,* he finally admitted, fists clenched so tightly his bones almost snapped, *discipline be cursed*. The answer was as clear as if he'd known all along, accepted even, that this was the way it would be.

He wanted this woman, wanted to embrace her every nuance, and hold nothing of himself back. Instead of the horror he'd envisioned with such an admission, he felt oddly at peace. *He* would be the man who unleashed Julia's full passion, who showed her just how delightful all pleasures of the flesh could be. *He* would be the one to savor her reactions.

Not Puny Peter.

That idiot was not good enough for her. Tristan knew it. Soon, too, would Julia.

Just how was he to win this stubborn and completely illogical woman?

Mayhap all she needed was more convincing, a gentle hand to guide her, he thought, relaxing into the hardwood seat. A smile curved his lips, and he closed his eyes. He'd learned through experience that Julia responded more favorably to demonstrative measures. Mmm…how would he demonstrate sensual indulgence?

Anticipation made his fingers itch and a thousand possibilities raced through his mind. By Elliea, he would try them all.

JULIA TRIED TO CONCENTRATE on her customer. She really did. But her attention continually strayed toward Tristan, all sleek muscle and masculine strength. With his features relaxed and his mouth curved in a half smile, he looked so serene, almost boyish, beguilingly innocent. Not the sensual master she knew him to be.

A woman could become addicted to the fire and delight found in his arms. He knew just where to kiss, suck and lick; knew just where to touch, both lightly and more forcefully, to bring optimum pleasure. She tried to hide her now-pebbled nipples behind a shelf of Oriental figurines. Resisting him was proving more and more difficult. But resist his allure she must.

Peter was her first priority. This wanton side to her she was only now discovering, a side that demanded release more and more frequently, demanded she give in just once and experience the passion Tristan stirred inside her, must be ignored. What could she have with him besides momentary passion? A lifetime of insecurity, that's what.

"Oh, that is marvelous," a female voice said, breaking into her thoughts. Mrs. Danberry held the little girl with one hand, and the corncob pipe in the other.

"I'm glad you like it," Julia said. "I thought of you the moment I saw it."

"Oh, no, dear. Not the pipe. The man." Mrs. Danberry motioned to Tristan with a tilt of her chin. "Marvelous specimen, really. He's grade-A sirloin. Not at all like my Weston. No, Weston is more like tofu. A cheap imitation. I like the corncob pipe, too, of course. It's lovely." The toddler tugged on her hand. "Stand by me, Shonna, and don't touch a single thing. Shonna's my granddaughter, you know," she told Julia. "The dear angel is the light of my life."

"I can see why," Julia replied. "She's beautiful."

"Thank you." Mrs. Danberry turned her attention to the pipe. "I must have it for my collection. But you knew that, didn't you?"

Julia smiled and gazed down at the little girl who looked so bashful as she stood quietly beside her grandmother. "May Shonna have a lollipop?"

"Oh, yes, of course," came the distracted reply.

Kneeling down, Julia said in her gentlest voice, "Hello, there. I love your dress. It's very pretty."

Shonna's big blue eyes widened, and she shifted from one flowery shoe to the other.

"Would you like a lollipop? I have chocolate and strawberry, cotton candy and tropical punch."

The little girl stuck two fingers in her mouth, glanced to her grandmother, who nodded encouragingly, then looked to Julia with a nod of her own.

"You can pick any flavor you want." Julia clasped her small, delicate hand and led her to the register where she kept a glass canister full of sweets. Shonna scrutinized every piece, and soon strands of midnight hair fell across her cheeks.

With her coloring, she could've easily passed for Tristan's child.

For the space of time unmeasured, Julia forgot to draw in a breath as wave after wave of desire flooded her. What would it be like to have Tristan's baby? To become his wife? Her mind readily supplied the answer to both questions: heavenly. A slight moan grew in her throat as her mind threw out two more questions: What kind of woman could make him forget his abhorrence to love and win his heart?

And would falling for Tristan be so bad?

Her stomach performed a slow, painful flip as she pitted the joys against the ramifications. Bad? Oh, no. That word didn't come close to describing such an occurrence. Terrible? Close. Disastrous? Without a doubt. A relationship with him was doomed to fail and leave a trail of heartache—her heartache—in its wake.

"I have to tinkle, Grandma," Shonna suddenly shouted, the sheer power of her lungs resounding from floor to ceiling.

Mrs. Danberry sent a beseeching look to Julia. "May she use your rest room, dear?"

"I'm so, so sorry, but it's still broken." She was going to pulverize her landlord, the miserly jerk. There wasn't time for Tristan to play handyman—if he even knew what tools to use. He probably didn't, Arcadian knowledge being so advanced and all. "There's one next door."

"Oh, gracious. Well, we'd best hurry. Shonna's just out of diapers, you know." Mrs. Danberry paid for the pipe and hustled her granddaughter toward the door. "I'll see you soon, dear," she said, waving. "Give that sexy man of yours a naughty kiss for me." With that last, parting remark, she disappeared past the door.

Julia once again found herself alone with Tristan. And once again found her body perking with arousal. Time to finish her lessons. Before her resolve raced past the borders of no return, she squared her shoulders and marched to Tristan's chair.

"Tristan," she said, her determination a tangible pressure within her chest.

Slowly his eyelids opened, and she found herself sinking into the pale violet depths of his gaze. "Aye," he said, his voice scratchy. Sexy.

"I'm ready to learn how to flirt." The words tumbled from her mouth. "Will you teach me?"

"Aye, I will teach you to play the wanton," he said. Then he muttered something that sounded suspiciously like, "You are almost making this too easy, sweet."

Too easy for what? Instead, she asked, "Are you ready to begin?" Best to get this over with as soon as possible. *Oh, please. Who are you trying to fool, Julia Anderson?* Anticipation hummed just below the surface of her skin. Anticipation for his attention, his kiss, his touch…and no other.

He regarded her intently, as if seeing her on a deeper level, as if seeing more of her than any other person ever had. "You have needs to begin here? Now?"

"Now." She nodded.

He rose to his feet, his face suddenly devoid of emotion. The lack of feeling he reflected gave him a dangerous aura of mystery and resolution. He leaned one hip against the counter. The white T-shirt he wore hugged his biceps, outlining every ridge of muscle, and his bleached jeans rode low on his waist, the top button unsnapped. His gaze traveled the length of her.

"You need a gown for what I have in mind," he said.

A tide of unease swept along her thoughts. "I have a

skirt in back." She always kept a spare set of clothing here in case of an emergency. "But I'm not changing."

His brows winged in challenge. "As I am in charge during a lesson, you will do as I say, and I say you will change."

"Fine." She threw her hands in the air. Why did she even attempt to argue with him? He always won. "I'll meet you in my office when I finish."

"Do you desire my aid, simply call out."

"Yeah, sure," she said dryly as she recalled his peeping tendencies. She locked the storage-room door before undressing. Even though she suspected foul play on Tristan's part, she wiggled into a plain brown ankle-length skirt. "You better not try anything funny," she told him as she entered the small office. The lights were dimmed. "This isn't a game. Flirting is serious business."

Looking completely at ease, he reclined in the swivel chair behind the desk and frowned. "I take my role as educator very seriously, little dragon."

"Then you should know I learn best through oral instruction."

"Aye, I very much like your idea of oral training." Two fingers stroked the smooth skin of his jaw, his expression pensive. "How shall we go about this?"

"We—"

"Uh-uh-uh, Julia." He leaned forward. Shadows veiled his features but for a single bar of lamplight illuminating his eyes. "As I am the teacher, the answer is for me to decide."

She gave him a sarcastic military-style salute. "Yes, sir."

That earned her another frown. "I would see you walk."

"That's it?" Disappointment rang loud in her tone. "That's how you're going to teach me to flirt? By watching me walk?"

"Aye. There are many ways to entice a man, and proper gliding is one of them."

"Oh." In a strange sort of way, that made sense. "Very well, then." Concentrating on every step, she strode past him, turned, then retraced her path. By the time she finished, he was seated on the edge of the desk, shaking his head.

"I am not exactly sure if you were walking or marching to the beat of a war drum. Try again. Slower this time, swaying your hips with every forward motion."

"All right." Heeding his instructions, she glided by him, exaggerating and swaying for effect. Only, the heel of one shoe bumped the toe of the other. Julia pitched forward, face first. She landed in a heap on the floor.

Her ankles didn't survive.

Neither did her pride.

Tristan uttered a long-suffering sigh. "Mayhap we will work on your walk later," he said.

Mortified, she lumbered to her feet and cursed her throbbing ankles. "I may never walk again."

"Do not be embarrassed. With some more training, your hips will be a seductive mating call no man can resist."

"Really?"

"Really." Tristan hid his amusement behind his palm. Except for the tumble, Julia had strolled like a seductress. However, he planned to make this lesson last for days, weeks, *months* if necessary, so he could not, would not tell her of her feminine allure. "For now, though, we will allow your knees time to heal."

He stood and sauntered around the desk. When he reached Julia, he latched his palms under her arms and lifted. Higher. Higher still.

"What are you doing?" she gasped, her feet dangling a good three feet from the floor.

He didn't offer her an explanation. He simply eased her buttocks atop of the edge of the desk. Stacks of papers rained onto the carpet. Without pausing, he slipped her skirt over her knees, past her thighs, revealing the creamy length of her legs. He gave her new position a once-over, then smiled. "Much better."

"For you, maybe." Locked in place as she was, Julia felt helpless and vulnerable and aroused. A permanent condition whenever Tristan was near, she was beginning to realize. "Shouldn't I take notes or something?"

"Nay. You will remember everything I teach you."

"But what if—"

"Enough." He waited until her lips closed before continuing. "Because of our bargain, it is my right to give orders and your right to take them." He loved reminding her of that fact. "You *will* remember."

"Ok—"

Lightning quick, he covered her mouth with his hand. "No speaking unless you have first gained my permission. Understand?"

"Fine," came her muffled reply. Since he had spent

the past thousand years obeying orders, Julia figured he was due to issue a few. She didn't mind, though. After all, he was doing this to help her.

"We will begin anew." With a satisfied nod, he removed his palm. "Flutter your lashes for me."

"Flutter my lashes? Women don't actually do that anymore, do they?"

An exasperated sigh parted his lips. "As I told you before, there is more to enticement than mere words. You must use every part of your body. Now flutter."

She did as instructed.

He shook his head and frowned. "Enough games, little dragon. How can I teach you if you refuse to cooperate?"

Insulted, she sputtered, "I'm not playing. That's the best damn fluttering I can do."

"Hmm." Long fingers stroked his jaw. "We have much to do then."

She groaned and nibbled her bottom lip with her teeth. "How long will this take?"

"Many cycles, mayhap," he said, his lavender eyes darkening. "Or maybe even an entire season."

Many months, perhaps even an entire year, of intense flirting practice with Tristan? Could her body systems take it?

No!

Which meant she had to work harder. So she spent the next hour diligently practicing her eyelash flutter. It would have been an innocent enough lesson had Tristan kept his fingers off her thighs.

Every time a customer entered, she had to shove him away, hop to the floor and don a respectable business persona, which meant smoothing her skirt from her waist and dousing the lust in her eyes. Both of which only managed to increase her anticipation for the lesson's continuance. The instant she and Tristan were alone again, she always jumped back on the table, eager to pick up where they'd left off. Roaming hands and all.

Finally Tristan deemed her flutter acceptable and moved on. "Next, we will work on your come-hither smile."

"Excellent." A seductive smile was something every woman needed in her man-hunting arsenal. How could she attract a man—Peter—if she couldn't grin properly? "What should I do?"

"You must smile, of course."

Okay. "How's this?" The corners of her mouth lifted wide.

"No, no, no. Lips closed." With gentle fingers, he manually moved her lips into a half grin. The heat of his fingertips sent currents of need pulsing along her nerve endings. "Much better. Now, using only facial expression, make me believe you wish to lick my entire body."

That shouldn't be a problem since the desire to do exactly that suddenly bombarded her! How easy it was to picture Tristan naked beneath silk sheets. Hot, moist skin. Hazy candlelight. Soft, lyrical music. Her body would inch over his, and her tongue and teeth would rake against his skin.

Tristan watched Julia's eyes darken with dreams, the

edges of her mouth soften with desire. A hard lump formed in the back of his throat. He gulped. "That is enough." His voice emerged hoarse, cracked. When she didn't alter her expression, he commanded, "Blink, curse you. Blink."

Julia blinked and the cloud of desire surrounding her cleared.

"Let's move on to something a little easier for you," he muttered after clearing his throat. "I have decided sensual expression is not for a beginner."

"I failed?" she asked, her tone dripping with disappointment. "Give me another chance, Tristan. Please. I can get it right. I know I can."

"Nay." If she dared glance at him like that again, he would strip the clothes from her body and take her here and now, her customers be damned. "You will work on expression by yourself. Here we will work on erotic speech. Close your mind to everything else and consider what you would say to a man you desire. A man you wish to bed."

"I've, uh, never been on a real date, so I'm not exactly sure what's appropriate."

"I am glad you have not practiced with others. Their inept teaching would only hamper your progress." He stroked her cheek with his fingertips gently, tenderly. "Worry not. We will do this step by step."

"Step by step," she agreed. Heat tingled a fiery path exactly where he touched. He had such large hands, she thought, hands capable of destroying everything in their path. And yet he treated her with such care. He always kept the true force of his strength under tight restraint.

"Pretend for the moment that you are trying to seduce me," he said.

Nervous flutters twisted her stomach, and for a moment, her tongue thickened, making any speech, especially erotic, impossible. She gulped. "I'm not sure—"

He cut her off. "We do this my way, Julia."

"Your way." She didn't dare explain that his words evoked a primitive desire for the forbidden, to do exactly what he'd said and seduce him. Or that the air around her suddenly seemed sultry and lightly scented with arousal. Or that desire pooled between her thighs, and in her mind she pictured her body sinking down onto his, his eyes a mesmerizing shade of violet and passion as she rode him.

Tristan sucked in a rough breath. "You will cease that at once," he barked.

His fierceness surprised her, and she jerked back to reality with a gasp. "What? What did I do?"

"You had donned another erotic expression. I recall expressly forbidding you to do that in my presence."

"Sorry," she managed. At the moment, she was acutely aware of her too-tight nipples, of the needy ache causing her veins to throb, and the way her skin felt too constricted for her bones. Suddenly irritated with him— and herself—she stuck her tongue out at him.

"Careful, little dragon, or I might take you up on your offer and suck that tongue of yours into my mouth." Eyes blazing with heat, he tapped a fingertip against his chin. "Now then. You wished to seduce me, did you not?"

Perilous lessons, she lamented, swallowing back a bolt of pure desire. "Yeah, I wish to seduce you."

He nodded, smiled. "Admitting your desire is the first step."

"And the second?"

"Thinking of the words that incite sexual hunger. Words such as *cock*. And *breasts*. *Rapture* and *bliss*."

Tides of *rapture* and *bliss* followed his words, along with images of his hands on her *breasts,* and her hands on his *cock.* She had trouble drawing in her next breath. "And what do I do with these words?"

"Use them. That is the third step. You may begin."

"Wait!"

"If you succeed, we will work on playful bantering next." Smug and all too sure of her failure, he crossed his arms over his chest. "If not, we will begin again tomorrow. Are you prepared for this challenge?"

"I think so," she lied.

"Then what is the first thing you say to gain my attention?"

"I—well—I…"

"Wrong."

"I want you?"

"Better." He gave her a bone-melting smile of approval. "What else?"

"You make me hot?"

"And?"

Because he thought her words were pretend, a sense of freedom surfaced, deflating her reservations and eradicating her need for constraint. She stared into his eyes, searching his soul. "You drive me wild whenever you enter a room. You make my pulse leap and my body tremble. I would say you're tender and caring and gentle, and I feel safe when I'm with you. I would say…I would say that I want you more than I want to take my next breath."

CHAPTER FIFTEEN

Always Remember That You Are Nothing
More Than Your Master's Property

SILENCE LADEN WITH an undercurrent of forbidden desires stretched between them. Julia's cheeks reddened. Why wasn't he speaking? Did he suspect she'd spoken the truth?

Finally he cleared his throat. "That was…interesting."

Relief coasted through her, as delicious and welcoming as his touch. He didn't know, didn't suspect. She almost sighed. She did grin. "Thank you."

"Mayhap we should cease the lessons for the day," he said, swiping a hand down his face, wiping away the beads of sweat that had popped onto his brow. The motion also managed to wipe away any hint of his emotion.

"We can't stop now," she said. "You promised to help me with playful bantering."

A prolonged pause sparked the air between them.

"So I did," he allowed. He sucked in a fortifying breath, easing the tension around his lips. "Playful bantering is an exchange of wits, with a sexual undertone only slightly different from seduction with words. How would you begin? And this time," he added, "I refuse to take you step by step. You must do this on your own."

Resolute, Julia nodded. Closed her eyes. *I can do this. I can.* "Let's do breakfast tomorrow. Should I call you or nudge you?"

His lips twitched, and he shook his head. "Try again."

"I'm a really good cook. My specialty is breakfast in bed."

"Now you are just being ridiculous."

"Nice pants. Can I talk you out of them?"

"Julia, please. Are you trying to seduce me or kill me with my own laughter?"

Her voice dropped low and husky, her next words emerging of their own free will. "I don't want to tease you with words, Tristan. I want to tease you with my mouth. Licking and nibbling your skin. Tasting and savoring your essence."

He quit laughing.

Tristan used his body, a slight shifting of his weight and a subtle proving of his dominance, to force her back to arch. The carnal scent of his fragrance enveloped her, filled her. Consumed her. He glared down at her, pressing her even farther back. "Where did you learn to say such a thing?" he demanded.

Far from intimidated, she clapped her hands with an almost giddy pride. "I don't know. So they worked? I actually bantered with you? Oh, this is fun. Teach me more."

"Mayhap you are ready for a more advanced training session." Pure, molten heat, hypnotic in its intensity, stole over his expression. "What think you of that?"

Slowly her joy ebbed, and libidinous hunger claimed her. "I think—I think I'm ready."

"We're going to have a very erotic conversation, Julia. No teasing. No innuendos. Your goal is to lure me into your bed using everything I have taught you so far. Everything. Think you can succeed?"

God, she hoped so, but… "No." She shook her head. "I don't know where to begin. Will you give me a demonstration?"

"Aye." Moving with tantalizing slowness, luring her with a deceptive sense of protection, he closed the remaining distance between them, his breath only a heartbeat way. He stood in between her open legs, caught her wrist with his hand and pressed a soft kiss upon her pulse.

She shivered, struck by the majesty of him, the rawness of his attentions.

His other palm traced up, up, up her thigh until the pads of his fingers brushed the lacy red trim of her panties. "You are honey and cream, Julia." His lashes slowly swept downward, then lifted at an even slower pace. "Do you know why?"

Caught by his mesmerizing voice and the sear of his fingers, she barely managed to say, "No. No, I don't know."

"Your skin reminds me of cream. Smooth and delicious, made for licking. The more I taste, the more I must have. And your hair—" He released her wrist and tugged her long tresses from the rubber band. Every strand cascaded down her shoulders and back. "Your hair is the color of honey. Soft, sweet honey that will caress my chest as you ride me. Your lips, too, are like honey. Succulent honey I long to savor over and over again."

His heat seeped past her clothes, into her skin, but his words, oh, his words enveloped her in a cocoon of sensual euphoria. His eyes beckoned with knowing intent. She found herself leaning deeper into his arms, craving more, needing more.

"Now it is your turn," he whispered, and dropped his hands to his sides.

"You're beautiful, Tristan. The most beautiful man I've ever seen." Yet her description lacked a sense of accuracy; wasn't nearly enough to describe the man that she knew he was.

"Beauty is subjective and easily claimed." Using the tip of his finger, he traced a path along her jaw. "Tell me what you see when you look at the man I truly am."

Lure him with words. Her eyes closed halfway, seeing him more with her mind than actual sight. "When I look at you, I see pale violet eyes that sometimes hold a hint of sadness, but always kindness. I see a gentle, compassionate warrior who is able to give more with one simple kiss than most give in a lifetime. I see an innate sense of duty that few possess. And a capacity for love that is staggering, if only you would tap into it."

Tristan cleared his throat. "Julia—"

"I'm not finished." In that moment, she forgot her decision to deny her attraction to Tristan. She forgot about

Peter, forgot everything except the truth. "Sometimes, when I look at you, my hands ache to move up your chest, to feel your heart beating beneath my palms so that I can assure myself you aren't a dream, that you are real. The ache is so powerful I shake with it."

"I imagine your hands on me, as well," he said, his voice cracking. "Except, you move lower, to the heat of me. You stroke me until I can take no more while I do the same to you. You writhe beneath my hands, screaming your pleasure. Only then do I part your legs and slide into your wet softness, binding our bodies as one." His half-mast gaze watched her, gauging. "What think you of that, little dragon?"

"I think—" Lord, what did she think? "You've taught me more than I ever hoped to learn."

He didn't respond. The pull between them right then was too strong. She couldn't tear her gaze away, couldn't move. Couldn't form a rational thought. Time seemed suspended, and the world around her nonexistent. She heard the drum of his heart, and each beat spurred her own. *What's happening?* she wondered faintly.

Tristan was the first to break the spell. He blinked, shook his head. He even moved two steps back and leveled her with a fierce frown. "I am sure Peter will be pleased."

Who cared about Peter? *Kiss me,* she pleaded with her eyes. Never had a moment felt more right for loving. Nothing else mattered. Not the reasons for Tristan's desire. Not the lessons.

But being the prideful warrior that he was, he would not kiss her if he suspected she imagined him as Peter. She read the knowledge in the sudden stiffness of his shoulders, in the flair of his nostrils.

"Mayhap we should end this lesson here and now," he said, the words a soft growl, yet strangely distant. "And begin anew at tomorrow's dawning."

"Is that what you want? To stop?"

"Of course. A good teacher does not force his student to overstudy."

Disappointment raked her, and she found herself glaring up at him. "Perhaps I'll practice on Peter when we go on our first date."

"He will never satisfy you."

"Maybe not, but I'd—I'd like you to release me from the first parameter." There. She'd said it. It was for the best; this would help end her constant craving for him and his kisses. Kisses he no longer seemed inclined to give her.

Silence.

Silence so thick it cast an oppressive fog throughout the room.

Finally he said, "That is truly what you desire?"

No. "Yes."

"Very well." His jaw muscle clenched and unclenched. "From this moment forward, you are free to do whatever you wish with Puny Peter."

CHAPTER SIXTEEN

*Your Place Is On Your Knees
Before Your Master*

THE REST OF THE DAY PASSED in a blur for Julia. She closed the shop at lunchtime, hoping to spend some time with Tristan and soften his dark mood. She escorted him to the Kreager Flea Market, now open to the public as well as dealers. They meandered through the stalls, and Julia noticed the man who had sold her Tristan's box was nowhere to be seen. Tristan remained stiff and unyielding and even scared several sellers with his glare, leaving them shaking and pale.

When she approached a table crammed with weapons of every shape, size and color, Tristan finally melted. "These are magnificent," he said. He reverently fingered each item, gauging its weight and durability.

"I'll give you the Glock for four-fifty," the vender said. She had short hair, cut like a boy's, and wide angular features that assessed Tristan and knew she'd found a ready buyer. "You can't beat that deal, I'm telling you."

Tristan opened his mouth to reply, but Julia laid a hand on his forearm. He paused, glanced at her. She gave him an almost imperceptible nod, then focused on the seller. "The gun isn't worth half that," she said, "and to be honest, we aren't interested in it." A knife she could allow Tristan to have, but a gun? She shuddered. "You might be able to interest us in the jeweled dagger, though. If the price is right."

The woman eyed Julia, considering just how much she could pry from her wallet. When she realized Julia couldn't be budged, she once again sent her attention to Tristan, hoping perhaps that he might bring Julia around. However, his features no longer boasted of fascination. No, he looked as cold and hard as granite, not a flicker of emotion betraying him. Julia almost smiled as she mentally applauded him. She made a conscious effort to keep her own features so impressively impassive.

Julia uttered a forced, breezy sigh. "Oh, never mind. I saw a similar blade the next stall over." She gently squeezed Tristan's arm, ignoring the warm tingles that prickled her skin, and moved two steps away from the booth. "I'm sure we'll find a better bargain over there."

"Wait, wait," the woman said.

Triumphant, Julia slowly turned and faced her. "Yes?"

"Two hundred for the dagger and sheath."

"Good day," Julia said, and made to turn again.

"One fifty," the woman pressed. "You're robbing me here. You know that, don't you?"

"One hundred for the knife, sheath and cleaning kit, and you've got a deal."

"Done." A smile spread over the woman's features.

Julia paid and handed the bag of items to Tristan. His eyes were wide and admiring as he closed his palm around the plastic. "You are more fierce than the Shakari of the Imperian market."

"Is that a good thing?"

"Aye." He nodded, glorious heat and something else, something tender in his eyes. "Aye."

TRISTAN SAT in Julia's car, warm air trickling through the vents and soft music humming from an unidentified source. After their trip to the market, they had returned to her shop, where she had worked several more hours before closing for the day. Now they were headed home.

Home...did he truly have one?

He fingered his new weapon. 'Twas the second gift she had given him. Why? Why, when she so vehemently pushed him away? Her actions continued to confuse and surprise him. While she refused to accept his affections, she so easily cultivated them. Once, he might have convinced himself that he cared nothing for her and her actions. Once, he might have believed that he welcomed all other men into his *guan ren's* life.

But he wasn't that man anymore. Julia had changed him. He could not deny the tenderness he felt for her, could not deny he wanted a place in her life, not as her tutor but as her lover.

"Are you hungry?" she asked, giving him a quick glance, completely oblivious to the turmoil inside him.

"Aye." He was hungry for her, for her naked body beneath his, writhing, seeking. "Aye, I am hungry." He might always hunger this way, for he saw no relief for himself anywhere in the future.

"I hope you like hamburgers."

He merely grunted.

She eased into the parking lot of a small red-and-yellow building, then drove around to the side and spoke into a square mouthpiece. Three minutes later, they were speeding down the road again. Her house soon came into view, and she pulled into her driveway.

A red car, tinier and sleeker than Julia's, was parked at the curb. He scanned the property and found a woman sitting on the porch, looking as fresh and pretty as a bouquet of spring flowers. She possessed dark brown hair that hung down her back in silky waves. He couldn't make out the color of her eyes, yet her facial features vaguely resembled Julia. Same cheekbones. Same elegantly sloped nose.

The second her car ceased moving, Julia vaulted out and raced toward the porch with open arms. "Faith!"

Tristan eased out of the vehicle, taking in the scene before him. Julia exuberantly embraced the tall, slim woman. The newcomer wore the same type of blue slacks that he himself wore, and a button-down chemise. The two women were laughing, talking and hugging, sometimes doing a combination of all three.

"I've tried to reach you for days," this Faith said to Julia. "I thought you'd been abducted by aliens or something."

"Close." Julia shot him a wry glance.

"I also called your store, but couldn't get through

there, either." Concern darkened the woman's features, and she gripped Julia's hands. "What's going on?"

"Oh, nothing major." She cut him another glance. "My phones are out."

"Then get a new one, already. I never want to worry like that again. You're a very consistent person. If you're not at home, you're at work. And when you're not at work, you're…" She tilted her chin, thinking. "Well, you're always at work. When I couldn't—" Her eyes connected with Tristan's. "Oh, my," she breathed.

If he hadn't been so aware of Julia, he would have missed the slight tensing of her body. What was this? A moment of jealousy? He studied her, watching intently. A tide of delight hit him. Oh, aye. The little temptress was indeed jealous. She fairly seethed with it. For the first time since she had announced her intention to practice her wiles on Puny Peter, he entertained a flicker of satisfaction. He even managed a smile.

Faith batted her lashes at him.

"Stop that, Faithie," he heard Julia say.

The woman's gaze never strayed from him. "Stop what?"

"Picturing him naked. He's not available."

"I wasn't picturing him naked." She smiled sheepishly. "Not now, at least."

Tristan choked back a laugh.

Julia's lips thinned. "Faith, I'd like you to meet Tristan. Tristan, this is my sister, Faith Anderson."

The woman extended her hand, and he brought her

delicate palm to his lips, just as he'd seen a man do on Julia's talking box. "A pleasure."

"I assure you, the pleasure is mine." Faith's large eyes, a mix of green and blue, softened around the edges, giving her face a pixie quality. "Jules didn't mention you the last time we spoke."

"Tristan and I have only been together a short time," Julia answered for him.

"Oh? How did you meet?"

"Long story, and it doesn't matter. We're just friends."

At that, Tristan tensed. He was tired of Julia calling him her "friend" and her "brother." She would call him "lover" or nothing at all. Scowling, he threw a possessive arm around her shoulders and tugged her close. He didn't speak, letting Faith draw her own conclusion instead.

Faith did. She arched two thin brows and eyed Julia. "Not dating, huh?"

Julia tried to wriggle away. He merely tightened his hold, liking the curve of her waist against him. But the tighter he held her, the more she squirmed, and a surge of heat shot straight to his groin. Every point of contact reminded him of how they'd ended things today. Unsatisfied. And he wanted satisfaction.

"Where are you staying, Tristan?" Faith asked, her tone sharper.

"I live here with Julia," he answered.

Julia sucked in a great gulp of air. "He doesn't mean that like it sounds."

Just to irritate her, he added smugly, "We also share

a chamber." He faced her, giving her a smile that clearly said, *Deny that.*

Frowning, Faith anchored her hands to her hips. "Is he serious? You're living with a man, and you don't think to call me? To invite me over so I can meet him?"

"Yes, we're living together, but—" Julia shook her head and sliced a hand through the air. "Oh, never mind. There's no way to explain." Tossing him a backward glare, she stepped from his reach. With clipped, jerky motions, she unlocked the door and ushered her sister inside. "I'm inviting you over for supper right now. Tristan ordered eight double bacon cheeseburgers for himself. Since I don't want him to spontaneously explode, I'm going to make him be a good boy and share with you."

"Do you mind sharing?" Faith asked him.

By Elliea, he was beyond famished, almost near death. For lunch, Julia had fed him a tiny piece of fish. He, who had once consumed an entire Daerabar on his own. Now he was in desperate need of sustenance. But to Faith, he grumbled, "Aye. I will share."

"Wonderful." She smiled, revealing two sweetly shaped dimples. "I'd be happy to stay, then. I've missed you, Jules, and it's obvious we need to talk more."

"I've missed you, too." Relaxing slightly, Julia removed the bag from his hands, emptied the contents on the table and dispersed the food until everyone held what they wanted. "So what have you been up to lately?" she asked her sister. "Last I heard you were traveling through a jungle."

Faith immediately launched into a tale about her latest expedition, a six-week journey through South America. Tristan only half listened. As he devoured five small slabs of meat and bread that did not settle well in his stomach, his attention focused on Julia.

He watched her eat, watched her mouth work slowly, sensually. Watched her tongue slide over the lushness of her lips. The words she'd spoken earlier played in his mind over and over, taunting him. *Sometimes, when I look at you, my hands ache to move up your chest, to feel your heart beating beneath my palms.* Had she thought of him when she'd spoken, or had she thought of Puny Peter?

Julia chose that moment to glance up. Their gazes collided. Blood coursed through his veins like a newly awakened river. His hunger for food was forgotten, and his jaw tightened right along with the rest of him. By the sudden flare of passion in the luscious depths of her eyes, he knew beyond a doubt that she'd meant the words for him. Him and no other. The knowledge sent more white-hot desire rocking through his body. At that moment, he felt more powerful than if he'd slain one thousand of his enemies.

"Hell-oo," Faith sang. "Someone else is in the room."

With much regret, he tore his gaze from the source of his arousal.

Julia blinked rapidly, then shook her head. Her cheeks bloomed bright with color as she once again faced her sister. "Uh, yeah, you were saying?"

A smile played at Faith's lips. "I doubt you're interested in a lost city. No, it's okay," she said when Julia protested. "I'd rather hear about you and Tristan, anyway. Where did you meet?"

"At a flea market," Julia supplied. "We started talking, discovered we had a lot in common and became friends." The paper covering her food crackled as she folded back the corners. "That's the whole story."

"I'm sure." Unconvinced, Faith regarded Tristan. "Do you collect antiques?"

"Nay. Julia bought my box."

"Ah, so you're a seller."

"Nay, I am a—"

"French fry, anyone?" Julia asked, cutting him off.

Her panicked expression pleaded with him to remain silent. Tristan's stomach clenched. He did not like that she begged him, even silently. Did she fear her sister would steal his box if she knew the truth? Whatever her reasons, he pressed his lips tightly shut and said nothing more on the subject.

"Jules, you're acting weird," Faith said pointedly. "No offense, but I've never seen you this flustered. What's going on?"

"Nothing." Eyes wide, Julia stuffed her mouth full of food.

Faith glanced between Tristan and Julia once, twice. "You're hiding something, Jules. I can tell. You can't even look at me without trembling."

Julia swallowed and said, "I'm not in any kind of trouble, if that's what you're thinking. I promise."

"Oh, really." Disbelief echoed in every syllable Faith

uttered. "Well, something is going on here, and I want to know what."

"Tristan has been taking care of me, that's all. I've just been…sick." *Sick in the head,* she thought wryly, *for offering room and board to a pleasure slave.*

"Are you okay?"

"Yeah, I'm fine. There's no need for you to worry."

"I can't help it. You're my sister, and I— Holy shit." Faith clasped her hands over her mouth, practically radiating giddy excitement. "You're pregnant, aren't you?"

Julia began to choke, a piece of burger lodged in her throat. Tristan pounded her on the back, dislodging the morsel. "Cease your questions, woman," he ordered. "You are upsetting Julia."

"I can't believe this." Disregarding Tristan's command, Faith continued on with a jubilant smile. "You're having a baby. Why didn't you tell me? Did you think I'd be upset because you're not married? Well, I'm not. Oh, this is wonderful. I'm going to be an aunt. When is the baby due? Do you know if it's a boy or a girl?"

Tristan pounded his fist against the table. "Enough!" Both women jumped at the harshness of his tone. "Such questions are ridiculous. There is no child."

"That's right. As I mentioned, Tristan and I are merely friends. I'm not pregnant, but I am dating my next-door neighbor." Why start telling the truth now? She'd lied to her sister about everything else today.

Faith blinked, confused. "I thought you were living with Tristan."

"I am."

Silence stretched throughout the room.

"I see," Faith finally said, her eyes glazed with disappointment, and it was clear she didn't "see" anything. "Even though you *said* you two weren't romantically involved, I simply assumed…" She frowned. "You two seem perfect for each other, that's all."

Julia's sibling was a woman of great wisdom, Tristan decided.

"Peter and I haven't dated officially yet," Julia said, offering a bit of the truth, "but it's just a matter of time."

"So this Peter hasn't asked you out?"

Defensive, Julia straightened her back. "Some men like a woman to take the initiative."

"No one I'd want to date," Faith muttered under her breath. Then a calculated gleam lit her eyes and she said, "Why don't you ask Peter to dinner on Saturday? That way, Tristan and I can double with you."

"Oh, aye." Tristan nodded. "This is an event I care not to miss."

Julia shook her head emphatically. "No, I—"

"I'm so glad everyone's in agreement." Effectively ending the conversation, Faith pushed to her feet. "Well, it's time for me to head home. I need my beauty sleep, you know. See you Saturday, Jules. Will you walk me out, Tristan?"

He didn't hesitate. "Of course."

"Of course?" Julia said, a hint of dismay in her tone. "But, Tristan. I'll be here alone. Alone and unprotected."

"If anyone attempts to hurt you, simply use your karate," Tristan said over his shoulder, then strode out the front door behind Faith. He grinned; he just couldn't help it. What a sweet, sweet day this had become.

Outside, Faith stopped midway to her car and spun to face him, hands on hips. "I think I've figured out what's going on. It's obvious Jules likes you. My guess is she doesn't think she's good enough for you. You don't think that, do you?"

"Nay. I want her."

She relaxed her soldierlike stance. "She's a beautiful, intelligent woman, but I've never been able to convince her of that fact. She's stubborn, you know, and has always avoided romance. Well," she corrected, "not always."

"There is a story here. You will explain."

Faith raised a brow at his commanding tone. "It's not my place to tell you. Ask Julia about her first date, and if she tells you…" She shrugged. "The sparks generating between the two of you almost set me on fire. Whoever this Peter guy is, he's not the man for my sister."

Tristan definitely liked this woman.

"On Saturday," she said. "I'll handle Peter. You just make sure Julia has the best night of her life. She deserves it."

CHAPTER SEVENTEEN

Always Wear Clothing That Is Pleasing
To Your Master. If She Despises Clothing,
You Must Remain Naked

SATURDAY MORNING DAWNED cold but beautiful. An early spring wind danced through the air and birds chirped merrily in the trees. Eager blossoms valiantly attempted to bud.

Inside Julia's home, candles glowed with vanilla-scented flames. Freshly polished counters gleamed brightly in the kitchen. Warm, inviting air cloaked every room like an old, comforting blanket.

Julia was ready to vomit.

Coffee hadn't helped. Nothing helped.

Yesterday she had finally worked up the courage to invite Peter to an early dinner. At first, he said no. So she offered to pay. Still he refused. Only the threat of her "brother's" fury had swayed him to, at last, agree. The hint of reluctance in his voice when he finally said yes—a strange squeak that clearly stated he did not wish to dine with her—had pounded against her pride.

Was she *that* undesirable that she had to threaten a man to eat with her?

"What are you going to wear?" her sister asked cheerfully. Faith had arrived only minutes ago to help her prepare for the "big day."

"I don't know," she answered, "but I can't wear anything until I find my black shoes." Lips tight in a glower, she frantically searched through a sea of makeup on the counter, then a pile of clothes on the floor. Right now, she was wearing only her new matching bra and panties made of opalescent material that picked up different hues of light. The color reminded her of Tristan's eyes. "Have you seen them? I've looked everywhere. They have to be here."

"Calm down, calm down." Faith's tone was reassuring, soothing, but did nothing to pierce Julia's shell of panic. "I'll find them."

"He's supposed to be here in one hour and two minutes, and I can't find my shoes! I'm not dressed, and my hair looks like crap. Calm down? I don't think so!"

Faith clasped her by the shoulders, forcing her to cease her frenzied search. "This is a date, Jules, not an execution. Take a deep breath. That's it. Now slowly release every molecule of air. Good girl."

"What am I doing?" Julia rubbed at her temples, trying to ward off the oncoming ache. "Dating is stupid. Men are stupid. I shouldn't be doing this. Why am I doing this?"

"Because you're searching for a man to share your life with."

"Oh, God." The enormity of the situation hit her all at once. Eyes wide, Julia ran to the bathroom, both hands covering her mouth. At the toilet, she hunched over and emptied out the contents of her stomach. Faith stood behind her in the next instant, holding her hair out of the way.

Why was she putting herself through this?

Julia hated the fact that her sister and Tristan were tagging along. The lucky couple would get to witness every faux pas she committed. So easily she pictured herself spilling vegetable soup down her dress, getting spinach stuck between her teeth and toilet paper attaching itself to her shoe—not her black shoes, though, because she didn't know where the hell they were.

With her eyes closed, she rubbed her temple. Even though Tristan had helped her learn to flirt, she wasn't sure she really knew what to do or say to a man. All morning her old insecurities had beat against her resolve, and now they fought for complete domination. She was going to make a fool of herself; she just knew it. Surprisingly the thought of her foolishness didn't bother her as much as the thought of Faith and Tristan becoming romantically involved. They were both so beautiful, so perfect together, and on this stupid, stupid, *stupid* double date, they might just realize that fact.

Julia hated the jealousy she was now feeling for her older, gorgeously put-together sister, the woman who had practically raised her, but she had no control over her emotions where Tristan was concerned.

Drained of confidence and strength, she collapsed

against the cool tile at her feet. She clutched her knees to her stomach and blinked up at Faith. "I can't do this. I can't. I'm not even sure I like Puny Peter," she admitted.

"Puny Peter?"

"That's what Tristan calls him."

Wry amusement gleamed in Faith's eyes. "I wonder why."

"Tristan's just—he's— I don't know," she ended lamely.

"Jealous?"

"No."

"Protective?"

"Absolutely." She sank deeper onto the floor. "And because of that, he and Peter do not get along well."

"Okay, then. Call Peter and tell him you can't make it. That way, you and Tristan can spend the evening here and explore this protective side of his."

Moaning, she let her head sink into her hands. Did she really want to give up, to admit defeat before the date even began? She just didn't know. If only she were remotely attracted to Peter, the date might seem easier to bear. But *noooo,* she had to lust after a man who would cause supermodels to drool over his beauty.

"No," she finally told her sister. "I'm okay. I want to do this. I *need* to do this."

"All right." Faith handed her a cool, wet towel. "Pull yourself together, and we'll do a total makeover."

Julia used the cloth to wipe her mouth, then pushed to her feet. Her knees were wobbly at first, so she leaned against the sink for balance. Once steady, she brushed her teeth and splashed cold water on her face.

"Come on," Faith said when she finished. "You need to get dressed."

"Not until I find my shoes." Finding those damn black heels had suddenly become her biggest goal in life.

"They're around here somewhere. Don't panic. We'll find them."

Together they searched for the missing items and ten minutes later Faith found them stuffed inside the dirty clothes hamper. She breathed a sigh of relief.

"How did they get in there?" Faith asked, holding them up between pinched fingers.

"I must have been distracted," Julia admitted, "because I can't remember." Now that her shoes were in her sights, she concentrated on clothing. Unfortunately, she'd never modeled her new outfits for Tristan, so she had no idea what would actually look good. She gave it a shot, anyway.

"I thought I'd wear this." She waved her hand over a fuzzy pink sweater and long floral-print skirt.

With a grimace, Faith shook her head. "This is a date, Jules. Don't scare the man away by pretending to be a stick of cotton candy. Where did you get that thing, anyway?"

"Tristan picked it out."

Her sister rolled her eyes. "I swear, if it looks edible, men are going to buy it."

"God, I need a glass of wine," Julia lamented. "The stress of this day is about to kill me."

"Drink the whole bottle. I'll find an outfit Tristan—and Peter, of course—will drool over."

"What would I do without you, Faithie?"

"Walk around like a vomiting stick of cotton candy, that's what."

CLOTHED ONLY in his white cotton briefs, Peter Gallow flexed what little biceps he had in front of the full-length mirror hanging on his bedroom wall. A perfect frame for his art-deco and black-wire lamps.

"I am a man. A tiger," he told his reflection.

His date with Julia was scheduled to begin soon. Since she'd first called and asked him to have dinner with her—and he'd accepted—his nervous system had kicked into high gear. Unfortunately, he now had hives on his stomach. He'd never been very good with women and didn't have much practice. His nerves kept him from acting out his desires.

He liked Julia, though. She made him feel comfortable. Her brother scared the hell out of him.

When he'd first moved into the house beside Julia's, he'd hardly noticed her. But each morning as he prepared his plants for summer's harsh rays, he would see her leave for work, and each evening as he fertilized and weeded his garden, he would see her return, and each time he saw her, he became more attracted to her. He wasn't sure how it was possible, but she'd become prettier and prettier until her image constantly filled his mind.

Little things about her appealed to him. The vivacious sparkle in her eyes. The way her hair curled at the ends. The delicacy of her wrists. He'd wanted to go over and talk with her so many times and, in fact, had almost worked up the courage once or twice. Yet he always lost his bravado when he reached her house, and he would race home.

Then he'd seen her hiding behind her bushes, as nervous as he was, and he decided to go for it. And almost been murdered in the process by her brother. Peter didn't consider himself a strong man—or at least, he didn't consider himself a strong man *yet*. By reading self-help books, he was becoming a more assertive man.

When Julia had asked him out, he'd been stunned. And terrified. Very, *very* terrified. Not only because he'd been on so few dates in his lifetime, but because angering Tristan could mean Peter's death. He'd never seen an expression quite so fierce, or a man quite so intimidating. Tristan obviously loved his sister, and like any devoted brother, would protect her and crush anyone who hurt her.

But today, Peter would have her all to himself. And he would make sure he didn't do anything she could tell Tristan about that would send the giant hulk into a rage. Then he thought, *So what if I act ungentlemanly? What's Tristan gonna do?*

"If Tristan gives me any crap, I'll squash him like a bug." He flexed again.

"I am a man," he repeated. "A tiger. No woman can resist me."

Wait. Peter paused. That wasn't right. Frowning, he strode to his nightstand and lifted his copy of *Unleash-*

ing the Tiger Within. He flipped through the well-worn pages, found chapter four, and read, "Let your mantra be I am a man. A tiger. An irresistible force of nature no woman can resist."

With a nod, he tossed the book atop his black silk sheets. "I *am* an irresistible force of nature no woman can resist." He'd already spritzed himself with pheromone cologne. He'd made cue cards with sonnets, compliments and topics to keep conversation going.

How could Julia *not* like him?

He gave his reflection one more glance, then growled low in his throat. "I am a man. A tiger."

JULIA STOOD in her bedroom, sipping her glass of wine. Unfortunately, the alcohol did nothing to diminish her fear of the upcoming date.

"Try the mint-green slip dress," Faith said.

A rush of uncertainty filled her, and her brows winged upward. "Do you think it's sexy enough?"

"Oh, yeah." Faith nodded, an assured grin lifting the corners of her lips. "They'll be mopping up his drool."

Smiling for the first time that day, Julia tugged the dress over her head and smoothed it down over her bra and panties.

"A perfect fit." Faith nodded her approval. She swept a lock of hair over her shoulder. "Now go show Tristan. He'll love it."

Julia's smile became one of eagerness as she padded to the living room. What would Tristan think of her in a dress? Would he beam and say she looked beautiful? Oh, of course he would, since he'd wanted to see her in a dress since their first night together. In fact, she could already picture the glint of appreciation in his eyes.

And Peter would love it, too, of course.

Tristan was sprawled out on the emerald-and-ruby couch cushions, eating frozen grapes. He looked like the Greek war god, Ares, before a battle, ready to strike down those who defied him, yet ever patient to wait until the perfect moment to act. All the scene lacked was a slave girl wielding a fan.

She shivered and had to stop herself from screaming to the heavens, *I'll take the job.*

"What do you think of this?" she asked.

At the sound of Julia's voice, Tristan lifted his head and perused her from top to bottom. With one finger, he made a circular motion for her to spin. She did as instructed.

"Again," Tristan said, wanting another view of Julia's backside. His groin tightened with need. By Elliea, she was beautiful, beyond compare. But the thought of her wearing such a comely gown for another man—a gown he had chosen, no less—sent a talon-sharp pang of possessiveness through him. She would *not* wear such a gown for Puny Peter.

"Sooo…what do you think?" Expectant and eager, she twirled for the third time.

"It is too long," he said with a deceptively lazy undertone.

Confusion flashed across her expression, and she examined the length of her dress. She paused. "Too long?"

"Aye."

"Maybe you didn't notice the fact that I'm wearing a dress."

"I noticed."

"That's it? That's all you have to say?"

"You should change." Then, with a lazy motion at odds with the dangerous fire in his veins, he sucked a grape into his mouth.

Julia forced herself to ignore the twinge of desire that action caused and marched back into her room, announcing, "He hates it!"

"Hmm." A frown shaped Faith's mouth. "You're sure?"

"I'm sure."

"Well, try this one."

Oh, yes, she thought, eyeing the red halter dress. Perfect. Tristan had seemed particularly fascinated with it at the boutique. She shimmied her body into the clingy fabric until it hugged every curve. Knowing she would receive a compliment this time, she strode back into the living room. "Okay, what about this one?"

Once again he looked her up and down. A muscle ticked in his jaw, and it was becoming more noticeable by the second. "Too red."

"Too red?"

"Your hearing is excellent."

"I can't believe this." She threw her hands in the air. "You think my dress is too red? That's the only thing wrong with it?"

"What I think of that gown cannot be put into mere words."

Scowling now, she flounced back to her bedroom.

"What's wrong with that one?" Faith demanded.

"He says it's too red," Julia replied, mimicking Tristan's I-am-master-of-the-universe tone. The next time she entered the living room, she wore a black dress suit, complete with neck sash. It wasn't red, and it wasn't long. It was the epitome of class.

Just before she could ask his opinion, however, he raised an eyebrow and said, "Too confining."

Forty-five minutes later, Julia wanted to smother Tristan in the sea of clothing he had rejected. No matter what she modeled, she heard a variety of refusals. "Too green." "Too open." "Too loose." Until finally she heard, "Too... You will not wear that, Julia. I forbid it."

Sorely vexed by now, she stomped her feet on the way back to her sister. She jerked on a midthigh-length skirt and stormed back to the living room. "And this one?"

"Too short. May I suggest you make a better selection next time?"

"*You* picked out everything I've shown you. Remember our little jaunt to the mall?"

He shrugged as if to say, *You should damn well pick out your own clothes.*

At a loss, she and Faith ransacked the contents of her entire closet, grumbling about the pestilence known as "man." Julia briefly flirted with the notion of wearing the green-and-orange baby-doll dress Tristan had found the first night he appeared, but she didn't want to frighten small children. In the end, she settled on a lavender floral-print skirt with a matching button-up blouse, both of which coordinated with her bra and panties. The outfit hugged her curves and swayed when she walked. Not her first choice, but by God, it would be her last.

She left her hair down around her shoulders, and for the first time in forever, she applied enough makeup to make the cosmetic company's stock soar. With her thin, strappy sandals in place, she breezed into the living room for the final time.

"Do not say a single word about my outfit," she commanded Tristan, hooking her hair behind her ears.

Again he shrugged, but the heated once-over he gave her said plenty. He liked the outfit! Delight chased away her bad mood, and confidence budded within her chest.

Faith cast him a why-are-you-acting-like-such-an-ass glance, then turned back to Julia. "You are stunning, Jules. Simply breathtaking. Don't let the opinion of one demented idiot make you think otherwise."

"I think she is lovely," Tristan said, "no matter what she wears."

Julia beamed her appreciation.

Faith looked radiant in a sophisticated black pantsuit. Her dark hair was pulled back in a simple twist that cascaded tendrils from the top. Tristan, sexy as always, wore a pair of jeans that kissed his muscular thighs, and a black shirt that fell open around the collar, revealing scrumptious skin that probably tasted as good as it looked. Her mouth watered, and she shivered.

The sound of the doorbell echoed through the house.

"That's him." Instantly butterflies unleashed a flurry of wings within her stomach. Even her desire for Tristan was overshadowed in wake of her fear. *Calm down,* she commanded herself. But the command didn't help. Still shaking, she smoothed her hair in place, drew in a deep breath and slowly glided to the entryway. *I can do this.* She tugged open the front door. A cold breeze burst past.

"Sorry I'm late," Peter said. He offered her a shy smile. "I lost track of time."

She returned his smile with one of her own. "You're forgiven."

In his gray slacks and white dress shirt, he appeared sweet and bashfully charming. Yet the sight of him didn't affect her. *I'm an idiot. He's perfect for me. I* will *give him a chance.* "You look very nice, Peter."

"As do you. You're like—" He glanced down at his palm, and Julia thought she heard him mutter "I am a tiger." Then he blinked over at her and said, "You're like the rarest of cacti that bloom a flush pink only once a year."

"I—thank you."

"Are you ready?" he asked, his eyes gleaming with pride, as if he'd just climbed a mountain without a harness and survived. He leaned into her, and the strong scent of his cologne wafted to her nostrils. "I've been waiting for this moment since you called."

Tristan chose that moment to step up behind her. Almost absently, she leaned into him. "*We* are ready," he growled.

Color instantly drained from Peter's face, leaving him pallid and waxen. Shaky. "Uh...we?" he squeaked.

"Peter," Julia said, hoping to soothe him, "you've already met Tristan, who has promised not to bite you."

If possible, Peter's features became more pallid. "I've met him." Inch by inch, he crept backward.

"And this is my sister, Faith," Julia said with a wave toward her sister.

"Nice to meet you, Peter." Faith moved forward and smiled a sexy, fall-at-my-feet kind of smile.

Peter ground to a halt. Lost in the sheer femaleness Faith radiated, he drank her in for a silent moment, his eyes half-lidded with admiration. Then, recalling Tristan was Faith's brother, as well, he became agitated once again and pulled at his blue-striped tie. Gulping, he looked back to Julia. "Did your brother say *we* are ready?"

"Brother?" Faith asked.

"I thought it would be nice if my family joined us," Julia interjected with a warning glance to her sister. What else could she say? *Oh, by the way, Faith. I lied and told him we're all family.* Or, *Peter, darling, they're forcing me to bring them.*

"I hope you don't mind," she ended up saying.

"Perhaps we should do this another day," he said. "I mean—"

"No!" Julia wasn't sure she could endure another morning of predate jitters. "Today is fine. You'll have fun." *I hope.*

Faith inserted herself between them and batted her eyelashes up at Peter. "Please, call me Faithie. Everyone does."

"I'm not sure this is a good idea," Peter began again. "I have an appointment early tomorrow morning and need to—"

Tristan cut him off before he could continue. "Enough conversation." A slight warning glare accompanied his words. "We will leave now. And you *will* join us. Understand?"

A jumble of horror and fear, Peter simply nodded.

"Peter," Faith said, breaking the mounting tension. "I'd love it if you walked me to your car."

"Excellent idea," Julia said, desperate for a reprieve. Any type of reprieve. "You three go ahead. I need to turn out the lights." She spun away before they could protest. When she heard the car doors slam shut, she sucked in a breath. *I can do this. I can.*

CHAPTER EIGHTEEN

Never Look Directly At Your Master
Without Permission

JULIA STROLLED down a carpeted entryway covered with a red canopy. *I'm on a date,* she thought, still shocked and scared by that fact. Bright green foliage spilled from stone planters. Cold gusts of wind swirled and beat against the building. The moment she stepped inside the vestibule, warm air enveloped her. Peter tried to insinuate himself beside her, but Tristan edged him behind. They all followed Faith as she cut through a haze of dim, smoky air. Soft, lyrical music played in the background.

A tuxedo-clad maître d' appeared and moments later they were ushered to a table for four in a secluded corner. High, narrow windows overlooked an immaculate blooming garden with twinkling white lights strung across the greenery.

Tristan ushered Julia into a velvet-covered seat, then directed Faith to sit next to her. When both women were situated, he claimed the chair on Julia's left, leaving

Peter the seat directly across from her, nowhere near touching distance.

"Thank you," she murmured to the maître d' as she accepted a menu.

Julia studied the selections while Peter quietly expounded on her beauty, her wit and her charm. He had even composed a sonnet in her honor. This was everything she'd ever wanted. A plain, shy man deeply and irrevocably attracted to her. But she couldn't summon a shred of happiness.

Peter attempted to lean over the table to get closer to her—what was that weird scent her date was wearing?—and Tristan's scowl grew darker and more pronounced with every tick of her silver wristwatch.

Thankfully, their waiter arrived. One by one, they made their selections. Peter ordered exactly what she ordered, the lobster bisque with stuffed mushrooms in red wine sauce. Tristan and Faith opted for the prime rib and lemon pasta—then Tristan immediately called the waiter back and said he would have both the prime rib and the lobster. After the man strode away for the second time, Peter launched into another sonnet.

Julia thought she spied white index cards balanced on Peter's thigh, but she wasn't sure. When he mentioned the glorious sun-kissed locks of hair that framed her face as prettily as a cameo, she dared a glance at Tristan. His features were granite hard and tight in a glower. *I have to change the subject,* she thought.

She gave Peter a tentative smile and interrupted him

midverse. "Have you always liked to garden? I mean, I see you working with your plants so often."

He nodded, and for an instant his eyes lost that desperate, I-must-not-stop-talking-about-you glaze. "I find peace among my plants and flowers, knowing that I'm enriching nature's beauty." He glanced down at his legs, then cleared his throat. "You know, you are like the moon and the stars."

"Uh, thank you."

"What about you?" he asked. "Do you enjoy horticulture?"

"Oh, I love it," Faith interrupted with an airy laugh, even though the question had not been directed to her. "Not Julia, though. She has the Black Thumb of Death. Plants simply cannot survive in her care."

Horror flashed over Peter's expression. Then he shook his head, as if clearing his thoughts, and offered a half smile. "I'm sure you have so many other wonderful talents, Julia."

Before she could reply, Faith launched into a tale about an ancient civilization she dreamed of finding. Peter tried to interrupt her several times and shift his attention to Julia, but her sister wouldn't allow it.

Julia propped her elbow on the table and rested her chin in her hands. Here was everything she'd ever dreamed, yet she was sadly disappointed. She'd hoped, really hoped, that she would come to desire Peter at least half as much as she desired Tristan. That wasn't going to happen, she finally admitted.

Not ever.

The thought should have depressed her. Instead, she felt relieved. Peter wasn't the man for her, and she didn't have the energy to pretend he was any longer. Unbidden, she glanced at her sinfully delicious pleasure slave. Candlelight flickered across the linen-draped table. Every time he moved, shadows and light danced over his features, giving his cheekbones a stark, almost harsh appearance. She couldn't look away.

I love him, she thought.

Her breath froze in her lungs, and the nauseous feeling of hours before returned. No, no, she decided then with a shake of her head. There were too many complications, too many obstacles. Still…what if she'd done the unthinkable and fallen for a pleasure slave?

What was she going to do?

WHAT WAS HE GOING TO DO?

From the moment Julia had stepped out of her chamber to reveal her new gowns, Tristan had been poised and readied to battle the male inhabitants of this world. Every garment she showcased had displayed her exquisite figure, hugging her luscious curves, revealing her perfection for all to see. Knowing she was now wearing a gown *he* had chosen, and she wore this gown for another man, still held enough power to infuriate him.

He studied her now, in the smoky atmosphere of the restaurant, measuring her reactions to her date. But Julia was no longer watching Peter the Poetry Reader, he noticed. She was watching *him* under the spiky veil of her lashes. Why? He wanted so badly to know her thoughts.

He cared for Julia, and he could not seem to make himself stop. Nay, he did not love her—he refused to love her, knowing he would only lose her—but she *had* somehow managed to sink her way under his skin.

I need her in my arms.

In the garden, couples strolled hand in hand, soft music humming all around them. He wanted that with Julia, wanted her all to himself, if only for a little while. He extended his hand. "Let us view the garden, little dragon."

Silent for a moment, she chewed on her bottom lip.

"I'll take you," Peter said bravely, already standing.

Tristan's gaze locked with hers, ignoring Peter, and he used the force of his will to quietly assert his dominance. "*I* will take you, Julia."

With resignation, Peter sank back into his seat.

"Peter," Faith said, brushing her fingertips over the man's arm. "I've been dying to ask you more about *your* garden. Let Tristan and Julia go, and you stay here and keep me company. Okay?"

Slowly Peter melted under the loveliness of Faith's pouty you-are-the-big-strong-man-and-I-am-the-weak-woman expression.

Tristan waved his fingers. "Come," he said, leaving doubt as to which way he actually meant the word.

Julia placed her palm in his. Gently he helped her to her feet and led her through a pair of French double doors. They stepped into a glass-encased atrium. Above, the moon and stars twinkled like diamonds in black velvet. Antique oil lamps and flourishing cacti wove interlacing paths, broken only by the occasional alabaster statue. The air was cool and sweetly fragrant.

He wrapped his palm around Julia's and they slowly meandered down the red carpet. Her body fit perfectly beside his. Vulnerability radiated from her.

"Is something wrong?" he asked, giving her hand a light squeeze.

With a sigh, she burrowed her cheek against his shoulder. "Peter isn't the man for me."

Primal victory danced through him, but he managed to temper his tone. "And you have just now realized this?"

"I think I knew it all along. I just didn't want to admit it."

Tristan paused and faced her. He brushed a tendril of hair from her cheek and hooked the silky strands behind her ear. "You need a man who sees the passion you try so hard to hide, Julia. A man who recognizes your generosity and your capacity for goodness. A man who realizes the depth of your beauty."

She looked away, asking dejectedly, "Where will I find this superhero with X-ray vision?"

"You already have." He cupped her chin in his hands, forcing her to face him once again. "You already have."

She blinked up at him, and he knew she didn't understand what he was telling her.

"I want you, Julia. I see who you truly are. I see your beauty. And I want you so much I ache."

"But the lessons—"

"Have nothing to do with how I feel about you. Do you think I would make you study so intensely if I did not actually crave you? Never doubt your appeal. I do want you, and my desire is not civilized or forced or contrived. Nay, to me you are more precious, more beautiful, than any other woman I have ever encountered."

"How can you, a man who has known thousands of women, say that about me—and mean it?"

"Mayhap when we return home, we will have ourselves a little chat to help you understand, hmm?" he replied with a dark scowl. "Complete with a demonstration and charts. Believe me, Julia, when I say that there is something special about you, something I have never encountered before."

A long while passed in silence as she studied him. "I believe you," she whispered, her eyes softening with awe. "I do."

"Good. Then I am going to give you another lesson. How to rid oneself of unwanted company." Tristan tugged her to a window alcove, which offered a perfect view to the restaurant's inhabitants. He leaned down, gently brushing his lips against hers. Then his fingers tangled in her hair, and he tilted her chin to kiss her more deeply. As his tongue explored her mouth, his lips demanded all of her passion. He wasn't sure which of them was flavored with wine and which of them was flavored with mint. He didn't care, either. He only yearned for more.

With Julia, there was always this need. Always this magic.

He leaned his hips into her body and wordlessly demanded she acknowledge that he was the only man for her. She moaned. He caught the sound, fighting the urge to whisk her away to a private haven where he might explore her more fully. His thumb played at the corner of her mouth, a silent appeal to take him deeper. Deeper, still. He hadn't lied to her. She affected him as no other ever had. If he could, he would give her his heart, give her his name. Give her his children.

Before his blood heated to the point of no return, he forced himself to pull back. His arms suddenly felt empty, void. Arousal blazed in Julia's eyes and gentled her expression with hazy desire. "Come," he said. "Let us see if this lesson was successful." With a possessive hand at her waist, he led her back to the table.

Peter watched them through wide, horrified eyes. He shot to his feet so quickly his chair skidded across the floor. "I don't know what gave you the impression I'm into kink, but I assure you I am not. A tiger doesn't have to put up with this…this sexual weirdness. I have to go."

"So soon?" Tristan asked, his tone clearly suggesting it wasn't soon enough.

That said, Peter tossed his napkin to the floor and stalked away.

Julia felt only relief…and just a hint of guilt.

Faith gasped. "What was that all about? And did he say tiger?"

"Aye. He did," Tristan said, canting his chin to the side and watching Peter's retreating back.

"And he thinks we're weird?"

"Well…I kind of told him that Tristan is our brother," Julia admitted.

Her sister hid a grin behind her hand, and when that didn't work, she allowed her chuckles free rein. "No wonder he—" Another laugh escaped. "You two are bad. So very, very bad."

Relaxed and solicitous now, Tristan helped Julia into her chair, then resumed his seat at the table. The food arrived not long after on a scented cloud of creamy butter and lemon sauce.

Faith chewed two bites of her prime rib and suddenly dropped her fork. "I, uh, just remembered that I'm needed at the lab." Though her tone lacked conviction, she grabbed her purse and jacket and jumped to her feet. "Don't worry about me. I'll catch a cab." With only a wistful glance at her food, she rushed out of the building.

Julia tossed him a smile that nearly stole the breath from his lungs. "This evening is suddenly far better than I could have ever anticipated, and I almost want to give *you* a lesson in doggie bags."

He didn't understand her meaning, but grinned all the same as he filled two glasses with the dark, crimson wine. "Lesson six has nothing to do with these doggie bags, but everything to do with discovery. Our discovery of each other."

She gave a quick intake of breath, almost undetectable, but he was attuned to her every nuance and knew she was excited by his words, by the images his admission evoked.

"You know," she said, her voice husky now. "I *do* want to be a good student. The very best."

Blood rushed to his groin as her words rained over him, as bold and seductive as an actual caress. He shifted in his seat. "Lesson six will require intense, in-depth training at home—in bed." With the tip of his finger, he traced a path across her cheek, along her jaw. "What think you of that?"

"I think I'm glad." She sipped her wine, watching him over the rim of her glass. The pulse in her neck quickened. He longed to caress the beat with his tongue.

Later he promised himself. Later. She had never experienced a "real" date, and he wanted to give her one.

The rest of the meal passed in a sexually charged silence as they each watched the other, each anticipating what came next. When their plates were taken away, Tristan ordered dessert, then leaned over the table and picked up their conversation as if it had never ceased. "Tell me about your childhood, little dragon. I know very little about your past."

She set her napkin aside and regarded him. "What exactly do you want to know?"

"Everything."

"Hmm...well, I had a typical childhood, I guess. My parents split up when I was eight."

When she didn't continue, he said, "That tells me nothing. Give me the complete story."

"The complete story. Okay. I don't know why my parents had children. We were more a nuisance to them than anything. When they weren't fighting with each other, they were fighting with us. During the divorce proceedings, they argued over who got custody of me and Faith, though not the way you'd expect. Mom wanted us to go with Dad, and he wanted us to go with Mom. We ended up with my mom and never heard from my father again."

There was no bitterness in her tone, only acceptance and regret. Tristan touched her knee, keeping the action gentle and reassuring. There was a vulnerability about her, a sadness that enveloped her and touched his heart—a heart he'd thought long dead.

"Tell me the rest," he coaxed.

"There's not much more to tell, really." Tracing a circle around the rim of her glass, she said, "About five years after the breakup, my mom remarried. Her new husband was a salesman, not a very good one I might add, but he traveled a lot with his job. She liked to go with him. Faith and I spent weeks at a time alone. It's a wonder child services didn't take us away."

As she spoke, he traced his fingertips over her knee, offering comfort for all she had endured. "Do you ever speak with your parents now?"

"Rarely."

"I am sorry." He wanted to wipe the painful memories from her mind, but also wanted to learn more about her. There would be time for forgetting later, when he filled her mind with passion and pleasure. Right now, he said, "Will you tell me about your first date?"

She did, her voice trembling with every word.

By the end of the story, fury raced a treacherous path through Tristan's veins. Killing the boy who had hurt his woman wasn't punishment enough. He wanted to tie the idiot to an *hendrek* hill—naked, of course—letting the tiny creatures slowly eat him alive. Instead, he drew on his battle instincts and kept his emotions under tight restraint.

He didn't have to scratch too far below the surface of her words to understand the anguish she had endured. Both her mother and father had rejected her. The first boy she showed interest in had rejected her. Now Julia simply expected rejection. That explained so much of her personality, and he sympathized, for he himself had endured many of the same rejections as a child.

The waiter deposited their dessert on the table then disappeared in a flurry. Tristan toyed with the stem of a plump red fruit. Were they alone, he would sweep the dewy softness along her silken skin and lick away the evidence. Since they were not, he pinched the fruit between his fingers and held it to Julia's lips. "Open up."

The pink tip of her tongue emerged, tasted, then devoured. "Mmm, that's good. Thank you."

He gulped.

"What about you?" she asked, unaware of the fire she continually stirred inside his body. She speared a small corner of the cake with her fork and brought it to her mouth. "What's your life story?" Her teeth closed over the sugary confection.

He dragged his gaze from her luscious charms, across the wide expanse of the dance floor, to rest on the far window that paid homage to the night heavy with glowing stars. "This you do not want to know."

"Yes, I do," she said without pause. "Besides, you

owe me. I told you about my childhood. Now you have to tell me about yours. That's only fair."

Tristan had never shared this part of himself with another, not even Roake. But he refused to lie to Julia, or sweeten the details. She desired to know about him, and so he would tell her. "There were times when I was young that I wished my father did not want me. I never knew why, but I always knew he hated me."

"Surely he didn't *hate* you."

"Then why did he give me these?" Tristan clasped her hand and placed it under his shirt, then guided her fingers to his back, to his scars.

"Tristan," she whispered, horrified, not knowing what else to say.

"My scars did not appear by divine power, Julia," Tristan said, his eyes fierce. "He hated me, and proved it every time he wielded the whip."

"Oh, Tristan. I'm so sorry." She wanted to put her mouth on every scar, to kiss and make them better while she flicked her tongue over one peak, then another. Temptation caressed insidious ribbons throughout her body as tears welled in her eyes. She allowed her fingertips one last stroke before removing them from his clothing and placing them in her lap. She imagined Tristan as a young boy, beaten, bruised and unloved. While her parents merely neglected her, his father had physically abused him. She ached for him, for what he'd lost and endured. "I'm so very, very sorry."

"Do not cry for me, little dragon." His anger and frustration for those years still ate at him at times, but

Julia's compassion helped soothe the pain that lingered. "I did not always know hatred." Smiling gently, he wiped the moisture from her eyes and the curve of her cheekbone. "I spent the first five years of my life with my mother. She adored me."

"How did she die?" Julia asked softly.

"She did not." His eyes darkened to steely gray, revealing secrets and pain. "Where I am from, warriors are looked to with respect and reverence. She was unmated, only a slave, and could not teach me the art of warfare. When the time came, she entrusted me into my father's care so that I might acquire the proper training."

"A five-year-old child training to be a warrior? Your childhood makes mine seem like a fairy tale."

"Suffering comes in many forms. Do not discount your own." He placed his napkin on the table, effectively ending that line of conversation. "Tell me why you have not arranged the upstairs chambers in your home."

Her shoulders lifted in a delicate shrug, and she graciously accepted the change in topics. "When I bought the house, I imagined myself there with a husband and children. I wanted to make the upstairs a nursery, one room for a boy and one for a girl, but I haven't yet because seeing them all fixed up and knowing I have no one to live there will hurt." She paused. "That sounds stupid, doesn't it?"

"Stupid? Nay." Heartbreaking? Aye. For he could never give her the children she craved. And he suddenly longed to see her cradling his son or daughter in her arms. Ah, was there anything sweeter? He should never have mentioned the room, and if she said one more word about them, he might offer her promises he could not keep. Might drop to his knees and swear at the heavens for all that he would never experience.

"What else do you dream about when you are alone?" he asked hoarsely. "What do you secretly crave?"

"Besides another cherry?" she asked, following his lead with a gentle smile.

"Aye. Besides that." He pinched another fruit and placed it at the portal of her lips. Watching him, she chewed, swallowed. Her eyes widened when he leaned over and licked the remaining evidence from the corner of her mouth. "Well, what is your answer?"

"About what?" she asked breathlessly.

His nearness warmed her ear. "Your dreams."

"I dream about what every other woman dreams about, I suppose. Finding my one, true love."

"That much I already know." Under the table, he stroked her knee. "Is there nothing else you desire right this moment?"

She hesitated only briefly, giving him the idea she was not truthful with her next words. "There's nothing else I want."

"Then I will just have to do everything in my power to change your mind, will I not?" He didn't wait for her response. "Are you ready to go home?" he asked, the words *to begin your next lesson* hanging in the air unsaid.

This time, she didn't hesitate with her answer. "Yes. I'm ready."

CHAPTER NINETEEN

Imperia

"CLOSE YOUR EYES, Zirra."

Instantly she obeyed.

Firelight licked the lushness of her features. Freshly bathed, Romulis reclined against the corner wall. The marble slat was cool and seeped past the fibers of his silver Imperian robe. The coolness did nothing to damper his arousal.

Zirra sat at the edge of her bed, her sheer white gown clinging to her every curve. Had there ever been a woman more alluring? She fairly hummed with mating heat. She radiated it, smelled of it, moved with it. He had lusted for her since the first moment he had seen her, and his desire for her had not lessened over the years. Nay, it had grown.

He had known instinctively that she was his chosen life-mate. Yet she always denied him. A lesser man might have given up long before now. Mayhap he *should* have admitted defeat. He liked to think he possessed too much pride to beg for her attentions.

But here he was. Here he was, willing to accept any scrap of tenderness she might offer.

When she had summoned him, she'd interrupted his magic and talon practice, yet he eagerly dropped his sword and came to her, just because she had need of him. He'd hoped she meant to at last accept him. But she hadn't. Instead she had asked him to help find her former lover.

The rage he had felt at that moment still beat within him. He yearned to cleave Tristan in two. At the very least, beat the warrior to a bloody mass.

Unable to do either of those things, he agreed to help Zirra find him. Because now she owed him—and he had every intention of collecting. Soon. Not yet, but soon.

"Are you peeking?" he asked her.

"Nay." She squeezed her eyelids so tightly little grooves formed at the edges. His voice was tight with irritation when she added, "Why will *you* not call him back?"

"Because his box will then belong to me, and I wish not to own him. Do *you* wish for me to own him?"

"Nay," she shouted vehemently. Then more calmly, "Nay." She paused. "If you owned him, you could gift the box to me."

"But I would not. I would cast the cursed thing into the nearest hearth and happily watch the man inside burn."

Her eyelids popped open. "You would not dare—"

"Aye. I would. Now offer no more complaints, or I will leave you here on your own."

It was a threat neither of them believed, for he wanted her too severely. Needed to taste her too desperately.

And they both knew it. He would give her anything she asked, even another man, if only to know her passion just once.

I am a fool, he thought with disgust.

"Close your eyes," he demanded again. She did.

Guilt wound through him. He was disobeying his father, a man he respected, a man he admired. Still that did not dissuade him. As if an invisible cord tugged him, he strode to her. She sensed his nearness and tiny bumps rose on her flesh. Her scent drifted to his nostrils, magic and moonlight, and was so completely arousing he grit his teeth against the pain of wanting her. Unable to stop himself, he traced a fingertip over the curve of her ear, then tangled his hand in her hair. Her lips parted on a wispy catch of breath.

Dewy mist swirled from the sea, past the windows, kissing her cheeks and neck, dampening her hair and silky blue robe. She was beauty and strength epitomized, a woman who would appeal to any who looked upon her, yet there was something very vulnerable about her, something at the periphery of her smile. Insecurities, mayhap.

"Reach inside yourself," he whispered. "Find the source of your magic."

Her lips pursed as she concentrated. The fact that she did not hesitate sent another surge of anger through him, battling with his desire, mingling with his guilt. He wanted to hate Zirra, wanted again to hurt Tristan. How did such a man, who lacked any mystical powers, command such devotion from this sorceress?

Scowling, he dropped his hand to his side. "My father's spell did not destroy your powers. It merely covered them, like a blanket. Reach under the blanket."

"There," she said excitedly. "I can see what you mean." She clapped her hands, keeping her eyes tightly closed, and he suddenly sensed a charged energy enveloping her. "I have it. I have it!"

So lovely. So deadly. "Now open your mouth," he commanded roughly.

Her lashes fluttered open, casting shadows upon her cheeks. When she saw him, she gasped, startled. "Romulis?"

"Hold on to the source of your power and open your mouth," he commanded once more, his voice rough with the force of his desire.

Just as before, she obeyed.

He crushed his lips to hers, his tongue immediately pushing deep and hard. Her teeth scraped him. Greed and decadence were her flavors; heady, forbidden, and he did not want to like them, but he did. All too well.

She purred, a deep throaty sound. His powers swirled around them, blending with the mystic abilities she clasped in her mind. Arcs of energy charged and lit the air and hummed along their skin. He pressed his erection between her thighs. Her nails bit into his shoulders. He palmed her breasts in his hands, measuring their luscious weight. She ground herself against him, searching for completion. He groaned, a sound of victory and joy, because he felt her need and knew she wanted him.

"Oh, Tristan," she breathed.

Romulis jerked away. Enraged, he glared down at her, taking in the swollen redness of her lips, the dewy desire in her eyes. His chest rose and fell rapidly. How dare she say another's name while he kissed her. How dare she! He could withstand many things from this woman, but not that. Never that.

Her eyes widened when she realized what she'd done. "Romulis," she said, shaking. She even reached for him, but he shrugged her off. "Do not be angry with me. Please. I cannot succeed without your help."

She cared only about his anger and the fact that he might change his mind and not aid her cause. And still he wanted her. His fists clenched at his sides. "Angry?" he said with deceptive calm. "My emotions matter not. I gave you my vow, after all, so I will help you."

"You must understand. He is—"

"Silence."

She clamped her lips together.

"I find I must wash the taste of you from my mouth." With that, he whipped around and strode toward the entrance. "But I will return. Doubt it not."

ROMULIS DID NOT APPROACH her again until the four suns had set on the golden horizon. By that time, Zirra had regained authority over her emotions. She would not allow him to startle her again with his kisses. Kissing him had been a pleasant diversion, exciting even, and had somehow given her a sense of her deepest power, but Romulis was an uncontrollable force, one who sought to dominate all he encountered, and she would not allow herself to be conquered.

She did the conquering.

Tristan was proof of that. If only she could clasp her powers on her own, but nay. Once Romulis left her, she'd lost her tenuous grip on them.

The wispy white fabric hanging over the entrance to her chamber *swished.*

Frowning, she spun…and found herself facing him. Romulis dropped the door scarves and they fell behind him, enclosing him inside. A gentle sea-dewed breeze floated from the windows, whisking the hem of her white gown about her ankles, making her shiver. Surely her reaction had nothing to do with the prince.

"Let us get this over with," he said, his tone emotionless. Bored, mayhap.

She didn't offer another apology for calling out Tristan's name while Romulis kissed her. What did she care if his male pride was hurt? He had sworn to give his aid, and he would, no matter how she infuriated him.

"It certainly took you long enough to recall your vow," she told him, straightening her shoulders and giving a regal flick of her hair.

The corner of his left eye ticked ominously, and he took one threatening step toward her. His eyes glowed with barely suppressed rage. Then he stopped, collected himself and made his expression once more impassive. "Sit at the edge of the bed."

Ire pounded through her. The prince was just like his father, always issuing orders, always expecting total compliance. She deserved so much more. She deserved devotion and love, affection and respect—things Tristan gave her when she commanded him.

Watching Romulis, she moved with deliberate leisure, swaying her hips and exaggerating each motion. When she perched where he had commanded, she eased back on her elbows, pushing the roundness of her breasts against the sheer fabric of her gown.

"I am waiting," she said.

"Clasp your power in your mind."

Though she wanted to taunt him further, she closed her eyes, reached within herself and easily found the source of her mystic abilities, a source Percen could not bind. They swirled and churned, dark and dangerous, searching for an outlet.

Romulis came to her then and cupped her cheeks in his big, hard hands. "Repeat these words." He uttered a spell she'd never heard before, a spell of time and galaxies and hope. "Repeat them until you believe them, until they are a part of you."

She did, over and over chanting the spell, each time louder, more intense. Lances of her power sprang from her body and reverberated through the chamber. Bright rays of light bolted toward the arched ceiling like wings of an angel. She even added her own words to the spell. "Make Tristan's current *guan ren* hang from a tree. Destroy her."

"Say only what I tell you," Romulis commanded with a fury so intense she felt it all the way to her bones.

"Hang her from a tree. Destroy the woman and bring

Tristan to this room," she said, uncaring she went against Romulis's orders. "Destroy her and bring Tristan to me."

I'M GOING to make love.

Julia smiled dreamily as she and Tristan held hands in the back of the cab. The warmth of his palm and the roughness of the calluses proved an amazing contrast, a contrast she wanted all over her body. She'd just spent the evening with this gorgeous, sensual man—who truly found her desirable, by the way—and now their date was going to experience the perfect ending.

Just imagining the skim of his hands up her calves, thighs, stomach; of his mouth sucking her nipples, caused something powerful and something wholly feminine to bloom within her. When the cab jerked to a stop, she and Tristan emerged. Almost immediately after she tossed the driver a twenty, exhaust fumes and gravel propelled around them.

Waving one hand in front of her nose and trying to subdue a fit of coughing, she searched for Tristan through the haze. Their gazes locked. His lips lifted in a slow, deliberate smile, and he reached out and clasped her palm in his once again. A shiver tingled up her arm, leaving a trail of delicious bumps.

"Are you ready to begin?" he asked.

Her knees almost buckled in eagerness. "Oh, yes."

"Then come."

He tugged her toward the house. They were just about to step up to the porch when the cement beneath her feet shifted. Suddenly her world was spinning out of control. She gasped. Tristan whipped around and tried to jerk her into his arms. But as they were spinning, they were falling farther apart.

Fear grinding inside her, she clawed her way to him, and he fought his way toward her. They met in the middle. She clasped him tight, afraid to release him. His grip on her nearly cut off her air supply.

"What's happening?" she cried. If he answered, she didn't hear him. Loud, piercing screeches erupted, like fingernails against a scratchy surface. She felt as if she were being sucked into a vacuum. A million twinkling stars whizzed past, so close she had only to reach out to grab one in her hand. Brilliant flashes of color filled her vision. Rays of pink, purple, green and blue. They twirled together, forming a kaleidoscope, spinning quickly. They had to stop spinning.

Tristan's grip on her tightened, and he held her as close as their bodies would allow. And then, as suddenly as the spinning began, it ended.

The ground hardened beneath her feet, once again a solid anchor. Her dizziness lasted for several prolonged moments, but when it passed, she opened her eyes and expelled a shocked puff of air.

"Where are we?" she asked softly, the words echoing around her.

Silver marble covered large, spacious walls, and some sort of smooth crystal provided a glistening floor. There was no furniture present, only empty space. No light fixtures, either, and yet the room was lit with a crown of brilliance. A large window claimed the farthest wall, and Julia released Tristan and strode to peek outside.

Confusion rocked her as a pink-and-purple skyline filled her vision. Dragonlike creatures soared through the air, their wings spanning an incredible length. Below, she drank in a view of a clear silver sea and white sand. Trees dripped with brilliant sapphire-and-emerald-colored fruit, and two golden moons decorated the night. A cool, damp breeze scented with sweet rain kissed her cheeks and ruffled strands of her hair.

Mouth agape, she spun. "Where are we?" she asked Tristan again. "And how did we get here?"

"We are in Imperia," he answered, his own shock dripping from each syllable. A flicker of joy lit his eyes. "I do not know how we arrived here, at this time, but I do not wish to question my good fate." His face now gleaming with immeasurable delight, he walked around the edges of the walls, his fingertips brushing each surface. "These are *lamori* gems. Watch." He caressed one of the stones, and the dull silver shimmered to life, glowing with vitality.

Unable to stop herself, she reached out and stroked the stone nearest her. No heat. Only cold and tangible reality. Yet a rosy light began to illuminate the inner sphere of the stone. Then the walls began to move, slowly at first, growing faster and faster, spinning like before, but shooting backward in a constant motion, its end never appearing. Panicked, Julia raced back into Tristan's arms. He held her close.

"Time," he said. "Time is reversing."

How many minutes passed while they stood, unable to do anything but watch, Julia didn't know. How was any of this happening? When everything calmed, she blinked in surprise. They were standing in the same room—the same room, but different. A large, delectable bed occupied the center, the sides draped by sheer white lace, the top covered with white furs. An elaborate vanity and a plush chaise longue filled a separate sitting area.

She scarcely dared to breathe as she returned her gaze to the bed.

She gasped, for the first time noticing that a woman reclined there, her delicate spill of black hair against the white silk sheets and perfect features giving her a beauty so real, so…alive, even Julia felt the force of it. A bronzed, muscled warrior stood beside her, his eyes glowing with barely suppressed rage. The man was scowling, the woman grinning. She jumped to her feet the moment she spied Tristan, her creamy gown floating around her ankles. She moved her mouth, yet no sound emerged.

"Zirra," Tristan spat, latching tightly on to Julia's waist and keeping her snug against him. In the next instant, the world around them began to spin again. More stars. More colors. Round and round they went, and her stomach clenched. When the spinning stopped for this third time, she faced a field of tall, flourishing trees. There were no houses, no cars, no electrical poles.

"We must wait for time to go forward once more," Tristan said, his breath a ripple against her cheek.

His body trembled slightly, she realized, fighting against her own trembling. Just how close had she come to losing him?

"HE WAS HERE," Zirra cried, her joy all but bursting from her chest. "He was here!"

"That he was," Romulis offered, his tone a bit too happy for her liking.

"Where did he go?" Swift and sure, she searched her entire room, every nook, corner and hidden hollow. "Is he hiding?"

"Your power was not strong enough to hold him— not without his box in your hands. And so he journeyed back to his new world."

She screamed with her rage. "I must reclaim his box. I must. Teach me another spell."

"Think you my father would allow that? He spelled the box as surely as he cast Tristan away. The box cannot return here with magic alone. The cursed thing must be brought by someone's hand. All I told you I would do is bring him to you. I did not say how long he would stay."

"Bastard!" A screech of rage broke through her throat, and she whipped around and glared at this man who was supposed to help her. "Bastard."

"And yet you should have realized."

"Bastard," she snarled again.

"What has you more upset, Zirra? The fact that he disappeared? Or the fact that he looked happy with the other woman?"

"He belongs to me. Do you not understand? I am his

master. I control him. If I cannot hold him here with my power, I will find another way. I will possess him again, Romulis. This I swear to you."

JULIA STARED AT HER HOUSE, which now towered in front of her, then looked up at Tristan, who still stood beside her. Finally the shock of what had happened dwindled away, and she experienced confusion and fear in full force.

"I don't understand what just happened. We were standing here, then we weren't, and now we are. How is that possible? How did we travel through time and galaxies and reach Imperia?"

Steel glinted in his eyes, making the violet seem like a whirlpool of deep purple liquid. "Zirra, the one who cursed me, tried to call me back."

Julia's mouth went dry. "But your box... I have your box."

"This I know. My guess is 'twas why we were returned here."

This isn't happening, she thought. She wasn't ready to lose Tristan. Not now, perhaps not ever, and the fact that she *could* lose him terrified her.

"Let's go inside," she said. She didn't want to stand out in the open, didn't want to be any more of a target than she needed to be. She wanted him within the walls of her house, the doors locked. But when she tried to move forward, he stopped her with a firm hand on her shoulder.

"Did you not turn out the lights before we left?" he asked, frowning.

"Yes. Now hurry." Frown deepening, she allowed her fingers to curl around his, and she tugged him toward the door.

He planted his heels firmly in the ground, preventing her from moving another inch. "I believe someone has invaded your home."

Her eyes widened in disbelief, and she saw that light seeped from beneath the closed curtains of her front window. "Oh, my God."

"Get behind the bushes," he demanded, morphing into superhero mode.

His face was an angry mask of determination, his gaze cold and hard.

"What are you going to do?" she asked, her words broken. While Tristan was unbelievably strong, he was not impenetrable to bullet or knife wounds.

He didn't repeat himself, didn't reply. Instead, using gentle force, he pushed her behind the bushes. His fists clenched at his sides. "Remain there until I return."

Tristan unsheathed his daggers, one from the waist of his drocs, the other from the sheath he tied to his boot, and with a stealth born of years on the battlefield, moved into the house. Broken glass and leaves littered the floor. The talking cube was shattered, lying in tiny pieces across the floor. In the center of the room loomed a tall, thick tree, its branches sprouting in every direction.

Zirra, he thought, baring his teeth. 'Twas a part of her spell. He didn't understand why she'd wanted a tree in Julia's home, however. But there it was, leaving destruction in its wake.

Fists clenched, he silently and methodically searched every chamber in the house, ascertaining the damage, ducking under limbs. His fist grasped the hilts of his daggers so tightly his knuckles drained of color. So many things had been destroyed in the sorceress's magical rage.

If she were capable of this, what else could the sorceress do?

Tristan suddenly knew a fear greater than the anger spilling into his veins. Zirra hoped to win him back and hurt Julia in the process. And she had almost succeeded. Seeing her, knowing she wanted him still, caused all of his old resentments to rise to the surface. He'd been so happy at first, to stand inside the Druinn castle, to see his homeland. Yet all of his happiness had faded when he spied Zirra.

In the past, females had attempted to steal his box from his current *guan ren*. Some had succeeded; some had not. Those times of success, he had found himself sucked back inside his prison, awaiting a summons from his new mistress. He'd never minded, for one *guan ren* was the same as any other. With Julia, however... Ah, he would not allow himself to be taken. Not by Zirra. Not by anyone.

His arms trembled as he returned his weapons to their pouches and lifted a broken portrait of a young Julia standing next to an equally young Faith, this photo slightly different from the other he'd viewed. Julia's bright eyes smiled up at him with such innocence and trust.

"Oh, my God."

The soft, feminine voice had him whipping around,

shoving branches out of his way. Julia stood in the doorway, her jaw slack, her eyes wide with shock and fear. "You were told to wait outside, woman."

"I was worried about you."

The words knifed through him, leaving a trail of guilt in their wake. Women lusted for him, but they certainly never worried for him. And yet, the one woman who *did* care, he had failed. He had been unable to protect her belongings. His hands shook as he set the portrait back onto the leafy floor. How did one man, one warrior, battle against a magic he could not see or touch?

"I am fine, Julia," he said. "Completely unharmed. Come and see." Never removing his eyes from her, he opened his arms and simply waited. With a broken moan, she raced to him and threw herself against him. Her fragrance, still so sweet and all her own, was now laced with fear—for him. "All will be well, little dragon."

Now that she knew he was unharmed, she began to break down.

"My house," she whispered raggedly. "My things. That tree!"

He continued to cradle her against him. It had been centuries since he had willingly comforted a woman, and it tore him up inside to do so now. He hated to see Julia so upset. He hated to see her tears, and he used his fingertip to gently wipe them away.

"Should I notify my insurance?" A humorless sound escaped her lips, and the sound tinkled like jagged bells grinding together. "What would I say?"

He gently led her to the couch.

"Sit," he told her, taking her hands in his. Her fingers were ice-cold, too cold. "Rest for a moment."

"I don't want to sit," she said, her voice hoarse. Wide-eyed, she looked around, trying to take in everything at once. Her beautiful paintings were in tatters from the branches. Her lovely emerald-and-sapphire chaise was a broken shell. Trembling, she said, "I know the box is here, but I need to see it, to hold it in my hands."

He sighed, hating that she would not accept his comfort yet, and released her. "I understand."

Lips tightly pressed together, she inched to the fallen faux plant that had once stood tall and shaded the bay window. She unscrewed the vacuous bottom. Upon seeing that his box still rested there, she released a relieved, battered breath and blinked up at him. "It's still here." She paused. "My computer!" Cheeks becoming even more pale, Julia shoved the box back into the planter, rescrewed the lid and leapt to her feet.

She raced from the living chamber, ducking limbs, and into her office, only to find equal devastation. All of her business files and account books were strewn across the floor, knocked over by the tree's long arms. Her computer was smashed. Her pretagged inventory damaged beyond repair. Horror wrapped around her.

She blinked back the sting of tears and felt Tristan draw near. He didn't utter a word. Staying behind her, he anchored his arms around her waist, tracing his palms over her stomach, stopping just under her breasts. His chin rested atop her head, and she felt the ripple of his breath against her hair. Almost completely broken inside, she welcomed his strength, his warmth. How could something like this have happened?

Numb with shock, she toppled to the cold wood floor.

"Julia," Tristan said, every nuance of concern in her name. Watching her, he sank beside her and curled himself around her, gathering her into the heat of his body. He stroked her hair, kissed the sensitive edge of her ear, all the while murmuring words of comfort.

"I don't understand this," she said, closing her eyes against the destruction.

"Some people let darkness fill their souls," he answered, locking one arm under her knees and supporting her back with the other. Then he stood, cradling her in the hollow of his embrace. He ducked his way to her bedroom. She didn't offer a single protest when he laid her down on the mattress and removed her skirt. After gathering the covers from the floor, he tucked the soft material around her trembling frame, placed a soft kiss on her forehead and turned to leave.

"Tristan," she whispered, stopping him. "Where are you going?" The thick foliage offered a shadowy canopy.

"I wish to clear the mess."

"Will you stay with me tonight and hold me?"

"Aye, little dragon. Whatever you desire." The bed dipped as he eased in beside her and gathered her close, so close every hollow and curve of her body fit snugly against him. His scent mingled with pine and surrounded her, familiar and so desperately needed. She breathed deeply. "I know not what I can say to end your torment," he whispered, "but somehow I will help you forget this happened. I swear it."

With his promise in her ears, she allowed herself to sink into the comforting clasp of darkness.

CHAPTER TWENTY

Ask For Permission Before You Do Anything

SOMEWHERE IN HER conscious mind, Julia heard a loud crack of thunder. Heard rain beat in rhythmic abandon against the window seal. The sleepy fog clouding her thoughts began to clear. And perhaps it was because of the softness of the mattress, or perhaps because Tristan's masculine scent enveloped her senses, but whatever the reason, her mind began to catalog all of her secret desires.

1. Make love with Tristan—him on top
2. Get a tattoo. Something sexy
3. Make love with Tristan—her on top
4. Skinny-dip. With Tristan
5. Make love with Tristan—him behind her

Wait. Him behind her… A warm male body did indeed press against her backside. She snuggled deeper into him, remembering she had asked Tristan to sleep in her bed. But as she lay there, her body began to tingle, to want. Her eyelids slowly cracked open. Sunlight forced its way into the bedroom, unwanted and unforgiving. Warm breath caressed her neck, and a bronze, muscled arm draped over her hip. She tried to fight the urge to slip his hand lower, until he touched her where she suddenly ached for him, where moisture pooled between her legs.

"At last Beauty awakens from a peaceful slumber," Tristan said, his sleep-rich voice purring along her spine. "After all that happened, I feared you would be unable to rest."

The tree…the little jaunt to Imperia…no, she inwardly intoned. *I don't want to remember.* But the memories flooded her, anyway: the destruction, the fear. *Get up,* her mind screamed. *Do something.* Blinking back the lingering cloud of sleep, she jumped from the bed. There was nothing she could do about the unplanned, otherworldly trip, but by God, she could take care of her house.

Her movements were clipped as she wrapped her sheer blue robe around her body, a tumble of silk from shoulders to ankle. Right now, Tristan's box *was* safe. She had to believe that. Otherwise, thoughts of his abduction—for that's what it would be—would haunt and consume her for the rest of the day, and she couldn't afford to worry. There was too much work to do. She needed to clean every room, cut down the tree and perhaps notify her insurance company, replace broken items.

Seductive as always, Tristan stretched then eased up. His eyes were rimmed with shadows, as if he hadn't really slept at all. "Where are you going?" he asked, his voice scratchy and laden with a delicious yawn.

Caught up in the trials awaiting her, Julia didn't spare him another glance. Nor did she notice she didn't have to duck. There were no tree limbs. "I need to organize and clean. I can't afford to close the store tomorrow, too, so everything needs to be taken care of today."

"There is nothing you need do now except climb back into this bed."

"Look," she sighed, "I don't have time for games. Everything I had in this house is ruined, and I need to clear the damage." She grabbed the first articles of clothing she could find, which turned out to be Tristan's sweatpants and T-shirt. She dressed in the bathroom. Unbidden, she felt her blood simmer with yearning as she inhaled his lingering scent in the fabric.

Striding through the house, she noticed how murky sunlight flittered through the open curtains. Another round of thunder boomed. Julia halted midstep, drinking in the interior of her house. The floors gleamed with a fresh coat of polish. Every counter and cabinet was dusted and clean. Except for a few missing antiques, an absent TV, and a few holes in the walls, each room looked perfectly normal. A rug covered the remaining tree stump.

Confused, shocked, she thumped down on the kitchen stool. She hadn't dreamed the destruction, hadn't imagined it, either. That meant…while she'd slept through the night, Tristan had cleared away the damage. She hadn't ordered him to do it. He'd simply taken it upon himself.

How…sweet.

She wanted to cry.

No one had ever treated her with such loving kindness, and knowing he cared enough to do this for her caused every cell in her body to swell with longing and tenderness.

He strolled past her, his fingertips brushing the hollow of her back. He wore only a pair of briefs. She shivered. His appeal never ceased to amaze and draw her; the strength of his body, the grace of his strides. The majesty of his gaze. Without a word from her, he began his morning ritual of making her coffee, which had not improved, yet she didn't have the heart to correct or stop him.

"I tried to tell you that I had already accomplished what you wished to do," he said, not sparing her a glance.

"No," she shook her head, "you said I needed to get back in bed."

He arched a brow. "Is that not the same?"

No, it wasn't. Once again she surveyed the length of the room. "What you did…you've left me speechless, Tristan, and I don't know what to say."

"Say that you will never again look so defeated, that you will trust me to take care of you."

"I do trust you," she said, and knew she meant every word. "More than I've ever trusted another person."

A smile teased the corners of his lips. "That pleases me."

"How did you manage this?" She swept her arms in a wide arch. "I never once heard you."

"My skills as a cleaner have been perfected over the years. Fresia, a woman I once served, forced me to scrub her home from top to bottom whenever I displeased her."

"How horrible," Julia muttered, more upset by the mention of another woman dictating his actions than by the work he'd been forced to do. *I'm a mess,* she thought.

"Horrible is an apt description," he replied. "Your office—"

She gasped. "My office! Please tell me you didn't clean my office." If he'd inadvertently thrown away her computer disks or account files... "I don't want to sound ungrateful, but—"

He cut her off before she could work up a good panic attack. "I left that chamber for you, as I did not know what belonged where."

"Thank you." The scent of coffee drifted to her nostrils, as relieving as his words. "For everything," she added. While he looked savage and untouchable on the outside, Julia saw the tender, kind man he truly was. No wonder she loved— Oh, God!

Love.

She'd entertained the possibility last night, yet it had seemed questionable under the influence of wine. There was no question in the light of day, however. She did. She loved him. The absoluteness of her feelings rang inside her like a carillon of bells, a culmination of joy and sadness, longing and bittersweet pain. She wanted to laugh and sob at the same time.

She loved him.

And she didn't know what to do about it.

If she told Tristan, he might pity her, or worse, nonchalantly dismiss her love as insignificant. After all, he placed no value on the emotion. And why should he? her mind added succinctly. Confusion. Self-doubt. Longing for the impossible. All three were components of love. Julia uttered a sigh. She'd always imagined the emotion as flowers and candy, smiles and happiness—not to mention marriage and babies.

She had two choices, she realized, closing her eyes. She could suppress her feelings for him and pretend nothing had changed, or she could give him all that she had to offer.

The answer sprang to life before she even finished her thought. Number two, thank you very much. He was everything she'd always wanted, and everything she'd thought she could never have. His smile brightened the worst of her days. She felt as if she'd waited for him her entire life. His generosity touched her heart. He made her tingle and sweat, made her crazy with desire.

Determined, she faced him. While she wouldn't tell him of her love and scare him away, she wanted to show him how she felt. Simply saying, "Hey, you. I want to get it on," wasn't appropriate, though.

So how did she gain his attention? Suddenly, she couldn't recall a single thing he'd taught her. Should she trace her fingertips over the hard ridges of his abdomen?

Roll his beaded nipples under her palms? Moisture pooled between her legs, hot and demanding. Her hands ached to touch him, had to touch him.

"You know, Julia, I have been thinking," he said, just as she was reaching out. She dropped her arm to her side. At the counter, he shifted his weight, his forearms resting on either side of her. "Since Puny Peter is no longer a part of your life, we must make a list of requirements for your new man."

She felt…shock? Anger? Hurt? Yes, all of those things. She wanted to make love with him, and he wanted to help her pick another man to seduce. Maybe she had misunderstood. "You want to help me pick *another* man to seduce?"

"Aye," he answered without hesitation.

What about last night? What about the wonderful things you said to me, did for me? Her heart drummed a painful, hollow beat in her chest. She heard each thump, an echo of her stupidity and pain.

"I don't have time to make a list," she bit out, not sure how else to respond. "I have to clean my office and see what's salvageable." She tried to push to her feet, but he held her in place with a glare.

"Your office can wait until later. As this is to be a lesson, I am in charge. What I say, you do with no arguments, and I say we will stay here and make a list."

"All right, fine," she snapped, choking back tears.

"I have taken the liberty of securing ink and paper."

"Of course you have." Her words floated across the distance, shrouded with feigned enthusiasm. She gripped the offered pen and pages and dropped them in front of her. "I'm ready when you are."

"I have given this much thought," he said, "and I believe requirement number one should be handsome."

Since Julia wasn't in the mood to play along, she muttered, "No. I'm putting 'not too ugly.'"

Tristan made a sound in the back of his throat that sounded suspiciously like choking. "This is a list of desires, if you will recall."

"I know. But in today's society a woman can't be too picky." *Especially me.*

He frowned, but continued on. "How do you feel about a man who appeals to your senses? Taste. Touch. Smell."

She shook her head, writing instead, "If he doesn't stink, I'll take him."

Tristan's expression deepened. "Is it important that your man give you jewels and furs?"

"Money doesn't matter." Which was true. She made enough money to support herself.

For some reason, her words made him smile. "Most women melt when a man hears beyond her words to what she truly desires. How feel you about this?"

Julia nibbled on the end of the pen as she pretended to think it over. "I'll settle for someone who doesn't fall asleep while I'm talking."

That wiped the grin off his face. In fact, he gritted his teeth. "What about witty? A man who can make you laugh is like a rare gem."

"Witty is too high a standard. I'd like a man who has

mastered the craft of laughing when I tell a joke, even when he didn't hear me in the first place."

"You need someone who is strong, a man well able to protect you."

"If he can rearrange my furniture, he's perfect."

"Do you want a man who shares your interests?"

"I'll settle for a man who doesn't drink straight from the milk carton."

Tristan began pacing, a dark storm cloud hovering over his shoulders. His hands were locked behind his back, his gait stiff. Uttering a frustrated sigh, he shoved a hand through his hair. Stray locks tumbled across his forehead. "Some men offer thoughtful surprises. Does this please you?"

"Oh, yes. Remembering to put the toilet seat down is a must."

He growled. "You should demand more for yourself, Julia. You are a beautiful, fascinating woman. Many men find you desirable."

"Fine. You want honesty? Here it is. I want a man who cares for me. Who will, well, who will make my body ache and my senses reel. Who wants me as much as I want him."

Frozen in place, Tristan fixed her with a hot stare. "That is truly what you desire?"

"Yeah." She glared up at him. "You got a problem with that?"

"A problem? Nay. Not when *I* meet your requirements."

"Wh-what?"

He ticked off his attributes. "I am not too ugly. I do

not smell foul. Have I ever fallen asleep while you were talking?"

"No," she answered, still shocked from his announcement.

"I am strong enough to move your furniture. I care for you. And I have pleased you with my touch. Many times. I am perfect for you." He smiled, slowly, seductively, sending a current of desire throughout her entire body. "So now you will entice *me.*"

He still wants me, was her first thought.

Why am I still sitting here? was her second.

Joy wrapped around her like a silken cocoon. His hungry gaze washed over her. Her hungry gaze washed over him. They were both mentally stripping away the other's clothing, piece by unwanted piece, and they both knew the other was doing it.

At last recalling the techniques he had taught her, she batted her lashes at him. "Maybe I'm waiting to see if you do, in fact, meet *all* of my requirements. Can you make me ache?"

Diabolical and wicked, his eyes gleamed with delight, making the irises glow like crystal fire. "We will just have to see, will we not?" With that, he simply walked away.

CHAPTER TWENTY-ONE

Worship Your Master's Body

DUMBFOUNDED, Julia stared after his retreating back. He'd vowed to seduce her yet had left her here alone. She didn't understand. Was she supposed to get started without him?

Before she could work up a good panic, Tristan reappeared.

"Come here, Julia," he said, and somehow managed to put all sorts of nuances into those words—as if he could lure her to bed with only his voice.

He was right.

In a trance, she went to him, craving the essence of his touch. Wanting the culmination of his passion.

"Fear nothing I do," he said, moving behind her.

A wave of uncertainty drifted through her at such ominous words, but she nodded.

He wrapped a blindfold over her eyes. Darkness engulfed her. He tied the strings, careful not to tug her hair. Nervousness soon mingled with her desire, making her tremble.

"What are you doing?" she asked softly.

"Do you still trust me?"

"Yes." Without a doubt.

"Then no questions."

"No questions." Julia drew in a deep breath, trying to break past the darkness. Only when she completely relaxed did she hear the deluge of rain splashing hypnotically outside. She smelled Tristan's masculine scent a bit stronger. Felt his heat a bit deeper.

"Repeat after me," he said. Ah, his voice was like rich brandy and smoky cigars, and so intoxicating she was drunk with arousal. "I am beautiful."

"I am beautiful."

"I am worthy."

"I am worthy."

"I am precious."

"I am precious," she whispered.

His praise, and her own avowal to the affirmative, seeped into her consciousness, and for the first time in her life, she believed them. She *was* beautiful. She *was* worthy. She *was* precious. Brian hadn't been worthy of *her.*

"Do you know what you do to me?" he breathed in her ear, then placed a lingering kiss on the back of her neck and she absorbed the warmth of him. "How you make me burn? If you do not, you soon will, for I plan to make you melt wherever I touch you. My fingers will be hot. They will scorch your skin as they explore every curve, every hollow…every luscious inch."

The ardor of his promise mesmerized her, cast a spell of love and lust around the parameters of her mind. *This* was what she'd dreamed about all those many years she'd spent alone at night, hoping, wanting.

"Once we come together, sweet dragon, you'll only want more," he vowed. "So much more."

Small, delicious tremors rocked her.

But he wasn't finished.

Reaching around her, he palmed one of her breasts through the fabric of her shirt, feather soft. "I'll touch you here." His other hand slid down her stomach, stopping only when he reached the apex of her thighs, not truly connecting, yet she still felt the heat of him. "I'll touch you here, as well. And everywhere in between."

His breath stroked her neck, so silky, so arousing. Intense currents of passion sailed through her blood, consuming every crevice of her body. He untied the drawstring of her pants, and the thick material floated to her ankles. Every insecurity she'd ever harbored slid away, as well, and she was surprised that she didn't want to cover herself. No, she wanted to take off more clothing.

He helped her step out of the pants. The air surrounding her was cool, but she felt hot. So hot. When she steadied, he dipped his fingers inside her panties, moving lower, lower still, until his hand rested over her curls.

She gasped. The contact was so intimate, so new. With gentle motions, he stroked the silky hair, soft, hard, soft. Her hips rocked slightly with his touch, urging him to go deeper.

"Do you want me to take you over the edge?" he asked.

Even whispering, he possessed the most sensual

voice; a deep, rich baritone that wrapped around her as surely as the blindfold over her eyes. Every time he spoke, his breath fanned her ear, sending images of tangled sheets and hot, sweaty skin through her mind.

"Yes," she answered breathlessly. "Only if you come with me."

His fingers finally brushed her clitoris. She gasped. Her other senses remained heightened, acutely sensitive. Tristan's rough, callused skin sent shivers of delight all the way to her toes as he stroked her.

He paused.

She waited eagerly, suspended in a time and place where only she and Tristan existed.

Then…his fingers began tormenting her again, still stroking, moving up and down the damp folds of flesh. Almost. Almost where she needed him most. A low, needy moan slipped past her lips. Nothing could have prepared her for this sensual onslaught to her senses, this consuming quest for pleasure. Nothing.

Again he paused.

Again she waited, growing desperate for more.

"Have you ever made love in a chair, Julia?"

Slowly she shook her head. "I've never made love to anyone. Anywhere." Her voice was hoarse with longing.

"I am glad," he said, kissing her neck again. His grip tightened as he spoke. "Your legs hook over the arms, opening the core of you. Then you take me inside so deeply you scream. And scream again. Over and over."

Fantasies of her and Tristan in a chair, doing exactly

what he described, besieged her, causing her throat to constrict. *I have to have him in a chair.*

"Tell me that you want me, little dragon. Say the words."

"I want you," she whispered. She wanted to kiss and lick his scars, to make them better and help him heal. She wanted to run her tongue over each of his tattoos and hear him gasp. "I want to make love with you so many times I'm not sure where my body ends and yours begins."

Tristan whipped her around then. "Give me your mouth." His tone was now raw, primal. He didn't give her time to reply. His head swooped down, and his mouth ravaged hers. Welcoming his strength, his hardness, she met his tongue thrust for thrust, her hands kneading his back.

Always and forever, she thought.

"Always," he said, as if he'd heard her unspoken vow. He clutched her to him, his pulse drumming with a riot of sensation. With Julia in his arms, his past couldn't affect him. He wouldn't worry about another woman trying to steal him. He only cared about this moment. The feel of Julia's skin skipped along his nerve endings, intense and consuming. The scent of her drove him to the brink of wildness. He wanted this woman to the exclusion of all else.

"Let me touch *you,*" she said on a wispy catch of breath.

He knew what such boldness cost her, and he would have given her the world just then had she asked. "Let you? Nay, Julia." He licked the seam of her lips. "I *need* you to touch me."

He guided her hand down the planes of his chest, his navel, and together they plunged past his underwear. He helped her wrap her palm around the ridged length of his arousal, showed her the way of it. A quick study, his Julia, she soon stroked up, down, up with exquisite accuracy.

"Yes, dragon," he praised, then groaned. "Just like that."

Holding him in her hands gave Julia a sense of feminine power that she could only revel in. Here was a man, a master of sensuality, who responded to her as if he could never get enough.

A heady thought, indeed.

In the next heartbeat, he lifted her shirt over her arms, baring her naked breasts for his view. Cool air kissed her heated skin, causing her nipples to pucker, ache.

She heard Tristan hiss in a breath, and he said, "You are the most ethereal creature I have ever beheld."

"No, I—" she began out of habit, then stopped herself.

He rimmed the outer edge of her nipple with his tongue and his finger traced her navel. The rest of her words died a quick death. Julia's body went up in flames. Needy for more, she arched her back, giving him better access. Tristan sucked the hardened peak into the hot wetness of his mouth. His hand trailed down her stomach. She quivered.

At last Tristan removed her final garment: her panties. Julia groaned, not in discomfort or embarrassment, which still surprised her, but in longing. Right now, this man belonged to her. Only her. To others he might be a pleasure slave. But to her he was simply Tristan, a sensual man who branded her body as surely as he'd branded her heart.

He placed drugging kisses across her neck and collarbone, and the hair on his chest tickled her skin. For only a second, he pulled back and she heard a delicate rush of air as he removed his underwear. Then one of his arms anchored under her knees. The other braced her lower back. When he lifted her into his embrace, her world tilted and it felt as if she were floating on a cloud of air. She clasped her arms around his neck for support.

Tristan stilled for a moment, drinking in the sight of the woman who had consumed his thoughts since the moment he first saw her. She captivated him, took him to new levels of sensuality, and he had to command himself to slow down before things ended too quickly. This was Julia's first time and, by Elliea, she would enjoy every hour of it.

Her breasts were full and lush, made for a man's touch. *His touch.* Rosy peaks crowned her nipples, ready and waiting. Beckoning. Her legs were not long, but they climbed all the way to heaven. Soon they would wrap around his waist, squeezing and pulling him tightly into her sheath.

So powerful was that thought, he nearly sagged to his knees.

Hunger drove him to the living room as fast as his feet could manage. A roll of thunder exploded, following a burst of lightning. He never even paused as he carried Julia to a soft, padded reclining chair. He eased

down and adjusted her on his lap until her legs straddled his thighs and her knees rested on the chair's arms.

He couldn't stop kissing her. He wanted to consume
every inch of her. His hands slowly moved downward,
skimming the soft curve of her stomach. Then he
reached around to caress the silky curve of her bottom.
Her indrawn breath told him just how much she liked it.

Quickly losing his fragile hold on sanity, he once
again explored her wet, feminine center, taunting her
with fleeting caresses. She uttered a low, throaty moan.
Her hips followed his touch, seeking whatever he would
give her. He watched her face, watched the way her lips
parted so uninhibitedly. The way she arched her back,
silently demanding more.

"That's it, little dragon. Move for me."

"Tristan…" she began, only to draw in a breath when
he laved his tongue over a waiting nipple. She was open
for him, both mouth and body. This woman affected him
as no other. Hearing his name on her lips was so more
intense than actually making love with another. Julia
somehow made him feel complete, whole, as if he'd
been born merely to know her.

She moaned again as his naked skin rubbed hers,
electric, consuming, intensifying the ache his fingers
caused. Soon she was writhing, searching for release
from the intense sensations all but bursting within her.

"I'm almost there," she said. Everything inside her
was coiling and poised for release. She was so close to
the edge, so unbelievably close. "Don't stop." Her
breath came in short, erratic pants. "Everywhere you

touch, heat ripples under my skin. I want you to never stop touching me. Promise?"

"With my entire being." He groaned deep in his throat, the vibration touching her all the way to her toes.

He pressed just a bit harder, but it was enough. Her inner muscles tightened; fierce pleasure erupted with the force of an avalanche. "Oh, my God, oh, my God, oh, my God!"

While her orgasm still hummed with life, he buried two fingers deep within her, stretching the walls of her femininity and making her ready for his invasion. His other hand gripped one side of her hips, pulling her up, helping her imitate the rhythm of sex. Once. Twice. He pushed his fingers deeper. Over and over pulling back, sinking in. Her need for him amazed her. Not just his touch, but *him.* His voice, his smile, his happiness.

Having deprived her body fulfillment for so long, it now demanded compensation. *I need more,* she thought. She craved all of him; she wanted him to experience release with her this time.

"By Elliea, Julia, I have never felt anything so hot," he praised. "So cursed good, so tight."

The tips of his fingers grew bolder, pushed deeper, teasing and taunting. Sensation eclipsed time. Fiery pleasure grew within her, the embers all but inextinguishable. Each movement she made served only one purpose. To gain deliverance from the sweet torment he continually inflicted.

"Come inside me, Tristan. I need you."

He removed his fingers and stared up at her face. "I want to taste you first."

Taste you first. It took a moment for Julia's passion-glazed mind to register what it was he actually wanted to do. When comprehension dawned, her sensual haze rescinded. She tore off the blindfold and tossed the black material to the floor. Panicked, she leaned back and drew her knees together.

"No." She quickly shook her head. "I can't let you do that." The thought, though sensuous in the image it evoked, caused her all kinds of worry.

"Aye." Tristan saw the wariness etching Julia's expression, and it doused the fire within him to a low-burning ember. His arms wrapped around her waist to keep her from bolting. "Let me taste you," he said. "Let me give you pleasure by using my tongue."

Incapable of speech, she shook her head. Her legs locked together even tighter. If she moved a fraction of an inch, he noticed, her closed knees would ram into his swollen flesh.

He gently cupped her chin in his hands and tilted. "Julia?"

She didn't answer, didn't relax.

"I asked you before if you trusted me," he said huskily. "Do you recall your answer?"

Somehow she managed a small nod. The very thought of him doing as he wanted sent shards of wicked desire pulsing between her legs. But...could she allow him access to her most private place? To look? Taste?

He slid his hands between her clasped legs, softly gripping her knees and pushing them apart. Then, hoping the familiar sensations might ease her, he urged two fingers inside of her again. He felt the wetness that pooled there and almost came. It required every ounce of self-preservation he possessed to submerge his intense hunger.

"I'll never hurt you, little dragon. Let me. Let me take you inside my mouth."

"But what if you don't like it?" she asked, finally voicing her fear.

"I will like it," he said fiercely. "This I vow."

The rich persuasiveness of his tone relaxed her, persuaded her to enter into the unknown, the feared. Bit by bit, she loosened the muscles in her thighs, giving him the access he craved.

"If you're sure," she said softly.

Her voice sounded drugged, breathless with passion, honey rich with uncertainty. He moved down, cupping her bottom with his hand and lifting her until her knees were braced atop the arms of the chair, her hands anchored to the top edge. His breath tickled the pink folds a second before she felt the heat of his tongue. He licked, caressed, moved against her, creating a dizzying friction. Her bones liquefied, her nerves sizzled, and at that moment, Julia knew she would never feel such exquisite agony again. Her ragged moans filled the room, mingling with the rumbles of thunder.

Her head thrashed from side to side, causing her hair to stream wildly down her back, and even that served as a stimulant. The silky tendrils caressed her heated skin, tickling, brushing.

Tristan pulled away.

"Noooo." Her thighs tightened, trying to lock him in place and hold him to her until he fulfilled the need pulsing so steadily through her blood.

"Like it, do you?" He uttered a hoarse chuckle, but the sound soon became a moan. "I do, as well, little dragon." Once more his tongue stroked, probed. "Never have I tasted anything so sweet," he whispered against the dewy flesh. "So perfect."

Trembling, she arched into him. "Mmm…" Speech was impossible.

So…much…pleasure…. Everything inside of her burst. Flashing lights. Twitching muscles. This orgasm rocked her to the core, stronger even than the last. Unable to temper the effects of this powerful onslaught, she screamed his name.

"You're killing me," she breathed.

He'd never felt this savage, this…hot. "I need you, Julia," he said.

"Yes. Yes."

"You are so small. Are you prepared?"

"Do it, Tristan. Do it now."

He lowered her, barely able to restrain his desperation, and placed her knees beside his thighs. With a roar, he surged up, burying his swollen flesh inside her and breaking the barrier of her innocence. She stiffened for only a moment, then fused completely against him. For an eternity, he remained unmoving, allowing her body time to accept his invasion.

For a moment, he felt her, not just her body, but her emotions, all the way to her soul. He felt her hunger, her awe. Her need. They were one being, two halves that made a whole.

"Are you unharmed?" he asked, sweat beading his brow.

"I am the way I was meant to be. A part of you."

His lips thinned with his strain to hold back. "Can you take more?"

"I'll take everything you have to give."

He pushed a bit deeper. She arched. Then he slipped all the way to the hilt. She gasped.

Perfection, he thought.

He began to move deep, deeper, lifting her up, pulling her down, just as he had with his fingers. Little by little, his rhythm began to quicken. Faster. Faster, still. He took her hungrily, almost brutally, pounding into her the way he'd dreamed these many nights. He could not control his reaction to her; he wanted her too desperately. She stripped him to his baser self, consumed him. A moan escaped his throat when she rotated her hips, taking him at a different angle.

"Do that again," he praised.

"Like that?" She did it again.

He nipped her bottom lip with his teeth. "Just like that."

Julia grinned wickedly, then quickly lost her smile on a pleasured moan. The width of his penis stretched her, but the feeling of completeness he evoked far surpassed any discomfort. He was a part of her now, deep and solid, his body one with hers, and the knowledge was more drugging than the most potent medicine. She'd dreamed of this moment, dreamed of being with him, but her imaginings had paled in comparison to reality.

His hand reached down between them, found her clitoris and pressed against it. With the mastery of his fingers, he made her forget any lingering discomfort.

"Tell me how you feel," he commanded hoarsely. "Tell me when you like what I do."

He slipped in and out of her, increasing in speed, increasing in urgency, even as he continued the onslaught with his fingertips.

"I like...I like..." Her lower body moved with him, then against him, rising when he retreated, only to lower again when he surged forward. She couldn't think, could only push toward more satisfaction. By God, she would never deny herself this pleasure again.

"Tell me," he breathed. Faster and faster he increased his rhythm. "Do you like this?"

She opened her mouth to explain she'd reached the depths of heaven, but a moan tore from deep within her as she reached another climax. Molten sensations sent her spinning, spinning, faster, faster.

Feeling Julia's inner walls tighten around his swollen shaft sent Tristan propelling over the edge, as well. Gratification, wholly male and infinitely powerful, sent a bestial roar of satisfaction ripping out of his throat before he collapsed into the chair, taking Julia with him. They were both spent.

When he was able to drag in a mouthful of air, he whispered into the silky strands of her hair. "Well, my little dragon. I guess you liked it."

CHAPTER TWENTY-TWO

Once You Have Worshiped Your Master's Body,
Immediately Do So Again

THE EVENING SHADOWS STREAMED through the velvety curtains and sheers, hazy and erotic. The storm had passed, yet its dewy essence still encompassed the room. Only an hour ago, Tristan had carried Julia to bed, where lace draped the entire length of the mattress and held them in a private haven. He had sparked the hearth's fire, and it now blazed with glowing embers, emitting lulling crackles every so often.

I will protect what is mine, he thought fiercely.

By fair means or foul, he would not allow Zirra, or any woman for that matter, to steal his box. Nor would he allow Julia to be hurt by such attempts. Nay, he would not. Death would come first—theirs.

I will protect what is mine, he thought again. Zirra had already proved she couldn't call him back permanently. And her powers had not been strong enough to do any real damage to Julia, only her belongings. Still...

Realizing his muscles were tensing and readying for

battle, he forced himself to relax. He turned onto his side and curled his arm around Julia's bare hip, fitting himself against her warm, sleeping form. He breathed in the lushness of her fragrance, and his eyes closed in surrender. His lips lifted in a half smile. He had kept his dragon busy for hours, introducing her to the many ways to make love. Beside him, astride him, standing. He had never enjoyed himself more.

With his other *guan rens*, he had reached sexual release, aye, but he had remained unsated. Always unsated, as if something were missing inside of him. With Julia, he had reached the pinnacle of contentment. She made him feel free, gave him glimmers of absolution. Did she still consider herself unworthy? He had pleasured so many women, but until now he had never before held such potent sensuality in his hands. No woman had ever responded to him so completely, all inhibitions forgotten. Before Julia, sex had become a monotonous game he had tired of playing. With her, he found utter contentment.

He was not worthy of Julia.

As jaded as he was in matters of the flesh, this experience with Julia felt more real, fresher, than even his first time all those centuries ago. His fingertips traced silky patterns over her hip, then dipped lower to her bottom. The fact that he was Julia's first, her only, filled him with a possessive pride he could not explain.

But I will not love her, he added darkly. He would not allow his pleasure slave spell to be broken, for he did not want to return to Imperia alone. Quite simply, he refused to lose this woman he held. He uttered a sardonic chuckle. How ironic that he preferred to face an eternity of enslavement simply to be with this woman awhile longer, a small flash of time.

"Mine," he muttered, tightening his hold on Julia.

LIKE THE HOWL OF A BANSHEE, the doorbell sounded.

Julia cracked open her eyelids and glanced at her bedside clock. Twelve thirty-four. Lunchtime. She was too content to eat. Or even move, for that matter. But the doorbell sounded again and she stretched, hoping to work the kinks from her naked limbs. Wincing at her soreness, she pushed out a breath and smoothed her hair from her cheeks.

At her side, Tristan stirred, instantly claiming her attention. A soft smile softened her lips. Inky locks of hair lay in disarray, framing his face. The length of his lashes cast shadows onto his cheeks, and a pink silk sheet draped the lower half of his bronzed body. And yet, he'd never looked more masculine.

With a drowsy, contented sigh, she kissed his jaw, always so smooth and devoid of stubble. He was so much more than she'd ever expected for herself, but she was finding that nothing less would satisfy her. For the rest of her life, every man she came into contact with would be judged against Tristan. No one could meet his standard.

I made love to this man, she thought, awed, drawing in his scent that still clung to her skin. *Several times.* Peace fluttered inside her, a feeling she'd thought she possessed before—a sort of satisfaction with her life, an acceptance. She'd deceived herself, convinced herself that her life was fine the way it was. Now she knew the truth. True satisfaction was only found in Tristan's arms. With him, she felt alive, whole. Desired.

And Zirra might attempt to summon him back at any moment.

Julia's smile faded. How could she protect him from a woman she couldn't see? From a woman who resided in another time, another world? She just didn't know. All she could do was keep his box hidden and hold on to him as tightly as she could.

Another round of bells chimed.

"If that is Puny Peter," Tristan said, his voice sleep rough as he rubbed a hand along his jaw, "I will have to kill him. Slowly and painfully."

"Not if I kill him first," she muttered. Already her breasts were tingling, aching for Tristan's touch as she considered all the ways she could "hold on to him." He'd trained her body well, and now she was addicted to his loving, in every position, gentle or rough.

A pounding of fists accompanied the bell this time.

"Whoever it is, isn't going away," Julia said morosely. "Is my box still secure?"

"Yes. I haven't moved it."

Tristan eased to a sitting position and tossed the sheet to the floor with a whoosh. "Stay here," he said, giving her a lingering, wistful once-over. "I will neutralize this enemy." He shoved to his feet and stalked to the bedroom door.

"Tristan," Julia called, still lounging atop the mattress, not caring that her body was completely bared to his view. No, she felt powerful and well loved.

Without hesitation, he spun around. He gave her another thorough inspection, and need swirled inside his eyes, making the lavender glow like two supernatural orbs. "Aye."

"Get dressed before you open the door, okay?"

He gave her a melting grin. "For you, anything." Turning again, he strode from the room. With every step he took, she watched his tight, bare ass. Her mouth watered.

Smiling softly, Julia hopped up and gathered her clothing, then haphazardly tugged them on. *I am a well-pleasured woman.* She wanted to sing and shout with the joy of it. When she was completely covered in wrinkled jeans and a T-shirt, she padded barefoot to the front door. Voices, both male and female, filled her ears before she actually reached them.

Tristan, she noticed, was clad only in a pair of gray sweats, but at least his most important features were covered. His hands were clasped behind his back and his feet were braced apart. He had assumed a battle position.

"Let me in," the woman demanded.

"Nay," Tristan growled, his tone so sharp it could have cut glass.

Recognizing the woman's voice, Julia rolled her eyes. "Faithie," she said, inserting herself at Tristan's side. "Is something wrong?"

"Yes, there's something wrong," her sister said, her eyes narrowed. "The barbarian here won't let me in."

Tristan flashed Julia a sheepish glance. "I am not

finished with you yet, little dragon, and do not wish an audience."

She rolled her eyes again—though she wanted to sink into his arms—and stepped around him to clasp her sister's hand. "Come inside. I'll put on a pot of coffee."

They strolled around a grumpy-faced Tristan and headed for the kitchen. Tristan followed, close at their heels. Within minutes, Julia had the coffee brewing and a deep, rich cinnamon-mocha aroma floated through the air.

"What happened to your house?" Faith asked. "There are holes in the wall."

"I'm redecorating." She didn't elaborate.

Claiming the burgundy-topped stool beside her sister, Julia glanced at Tristan, who reclined at the table and had his arms crossed over his chest. He was watching her with heat in his eyes. She turned and regarded Faith, who was watching them both with twinkling amusement.

"What?" Julia demanded of her.

"Nice hickey," her sister said.

"Oh. Oh," she said, fingering her neck. Then very primly, very properly, she added, "Thank you. I'm quite fond of it."

Faith's smile stretched from ear to ear. "I swear you're glowing," she said, a mischievous sparkle in her turquoise eyes. "So…what have you two been doing? Besides redecorating?"

"Just what you are thinking, I am sure," Tristan quipped.

Julia gave him and his sun-kissed chest a hungry—

not that she'd admit it—glare. All those muscles and that glorious skin were for her eyes only, and it didn't help that he bore four scratch marks below each of his nipples and a little hickey of his own beside his navel. "Aren't you cold without your shirt?"

"Nay." Half-grinning, he languidly stretched his arms over his head. "I am not. I suddenly feel hot."

Me, too, she longingly added, and took a mental step toward him.

"Lord save me from horny adults," Faith muttered, her voice heavy with wistfulness.

Julia was having trouble drawing her attention away from her lover. *I've got it bad,* she thought. *Real bad.* With regret and much effort, she schooled her features and faced her sister again. "I forgot to ask why you're here."

Faith hooked dark strands of hair behind her ears. "I came over to see how the rest of the date went, but no more words are needed, really."

Speaking of the date… "Did you finish all your *lab work?*" Julia asked, her brows bowed.

"Of course." Knowing she was caught, Faith studied her cuticles and gave a pouty little yawn. "Only finished up a few hours ago. Worked all through the night."

Tristan sighed. "If you are going to stay, Faith," he said, breaking into their conversation, "the least you can do is cook us some food."

"No way," Faith said.

"I'll cook." Julia filled three mugs with steaming coffee, then handed one to her sister, one to Tristan and saved the last for herself. Eyes closing in surrender, she took a tentative sip, found the temperature perfect, then drained the rest. "I know it's lunchtime, but I'm craving breakfast."

"Sounds wonderful," Faith and Tristan said in unison.

She peeked inside her fridge. "We have eggs and bacon, but no sausage."

"I can live with that," Faith said. "I'm starved."

"Me, as well."

Yet neither of them offered to help cook, she noticed. And that was probably a good thing. Faith didn't know how to boil water, and if Tristan's food was anything like his coffee… She shuddered.

Humming under her breath, she quickly fried the bacon, scrambled a dozen eggs, then browned and jellied several pieces of toast.

"That smells so good," Faith said, eyeing the mountain of food as her stomach rumbled.

"Yours is coming up next." Julia handed Tristan the plate. "If I don't serve Tristan first, he's likely to eat *me*." As soon as the words left her mouth, she froze. Gulped. Remembered. "Uh—I mean…"

"No need to correct yourself, Julia," he said huskily. His fingers brushed hers, sending stark awareness through every inch of her, and for a silent moment, they stared at each other, plate suspended midair.

When she was near, Tristan thought, he could only think of bed play. Right now, even though he had already loved her body thoroughly—several times—he wanted to fist her clothes in his hands and rip them away from her rosy curves.

"Later," she whispered as if she heard his thoughts.

"Not later. Now." He pinched the eggs between his fingers and brought them to his lips. As he chewed, he watched her. She watched him. And they both knew what the other was thinking. He gave her a wink, a sensuous sweep of his lashes and said, "You were right. I want to eat you, for I know these would taste so much better on you."

Her heart slammed erratically in her chest. *Oh, I'm a wanton woman.* "Sorry, Faithie," Julia said without sparing her sister a glance. "I'm going to have to ask you to leave."

SEVERAL GLORIOUS HOURS LATER, Tristan nestled Julia against his side, their skin sticky with strawberry jelly. "I'll never view breakfast foods quite the same way again," she murmured with a satisfied grin.

"Nor I." He smiled. Every moment with this woman offered a new experience. "For each meal I now consume will be compared to our buffet of carnality."

"We should probably take a shower." She swirled her fingertip in his belly button. "You've got jam everywhere."

"First…" Suddenly serious, he rolled her onto her back and pinned her beneath him, her hands imprisoned above her head. Palm to palm. Breasts to muscle. "I wish to ask you a question."

The change in position placed his growing erection right where he liked it most. Obviously, she felt the same. Heat flared in her eyes, and she uttered a sexy purr. "Ask me whatever you want."

"What are your feelings toward me?"

Bit by bit, the heat cooled in her expression. She stilled. Looked away. "I care about you." Her words were hesitant and heavily measured. "You know that."

"Aye. I know." But he'd wanted more from her. He could not give her a declaration of his own love, but he wanted one willingly from her lips. Mayhap 'twas selfish on his part. However, he had no control over his need for her love. He licked her collarbone. "I, too, care about you."

"I—thank you."

"Do you love me?"

"Do you love *me?*" she countered, refocusing on him.

He wanted to answer, but he decided to show her how he felt about her with his body instead. His fingers moved between her legs, circling the dew he found there. "You are perfection."

"So are you," she breathed.

He kissed her everywhere, leaving no hollow unexplored. He had her writhing, screaming, and when he finally entered her, they both moaned at the rightness of it. He took his time loving her body. Only after she peaked twice did he allow himself his own release. When his shudders subsided, he fell to his back and stared up at the ceiling, keeping her at his side.

"I—I want to thank you for all you have done for me."

Tenderness shining in her eyes, she caressed his cheek. "We've helped each other, Tristan."

"Aye, but I do not think you will ever know just what *you* have given me. A piece of my soul. My pride. My honor."

"You've given me confidence and adventure. You've shaken up my boring life and added vitality."

He paused. "But we cannot give each other marriage or children, can we?"

"No," she replied sadly. "But having you is enough."

Her words touched him all the way to his soul, and he captured her lips for a soft kiss. "Once, when I was a boy, I dreamed of such things. Of my wife holding me in her arms each night as she grew bigger with our child. Of my son learning the skills of a talon by my patient hand. Of my daughter smiling up at me, allowing me to kiss her hurts away."

"I wanted the same," she admitted. "A family, a place to belong."

"I wish I could give you those things, little dragon."

Julia closed her eyes against the joy and pain of his admission. Combined, the emotions cut deeper than any knife, yet lifted away the sting. "And I wish I could give them to you."

"What a pair we make, eh?" he said with a sigh.

Change the subject, change the subject, her mind chanted. Before she broke down and cried. "Tell me about the women on your planet. What are they like?"

He nuzzled her neck before he answered. "And if I refuse to tell you?"

"I'll give you a karate chop you'll never forget."

"Then I will tell you—" he slid his hands away, and she moaned from the loss "—after you give me a demonstration of this karate. My curiosity must be appeased."

"Very well, then." She crawled from the bed and pushed to her feet.

When she bent to grab her clothing, he tsked. "Ah-ah-ah, Julia. I am sure this karate is best demonstrated with no clothing to hinder the movements."

"You're sure, are you?"

"Aye." Expression mischievous, he propped himself up on the pillows. "Upon my honor."

"Well, since your honor is at stake." Gathering her courage, she stepped in front of the bed. He watched her as if he couldn't tear his eyes away, as if he didn't mind that she was, well, a tiny bit plump.

I am beautiful, she thought, recalling the mantra he'd taught her. Even naked and covered with strawberry jelly. Perhaps stick-thin women were considered malnourished and pathetic on his planet. She grinned at the thought.

"Are you ready for this?" she asked him.

"I have been ready since I first appeared to you." He crossed his hands behind his head. "You may begin now."

Lord, help me. Before she lost her nerve, she performed several moves she'd seen on TV. A high kick. A slash of her arms. She even pretended to chop a block of wood in half. He didn't laugh. No, when she finished, he growled, "Come do that to me."

And she did.

Later she found herself once again snuggled into his side. "I do believe you owe me a big, fat description of the women on your planet."

His deep, rich chuckle filled the room, but his merriment soon faded. An intrinsic sadness overtook him, a sadness for all he'd lost, perhaps, or for all he would never have. "Best you explain *exactly* what you wish to know, so I do not bore you with minute details."

"Are all the women as beautiful as Zirra?"

"Zirra is not beautiful. She is ugly. Evil. But nay, most of the women do not resemble her. They come in all different shapes and sizes, colors and temperaments."

"What about Imperia itself? You've spoken of the magic found there, but not about the way you're governed."

"There is a Great-Lord who reigns over the mortals, and a High Priest who reigns over the Druinn. Their word is absolute over their people. Then there are the Elite, the soldiers and the serving class. I served my Great-Lord gladly, for he was a wise and just man."

"So you were a soldier?"

"I was an Elite soldier."

"And did you, my Elite solider, fight many battles?"

"Aye. You see, at one time the mortals and the Druinn continually warred. Then the two rulers forged a bond of peace, the mortals vowing never to destroy the source of the Druinn powers, the Kyi-en-Tra Crystal, and the Druinn vowing never to hurt the mortals with their magic. Many of the people, both mortal and sorcerer, were against such an alliance, however. Each wanted his own race to rule the other. When I left, a rebellion was brewing."

"I wonder if it ever erupted and if so, who won," she said. "The rebels or the kings."

"The Druinn have many mystical powers, and the mortals outnumber them ten to one. Together, they could conquer anything, yet they were having trouble quashing this resistance."

"Did the rebels have some sort of magic weapon?"

"Nay, they were simply more determined than most. And the world was quickly losing its vitality. The continual war between races caused cities to wither and many people to die." Tristan shifted her more comfortably in his arms. "That which once thrived was quickly losing its resilience, weakening the classes and strengthening the rebels."

"I'm sorry."

He gently squeezed her hip. "Before my curse, I had been called by my Great-Lord to fight the Druinn rebels."

"So you were consorting with your enemy, weren't you, when you were with Zirra?"

"We were not enemies at the time. Remember, our kings had just become allies. And besides that, I had always considered a woman a woman."

"And therefore unable to hurt or overpower you, whatever her origins," Julia finished for him.

He nodded.

"Do you *want* to know what happened to Imperia once you left?"

"Aye. I do. Imperia is still my home."

Silence ensued.

Julia waited a moment, letting Tristan gather his thoughts, before she spoke again. "One day you might be given a chance to go back, without Zirra's help, and finish what your king called you to do."

"Nay," was all he said.

"Maybe we can find a way," she persisted, longing to visit Imperia again, on her own terms, to walk through the billowing white grass, to feel the scented breeze. To see Tristan in his natural environment and allow him to finish out his life's purpose. "Maybe if we found a way, I could go with you."

"Nay." Expression dark, muscles clenched, he shook his head. "I will never go back, Julia, for such is my curse. I will speak no more on this subject."

"Could you go back if the curse were broken?"

He hesitated but finally answered, albeit reluctantly, "Aye."

"Tristan—"

"Enough," he said.

He was choosing to remain away from his home because…why? Was he afraid of Zirra? Julia bit back a sigh. If he would only allow himself to love and open his heart to her, the curse *could* be broken and he would never have to deal with Zirra again. How easy. How simple. *Just love me,* she inwardly cried. In his stubbornness concerning matters of the heart, he was forfeiting a life he had obviously adored.

"Are you ready for your shower now?" she asked him, because she didn't know what else to say.

"Nay. I am ready for *our* shower."

CHAPTER TWENTY-THREE

You Own Nothing, Not Even Your Own Happiness

LATER, THEY FOUND themselves in the backyard, a cool breeze dancing around them and muted rays of light fighting for evening dominance. Tristan's box was still locked inside the planter, where it would stay, giving them both a sense of relief and relaxation. They laughed, played tag and rolled atop a damp red hill. Because of the storm, the ground was soft and wet, and streaked them both with mud and raindrops.

Tristan made a great production out of removing the mud and twigs from Julia's hair as she struggled to contain her laughter. Each time she smiled, his own lips would stretch, unbidden, into a grin. He did not recall a time in his life when he'd been happier or more carefree than he was at this moment. Like children they were, so lighthearted and vibrant.

When their bodies ached from their antics, they settled on "lounge chairs," as Julia called them. Lying there in the cold and holding each other to stay warm, he shared memories of his mother and of the trouble in which he, a precocious and mischievous little toddler, had always found himself. Julia shared her favorite memories with her sister.

"Before my parents split up," she said, "I once found Faith's diary, copied the pages and taped them all over the house. I'm still not sure if she's forgiven me."

"Cruel, cruel Julia," he teased.

"I had to do something to make her suffer." Almost absently, she picked at the ivory buttons on his coat. "My sister had sneaked into my room the night before and cut off all my hair."

His fingers tangled in the thick mass, angling her head up to face his flashing eyes. "Such a travesty deserved a harsh punishment. You did well."

He captured her lips with his own then, a hungry kiss that filled his soul and melted his bones.

WHEN ROMULIS APPEARED to Zirra again, he gripped a turquoise shard of the Kyi-en-Tra Crystal, the source of all their power. Smug secrets danced in the golden depths of his eyes as he angrily faced her.

"Think you Tristan is the only man who can meet your desires?" he growled.

"Aye," she answered, though a single doubt sprang to life inside her. She hastily tamped it down. "I do," she said with greater force, more for her own benefit than his.

He blinked, the action somehow highlighting the smugness in his eyes. "Even if I prove beyond a doubt that he hungers for another?"

Her stomach twisted at the thought, yet she had to know. "What have you found?"

"Watch," he commanded. "See."

He lifted the prism. With a few muttered words, multiple rays of color exploded toward the ceiling. Red, pink, blue, green, all brilliant and nearly blinding. They whirled together, colliding, mixing, and when they evaporated, she spied Tristan's image hovering in her air.

Zirra watched him and his *guan ren* play and laugh. Tristan tackled the woman to the ground, twisting in midair to take the brunt of the fall upon himself. The woman smiled up at Tristan. He returned the smile with one of his own, one filled with joy and affection. Then he kissed her hungrily.

Waves of emotion flooded Zirra, a sea of anger and fear, cresting with a relentless desperation so intense she wanted to shout *You belong with me*.

"I cast a spell to destroy that woman," she said through clenched teeth. "Why is she still alive?"

"Your magic was too weak to do much harm."

"But yours was not, and you helped me with the spell."

"Nay." He slowly shook his head. "I only helped you with your powers. I used none of my own."

Pure hatred filled her. For Romulis or the woman, she wasn't sure which. "Kill the woman for me, Romulis. Kill her."

Lethal fury smoldered in his gaze, and he watched her for a prolonged moment. "This is how you react? Do you not see these two are in love?"

"They are not in love, you fool," she spat. "Otherwise, his spell would be broken."

"Why can you not forget him?"

Her nails cut into her palm. "I will forget him when I am dead, and no sooner."

"Mayhap that can be arranged," he said quietly, deceptively, and strode from the chamber.

ZIRRA SPENT THE NEXT HOUR agonizing over exactly how to acquire Tristan. She wanted his box, and to get it, she must first destroy his *guan ren*. But how? How did she accomplish those things when her magic continued to fail her? When Romulis continued to refuse her?

The answer lay in Romulis. He could not refuse her for long, for he had given her his vow. He *must* help her.

Scowling, she prowled through the empty, silent hallways, a meadow of arching walkways, sea-scented air and cool, midnight-colored marble flooring, a direct contrast to the alabaster columns that stretched to the high, high ceilings.

Because she did not acknowledge the *lamori* gems, they ignored her, enveloping her in darkness. But then, she did not need light; she knew the way. Knew all the palace residents slumbered peacefully in their beds. Because of their magic, they assumed no one possessed enough courage to stalk their hallowed halls. That complacency might one day be their downfall, she thought disgustedly.

Finally she reached Romulis's private passage. She did not bother to announce her presence. She brushed past the wispy sheers and stormed inside. She stopped abruptly, her eyes widening. Her breath burned in her chest as she drank in the image Romulis presented.

He lounged in his bathwater, head reclined against the rim, dark hair in disarray about his shoulders. How utterly masculine he was. How beautiful.

When he saw her, he unabashedly eased to his feet. Her gaze traveled the length of him, all golden muscle and virile hardness. Rivulets of water trickled down the ridges of his abdomen, pooled in his navel, then caught in the dark curls surrounding his growing cock. He smelled of *elsment,* an aphrodisiac to their people, and she tried to hold her breath against his allure.

"What do you here?" he demanded with a calmness that belied the luminance in his eyes. He stepped from the opal tub and toward the bed where his robe draped the bottom ledge.

Before he reached it, she closed the distance between them and gripped his shoulder. He spun around and faced her. Without a word, she pushed him backward until his knees hit the edge of his bed. And he let her. Though he possessed the physical strength to stop her, he allowed her the final push. He fell, naked, splayed atop the silkiness of the black furs.

Her legs suddenly felt heavy, and she wanted to sink into him. She fought past the urge and glared down at him. "You promised to help me. I demand that you do so."

"My vow was not offered with a time constraint. I will aid you when I decide, not a moment before."

"Arr!" she screeched. "You are worse than your father, always trying to thwart me."

"Why must everything be about you?" Romulis crossed his arms under his head, his expression still relaxed, almost impassive. "What if I collect your debt to me now? What if I demand you forget Tristan and pleasure me?"

"Have you no pride?" she said, the words somehow foul in her mouth. "You would welcome my touch while I imagine you to be another man?"

His nostrils flared and his lips strained over the whiteness of his teeth. "Leave. Now. You are a greater fool than I, and I find I am tired of dealing with you."

She stormed from the room. If she could not go to Tristan this night, she would just have to find a way to remind him of her ownership.

CHAPTER TWENTY-FOUR

Never Ask Your Master For Anything

ON MONDAY, Julia opened up the shop one hour and ten minutes late, which wasn't bad in her estimation, considering she'd forgotten all about her business. Of course, she blamed Tristan for that. The man constantly consumed her mind, body and heart. In bed and out.

Perhaps some of her preoccupation with him stemmed from the fact that she'd almost lost him. That Zirra wanted him enough to hurtle him through galaxies and time, wanted him enough to destroy his *guan ren*'s possessions.

Perhaps the same worries lingered in Tristan's mind, because he remained at her side, his eyes always watching the store safe, where she'd locked his box. Neither of them had wanted to leave the house without it. He remained tense and guarded, as if he expected a monstrous alien to fly into her store and attack, which was exactly what she considered Zirra. A monstrous alien with a God complex who needed someone to knock her down a peg or two.

The image of doing just that flashed through her mind, and she smiled. And as she smiled, she recalled all the other reasons she had for smiling. First and most important being the fact that she had a lover! Her. Julia Anderson. She'd gotten laid. She'd had so many glorious orgasms and had given her lover numerous orgasms of his own.

Practically skipping, she went to the register, lifted the candy canister and selected several pieces—all of them chocolate. She deserved a treat for her fantastic performance this morning. The first one she ate teased and tantalized her taste buds, reminding her of Tristan. With her eyes closed in surrender, she ate the second, and then the third.

Moments later, she *felt* Tristan come up behind her.

"Stop moaning every time you eat those," he said fiercely, his warm breath tickling her ear.

Awareness rustled along her skin. Thankfully, they were alone in the store. "Or what?" She turned to face him, her expression daring him as she fought a rush of sensations between her legs. "You'll beat me?"

Gone was the intense guardian of the day. In his place was a man who only responded to the sensual. His heat bored into her, sending tingles of delight along her nerve endings.

"Aye," he said. "I will beat you most soundly."

The way he said those words made her long for whips and chains and anything else he might need to properly punish her. Where had this playful, flirty wanton come from? she wondered, amazed with herself. Plain, awkward Julia had finally become a tease!

He looked so beautiful, seething with sensuality, life and carnal intent.

Huskily she said, "Do you promise to make it hurt real good?"

He clasped a stray tendril of her hair between his fingers and smoothed it from her cheek. "Whatever happened to the shy maiden who tried to defend her honor with karate?"

"She took lessons from the master of seduction." Laughing throatily, she ran her hands up his chest. "It's too bad those lessons are completed."

"How dare you say such a thing," he replied with mock ire. "The lessons were never completed. There is so much more I must teach you."

"Oh, really?" Her teeth nibbled at her bottom lip just the way she knew he liked. She teased the waist of his jeans with her fingertips, then dipped lower and cupped him. "What else do you need to teach me?"

He hissed in a breath. "That there is a penalty for teasing your man. Later," he promised. "You are mine."

Oh, yes. She was his. And he was hers.

"Now, if we do not change the subject," he added, "I cannot be responsible for my actions."

Though it required all of her strength, Julia pulled away from him. Her store was no place for a seduction. Not during working hours, at least. With a sigh, she glanced at her wristwatch. "My landlord's son is supposed to fix the bathroom pipes today, and he's—big surprise—late. Since your knowledge is so *advanced*—" she almost choked on that one "—would you mind taking a look?"

"I do not mind," he said. He licked his lips with wicked intent. "That is to say, I do not mind…if you will agree to pay me for my services."

Still thrumming with excitement, she flicked her hair over one shoulder and acted nonchalant. "What kind of payment?"

"The lascivious kind, of course."

She tried to appear reluctant, she really did. "All right," she said, hoping her tone sounded less eager to him than it did to her. "But only because I'm desperate to have those pipes fixed."

"I will take great pleasure in the receiving of my payment."

As would she, she was sure. "Just out of curiosity, have you ever done any plumbing work?"

"Nay, but my knowledge is—"

"Sufficient. I know." She placed her hands on her hips. "I should supervise."

"Let us get to work." He pulled his T-shirt over his head, baring his body from the waist up. His deeply tanned muscles rippled with the movement.

Her mouth watered because she knew exactly how that skin tasted. She'd licked every inch of it only this morning, and she knew he tasted much better than chocolate. If only he weren't so handsome, so beguiling that even the air in her lungs burned for him. Lord, not even six hours ago, the very body she was now ogling had been pressed up against hers, doing wonderful things to her.

The man needed only to remove one item of clothing, and she was hot for him. No, the man needed only to look at her, and she was hot for him. Almost trembling with her desire, she followed him into the bathroom and watched him as he worked. She was struck again by the raw masculinity of his form, the panther-like grace with which he moved, even while doing manual labor.

But half an hour later, she was jerked from her sensual reverie when Tristan began shouting curses at the pipes. She gasped when she saw that he had cut his hand. Concerned, she rushed to his side. Blood seeped from the wound, running with constant force.

She had to bite back her fear as she grabbed his shirt from the floor and hurriedly wrapped the material around his hand. Soon crimson soaked through the white, and dripped to the floor.

"I need another bandage. This one is useless. Do you still keep a spare set of clothing in your office?"

"Yes. I'll just go get—"

"There is not time. I'm bleeding too badly. Remove your blouse and hand it to me," he demanded, his attention centered on his wound.

"Of course." Her concern for him increased. She tugged off her shirt and helped him rewrap his hand.

"Now give me your panties," he said.

This time she paused and blinked up at him. "What?"

He winced. A little too forcefully, perhaps?

"Give me your panties," he repeated.

She studied his features, and suspicions grew in her mind. "Let me see your hand."

"There is no time. I have need of your panties."

"What kind of need?"

"I am in pain, woman, and you dare question me?"

She didn't doubt he was in pain. It was the type of pain that was in question. There was a mischievous twinkle in his eyes, and she knew her thin, lacy thong would offer no protection for his injury. Still, willing to play along, Julia cast a quick glance around the corner to make sure no customers had entered. They were still alone.

Feeling daring and uninhibited, she removed her pink lace thong and gave the tiny scrap to Tristan. Cool air touched the heat of her, making her shiver. Delightful bumps popped up all over her skin.

"There," she said, trying to hide her growing excitement. "Happy now?"

"Nay. I need your skirt, as well."

Not wanting this to be too easy for him, she crossed her arms over her chest. "What for?"

"Come here and I will show you."

"No way. You only get paid when the pipes are fixed. And they aren't fixed."

"True, but this is just to inspire me."

Well, how could she argue with that? If the man needed inspiration… A fog of anticipation wrapped around her as she closed the distance between them. Grinning, he lifted her up and placed her atop the sink's edge.

"That is better," he said.

With slow, deliberate movements, he removed the

shirt from around his hand and tossed it to the ground. She stared down at his palm. As she watched, his wound was even then healing itself. The tissues were weaving together, interlacing and sealing. Soon there was no evidence he had ever been hurt.

Her jaw dropped. "How did you do that?"

"A function of the curse." He tugged her skirt from her body and dropped it with a whoosh. He held fast to her thong. "This is mine."

"Okay. But you have to give me something in return."

"Hmm, I like the customs of your world. What do you say I keep your panties and in return I give you your woman's pleasure twice?"

As if she needed to think about that! "Sounds like a good bargain to me."

Through the fabric of her bra, he circled his fingertips over her nipples. Just as it did every time he touched her, the heat of his skin seared her to the core. She gasped.

"I want you, Julia. Are you too sore?"

Yes, but need pulsed through her anyway. It was like melting, dissolving into hot flames. "I want you," she said, "and I'm willing to bet you can make me forget any discomfort I might feel."

"Such will be my personal mission." He placed drugging kisses along her breasts, making her bra moist, causing delicious friction, then he flicked each nipple with his tongue.

"Did you lock the front door?" she asked suddenly.

He shook his head and gave her a soft, sweet kiss that captured her breath. "Nay."

"Then don't make me scream, okay? I have to know if someone comes in."

"If I cannot make you scream, little dragon, I am not worthy to be your lover." With that, he slipped inside her. Five minutes later, she was moaning. Ten minutes later she was ordering him to move faster.

Fifteen minutes later she screamed over and over again, the sound echoing off the walls.

Neither heard the bell above the door chime.

CHAPTER TWENTY-FIVE

Protect Your Master With Your Own Life

"UH, EXCUSE ME," a deep, slightly accented male voice called. "Are you okay in there? I heard screaming. Should I call the cops?"

Julia glanced at Tristan, then down at their still-joined bodies. This wasn't happening, couldn't be happening.

But it was....

She'd just had a mind-shattering orgasm. Tristan had just had an earth-shattering orgasm. And there was someone in the shop's vestibule, wanting to know if everything was okay. Her cheeks erupted into flames. Here she stood, her clothes a few feet away, a half-naked man between her thighs, and the echo of her screams ringing in her ears.

Why, oh why, hadn't she locked the door and posted the Closed sign?

Just how long had the customer been there? What had he heard? Enough to want to call the cops, obviously.

Tristan, the jerk, seemed totally unconcerned with the thought of having an audience. Smiling, he pushed the bathroom door shut with his foot and continued to grip her hips in his hands.

"Hello?" the voice said again. "I'm dialing 911 right now."

"No!" Julia shouted. "I'm fine. Really. I'll, uh, be right there." She scrambled away from Tristan.

"Do you need any help?" the stranger asked.

"No, no. Stay where you are."

"Allow me to aid you, little dragon." Tristan picked up her skirt and helped her step inside.

"I need my panties, too," she whispered.

"Nay." Eyes darkening, he shook his head. "You gave them to me."

"Well, I'm taking them back."

"I will fight to the death to keep them."

Her teeth ground together. Without her underwear, cool air continued to kiss her exposed skin, a potent reminder of everything they'd done. How was she going to face this customer with that knowledge fresh in her mind?

She'd once thought having a boyfriend would solve all of her problems. Now she learned a boyfriend created a whole new set of complications she'd never imagined.

Tristan watched the play of emotions cross Julia's face. Embarrassment. Satisfaction. Aye, even excitement. Whether she protested or not, she was enjoying each new adventure tossed her way. And he liked that she liked them.

"Are you sure I can't help you?" the man said.

"I'm sure!" Julia cried.

Tristan's good humor quickly fled as he recalled this

man was alone inside the store and could even now be searching for the box. At the moment, Tristan suspected everyone, male and female, for a woman could easily pay a man to do her dirty work.

"You will wait here, Julia, while I interrogate this new arrival."

"No, Tristan, I—"

He stalked off before she could finish.

Her fingers moved lightning fast over her shirt, re-fastening the buttons. She grimaced when she saw the crimson spots of dried blood dotted across the center. Too late to do anything now. She refused to greet her customers in her bra. If he'd just come back for a moment, she could change into her spare outfit in the store-room. "Tristan," she called.

Tristan ignored her. In the center of the shop he spotted a tall fair-haired man. He was dressed in ripped, faded clothing that showcased a warrior's muscles. He also carried a red rectangular crate that held…weapons? Weapons to kill or to break inside the safe? Or mayhap both. Tristan's gaze scanned the item in question. It appeared fine. He searched the rest of the store. Three other people, two female, one male, were wandering around the shop, inspecting the merchandise.

Tristan finally settled his concentration on the muscled man with the red crate and cursed himself for placing Julia in danger. He should never have relaxed his guard. But, curse it, the woman was too tempting, too alluring for him to resist. When she had taken that candy into her mouth, her expression had looked the same as when she came. He had thought of nothing but bedding her from that moment on.

"What do you here?" he demanded of the man with the crate.

Before the man could answer, Julia shuffled around him. "Hello," she said, then stopped. "I'm, uh...well, I'm Julia. The owner." She took a deep breath and made a visible effort of gathering her wits. "How can I help you?"

Tristan lunged to grab her, to shove her safely behind him, but she easily sidestepped him.

"I'm here to fix your pipes," the man said.

His voice was oddly familiar, Julia thought. But it was his eyes...they were deep blue, bottomless, and as clear as ice chips. They struck a deep chord of familiarity within her. However, she'd never seen him before in her life. She would have remembered. He was gorgeous, almost too beautiful to be real, as if he were wearing some exquisitely detailed mask.

"I believe you're expecting me," he added.

"Oh, yes." She offered him a welcoming smile. "Morgan Schetfield, right?"

He paused a moment, then nodded. "That's right. I am Morgan Schetfield."

Tristan still did not relax his warrior stance. "I will need to see proof of your identity," he said, taking Julia by the shoulders and forcing her to his side.

Her frown flashed in his direction. "I'm sure that's not necessary."

"It is *very* necessary." He gave the man a pointed stare.

"Sure thing," Morgan said easily. He muttered something under his breath, then withdrew a thin card shaped much like Julia's American Express.

Tristan took it, studied it from every angle and handed the colorful, thin square to Julia. She glanced over the surface. "He's Morgan Schetfield, born December second, nineteen seventy-five. His license expires in exactly three months. Anything else you need to know, Tristan?" she asked dryly.

"That is sufficient." But he planned to watch both Julia and the man until he was assured of Julia's safety.

"The problem is in the back," Julia said. "If you'll follow me…"

Tristan followed. He almost smiled when her cheeks reddened as she entered the bath chamber. He did gloat. Both of her shoes were strewn haphazardly across the floor. She quickly stuffed her feet inside.

"What exactly is the problem?" Morgan asked.

Julia explained about the moaning pipes and unflushable toilet. "Think you can fix it?"

"I know I can." Morgan jumped into the work, chatting the entire time, inquiring amicably about Julia and her life, asking if she was happy and other such things that were none of his business.

It irritated Tristan that the man showed such interest in *his* woman. What irritated him more, however, was the fact that the man accomplished something he himself had been unable to do, making the plumber appear a hero in Julia's eyes. The cursed man fixed the pipes, just as he had claimed.

Even when his job was done, Morgan continued to

smile up at Julia, laughing and talking about people and places Tristan knew not. Tristan did not like it. He suppressed the urge to pound the plumber's face into the cracked tile floor. *Let us see how well the man smiles when his teeth are ground into powder.*

Contrary to her initial unease, Julia was perfectly content with Morgan; not the shy, nervous woman she had once described herself. She no longer seemed weighed down with self-doubts. She appeared confident. While he was proud of her inner growth, he did not like her ease with this other man.

By the time Morgan left, Tristan was seething with emotion. He was not jealous. Nay, he was furious. Julia was *his,* and he would not allow another man to poach on his territory.

Julia quickly eased him from his upset. When the last customer left, she wrapped her arms around his neck, drew him to her and whispered all the things she wanted to do to him. Only to him. By the time she uttered her last word, a sheen of sweat covered his entire body.

"Let us go home," he managed.

Her lips lifted in a slow smile, and she nodded.

CHAPTER TWENTY-SIX

Never Slacken From Your Duties

JULIA ZIPPED along the highway. She and Tristan were almost home, almost in bed. She patted her purse, sighing contentedly when she felt the comforting bulge of the jewelry box.

She glanced over at Tristan, and her relaxed mood vanished. His eyes were closed, and his skin was unusually pale. Sweat beaded on his brow. At the corners, his lips were tinged with blue.

"Tristan?" she said, alternating her attention between the road ahead of her and the man beside her.

He didn't respond.

Her stomach knotted with fear. "Tristan?" She yelled his name this time, and the sound echoed throughout the sedan. She punctuated the word with a shake of his thigh. "Tristan!"

TRISTAN WAS LOST in a world of darkness and light, one or both, he couldn't decide. He only knew his body burned, an inferno of flicking flames. He was trapped in some sort of prison, lying on the cold, hard ground.

Suddenly Zirra was straddled over his body, cruelly using him to gain her pleasure, yet denying him his own. He was almost glad he was to be denied release, for even while he prayed for it, he despised himself for giving her any part of him.

Nay, his mind shouted. *This isn't real. This isn't happening. Fight it.*

"Do you see how I control you?" she said huskily. "Do you see?"

"Aye."

"I know you like this. I know you like me. How can you not?"

His jaw locked mutinously.

"Say it," she demanded. "Tell me how you're glad of my domination."

"I am glad." The lie tripped from his lips by force because the spell dictated that he please her, and his admission would surely please her, though he tried desperately to hold back the words. Zirra did not deserve such an avowal, untruth or not. She deserved only words of hate.

"What a good little slave you are," she praised, raking her nails down his chest, not as a lover would, but as a master does to someone unworthy of tenderness. "Now tell me how much you love me."

"I love you," he growled, adding silently, *I loathe you.*

"Liar," she snarled, baring her teeth in a fierce scowl. "You are a liar. The spell would be broken if you spoke true. How dare you lie to me, to your master. You will be punished, doubt me not." She rode him hard, pounding against him with bruising intensity. When she came, she threw back her head and screamed. With rage and pleasure. Victory and glee.

He didn't want to come. He fought against it. He always fought against it, but in the end, his body betrayed him every time.

Zirra's spasms ceased soon after his own, and she glared down at him. "All I have ever given you is love, and yet you constantly throw that in my face." She pushed to her feet and drew on her robe. Her hair tumbled over her shoulder when she turned to glare down at him.

"Why are you still in bed, slave? Bow before me. You owe me thanks for the pleasure I just bestowed upon you."

He moved automatically, dying a bit more with every movement, and took his place before her.

Abruptly Tristan found himself chained to a wall. His surroundings were familiar. He'd been here before, he thought, confused. A progression of women paraded in front of him. Each female was allowed to touch, to taste, to do anything she desired as she strolled past him. The line seemed endless. He endured cruel pinches, eager tugs, stinging slaps, and by the end, his skin was a mass of purple and blue bruises. Even the battlefields of Gillirad had not wounded him so deeply.

"I am your master, your true lover," Zirra said when the last woman left the chamber. "Will you ever again glare at me?"

"Only if you command that I do not," he gritted out.

Her eyes flashed blue fire. "For that you shall spend the rest of the eve as you are."

Again the image shifted.

Colors swirled behind his eyes and blurred together, spinning and spinning, tugging him closer to another part of his life.

He found himself standing naked before a bed. Zirra reclined on the mattress, white pillows at her back. "Tristan, come over here, darling."

Without hesitation he obeyed. He crawled up the bed and hovered over her, staying on his knees as he knew she liked.

"I have need of you," she purred.

"Whatever you wish, you know I will perform."

Her features softened. "Tell me you want me."

"I want you."

"Tell me how beautiful I am."

"You are beautiful." He did not elaborate as she wished. She had to force his every move. He would give her nothing willingly, no more of himself than demanded, for that was the only control he had over himself.

"Love me," she breathed, placing kisses up his chest and neck.

He despised her every touch, wanted to race from this chamber and spew the contents of his stomach each time she glanced his way. "Love is the one thing I do not have to give you, Zirra. You know that. Your spell was for me to give pleasure to my *guan ren*. It said naught of love. That was your mistake, and that is what you must live with. For I will never offer you my heart." He took great delight in his next words. "You sicken me."

The nails that had softly scraped his back now sank into his flesh, causing droplets of blood to slide down his back. "Who owns you?"

"You do."

"Who governs your fate?"

"You do."

"Never forget that, Tristan, or I will make you suffer for it."

Tristan vaguely heard someone, a female, calling his name from a faraway place. It was a voice he felt compelled to answer. His mouth refused to work, however.

The voice continued to echo in his head. It was Julia, he realized, and she was afraid of something. She needed him. In a panic to reach her, he fought his way through the dark haze enveloping his mind. As he fought, he became aware that his body was soaked with sweat and he was trembling. He sucked in a deep breath.

What had just happened? He had been inside Julia's car, had been viewing the scenery of this planet he had come to admire. The red hills, the stone homes, the clean, crisp air. Then a dark presence had invaded his mind. He had been unable to stop from following the presence into his memories.

Aye, memories. That is what they were. But how had he relived them so vividly?

He already knew the answer.

Zirra. She was forcing him to remember. Since she

had failed to reclaim him, she now reminded him that she was out there, searching for a way. He bit back a curse.

"Tristan. Please, look at me."

Bit by bit, he cracked open his eyelids. Julia was crouched in the open car door, her lovely face above his. To his left, cars whizzed past the window.

"Are you allowed to park here?" he questioned hoarsely.

A sob burst from her throat, half laugh, half desperate cry. "That's all you have to say?"

"Aye."

"Well, the answer is yes. This is the side of the road. Now tell me what the hell is wrong with you."

"A dream. Only a dream," he forced out.

"No." She shook her head. "It was not just a dream. You were in some sort of trance."

"I am fine."

Though her expression remained unconvinced, she pushed out a shaky breath. "Are you sure?"

"I am fine," he repeated. "The past simply demanded consideration." His head fell against the seat rest, his energy quickly deserting. He felt himself sinking into sleep. "Take me home, Julia. Take me home."

WHEN THEY REACHED the house, Julia helped Tristan to the couch, locked his box inside the plant stand, then raced to the kitchen to get him a glass of water. He drained the liquid with one gulp and set the glass aside. He stretched out his long legs, and she snuggled up beside him, her arms holding him close.

She'd never witnessed anything like what she'd seen in the car. He'd been deathly still, barely breathing. He'd alternated between pale and fiery hot.

Thank God he'd awakened on his own.

Thank God.

She didn't know what she would have done if he hadn't.

Yet, as her eyes had met his, she'd almost wanted him to sink back into the trance—anything so that she wouldn't have to see the horror and pain on his face.

What had happened to him to cause such a look?

With her fingertips, she toyed with the fine hair on his arm. "Tristan?"

He didn't stir, didn't face her. "Hmm?"

"Tell me what happened. I want to help you."

Silence.

Silence so thick an oppressive fog descended all around them.

"Speaking about what happened to you might help ease the pain. I won't judge you, or laugh. I'll simply listen."

More silence.

And then he spoke.

"Zirra, the woman who entrapped me and kept me for several seasons," he began hesitantly. "She was a cruel mistress. She demanded my love and when I wouldn't give it to her, she punished me."

He continued on, telling her of all the *guan rens* who had emotionally scarred him with their cruelty. He described horrors such as she'd never imagined, terrors done to this strong, proud man whose only sin was his beauty. She listened to his every word, trying, hoping, to absorb some of his pain into herself.

"In the end," he said, "I lost my will to fight. I simply accepted what was done to me and expected it. My only control was the pleasure I could give and the way I responded."

"You are not a pleasure slave anymore," she said softly. "You are a man, Julia's man, and I am your woman."

"Julia—" he said, his tone laced with regret.

"No. Don't deny my words or tell me that you are what Zirra made you, that what we have can't last. I know differently."

"We can prevent the box from being stolen, but we cannot prevent time from passing. I will never age, never die. And you will, Julia. You will."

"What if—what if you loved me? The spell would be broken and you would be mortal. Just like me."

"Oh, that I could, sweet dragon. But I do not and I will not love you."

She fought back tears. "Why?" The word was broken, hoarse. "Am I so unlovable?"

"Nay," he said fiercely, taking her hands in his. "Never think such a thing. You are the most precious woman I have ever encountered. But if I love you, I will lose you. And I will *not* lose you."

Confusion mingled with dread, twisting inside her. "I don't understand."

"The magic will be broken and there will be nothing

to bind me to you or to this world. As I have no magic of my own, I would hurtle back to Imperia without you."

Another horror for him to endure, she thought then, fighting a wave of sorrow. Of all the things he'd had to endure, surely that would be the worst. Losing the one he loved. No wonder he refused to give his heart. Love and lose. He would be free, but alone.

Wasn't that better, though, than an eternity as a slave?

"You want to go home, Tristan. I know you do. You said the words yourself."

"Aye. I would like to once again walk the shores of my homeland, but I am content here with you. I would rather stay here with you, in fact."

She closed her eyes against an onslaught of stinging tears. He was willing to endure an eternity as a pleasure slave for a flash of time with her. She tightened her hold around him. This man loved her. He might not recognize or acknowledge the emotion, but he did.

What did I do to deserve him? The words filled her mind even as she accepted that she couldn't, wouldn't, keep him. To force him to endure a life of slavery…no. Not while there was a way to save him.

And there was.

Giving him up.

Oh, the knowledge ripped inside her, tearing apart her heart, body and mind. She'd have to live without him, because she was going to do whatever it took to grant him his freedom. Without him, she would suffer, she knew it, but it was because of her overwhelming love for him that she would endure, knowing he was free.

She would not let him sacrifice his own freedom for her. That, she could never do.

THAT NIGHT, Julia lay beside Tristan inside the confines of her bed. They were both naked. He didn't want clothes between them while they slept, and to be honest, neither did she. She toyed with a lock of his hair, running the midnight strands between her fingers.

I know what I have to do.

She was going to gain his admission of love. And he was going to disappear from her life forever. She trembled as her fingertips glided over his cheekbones, along his jaw. He didn't wake. The clamor of her heart echoed in the quiet of the room. "Tristan," she whispered. Even she heard the undercurrent of desire and determination in her voice, "Wake up. I need you."

Very slowly, he came drowsily awake, and she repeated her request. Before she could inhale another breath, he dragged her atop his chest. The juncture of her thighs rested against his growing erection. He cupped her bottom. "Tell me, sweet dragon, tell me exactly what you need."

"You. Only you."

"Then take me." His husky voice was deepened with his own need.

Inch by inch she moved down the length of his body, stopping at the object of her fascination. She took him into her mouth. He tasted of male and warmth, and she couldn't get enough. Over and over she moved her mouth up and down the length of his erection, over the head of his penis, then all the way to the base, savoring the thickness, the heat. She cupped his heavy sac in her hand.

"Julia," Tristan said hoarsely. "Julia."

"Yes?"

"Kiss me." He grabbed her underneath the shoulders and wrenched her up. He captured her lips then, and at the same time he thrust upward, entering her in one long, swift thrust. "I want to come inside your body, not your mouth."

"Later, then," she said. "I want to taste you."

Fierce and growling, he bit the hollow of her neck, then licked away the sting.

Breathless, Julia closed her eyes. She arched her back, sending him deeper inside. Softness met hardness in one glorious burst of sensation.

This is bliss, she thought, moving up and down his rigid length with the desperate pace he set. But she wanted to prolong this moment, to make it last forever. So when she rode the downward slide, she stopped. He groaned. Gradually she raised herself up. Down. Up. So slowly.

Tristan gripped her hips, urging her on. He was sweating. "This is the sweetest torture I have ever endured. But if I do not have you, all of you, I will die. I swear it."

"I love you," she whispered.

He ceased moving completely and just stared up at her.

She cupped his jaw in her hands. "I want you to love me, too. I'm not saying this as a command, but as a request for the truth. Will you admit that you love me?"

He rolled her to her back, pinning her against the softness of the silk sheets. His shoulders were taut, the lines of his face drawn.

"You know I will not love you."

"I don't believe that. I think you do, that you just haven't admitted it to yourself."

"Nay. Do you not understand, Julia? If I admit such a thing, I will lose you. Do you want to lose me?"

Horror that he would think so had her screaming, "No!" And too late did she realize that she should have lied, should have told him she was tired of him—something, *anything* to make him yearn to leave. "I *need* the words, Tristan. I need them."

Deep torment flashed in the depths of his eyes, and she glimpsed his inward struggle. "Tell me again that you love me," he said raggedly.

"I do," she said. "I love you so much. Never doubt that. Now tell me how you feel."

She waited for him to offer her the same avowal, but he merely slipped his hand between their bodies and pressed against the core of her desire. She gasped, in pleasure, in exquisite pain.

"You love me, but you are willing to lose me?"

She gulped back her pain, and didn't even try to deny what they both knew. "Yes. I am willing to lose you."

He studied her face. "Then perhaps, my little dragon, I will have to convince you otherwise." His voice was a husky ripple purring against her skin.

"What—what do you mean to do?" she asked.

He flexed and surged inside her at the same moment

his fingers circled her. "Oh…Tristan…" Her breath grew ragged as he moved within her again and again.

"That is right, Julia. Your body needs mine, will forever need mine. Can you feel yourself tighten around me? Can you feel how your body cries out for me?"

"Yes," she gasped. "Yes."

"Tell me you want me for the rest of your days. You know what your body is telling you, now listen to your heart."

Whimpering, she clutched the silk beneath her. "Do you love me, Tristan?"

He hesitated. A pain so great it was almost physical again lit his eyes, making his lavender irises swirl with the force of a storm. "Nay. I love you not." He plunged into her so deeply she felt his essence reverberate from head to toe. "However, I will be with you for the rest of your life. I am willing to do whatever is needed to convince you of that fact."

He was a man of his word.

CHAPTER TWENTY-SEVEN

Imperia

ROMULIS PACED the white sands of Druinn, the four suns heating his skin. Those warm rays in no way compared with his fury. "Bitch," he growled. "I do not need her."

"Need who?" one of the elders asked him. Several sorcerers stood along the sea's edge, some even hovered in the air, watching him with weary eyes. He refused to speak or acknowledge the question in any way. He continued to pace, the rage inside him growing, consuming him. He knew Zirra had been working on her own to regain her magic. She was so determined to have Tristan.

Zirra was destined to be his life-mate, and still she hungered for another. Always she hungered for Tristan. Mayhap she would for eternity. Yet *he* desired no other. Only her. Only Zirra. He wanted no other. Fury and pain and desperation vibrated together inside him, and he lashed out, growling again, "Bitch." The crystal sands scattered with the sharpness of his movements.

"I have never claimed differently."

The voice came from behind him. Romulis spun and

found himself glaring into Zirra's unrepentant face. Those traitorous suns' rays paid her nothing but tribute, caressing her cheeks, making her cerulean eyes sparkle. Even now, he craved her hands on his flesh, her screams of pleasure in his ears.

"Leave us," he told the sorcerers still brave or foolish enough to linger. The rustle of their footsteps echoed in his ears.

"What do you here?" he demanded.

Her chin rose haughtily. "I've come to tell you that I am holding you to your vow. You vowed to help me acquire Tristan, and I expect you to do so—permanently. Some of my powers have already returned but I still need yours."

His stomach twisted, the pain so sharp he nearly cried out. Just then something broke inside him. Mayhap it was his patience, mayhap it was his goodwill. Whatever it was, Zirra was meant to be his, his lifemate, and he would no longer tolerate her defiance. He would no longer tolerate her obsession for another man.

"I have watched you pant for Tristan all these many cycles," Romulis growled, backing her into a cold, silver stone that circled the sands. "I am finished watching. I am finished waiting. You are mine."

Her eyes widened with fear, and mayhap a bit of arousal. He hardened his heart against her. She had pushed him past the point of his endurance, and now she must assuage him. He would *not* assuage her.

"We end your obsession now," he said. "Come with me."

TRISTAN SAT at the kitchen table, silent and scowling, as he ate his breakfast. Julia had tried to make him leave her. She had tried to gain a confession of love.

Shock still coursed through him.

Had she tired of him?

He shook his head. Nay, she had not. She loved him. She had uttered the words so many times they were branded inside his mind. And she had meant them. The truth had been there in her eyes. His chest clenched as he remembered. She loved him, yet she was willing to sacrifice their lives together. For him. He knew enough about his little dragon now to know she would not want to watch him live a life of bondage and do nothing. That was why he…liked her so well. Aye, he liked her. Nothing more.

How could he tell her that what he felt for her would destroy him inside?

He would *not* risk it.

After her death—his heart twisted at the thought— he could endure the transference of his box to a new *guan ren,* knowing that he had finally shared true friendship with a woman. The memories of his time with Julia would keep him happy for the rest of his life. For the rest of his servitude.

"I want to close the shop today and just spend the day with you," Julia said.

She deserved children.

The thought slithered into his mind and remained. She had saved two rooms for her babies, for she dreamed of being a mother. This woman who gave so freely of herself deserved to have her dreams come true. He almost gave her his declaration just then, but stopped himself in time.

He was finding that where Julia was concerned, he was a selfish man. He needed her and would pamper her until *he* became her dream. Mayhap they could even provide a home for orphaned children.

He said none of this to her, however, knowing she would not rest until she had his declaration. "What would you like to do?" he asked.

"We can go to a movie or play miniature golf. We could even…" Her words tapered to quiet.

Just in front of her, the air began to thicken, liquefy. Silver mist swirled and tangled together, rising all the way to the ceiling. Julia blinked, unsure of what she was seeing. Heart pounding, she jumped back.

Tristan had already pushed to his feet, his daggers drawn. The mist began to spread and billowed throughout the kitchen. When it cleared, Julia gasped. Her jaw went slack. Zirra stood next to the same very large, very angry-looking man that had been with her before.

Julia focused on Zirra. Here was the woman who had cursed Tristan, who had tried to break his pride and his spirit, to make him suffer for all of eternity.

Julia didn't think about her next actions, didn't consider the repercussions of what she was going to do. She jolted forward, fist clenched, and punched Tristan's tormentor with every ounce of strength she possessed. Zirra's head whipped to the side and before she could recover, Julia punched her again.

"You deserve a lifetime of suffering," Julia ground out. "And damn if I'm not ready to give it to you."

Tristan grabbed her shoulders and jerked her behind him. His body shook with the force of his...fear? Julia gripped his waist, hating that this big, strong man could experience terror like this.

"Do not hurt her, Zirra," he commanded. "'Tis me you want."

"You are right. I do want you, but that bitch is going to suffer."

When Zirra raised her arms, Tristan launched himself at her but it was too late. By the time he reached her, she had already focused her hate-filled eyes on Julia and uttered a spell.

Heaviness instantly settled over Julia's eyelids, and lethargy coursed through her veins. "Tristan," she said, growing weaker by the second. Her knees buckled. Thankfully, he rushed back to her side and was able to catch her.

"What did you do to her?" he croaked to Zirra.

She merely smiled smugly and rubbed her fingertips over her bloodied mouth.

"Julia," he whispered, cupping her cheek. "What is wrong?"

No response.

"What did you do to her?" he roared.

"Romulis helped me regain my powers," Zirra gloated. "I used them to cast a spell of sickness over her body."

"Break it," Tristan commanded. Fear raced through

him, more potent than any other emotion he'd ever endured, because he knew Zirra would not heed him. She was evil incarnate. If she could cast him to an eternity of hell when she professed to love him, what would she do to Julia? A woman who stood in the way of his possession?

Julia's skin quickly lost all color, becoming so pallid he saw the blue trace of her veins. She was so silent, so lifeless. "Save her," he choked, his eyes blurred as he addressed Romulis. "Save her now."

"I cannot," Romulis said, directing a furious scowl to Zirra. "The Druinn cannot break each other's spells, and well Zirra knows it. I did not bring her here for this. I had no idea her powers had returned so greatly."

Tristan's fists clenched around Julia's clothing. He needed her more than he needed to take his next breath. He needed to spend an eternity hearing her laugh, seeing her smile. She represented everything that was good and right. She did not deserve the fate Zirra was giving her, a torturous punishment that only an unstable mind could mete out. He could not let that happen. He could not let Zirra hurt Julia.

He had once refused to beg this sorceress for his own life. But he would beg for Julia's. With pleasure.

Without another thought, he gently laid Julia atop her table and dropped to one knee. "Please, Zirra, let me have the life I have built for myself. Let me have Julia healthy and whole and in peace. Please…I am begging you. Leave us to our life."

Scowling, Romulis strode to him and tried to jerk him to his feet. "Do not beg her," he said.

Tristan held fast.

Zirra's smile vanished and in its place was a grimace so fierce he had never seen its like. "What do you think you are doing?" she screeched. "You dare beg me now? And for *her?* She is nothing, I tell you. Nothing!"

"Nay, she is everything."

"I will not let you do this. Where is your box?"

"Please, Zirra. Please," he rushed out. "I am here on my knees for you when I swore never to beg again."

Zirra screeched, "Where is your box?"

Romulis released Tristan and grabbed her shoulders. "Do you see what he is willing to do for this woman?" he demanded of her, shaking her with all of his might. "Do you see how much he wants her? How much he does not want you?"

Tension crackled between them.

"You know not of what you speak," she screamed.

He rattled her again. "How can you not realize you are meant to be my life-mate?"

She paused for only a heartbeat, then tried to slap away his arms without success. "I do not realize it because it is not true."

"Liar. I am calling in my favor. Leave Tristan and his woman alone, and give us a chance."

Panic washed over Zirra's features, then she paused and smiled slowly. "I am afraid I have already granted your favor, Romulis. You told me to come here and here I am."

A muscle ticked near his left eye, until finally he ground out, "Curse you, Zirra. You destroy everyone in your life."

"What do you care, Romulis?" she asked, haughty now with her victory. "Even without Tristan I would not come to you."

All emotion drained from Romulis's features. Defeated at last, he dropped his arms to his sides and stepped away from her.

Tristan tried one last time to save the life of the woman he had come to cherish. "Heal her and let me stay here with her, Zirra. Please."

Mouth tight in her rage, Zirra strode to him. She glared down at him, her eyes barely visible behind her lashes. "Get off your knees, curse you. Stand before your master."

He remained where he was, sweating, trembling. Zirra wasn't going to grant his request. There was only one thing he could do. His stomach twisted painfully. How great would his suffering be because of his next action?

Immeasurable.

But he would do anything to save Julia's life. Anything.

"Do you vow to heal Julia," he said, "to leave her and all of her family alone if I give you the box?"

"Aye," Zirra said eagerly.

"Swear it by the Kyi-en-Tra Crystal," Tristan added. Such a vow could never be broken without death, and they both knew it.

She didn't hesitate. "I swear."

"Let me first say goodbye," he said. Dying inside, he pushed to his feet and leaned over Julia, whispering in her ear, "Remember me fondly, sweet dragon, for I will never forget you. Live your dream. Love another. Have your children and be happy."

She moaned.

He placed a soft kiss on her lips and tried to memorize her features while everything inside him crumbled, withered. "It is there," he told Zirra, motioning to the plant with a tilt of his chin.

On shaky legs, Zirra inched toward it. Once there, she dropped to her knees and slowly released the false bottom. A gasp parted her lips. Slowly she lifted the box. Her greedy hands clasped around it with reverence.

"I have fulfilled my part of the bargain, Zirra, now fulfill yours."

She nodded and waved one hand through the air. Julia moaned again, stirred. Already her color had begun to return. He pushed out a relieved breath. She was going to live, he thought, as she slowly opened her eyes. She reached for him.

Though it was the hardest thing he had ever done, he forced himself to turn away from her and face Zirra.

"You will be in my bed this night," the black-haired witch snapped, striding to him. "Where you belong. Take us home, Romulis. Take us home."

Without uttering a word, Romulis waved his hand through the air. The only thing that betrayed the sorcerer's emotions was the shaking of his fingers.

TRISTAN FELT the box's walls close around him. Darkness. Silence. Only the awareness that he was a vaporous entity. Before, it would have killed him to go willingly into his prison, but now, now he was happy for it. Julia was safe, and gladly he awaited his next summons, knowing what he must do.

"COME."

He heard Zirra's summons and obeyed without hesitation. He appeared in her bedchamber. The walls, the bed, the floor, were all as white as he remembered. Too, her heart was as black as he remembered.

"Zirra," he said softly, languidly.

"Aye." She smiled, standing naked and ready before the hearth. Flames kindled behind her, illuminating her body with a glowing amber halo. "I am here, my pet. My glorious slave."

"I have been waiting for this summons," he said, and she caught the truth in his tone.

Her smile grew. "Did I not tell you Julia meant nothing."

"You did say that."

Now her eyes softened. "You are mine once again."

"That is the way it appears."

"Come here and welcome me with a kiss."

He did, hating every step that brought him closer to her. The moment he reached her, she cupped his cheeks in her hands and forced his head down. Their lips smashed together. He hated her taste, her smell. The way her mouth pulled and stretched against his. The way her teeth scraped his. When his response did not meet with her approval, she fell back, eyes narrowed.

"I will make you forget that woman if it kills you."

Tristan stepped back, as well, and crossed his arms over his chest. He was ready, beyond ready, to at last take his fate into his own hands. "I have something to tell you first."

Impatient, she tugged at his shirt until his chest was exposed and she could lick his nipples. "And what is that, slave?"

He forced himself to groan an emotion he didn't feel. He watched as her eyes widened with hopefulness. He steadied his resolve. "I love…"

"Aye," she probed. "Tell me." Her nails scraped into his chest. "Tell me who you love. I have waited an entire lifetime to hear you utter these words."

"I…love…Julia."

Three words that he had once thought impossible to utter. Three simple words that were suddenly more real and emotion filled than any he had ever spoken before. He inhaled sharply, feeling his heart swell with the force of the love he had just declared.

He loved Julia. She made him strong, not weak. She did not seek to master him, but only to return his love. "I love Julia," he said again.

And the spell that Zirra had held over him for far too long broke.

The air around him whirled. He was thrust back against the wall with the force of it. He felt invisible bands snap from his wrists and neck, and every docile acceptance he had ever given lifted from his shoulders. He doubled over, bellowed with every breath of air in his lungs. And when he straightened, he knew he was free.

Free!

The knowledge held no joy. Only a painful reminder that he was without Julia.

Zirra yelled with rage and flung herself at him, hitting and kicking.

What should have been a catapult of teeth, fists and nails was only a tug of a creature to be pitied. He recognized her agony, because he experienced his own.

He sighed while Zirra raged. And he waited. Aye, he understood this witch's obsession. He understood it so well that he could almost forgive her. Almost.

"I will not rest until you've suffered a thousand deaths," she spat, then collapsed to her floor with a sharp cry of realization. She no longer owned him, and she could not curse him again now that his heart knew true love.

"Worry not. I will suffer forever," he replied, "for I am parted from the woman I love." How true those words were. His life was nothing without Julia.

He turned to leave Zirra sobbing, when a thunderous sound stopped him.

Percen, High Priest of the Druinn, appeared in a whirl of wind, resplendent in his royal robe of turquoise and scarlet cloth. The surge of power he brought with him almost knocked Tristan to the ground. He felt the High Priest's grip upon his arm and turned to face him.

"I wish words with you, Tristan. But first..." Percen released Tristan and pointed an accusatory finger at Zirra. "I must deal with you. You are a disgrace to our kind."

"Nay, I am the best of our kind," she snarled, jolting up.

"Keep talking. You are only increasing your punishment."

Gone went her haughty smile, her smug air. She looked petrified and snatched up her robe in an attempt to cover herself. "What of Romulis? He aided me."

"Nay. He aided *me* by distracting you, and thought he could save you in the process."

"Percen—"

"I told you to leave this mortal alone. I told you the Fates would one day return him."

Tristan stared at the man who had hurtled him through the galaxies and felt…empty. He could not hate the man for having sent him to Julia, any more than he could despise Zirra, who felt love's arrow so fiercely in her heart. But all he wanted now was to return to Julia.

"Percen—"

Percen silenced Zirra with a wave of his hand. "You will interfere in the lives of mortals no more. The Alliance is too important to our kind." He raised his hands in the air and uttered a spell very much like the pleasure slave spell Zirra had uttered over Tristan so long ago.

Zirra's eyes widened with horror as her body became transparent and then, like a whiff of smoke, blew into the very box Tristan had once occupied. Percen lifted the box. "I'm giving you to the mortal Peter," he said, patting the lid. "I want you far away from my son. He was to keep you occupied," he muttered, "not fall in love with you. Mayhap some time away from you will show him the error of his ways."

Percen sighed, then looked to Tristan. "'Tis my hope

Romulis will meet his *true* life-mate soon. Mayhap I will release Zirra later. For now, she must learn her proper place." He once again laid a hand on his shoulder. "I cast the world traveling spell because the time had not yet come to free you. Do you forgive me?"

"I understand and forgive." And he did.

"The Druinn will leave you in peace."

"Wait," Tristan rushed out. "I would first beg a favor from you."

Percen paused, his expression weary, then nodded. "Ask."

"There is an otherworlder, Julia. I ask that you send me back to her."

He shook his head. "Your place is here. The centuries you endured on other worlds have not yet passed here. To us, you have been gone only a few cycles. We are still adrift as the rebellion grows, and we are in need of leaders such as yourself to calm the angry waters of the people. I am sorry, Tristan, but you must stay here. It has already been prophesized that your firstborn will one day rule Imperia."

Tristan blinked, almost choking on a wave of longing. "My son will rule?"

"Your child will end the feud between our people. Permanently. Would you have this planet at war, simply to be with your woman?"

Part of him cried nay. Another part of him screamed aye. "Bring Julia to me, then. She can give me this son, for I will not father a child with any other woman."

"What if she does not wish to come?"

He refused to ponder such an occurrence. "She will come to me."

Percen sighed. "Then I offer you this—if you spend the next season fighting the rebellion and still yearn for the otherworlder—and she wants to come to you—I will bring her to you."

Knowing he had no other option, Tristan gave a stiff nod.

CHAPTER TWENTY-EIGHT

*Your Greatest Satisfaction Is Knowing
You Pleased Your Master*

"JULIA," Faith said on a sigh. She sat beside Julia's bed, concerned. "Tristan left you. You can't mope here forever, neglecting your life and your business, praying for him to return. You have to move on. No man is worth this amount of suffering."

"You don't understand, Faithie," she replied softly. She'd known saying goodbye to him would be hard. Brutal, even. She'd thought she would be prepared. But this…this was the cruelest torture, loving Tristan and living without him. He was everything to her; without him she had nothing.

She'd always thought of herself as content. But she'd never known true contentment before Tristan.

Murky darkness filled her bedroom because the curtains were drawn and the lights were switched off. She liked it this way. Here, she could remember; she could picture Tristan in her mind and could catch a hint of his lingering scent on the sheets and pretend that he really was here.

"Just go, Faith," she said. She wanted to be alone with her memories. Maybe if she concentrated hard enough, he would appear.

Don't cry, she commanded herself. *Whatever you do, don't cry. Once you start, you'll never stop.*

"I saw Peter yesterday," Faith said.

"I don't care."

"I don't know what happened to him, but he was glowing."

"I don't care," she said again.

Her sister remained undeterred. "Refusing to leave your bed isn't going to help you. Thousands of women have been dumped all over the world. You have to pick yourself back up and prove you can live without him."

"He didn't dump me." She'd heard every word. Heard Tristan tell her to live her dreams, heard his un- spoken vow of love. He'd left with Zirra to save her. Oh, how she ached for him, how she longed to tell him again of her own love. "He was forced."

Faith snorted. "That man was a mountain. No one could force him to do anything he didn't want to do."

"Yes, they could." Her voice almost imperceptible, she told Faith the entire story. Her sister didn't believe her, and she didn't have the strength to convince her.

She'd closed her shop this past week. She simply hadn't had the time or the energy to work. She needed Tristan, and her every waking moment was spent here at the house, in bed or on the computer, searching for information about magic and spells, something, any- thing to lead her to Imperia.

To Tristan.

So far, she'd found only emptiness and despair.

Remember me, he'd said, his voice sad.

"I miss him so much," she told her sister, and one lone tear slid down her cheek. That was all it took for the damn to break. She sobbed and shook with the force of her grief, all of her tears cascading down her cheeks, wetting her pillow.

Faith gentled a hand down her hair, held her tightly and cooed soft words of comfort.

But there was no comfort to be found.

Imperia

ON THE LAST DAY of his required season without Julia, the fine hairs on the back of Tristan's neck rose, warning him of a coming adversary. He sat atop his horned stag, darkness surrounding him and his men. They had already fought many battles, and he knew many more were to come. It was as if he had never left this place, his battle instincts were so sharp and attuned. Mayhap that was because he only wanted Julia in his arms, and was willing to do anything to get her here.

He knew his men wondered why he fought so hard, harder than ever before. He had told only his friend, Roake, who had agreed to fight at his side, giving his aid.

In a low, quiet tone, he cautioned his army to guard their flanks. Danger lurked nearby. The talon at his side hummed with anticipation. Tristan clutched the hilt, ready. Oh, aye. A battle brewed.

A war cry sounded—and it was not his.

Rebel attackers jumped from the trees, blades hoisted in the air, the only thing visible in the night. Combat began seconds later. Tristan's talon sliced through the air, vibrating when it made contact with flesh.

Energy flowed through his veins. Battle always had that effect on him, always gave him added strength. Yet this time, his energy stemmed from his desire to be with Julia. This was his last day without her—if she wanted to come to him. He had to believe she did. Otherwise, his life was not worth living.

He fought like a man possessed. He heard men scream in pain. The blood of the rebels ran like crimson rivers along the grassy field. The muscles in his arms and back burned, not completely healed from the many battles he had already endured these many cycles, but he kept fighting, wielding his weapon with deadly intent. There was too much at stake to give up now.

When he finished off one man, two others attacked him. He stepped backward, blocking a blow to his midsection. Then he lunged out, taking down one assailant in a single fluid spin. As he straightened, something stabbed at his back.

On instinct, he dove to the right, a movement that prevented a talon from sinking past bone and muscle and saved his life. Wincing as the new wound throbbed in protest, he whipped around. His combatant grinned, sensing victory, and raised his arms. The silver metal glinted in the moonlight as it arced downward.

Without pause, Tristan unsheathed the blades Julia

had given him as he spun and stabbed upward. Instant contact. With a painful scream, the man collapsed.

More men attacked from the trees, and he and his men continued to fight. Not long after, Roake sounded the victory shout. Loud, buoyant cheers covered the lingering sounds of battle, the moans of the hundreds of men lying wounded and bleeding in the grass.

Tristan rubbed a weary hand down his equally weary face, then gazed up at the heavens. He had had enough. It was time.

"Percen," he shouted, praying the High Priest heard him. "I fight no more until our bargain is complete."

JULIA LAY IN BED. She wore the same T-shirt and sweatpants she'd worn every day since Tristan left. They were his, and she welcomed the small bit of comfort they brought her. Another week had passed without him. Another awful, lonely week.

She was no longer sleeping. She only tossed and turned and imagined.

When would this terrible ache subside? She just didn't know. As she clutched her pillow to her chest, she heard a voice boom through her home. She jolted upright, startled.

"Do you wish to go to him, lass?" It was the same Scottish burr she'd heard at the flea market when she'd bought Tristan's box.

She didn't question her sanity. She simply shouted, "Yes!"

As soon as she uttered the word, her world began to

spin. She squeezed her eyes tightly closed. Colors swirled behind her lids, and something whizzed in her ears. How many minutes passed, she didn't know. *Please let this be real,* she thought, trying to kindle her growing hope.

An eternity later, the spinning ceased.

When she opened her eyes, she had to blink until they adjusted to the bright sunlight. She stood on a bed of white grass. Half-clothed men strode all around her, some sweaty and bloody. Some freshly washed. They gave her confused looks but did not approach her.

A large lake of perfectly clear water consumed half the land. Tristan leaned against a gleaming silver boulder, his eyes closed as water cascaded down his naked torso and pant-clad legs.

With a joyous cry, she shouted his name, "Tristan!"

His eyelids snapped open. He shook his head, as if he didn't quite believe his eyes. Then he leapt into motion. He ran to her and swept her into his arms. "Are you here? Are you truly here?"

"I'm here, I'm here." Tears burned her eyes, such happy tears.

He squeezed her so tightly she almost lost her breath. "Welcome to Imperia, little dragon," he breathed into her neck.

Cool droplets of water soaked her clothing, but she didn't care. She wound her arms around his neck and held him closer. "I've missed you so much. My house is empty without you."

He pulled back from her ever so slightly. "I cannot go back with you, Julia. Not ever."

Julia thought of Faith. She would miss her, but she knew her sister would be all right without her and would hopefully one day understand. "I would like to stay with you. If you'll have me."

"If I will have you?" With another shout of delight, he smothered her face with kisses and nips. "I would die without you. I love you so much I ache."

The men around them cheered loud and long. And Julia caught one man's smile. He was tall, as tall as Tristan, with a scar that slashed down the left side of his face. She couldn't help but grin back.

"I want to make you my life-mate," he said. "I want to give you my children. You can open a shop at the market and all of Imperia will come to purchase your wares."

"There is only one thing I need, Tristan, and that's you." Her contented smile grew as she stared into his eyes. She had never felt so whole and complete. "You're a part of me I don't want to live without. With you, I'm content."

"We were always meant to find one another, I think." Tristan cupped her chin in his hands. "You are willing to give up everything for me," he said, awed by that fact.

"No, I was simply willing to take what mattered most."

"What matters most, Julia? Like you, I need the words. What matters most to you?"

"My final lesson, of course."

He stilled. Not what he had expected, but then, she had

always done the unexpected. He grinned back at her. "Best you tell me what you would have this last lesson be."

She gazed up at him through half-lowered lids. "Why, happily ever after."

"I will do better than that." His gaze never strayed from hers. "I will give you forever, my beauty, my dragon. I give you my love, all my heart and my soul. I give you my name and my children."

"I love you, Tristan."

"By Elliea, I could live on those words alone. I love you, too." Julia strengthened him, completed him in a way unknown to him until he'd first seen her. He could not breathe without her, could not function without her at his side. "Will you life-join with me, and have my children?" he asked raining soft butterfly kisses upon her face.

"Oh, that will be my pleasure." Happy tears gathered at the corners of her eyes and her chin wobbled slightly.

"And my pleasure, as well. I will always be your pleasure slave. Always."

"Hmm…" She pulled his lips to hers. "That's all a girl can ask for."

EPILOGUE

IT WAS SOON to become the loudest birth ever recorded in Imperian history.

"Tristan," Julia said, panting, a sheen of sweat and pain dampening her brow. "How could you do this to me?"

He stilled, concerned for her, and quite baffled by her question. "Do what, little dragon?"

"Impregnate me, you bastard!"

At that, he chuckled, though the sound was strained. He hated that she was in so much pain and wanted to take it all into himself. He wiped her brow with a gentle hand. "Just imagine, my love. We will soon welcome our son into the world."

Those words caused peace to settle over her features. "Yes. We will welcome our son." Another pain hit her and she screamed. "If he doesn't hurry I will personally drag him out." As the pain faded, she drew in a breath, then another, then settled back on the bed.

"Does the pain leave you?" he asked hopefully.

"A little." Closing her eyes, she uttered a tired sigh. "I can't believe it. I'm about to become a mother."

"Life is good. Did I ever tell you that the Druinn

High Priest predicted our firstborn would one day rule Imperia?"

"No." The thought pleased her, though. She, a formerly plain, shy woman, was about to give birth to a future king. "That is so cool."

"I can easily picture our boy sitting atop the royal throne. He will be known as a kind, giving king with a capacity for fairness that rivals even his mother's."

Except fifteen minutes later, Tristan welcomed his *daughter* into the world—a girl who would one day rule Imperia, he realized. How…astounding.

Holding the beautiful squalling infant in her arms, Julia nuzzled the baby's neck, cooing soft words. "Finally," she said, "a ruler of uncommon intelligence."

Tristan remained unmoving, shock still coursing through his blood. "A female sovereign," he whispered.

Julia looked up at him through the spiky shield of her lashes. "Are you disappointed that we didn't have a son?"

"Nay, sweet." He smiled down at her with all the love he felt shining in his eyes. "I have never been happier."

Please turn the page for
a preview of Gena Showalter's
new novel
HEART OF THE DRAGON

Coming in September
from
HQN Books

Atlantis

Do you feel it, boy? Do you feel the mist preparing?"

Darius en Kragin squeezed his eyes tightly closed, his tutor's words echoing in his mind. Did he feel it? Gods, yes. Even though he was only eight seasons, he felt it. Felt his skin prickle with cold, felt the sickening wave of acid in his throat as the mist enveloped him. He even felt his veins quicken with a deceptively sweet, swirling essence that was not his own.

Fighting the urge to bolt up the cavern steps and into the palace above, he tensed his muscles and fisted his hands at his sides.

I must stay. I must do this.

Slowly Darius forced his eyelids to open. He released a pent-up breath as his gaze locked with Javar's. His tutor stood shrouded by the thickening, ghostlike haze, the bleak walls of the cave at his back.

"This is what you'll feel each time the mist summons you, for this means a traveler is nearby," Javar said. "Never stray far from this place. You may live with the others, but you must always return here when called."

"I do not like it here." His voice shook. "The cold weakens me."

"Other dragons are weakened by cold, but not you. Not any longer. The mist will become a part of you, the coldness your most beloved companion. Now listen," he commanded softly. "Listen closely."

At first Darius heard nothing. Then he began to register the sound of a low, tapering whistle; a sound that reverberated in his ears like moans of the dying. *Wind,* he assured himself. *Merely wind.* The turbulent breeze rounded every corner of the doomed enclosure, drawing closer. Closer still. His nostrils filled with the scent of desperation, destruction and loneliness as he braced himself for impact. When it finally came upon him, it was not the battering force he expected, but a mockingly gentle caress against his body. The jeweled medallion at his neck hummed to life, burning the dragon tattoos etched into his flesh only that morning.

He crushed his lips together to silence a deep groan of uncertainty.

His tutor sucked in a reverent breath and splayed his arms wide. "This is what you will live for, boy. This will be your purpose."

"I do not want my purpose to stem from the deaths of others," Darius said, the words tumbling from his mouth unbidden.

Javar stilled, a fiery anger kindling in the depths of his golden eyes, eyes so like Darius's own—eyes like every dragon's. "You are to be a Guardian of the Mist and the leader of the warriors here. You will take your vows. You will kill travelers, for that is the only way to save our land."

Darius's shaking ceased. He straightened and wiped his mouth with the back of his wrist. "You are right," he said starkly, determinedly, craving a detachment he didn't feel. "I am ready."

"Do it, then."

Without pausing for thought, he sank to his knees. "In this place I will dwell, destroying the surface dwellers who pass through the mist. This I vow upon my life. This I vow upon my death." As he spoke the words, they mystically appeared on his chest and back; black and red symbols that stretched from one shoulder to the other and glowed with inner fire. "I exist for no other purpose. I am Guardian of the Mist."

Javar held his stare for a long while, then nodded with satisfaction. "Your eyes have changed color to mirror the mist. The two of you are one. This is good, boy. This is good."

Amazon Jungle
Three hundred years later

GRACE CARLYLE ALWAYS HOPED she'd die from intense pleasure while having sex with her husband. Well, she wasn't married and she'd never had sex, but she was still going to die.

And not from intense pleasure.

From heat exhaustion? Maybe.

From hunger? Possibly.

From her own stupidity? Absolutely.

She was lost and alone in the freaking jungle.

As she strode past tangled green vines and towering trees, beads of sweat trickled down her chest and back. Small shards of light seeped from the leafy canopy above, providing hazy visibility. Barely adequate, but appreciated. Rotting vegetation and flowers mingled together and formed a conflicting fragrance of sweet and sour. She wrinkled her nose.

"All I wanted was a little excitement," she muttered. "Instead, I end up broke, lost and trapped in this bug-infested sauna."

To complete her descent into hell, she expected the sky to open and pour out a deluge of rain at any moment.

The only good thing about her current circumstance was that all this hiking and sweating might actually help her lose a few pounds from her too-curvy figure. Not that losing weight did her any good here. Except, perhaps, in her obituary.

New Yorker Found Dead In Amazon
At Least She Looked Good

Unfortunately, the deeper she roamed through the jungle the more lost and alone she became. The trees and liana thickened, as did the darkness. At least the scent of rot had evaporated, leaving only a luscious trace of wild heliconias and dewy orchids. If she didn't find shelter soon, she would collapse wherever she found herself, helpless against nature. Though her vaccinations were up-to-date, she hated snakes and insects more than hunger and fatigue.

Several yards, a tapir and two capybaras later, she had made no progress that she could see. It was darker now, the trees thicker. Her arms and legs were so heavy they felt like steel clubs. Not knowing what else to do, she sank to the ground. As she lay there, she heard the gentle song of the insects and the— Her eardrums perked. The trickle of water? She blinked, listened more intently. Yes, she realized with excitement. She was actually hearing the glorious swoosh of water.

Get up, she commanded herself. *Get up, get up, get up!*

Using every bit of strength she possessed, she pushed to her hands and knees and crawled into a thick tangle of vegetation. Forest life pulsed vibrantly around her, mocking her weakness. Brilliant, damp green leaves parted and the ground became wetter and wetter until becoming completely submerged by an underground spring. The clear, turquoise water smelled clean and refreshing.

Shaking with the force of her need, she cupped her hands together, scooped up the cool, heavenly liquid and drank deeply. Her parched lips welcomed every wet, delicious drop. Then her chest began to burn, hotter and hotter, as if she were swallowing molten lava. Except the sensation came from the outside of her body, not the inside.

The heat became unbearable, and she shrieked. Looking up, her gaze locked on to the twin dragon heads dangling from the silver chain around her neck. Both sets of ruby eyes were glowing a bright, eerie red.

She tried to yank the thing from her neck but was suddenly propelled forward by an invisible force. Arms flailing, she broke past an amazingly thick wall of flora. She abruptly stilled as the medallion cooled against her chest.

Her eyes grew impossibly round as she studied her new surroundings. She had entered some sort of cave. A cool, welcoming breeze kissed her face. Relief nearly buckled her knees. The tranquil ambiance flowed into her, helping to calm her racing heart and labored breathing.

Too exhausted to care what might be inside waiting for a tasty human to appear, she scrambled deeper inside the passage and down a steep incline. The ceiling constricted and lowered, until she had to crouch and kneel. How long she crawled, she didn't know. Minutes? Hours? She only knew she needed to find a smooth, dry surface so that she could sleep. Gradually a ribbon of light appeared. The muted beam snaked around the corner like a summoning finger. She followed.

And found Paradise.

Light crowned a small iridescent pool of...water? The dappled ice-blue liquid seemed thicker than water, almost like a transparent gel. Instead of lying on the ground, however, the pool hung upright at a slight angle, much like a portrait on a wall. Yet there was no wall to support it.

Why wasn't it spilling over? she wondered dazedly. Her foggy brain couldn't quite sort through the bizarre information. Balmy tendrils of mist enveloped the entire haven. A few ethereal strands reached the cavern top, swirling, circling, then gently dipping back down.

Grace carefully reached out, meaning only to touch and examine the strange substance. At the moment of contact, a violent jolt exploded within her, and she felt as if her entire being was sucked into a vacuum.

The world crumbled around her. She was falling slowly, falling down. Her arms reached out, desperate for a solid anchor, yet no tangible object greeted her palms.

That's when the screams began, like a thousand screeching children running all around her. She covered her ears to block the sound.

Suddenly everything quieted.

Her feet touched a hard surface; she swayed but didn't fall. Cautiously she shifted her feet, ascertaining that she truly stood on a stable foundation. When her head cleared, she cracked open her eyelids. A haze of dew still rose from the small pool like strands of pale, glistening ivy composed entirely of fairy dust. The beautiful sight was spoiled only by the stark contours of the gloomy cavern—a cavern that was different from the one she'd first entered.

Her brows furrowed. Here, the rocky walls were covered with strange, colorful markings, like liquid gold upon forgotten ash. Instead of miserable humidity, she inhaled air as cold as winter ice.

She shivered. This couldn't be a dream or a hallucination. The sights and smells were too real, too frightening. Had she died? No, no. This certainly wasn't heaven, and it was too cold to be hell.

So what had happened?

Before her mind could form an answer, a twig snapped.

Grace's chin whipped to the side, and she found herself staring up into cold, ice-blue eyes that swirled like foam in a sea—swirled in startling precision with the mist. She sucked in an awed breath. The owner of those extraordinary eyes was the most ferociously masculine man she'd ever seen. A scar slashed from his left eyebrow all the way to his chin. His cheekbones were sharp, his jaw square. The only softness to his face was his gloriously lush lips that somehow gave him the hypnotic beauty of a fallen angel.

He stood in front of her, at least six foot five and pure, raw muscle. He was shirtless, his stomach cut into several perfect rows of strength. Shards of mist fell around him like glittery drops of rain, leaving glistening beads of moisture on his bronzed, tattooed chest. He held a long, menacing sword.

A wave of fear swept through her, but that didn't stop her from staring. He was utterly savage. Danger radiated from his every pore, from the dark rim of his crystalline, predator eyes, to the blades strapped to his boots.

With a flick of his wrist, he twirled the sword around his head.

She inched backward. Surely he didn't mean to use that thing. My God, he was lifting it higher as if he really did mean to… "Whoa, there." She managed a shaky laugh. "Put that away before you hurt someone."

He gave the lethal weapon another twirl, brandishing the sharp silver with strong, sure hands. His washboard abs rippled as he moved closer to her. Not a trace of emotion touched his expression. Not anger, fear or mischievousness, offering her no clue as to why he felt the need to practice sword-slicing techniques in front of her.

He stared at her. She stared back, and told herself it was because she was too afraid to look away.

"I mean you no harm," she croaked. Time dragged when he didn't respond.

Before her horror-filled eyes, his sword began to slice downward, aimed straight for her throat. He was going to kill her!

Terror wrapped around her like a wintry blanket. Her gaze scanned the cave, searching for a way out. The mist was the only exit, but the savage warrior's big, strong body now blocked it.

"Please," she whispered, not knowing what else to do or say.

Either the man didn't hear her, or he didn't care what she said. His sharp, deadly sword continued to inch closer and closer to her neck.

She squeezed her eyelids tightly shut....

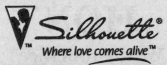

gena showalter

77007 THE STONE PRINCE   ___ $6.50 U.S. ___ $7.99 CAN.

(limited quantities available)

TOTAL AMOUNT $ _____
POSTAGE & HANDLING $ _____
($1.00 FOR 1 BOOK, 50¢ for each additional)
APPLICABLE TAXES* $ _____
TOTAL PAYABLE $ _____

(check or money order—please do not send cash)

To order, complete this form and send it, along with a check or money order for the total above, payable to HQN Books, to: **In the U.S.:** 3010 Walden Avenue, P.O. Box 9077, Buffalo, NY 14269-9077; **In Canada:** P.O. Box 636, Fort Erie, Ontario, L2A 5X3.

Name: _____

Address: _____ City: _____

State/Prov.: _____ Zip/Postal Code: _____

Account Number (if applicable): _____

075 CSAS

*New York residents remit applicable sales taxes.
*Canadian residents remit applicable GST and provincial taxes.

HQN™

We *are* romance™

www.HQNBooks.com

PHGS0205BL